A MAN ABOUT THE HOUSE

WAR ECONOMY

THIS BOOK IS PRODUCED IN COMPLETE CONFORMITY WITH THE AUTHORISED ECONOMY STANDARDS

FIRST PUBLISHED JULY 1942
REPRINTED JULY, AUGUST, OCTOBER 1942

PRINTED IN GREAT BRITAIN AT THE WINDMILL PRESS
KINGSWOOD, SURREY

THE NOVELS OF FRANCIS BRETT YOUNG

UNDERGROWTH
(with E. Brett Young)
DEEP SEA
THE DARK TOWER
IRON AGE
THE CRESCENT MOON
THE YOUNG PHYSICIAN
THE TRAGIC BRIDE
THE BLACK DIAMOND
THE RED KNIGHT
PILGRIM'S REST
WOODSMOKE
COLD HARBOUR
SEA HORSES
PORTRAIT OF CLARE
MY BROTHER JONATHAN
BLACK ROSES
JIM REDLAKE
MR. AND MRS. PENNINGTON
THE HOUSE UNDER THE WATER
THIS LITTLE WORLD
WHITE LADIES
FAR FOREST
THEY SEEK A COUNTRY
DR. BRADLEY REMEMBERS
THE CITY OF GOLD
MR. LUCTON'S FREEDOM
A MAN ABOUT THE HOUSE

FRANCIS BRETT YOUNG

A MAN ABOUT THE HOUSE

AN OLD WIVES' TALE

WILLIAM HEINEMANN LTD
LONDON :: TORONTO

For

FAITH COMPTON MACKENZIE

My dear Faith,

Twenty years ago—long before you had learnt to write such charming prose—I remember your husband accusing me of being unable to 'draw' a convincing villain. Mr. Furnival, in Cold Harbour, *was my immediate reply to that challenge, and the fact that that strange little book is alive to-day suggests that he still has his admirers. The background of this new villain of mine doomed you, from the fifty-seventh page, to a dedication; for we have both of us lived in Arcadia. Shall we ever return there? I hope so. The bastions of your sequestrated Ventrosa still look down (not too superciliously, I hope) on our sequestrated Casa Fraita; but I think we have both had good value for our money; and there are some things the Facists cannot sequestrate.*

Yours always,

F. B. Y.

PART ONE

I

THE house had lain empty and neglected for many years, I suppose, before I became aware of its existence on the day when first I rode in to school on the top of one of the North Bromwich Corporation's electric trams. It stood back—but not very far back—from the street still called Enville Lane, which had been straightened and widened at this point when the tram-lines were laid; and this widening had undoubtedly cut off the greater part of a sweep of gravel drive embracing a semicircle of lawn, with a cedar of Lebanon in the middle of it. The stump of the cedar, which must have been a noble tree, still stood, cramped up against the wall the corporation had re-built, along the edge of their new footpath, at its original height—so high, indeed, that nobody walking along the pavement would ever have guessed that there was a house behind it, since the drive-gates (one could see there had once been two of them) had been replaced by a single narrow archway let into the wall and filled by a wooden door, impenetrable to the sight, that was never seen open. On either side of this door the high wall was continued for twenty or thirty yards to enclose a front garden clogged with shrubberies of sooty laurel that had overgrown the disused drive; and above this wall, at either end of the property, rose a weather-beaten notice-board from whose faded inscription one might learn with difficulty that the house was called 'The Cedars', and was To Let.

I never saw 'The Cedars' for more than a few moments at a time; for there was no tram-stop within fifty yards of it, and the trams usually ran past it gathering speed. Yet that house had always impressed my imagination. It was, to begin with, so secret, so withdrawn behind its high wall. There ought not, by rights, to have been any house there at all; for the neighbourhood, which had once been fashionable, had deteriorated long before I was born, and the lane (as it was still inappropriately called) which had once, no doubt, run through open fields, and later become part of the comely suburb of Alvaston, was now bordered on either side by mean rows of mid-Victorian brick and had become indistinguishable from the hundreds of other slummy cañons of working-class dwellings interspersed with sordid pubs and fried-fish shops, which intensified the drabness of the industrial age.

But the character of this house was even more remarkable than its persistence. It was, relatively to its surroundings, enormous, and unusually dignified: a square, stuccoed Regency villa, in a style reminiscent of Adam, enriched with swags, urns and medallions, and entered from beneath a massive portico supported by Corinthian pillars and obviously planned for the reception of the occupants of a carriage and pair, whose eyes should have surveyed a wide expanse of parkland rather than a blank factory-wall and an unending vista of chimneys and smoke-blackened brick. No doubt, at the time when it was built, 'The Cedars' had had neighbours with equally genteel pretensions. (At the beginning of the nineteenth century North Bromwich had grown rich on the wealth released by the Napoleonic wars.) But the owners of these had made good their escape from the city's advancing smoke-screen before it was too late, and had sold the land on which their mansions stood to build manors of Victorian Tudor in the green recesses of Alvaston. Only 'The Cedars' had remained, rarely painted and unrepaired and, at last, uninhabited, while the surface gradually shed from its wall in flakes, like the bark of a wintry plane-tree, and the stucco, green-streaked here and there by the drip from leaf-choked rain-pipes and sagging gutters, became pocked and scabrous, until the house, with its blank, soot-blinded windows, resembled in its raffish distinction the corpse of a Regency buck whom his relations had forgotten to bury. It was this charnel air, this suggestion of a mausoleum, which made me privately decide that 'The Cedars' was haunted, and through the curiosity with which I viewed it from my exalted tram-top ran a delicious shiver of dread which I felt less pleasant on the rarer occasions when I walked past it in the dusk. In my youthful mind, it had long since been established as *the* haunted house, when, one morning, in my swift passage, I saw that it was coming to life. The notices which had so long and so ineffectively proclaimed its vacancy, had been removed; the door in the wall stood wide open; a forest of ladders and scaffolding-poles now topped the façade, and workmen, suspended in mid-air, were scraping the leprous walls. Fresh air, which had so long been denied entrance, swept through open doors and windows to blow away its mystery. Though the spectacle was exciting, I must confess I felt rather hurt by this desecration which had violated one of the dearest of my private illusions. The house, I considered, should have been left to moulder in peace. For my own part, I knew that nothing could have induced me to live in it, and I shuddered at the blindness of those who were making so rash an experiment, whoever they might be.

2

My curiosity was soon to be satisfied through a visit from our solicitor, Ernest Wilburn, an old friend of the family who occasionally dropped in after dinner to smoke a cigar and talk with my grandfather, who was an unrivalled authority on his favourite subject: the fauna and social history of North Bromwich in the middle nineteenth century. There had been giants in those strange, harsh, full-blooded days; and I had often sat spellbound listening to the old man's mythological tales of the beginnings of the Hingstons, Willises, Astills, Hacketts and the rest of them: those legendary figures who had laid the foundations of an industrial aristocracy that was already sliding into decadence. Most of these were clients of Wilburn's firm, and as a lawyer no less than as a student of humanity, he often sought this short cut to information on their family history.

That evening, as I sat listening and pretending to read in the shadowy warmth of my grandfather's library, which smelt so comfortably of ancient leather and Havana cigars, I pricked up my ears at the sound of a familiar name.

"Do you remember a house called 'The Cedars'?" Ernest Wilburn was saying.

" 'The Cedars'? Isn't there a house of that name at the top of the Halesby Road?"

"Yes, I think there is; but that isn't the one I mean. This is in Enville Lane; more or less in the middle of a slum."

"Ah, yes. Now I know what you're talking about. 'The Cedars' . . . Dear me! I'd quite forgotten that place was still in existence. When I was a lad it belonged to people named Isit."

"It still belongs to them. An odd name, Isit, isn't it?"

My grandfather chuckled. "The Isits were an odd family. To tell you the truth I hadn't realized that there were any of them left."

"Tell me about them. I'm interested because they're clients of mine."

"Well, they're an old North Bromwich Unitarian family, members of the original gang. They came here, I suppose, with the rest in the days of the Five Mile Act, which forbade their meeting within that distance of a corporate borough. North Bromwich, of course, had no corporation then . . ."

"And no Lord Mayor . . . Fortunate city," said Wilburn.

"The name of the first Isit, I think, was Abraham. He was a member of the New Meeting, a disciple of Joseph Priestley, and took part in the Constitutional Society's famous dinner, commemorating the Fall of the Bastille, at Dadley's Hotel; and I rather think he was concerned in Priestley's flight from the anti-Jacobin mob. That was in

1791. He probably built the house you were speaking of. It's Adam, isn't it?"

"Well . . . Adam after the Fall, if you like. I should put it later."

"Then or thereabouts. At that time the city had not grown much on this side, and a number of those rich, cultured Radicals built what were to all intents and purposes 'country houses' between it and Alvaston, most of them were demolished to make room for a denser population when I was a boy. I imagine 'The Cedars' must be the only one left. As a young man I can remember an elderly Mr. Isit living there, rather a recluse. I don't know if he had any family . . ."

"Quite possibly not. He had nephews, though. One of them came to see me the other day. His name's Arthur Isit, Lieutenant-Colonel, R.E. Not exactly 'mad, married or methodist', as sappers are supposed to be, but a widower, a Unitarian, and decidedly queer."

"Queer in what way?"

"Well, first of all, he wants to live at 'The Cedars'. Surely it's queer for a soldier, retired from India, to want to live in a slum?"

"What is he like?"

"Like a late El Greco. The most elongated thing you ever saw in your life, straight off the walls of the San José church at Toledo. I knew nothing about him, except that he existed and was a client of ours with whom we corresponded occasionally about the house, which belongs to him, and which he had been trying to let, unsuccessfully, for the last twenty years—ever since I came into the firm. My clerk opened the door and in came this apparition which might have walked out of a tailor's fashion-plate of the eighteen-eighties. He's probably not so tall as he looked, but he was wearing tubular trousers, a tightly-buttoned frock-coat, an enormously high starched collar, above which rose an extraordinarily long, narrow head, with a high forehead that looked as if it had been screwed down sideways in a copying press. You know I like 'period pieces'. Well, this one was so perfect that for a moment it took my breath away. When I recovered it, I told him how delighted I was to make the acquaintance of a client whose family, etcetera, etcetera. As luck would have it, there's an old tin deed-box with the name 'Isit' inscribed on it on a shelf behind my desk. I showed it him, and that pleased him no end. Then I asked what I could have the pleasure of doing for him. He said he was just home from India, having retired from the army, and had been having a look at his property."

" 'The Cedars'?"

" 'The Cedars' . . . Of course I condoled with him, and made all the excuses I could for our not having been able to let it. That wasn't difficult. I explained how old Joe Astill had bought up all the land in that part of the city and built slums to house people to drink his beer, and how all the other decent houses had been gradually demolished. I tried out the little joke that you laughed at just now, about Adam after the Fall, but he didn't rise to it. Then I told him quite frankly that the best advice I could give him was to sell the land for what it would fetch. I said I thought we might possibly induce the Astill Estates Limited to make him an offer by pointing out to them that it was rather a pity to have a desert island in the middle of their property. If he thought it worth while, he might sell the house first for demolition; but I doubted if the building materials would be worth much: that Georgian stucco covered a multitude of sins.

"During all this time Colonel Isit hadn't uttered a word. I'd been talking, as I often do, looking up at the ceiling, and taking it for granted that he was listening sympathetically. Then I suddenly lowered my eyes and caught sight of his face. It gave me a shock. There was a great blue vein bulging in the middle of his narrow forehead, and his eyes, on either side of his bony, hooked nose—which I don't think I've mentioned—were positively malignant, like those of an angry bird. I saw that I had to deal with a touchy client, and drew in my horns.

" 'Of course,' I said, 'if you have any other idea . . .'

" 'I have no intention of selling 'The Cedars', he said. 'I have decided to live there.'

"Well, I couldn't honestly leave it at that: after all I was his legal adviser. I told him I quite understood that he might be sentimentally attached to the house as an old family property and all that, but I did think I ought to warn him of some obvious disadvantages. The surroundings, to say the least of it, were sordid and might be unpleasant. He would have no neighbours of his own class, and, apart from all this, the house had no modern comforts and few conveniences.

"He bridled at that, and said rather haughtily that the lack of unnecessary luxuries wouldn't trouble him. 'I'm a soldier,' he said, 'and not used to them. What was good enough for my uncle and my grandparents will certainly be good enough for me. We are a hardy family, Mr. Wilburn. My poor wife, as you probably know, was a Vaughan of Tregoyd, a member of a rough border family and a lineal descendant of King Cadwallader.'

"I agreed that this was most interesting, but reminded him that he couldn't possibly live in the house as it was, and it might cost him a deuce of a lot to make it habitable. He thought for a moment; then asked me point-blank 'How much?'

"That, of course, I explained, I couldn't answer. After all, if he had made up his mind it wasn't my duty to persuade him—and 'persuade' was hardly the word one could reasonably apply to the brain concealed behind those arrogant eyes, compressed within that high forehead, which surely had no room for more than one idea at a time. It was the most obstinate head, you know, I've ever set eyes on: the kind that is congenitally fated to run into brick walls. Still, I liked the old chap. He was a museum-piece, and I love museum-pieces.

" 'I'll tell you what we'll do,' I said. 'I know of a practical builder, a client of ours, whom you may rely on to tell you the truth and treat you fairly. If I can get hold of him this afternoon we'll take him round to look at your property and give us a rough idea of what the job's likely to cost.' I saw he liked the idea, so we fixed it up, and drove round together to 'The Cedars' that afternoon to meet Higgins, the builder.

"The house, at close quarters, has a good deal of charm; but Higgins didn't regard it æsthetically. As we climbed to the empty attics I heard him sniff and saw him shake his head. 'Dry rot,' he said. I looked at old Isit: he didn't utter a word. 'I suppose that means a biggish job, Mr. Higgins?' I said. Higgins wouldn't commit himself. 'You see, Mr. Wilburn,' he said, 'you can't rightly say where a thing like rot ends or begins, not until you start cutting it out. If it's left as it is, I can guarantee the whole blooming roof will be coming down sooner or later; and I wouldn't answer for the stairs or floors either, not till I've looked at the j'ists. Then there's the drainage: we would have to look into that as well. The Council is getting a regular terror on drains. No, sir, taking it altogether,' he said, 'I couldn't recommend anyone who was a friend of mine or yours to take on this house. I could build him a tip top new one in a respectable neighbourhood, land and all, for far less than you'ld have to spend putting this right.'

" 'It isn't a question of buying,' I told him. 'This gentleman here is the owner.'

"Mr. Higgins screwed up his eyes and had a good look at him, then shook his head. 'If this place was mine, sir,' he told him, 'I should have it pulled down and run up a row of working-class houses on the land. Then you might get your money back.'

" 'But supposing I decide to repair it,' the old man asked. 'How much will it cost me?'

"I could see that Higgins was sorry for him—and so was I. 'I'll tell you straight, sir,' he said. 'It'll cost you a fat lot more than it's worth or ever will be. You'll want a new roof, to begin with. You'll want new sanitation and plumbing for baths and domestic hot-water—to say nothing of the electric-wiring and central-heating—which is the only thing that'll keep the damp out as I see it: in the days when this house was built they didn't go in for damp-courses. Then there's painting, two coats all over outside and in, and plastering, and generally making good as we say in the trade. Two thousand seven hundred. That's my rough estimate. That's a packet of money, sir; and in my opinion it's throwing good after bad.'

"I looked at old Isit. He hadn't batted an eyelid. 'Two thousand seven hundred,' he said. 'Very well, Mr. Higgins. I shall be obliged if you will make a survey and prepare an estimate. I should like the work started as soon as may be convenient; but I want no bathrooms, hot water, or any nonsense of that kind. As for references . . .'

"I told him he needn't worry about those. Mr. Higgins looked glum. 'If I take on this job, sir,' he said, 'remember, I shall be doing it against my own better judgment.' The old man smiled grimly. 'That will be my funeral, Mr. Higgins,' he said. And, d'you know, it sounded prophetic. I think the decision must have shaken him: at that moment he looked extraordinarily old and frail. When the builder had gone, he stood in front of that gloomy place and stared at it with an affection and pride that was positively harrowing. 'It's a pity they cut down that cedar, Wilburn,' he said. 'It was a magnificent tree. I remember it well as a boy. My great-grandfather planted it. My girls will be disappointed. I have often told them about it.' "

"His girls?" my grandfather said. "I don't think you mentioned them."

"He hadn't mentioned them himself before that," Ernest Wilburn said. "Apparently there are two Miss Isits. I've been wondering ever since what on earth they'll be like. More El Grecos, I'm afraid. It's an odd heredity."

3

We were destined to wait a long time before anyone saw the Miss Isits. The necessary repairs to 'The Cedars' must have proved to be more expensive than Mr. Higgins at his most doleful had ever anticipated, for the thickets of scaffolding-poles continued to surround 'The Cedars' for several months. In the meantime the door-way in the middle of the wall was bricked up, and the openings to the drive on either side of the diminished front-lawn restored and fitted with wrought-iron gates that had probably been rusting for years in the dripping stables. Colonel Isit had evidently decided to keep a carriage. As for the house itself: now that workmen were busy about it and the windows open, it had lost, for me, a good deal of its mystery, though indeed, when Mr. Higgins had finished the job with a shiny coat of a bilious cream-colour, it looked more like a mausoleum than ever and almost more sinister than in its dingy past.

After this I caught sight of loads of furniture arriving from the repository in which, since Colonel Isit's uncle's death, it had been stored: pieces of massive mid-Victorian mahogany upholstered with horsehair, as "period" as anything Ernest Wilburn could desire, and as round and shiny as the horse-chestnuts which, to our great delight, at that season were falling to split their prickly cases on the mosaic of trampled leaves. Then, one day in November, when trophies of Roman candles and squibs and backa-rappers suddenly appeared in the shops behind window-panes misted by the cold outside, I saw the smoke of a fire ascending from the central cluster of chimney-pots, which meant that life had returned to the empty hearths; and when a few days later the front windows broke out, one by one, into festoons of lace curtain, I guessed at once that the Miss Isits must be in residence.

In my adolescent mind Colonel Isit's girls were already invested with an exotic fascination. They had come from India, the scene of the *Plain Tales from the Hills*, which everybody had been reading, and I expected them to be as dashing and as romantically inclined as Kipling's heroines. When my mother announced that "she must really go and call on those Miss Isits", I wished fervently I could find some excuse to go with her, and waited eagerly for the report on their charms she was certain to give my grandfather on her return.

The result was disappointing. The Miss Isits, she told us were not, strictly speaking, girls at all: the elder, Agnes, was probably in the neighbourhood of forty, and her sister Ellen some five or six years younger. They were certainly "ladies". Both, she gathered, had been educated at boarding-schools in England, and Agnes had evidently also been sent to finishing schools abroad: she had talked—rather gratuitously, my mother considered—of France and Italy, declaring that the world was divided into people who knew Rome and those who didn't. (My mother happened to belong to the second class.) Altogether she felt that the elder Miss Isit was a bit too superior for her liking, as a result, no doubt, of having been made to seem unduly important as the principal lady, the *burra memsahib*, in the limited community of a small station in India where such things counted. They certainly wouldn't count for much in North Bromwich, where professional soldiers were rare, and the wearing of military titles or uniform deprecated as evidence of 'swank' or 'side'. The Isits, she thought, would have felt much happier and more at home if they had settled in Bath, Leamington, Cheltenham, or some genteel watering-place with a reputation for a mild climate and the formal sort of society in which retired service people can exchange reminiscences with others who 'speak their own language' and share their grievances.

"I'm afraid," she said, "they're going to find us exceedingly dull."

"You haven't yet told me what they look like," my grandfather said.

Well, Miss Agnes, the elder, was handsome in a big, bony way—(I remembered Ernest Wilburn's description of the Colonel)—with dark hair, a rather sallow complexion, and extremely fine eyes with strongly-marked eyebrows. She certainly looked distinguished: the sort of woman a man had to look at twice. Whether he would look at her more than twice was another matter. Though she wasn't exactly unwomanly, her handsomeness had a decidedly masculine cast: she would look splendid in fancy-dress as a gentleman at the court of

Queen Elizabeth—or, if she put on a ruff and a red wig, as Queen Elizabeth herself.

"A trifle too queenly, in fact," my grandfather said.

"No . . . that wouldn't be fair. She was really quite agreeable, particularly when I told her that Ernest Wilburn had asked me to call. Before that she had no idea who I was; and I think she was anxious not to make the mistake of knowing the wrong people. Her sister was as different from her as chalk from cheese—or rather as cheese from chalk: much softer in every way and more feminine, without any unnatural constraint. If she'd been alone, I'm sure she would have let herself go and fluttered and talked quite a lot; but the presence of her sister subdued her and made her shut her mouth as soon as she'd begun to open it. Compared with her sister she's small, and she's not the least bony. Rather plump—you might almost say pretty, with soft, wavy hair and blue eyes, the colour of love-in-the-mist, and a quiet, rather plaintive voice. She hasn't a quarter of her sister's distinction; but I liked her the better of the two—partly, perhaps, because I felt sorry for her, though in fact she looked less like a fish out of water than the other one. If one got to know her well, one would probably find her too sentimental. She ought to have been married long ago to some not very ambitious man with a comfortable income and inexpensive tastes: she'ld have had lots of children and made a great success of life in a small way. Her sister looked positively magnificent in maroon satin. As I said before, she only needed a ruff to make Ernest Wilburn call her a perfect Vandyck. Of course they were both of them frozen."

"*Frozen?* What do you mean?"

"Well, that house is an ice-box in winter. When the maid opened the front door, you could feel a wave of cold air sweeping out to meet you over the stone flags. There was no furniture to speak of, and no carpet. It felt more like a family vault than an entrance-hall; and the drawing-room into which she showed me seemed even darker and colder, with the miserable remains of a fire just burnt out under an enormous black marble mantelpiece that looked as if it might have been designed as the entrance to Napoleon's tomb. They kept me waiting quite a long time, so I had a good look at the furniture. Very grand and rather jaded and dreadfully uncomfortable. There were a lot of gilt Empire chairs, upholstered in crimson brocade, and gilt ormolu cabinets and a clock that had stopped at a quarter to three, heaven knows how many years ago; and a piano—you know the kind—faced with pleated silk; and one of those threefold settees, of the kind they call 'sociables', on which people can only sit most unsociably back to back. And right in front of the fireplace there was a tiger."

"A tiger?" my grandfather protested.

She laughed. "You know what I mean. It wasn't alive. In fact it must have been dead a long time, the skin was so worn and mangy. But its left eye, which caught the light from the window, was dreadfully baleful and lifelike, and I'm sure it hated the cold and the darkness of that room as much as I did. You see the ceiling was so high that no fire could possibly have kept the place warm on such a raw day; and the windows, big as they were, admitted no light, because the factory on the other side of the road blocks out most of the sky. I just sat on the 'sociable' and looked at the tiger and shivered, while the maid, who had scrambled into a black uniform and a starched apron and put on a cap with streamers, brought in one of those bamboo trestle-tables with a tray of beaten Benares brass on the top of it, and a really exquisite Green Rockingham tea-set. I'm sure they have lots of lovely things like that if you could only see them, but the room simply bristled with grotesque oriental oddments: a huge ivory elephant trumpeting in the middle of the mantelpiece—which is genuine Adam, by the way, with its enrichments (is that the word?) hidden by a macramé mantel-border—with a whole family of baby elephants advancing on either side of him. Then there were brass Buddhas and many-armed Hindu idols and trophies of queer-looking weapons and useless, rickety bazaar-stuff of the kind that steamer passengers pick up at Port Said. All the gorgeous East in fee! And then Miss Isit surged in like the Queen of Sheba . . ."

"Queen Elizabeth, surely?"

My mother laughed. "Well, like Royalty anyway. I never felt more provincial and humble in my life. But that wasn't really her fault. I'm sure she's quite nice. It's only that she's missed her vocation and doesn't belong here. She ought to have married the Viceroy or the Governor of Bengal, and stood at the top of the Stairs while the band played *God Save the Queen*."

"You didn't see Colonel Isit?"

"Oh no. 'Papa,' as they call him, doesn't take tea. After tiffin he smokes a cheroot in the library and reads the *Times* of India, three weeks old. Then he goes for a ride, or shuts himself up in his workshop where nobody is ever allowed to disturb him on any account. I asked what he did there, but the sisters were rather mysterious. He works with a lathe at what they call 'his inventions'. It seems that he takes himself very seriously, but not half so seriously as they take him. Though they obviously venerate him and adore him, I must say he sounds to me like a difficult old man. He had no right to shut them up in that awful house in any case. That's enough in itself to cut them off from anything like a normal social existence. I don't want to go near it again if it can possibly be helped, though I feel it would be mean to desert them."

"Better have them to dinner next week and invite some nice people to meet them," my grandfather said.

4

I DON'T know how far my mother's sponsorship helped them, but by the following summer the Isits had been absorbed and had made a place for themselves in the society of Alvaston. No doubt they were given a social *entrée* by the fact that they belonged to one of the old North Bromwich Unitarian families, which are our local substitute for an hereditary aristocracy. In the church which his forefather Abraham had helped to found, Colonel Isit himself became a respected figure. Every Sunday morning he and his daughter Agnes, respectively resplendent in a frock-coat and a gown of black satin, drove down there in state in a victoria drawn by the old chestnut mare on whose back, during the remainder of the week, the Colonel took his daily afternoon ride. Miss Ellen did not accompany them, but humbly preceded them on foot to the High Anglican chapel of St. Jude. This unhappy lapse, of which the less said the better, was, it transpired, the result of Miss Ellen's early attachment to a boarding-school mistress who had seduced her from her family's more robust faith.

"The shock nearly killed Papa," Miss Agnes said, "and though he never mentions it now, I don't think he has ever got over her being baptized in secret by a wretched missionary in Poona whom nobody liked. Of course, as Unitarians, we pride ourselves on our liberality; but, as I told her at the time, I *do* think she might have considered her dear Papa's feelings."

This was the only outward sign of a breach in the solidity of the Isit façade; but though both sisters were firmly united in their loyalty, devotion and subservience to their exacting father and presented to the outer world the front of an affectionate and united family, there was between them, I fear, a strong, unconfessed antagonism, partly physical and temperamental, and partly the result of events of which, at that time, we had no inkling. These would have remained unknown but for the natural and usually suppressed effusiveness of Miss Ellen, whose innocent and spontaneous tongue, in revolt against the controls clamped on it by her sister's habitual reserve and her fear (for it was nothing less) of her dear Papa, was inclined to blab out all sorts of intimate confidences when encouraged by the least sign of human sympathy. No doubt it was this need for expression that lured her from the pragmatical faith of her fathers into the emotional atmosphere of the confessional at St. Jude's. Be this as it may, it was not long before the ladies of Alvaston became acquainted with most of the two Miss Isits' romantic history.

Both had had 'disappointments' in love, though in Agnes's case the disappointment had been tempered by a stern satisfaction in the maintenance of her caste.

"Of course," Miss Ellen said, "my sister always had scores of admirers. She is handsome and stately now, but fifteen years ago, when I was little more than a schoolgirl, just out from England, her beauty was really remarkable. If we had lived in important stations, like Simla or Rawal Pindi, I'm sure she could have made her choice from dozens of eligible men. But we never did, you know. You see Papa was always so forthright and independent, and nothing could ever induce him to truckle to superiors who were so much beneath him in fineness of character and intellect; and the result was, we always seemed to move about from one small station to another, little out-of-the-way posts where the society was very limited and *terribly* mixed. In places like that, of course, Agnes was simply a queen. How I wish you could have seen her! When she was present no man could dream of looking at anyone else: such a glorious figure, you know, and such fine eyes! A wife like her would have been the making of any man's career. She could have held her own in any rank of society: you see, she was not merely beautiful but so gifted and highly cultured—you've probably heard she was educated in Paris and Rome?—and she could talk about all sorts of things that are quite beyond me. And yet, somehow or other, the right sort of men, really coming men, never took to her. I think she was so dazzling that she must have frightened them; and the only admirer who ever proposed to her was—would you believe it?—a mere civilian: a doctor who had been sent out by a firm of druggists to experiment on the treatment of tropical diseases. A fine-looking, manly man, rather older than her, and very well-paid, I believe, but, all the same, very nearly what *we* call a 'box-wallah'. It would have been different if he had been in the I.M.S. His name—though I suppose I oughtn't really to tell you—was Benjamin Dench, and he's since been knighted, but nobody could have foreseen such a thing, and of course that plain sort of knighthood is never the same as a K.C.S.I. or a K.C.I.E. He wasn't, at that time at any rate, at all the sort of man a girl like Agnes, who came from a service family, could consider, and I'm sure Papa was relieved when she nipped the affair in the bud. Though she resembles Papa in never showing her feelings, I believe Agnes was fond of him in a way. Of course I had my own disappointment too . . ."

Miss Ellen sighed as she spoke of it, and her blue eyes grew mistier than ever as she glanced at a garnet ring she wore on her engagement-finger. She had been very young, ridiculously young, at the time. It was no more, she confessed, than a boy-and-girl affair, and had happened in 1895 almost immediately after her sister's double self-sacrifice on the altars of caste and filial duty. The young man who had fallen in love with her was in some ways a more desirable suitor than Mr. Dench, being a subaltern in the Two hundred and ninetieth, a not-very-good Madras infantry regiment, a detachment of which had recently arrived at their station. No doubt they had been very deeply and pathetically in love with one another, and might even have made their 'understanding' public, had not Agnes, newly aglow with conscious virtue, nipped their tender shoot of romance in the bud as well as her own. Her objections, this time, were not social but financial. Ellen's admirer, though more eligible socially than Mr. Dench, had no income beyond his pay and faint prospects of early promotion. They were both of them far too young, Agnes said, to know their own minds, and a protracted engagement would not be fair to either of them. Considering their age, they would have plenty of time to think the matter over for four or five years and avoid any rash commitment which they might later regret. Finally, Ellen ought always to remember that, however strong her inclinations might be, Papa, to whom they owed everything, must come first.

The young man had been furious. He couldn't for the

life of him see what Papa, whom he regarded as a tiresome old stick, had to do with it. 'Can't you see,' he had said, 'that your sister is jealous of our being happy?' Ellen couldn't—or wouldn't. She had scorned to believe that a woman so gifted, so handsome and so high-minded as Agnes could be jealous of anybody. They quarrelled over Agnes; they quarrelled over Papa. And in the midst of these pathetic dissensions a wire had come through from Simla ordering the Two hundred and ninetieth to proceed forthwith to the North-West Frontier, where trouble was fermenting in Chitral.

At this point it had been touch and go. If she wouldn't marry him there and then, as he wished, let them at least, the young man implored, be officially engaged. In the end Ellen had compromised on a secret engagement: it was the first time in her life she had ever done anything important unknown to her sister. On the last day before the unit entrained for the North on their way to Gilgit, he had bought her a poor little garnet ring, on tick, from a Parsee in the bazaar. Ellen dared not show it on her finger, but threaded it on a slender gold chain that had once been her mother's, and wore it on her breast, concealed by the high-necked costume of the period, and kissed it devotedly every night before she went to sleep. The next thing she heard of her lover was the news of his death in the Chitral rising. Though she felt her own life was as good as ended, she consoled herself, as she believed a soldier's daughter should, with a bitter pride in the thought that her lover had died heroically for his Queen and Country; but she often cried as she kissed her ring at night.

"You see," Agnes had said, "it was all for the best. Where would you be now if you had been married to that poor boy? Just imagine yourself; a widow at twenty-two . . ."

Perhaps she was right. Agnes was usually right, being so much cleverer and more logical than she; yet Ellen couldn't help feeling for the rest of her life that she had been cheated out of a happiness that was her due. Though she could never bring herself to accept her lover's diagnosis of Agnes's motives, their relations, from that day forward, had never been quite the same. It was about this time that, feeling the need of spiritual consolation, she had plucked up courage to join the Church of England, and the shock this administered to Agnes and her dear Papa had given her the unconscious satisfaction of an act of rebellion if not of revenge. It was not until many years later, when she was older and more sure of herself, that she had dared to wear the garnet engagement-ring on her finger, as she did now. And Agnes, although her keen eyes saw it was there, had never mentioned it, while Papa was too deeply wrapped up in his professional work to notice small things like that.

Now, of course, that was all ancient history. They had both of them settled down to live their own lives, joined together in a sort of social defensive alliance as a united and self-sufficient family whose main purpose it was to see that nothing they did or said adversely affected Papa's comfort and dignity. He was growing an old man now, and had greater need of their devotion than ever before. The sisters paid this debt willingly—even to the uncomfortable extent of encouraging and abetting his whim to settle down for the rest of his days in that cold Midland city, where neither of them knew a soul, and in that dark, dank, melancholy house which they both detested but which he loved because it had been the home of his family and the enchanted scene of his boyhood. So long as he lived they might—and indeed could—be counted upon to do their duty. After that—but this would not bear thinking of, and they didn't think of it. It would not be so easy for two middle-aged women who had lost the only thing they had in common to begin life all over again.

It must be admitted that the Miss Isits made a fair job of it. Agnes, at least, had a good deal of social *savoir-faire*, and Ellen, whom one couldn't help liking, gained by contrast with her sister. As a family they were not merely full of character but picturesque, and picturesqueness was not a common quality in North Bromwich, where the whole duty of man was to make money and spend it unobtrusively. Though when first he rode out from the wrought-iron gates of 'The Cedars' the women in the neighbouring slums flocked to their doors to laugh, and a crowd of children ran jeering after him, the slim, erect figure of Colonel Isit in polished black Wellingtons, full-skirted riding-coat, top-hat and yellow dogskin gloves made a startling spectacle in our prim suburban streets; for to diverge from the leaden mean of normality in appearance was more than any other man in Alvaston (save perhaps Ernest Wilburn, whose manners were frowned on) dared to do. Colonel Isit carried it off and was even admired for it because he was so completely unselfconscious—because he was not 'showing off' in the least but just being himself. If they didn't, like Wilburn, recognize him as an El Greco on horseback—perhaps an unknown portrait of Don Quixote?—they knew 'style' when they saw it.

And the Miss Isits too, clop-clopping along side by side in their old-fashioned victoria (on afternoons when the horse wasn't needed for riding) to make 'calls', at a time when everybody in Alvaston who could afford it and many who couldn't had begun to support the latest local industry by buying motor-cars, commanded more notice and respect than Lady Astill swishing past them in the largest of her husband's 'fleet' of hearse-like Daimler limousines. Their manners and speech were not bogus 'old-world', but the genuine mid-Victorian article inviolably preserved in the remoter recesses of British India—like the Elizabethan English which (we are told) still survives in the Kentucky mountains. When Lady Astill said 'ain't it?', the phrase betrayed her vulgarity: when Miss Agnes Isit used the same words they were merely a polite archaism: she was speaking as all the 'best people' had done in the eighteen-seventies, just as she and her sister persisted in wearing gloves at the dinner-table and slipping out the thumbs of both hands when the fish was served.

Once a month they gave dinner-parties at 'The Cedars'. In North Bromwich the fashion of formal entertaining had waned—if indeed it had ever existed. We were a bourgeois community, and prided ourselves on our lack of ceremony. People were invited to 'drop in for supper' on Sundays and take 'pot luck', and only 'dressed' for the Assembly-Room dances in winter. But the Isits' dinners were as formal as those of a Residency or a Government House. Even the menu was standardized, beginning with clear soup flavoured with chill vinegar followed by poached turbot and a chicken pilaff, and ending with a sardine savoury sharpened with sweet mango chutney—a refinement unknown to our provincial palates. Miss Agnes always wore 'her brocade' and Miss Ellen black lace; the Colonel looked taller and thinner than ever in 'tails', a white cambric tie (which he knotted himself) and a black moiré waistcoat. The seating at table was arranged with the strictest regard to precedence—a difficult problem in such a mixed community as ours. A mediocre claret was served cold in heavy cut-glass (the Colonel protected himself by drinking whisky) but the ladies of the party were expected to drink water or lemonade. After the savoury, when Miss Agnes, rising superbly, gave them the signal to retire, Colonel Isit passed round a decanter of excellent Madeira, matured by a voyage round the world, and offered his guests the choice of cheroots, which he favoured, or cigars. But no cigar was ever smoked in the drawing-room, where the ladies (resembling, as Ernest Wilburn said, a conversation-piece by Winterhalter) waited freezing round the fringe of the tiger-skin on which, later, the Colonel, taking the centre of the picture, stood bolt-upright distributing well-turned compliments to his female guests with a frigid, toothy smile on his bluish lips, or describing, at a hint from Agnes, how and when the animal had been shot, till, at ten precisely, the maid brought in the bamboo trestles and a tray of weak tea, which, it was learnt, had been sent specially from Dharjeeling. It was understood that the guests who had dined should leave cards on the following day, to prove, as Ernest Wilburn mischievously suggested, that they had survived the Colonel's chilled claret. Those who neglected this act of formal politeness were never invited again. And rightly: no doubt it was little things like this that had made the British Empire; and though these dinners at 'The Cedars' were not, as you can imagine, precisely festive, most people in Alvaston considered it an honour to be invited to them. Colonel Isit, it was generally conceded, was a 'grand old gentleman', the last exemplar of all those gracious forms and proprieties which our commercial age had so lamentably outgrown. He was not merely regarded as odd, but respected and prized for his oddity. Whatever he said or did was stamped with the hall-mark of style.

Naturally enough—for North Bromwich people are incurably inquisitive about each other's incomes—there was always a good deal of speculation on the subject of Colonel Isit's financial position. He had certainly spent money lavishly, and unprofitably, on the rehabilitation of that uncomfortable house in that shocking neighbourhood; and though his standard of living, apart from his rare entertainments, was unpretentious and without any obvious extravagance, it was generally supposed that he must be a 'pretty hot man'. At the club, where men talked about little else, he had never been known to speak of money or investments, and Ernest Wilburn, who handled his affairs, was far too good a solicitor to give anything away. His rank, of course, entitled him to a moderately good pension, but hardly enough to sustain such a large establishment—to say nothing of his carriage and groom.

In our ignorance of conditions in modern India I think we imagined that he had probably been loaded with jewels and lakhs of rupees by grateful native princes, like the 'nabobs' who bought estates and built country-mansions at the beginning of the last century. Of one thing we felt certain, that no man so constrained and rigid in his manners and principles as he, could ever be suspected of being a spendthrift. When, six years after settling at 'The Cedars', he returned from his usual ride, went to bed without telling anyone, and died, the same evening, in his sleep, people were naturally interested to know how much he had left. It came as a shock to most of North Bromwich to learn that his net personalty had been proved at less than three thousand pounds. I imagine that Ernest Wilburn was shocked even more deeply when he discovered that not a penny had ever been settled on the Miss Isits, and that 'The Cedars' was mortgaged for rather more than he considered it was worth.

5

If this startling figure gave a mild shock to people in Alvaston, it meant nothing to the Miss Isits. They had been living for years in a water-tight compartment—if such a phrase could rightly be applied to 'The Cedars', whose roof, in spite of Mr. Higgins's repairs, was already beginning to leak. In spite of their social activities, they had discouraged intimacy, and made no friends who could be counted upon to give them advice or comfort, with the exception of Ernest Wilburn. He, indeed, far exceeded his professional obligations, and was, as Miss Ellen declared, a 'tower of strength' and 'kindness itself', partly, no doubt, because he liked them, but even more because he regarded them as items in his collection and as characters in his private human comedy.

He found 'The Cedars' more hushed and dank and dismal than ever. Outside, soot and rain had already streaked and blackened Mr. Higgins's bilious cream paint, and the bleak drawing-room in which he awaited the Miss Isits' pleasure was so dark that it was hard to believe that the blinds which had been lowered on the day of the Colonel's death had yet been raised. As he sat there shivering, and submerged in a sort of subaqueous gloom, he couldn't help feeling that Colonel Isit's influence permeated it even more strongly in death than when he had been alive. It would hardly have surprised him if, raising his eyes, he had suddenly seen that odd, elongated apparition smiling at him from its accustomed place on the tiger-skin in front of the empty hearth; and indeed, when the door swung open at last with a metallic rattle of curtain-rings and the ghostly swish of the portière, and Miss Agnes, made taller and paler than ever by her mourning, gave him greeting in the strangely hushed tones to which human voices are habitually subdued in the neighbourhood of death, he found it hard to believe that the coffin he had seen duly lowered into its grave in Alvaston churchyard was not still in the house. Only the shy, sweet smile of Miss Ellen and the quick pressure of her warm hand reassured him and put him at ease.

Both the sisters were obviously still dazed by their loss. Their devotion to their father had been not merely the only interest they had in common but the mainspring of their separate existences. They had both given so much thought to their idol's caprices and comforts that, lacking these objects, they had nothing left to think about—and indeed seemed incapable of thinking of anything else, including their own situation. The Colonel, it seemed, had persisted to the end in treating them as children, and had never—for the best of reasons, as it now appeared—admitted them to his confidence in financial affairs. He had allowed Miss Agnes so much every month for household expenses, an estimate which she had never exceeded; but even so he had insisted on scrutinizing and paying every single bill himself. This fixed sum had been expected to cover not only the wages and housekeeping but also the two sisters' modest personal expenditure. They had never enjoyed the liberty of an allowance or handled money themselves. If they needed it for any particular occasion or purpose, they had had to ask him for it; and such demands had not been encouraged. As a result of this discipline, they were not merely unused to thinking of money but lamentably ignorant of its value and incapable now of appreciating the condition in which the old tyrant's selfishness had landed them. Ernest Wilburn, with admirable tact and patience, did his best to enlighten them and to let them down gently.

"I have carefully examined all your father's affairs," he told them, "and I think the general picture is now fairly clear. It isn't exactly cheerful. You will be faced with decisions that will certainly be difficult and may be painful. As your friend no less than as your lawyer, I shall naturally do my best to advise you; but, to tell you the truth, I would much rather share the responsibility with some member of your family—a male relative for preference."

"We have no relations at all," Miss Agnes replied in a tone which suggested that she was proud of it, "with the exception of an uncle, my dear mother's brother, who succeeded to the family estate in Radnorshire. As you probably know," she added with conscious dignity, "my mother was a Vaughan of Tregoyd. The family is in direct descent from King Cadwallader."

"Of course, of course," Wilburn murmured sympathetically.

"But I have no idea," Miss Agnes went on, "if this Mr. Vaughan is still alive. Papa had differences of opinion with him. I don't know what they were, but I'm sure they were justified. And after mother's death they did not correspond, so you need not consider him. Still, in any case, Mr. Wilburn, I think that my sister and I are competent to make any decisions that may be necessary. We are no longer children."

"Oh, quite, quite. . . . I entirely agree," Wilburn said. "Of course you already realize that, up till now, you have mainly been living on your father's pension. And that, naturally, will no longer be available. In fact, when all the estate's outstanding debts have been paid . . ."

Miss Agnes flushed quickly. She straightened her back and her fine eyes hardened.

"Did I hear you say 'debts', Mr. Wilburn? I am positive that Papa would never have allowed a penny to remain unpaid beyond the end of the month. He was a man of unshakable principles in this, as in everything else."

"Of course, of course . . ." Wilburn agreed. "I shouldn't for a moment dream of suggesting he wasn't. But you must understand that the settlement of every estate involves a number of unavoidable expenses—for death duties, probate, and so forth; and before it is 'wound up' it is my duty as your lawyer to see that every outstanding item of indebtedness has been discharged—as indeed I have done. I am only afraid that you and your sister may be disappointed by the result. Your father was not a rich man, Miss Isit. What is more, he lived up to his income; and I'm sorry to tell you that you will have to adapt yourselves to a much more modest standard of life than that to which you have always been accustomed—unless, that is, you have private means of your own of which I am unaware."

"We have *no* private means," Miss Agnes said emphatically, "and I hardly think, Mr. Wilburn, if I may say so, that our standard of life could be much more modest than it has been. We have managed to maintain it quite comfortably on the forty pounds a month Papa allowed me."

"Ah yes. Forty pounds a month. That's ten pounds a week, isn't it? Very moderate too, considering the size of the house, with your carriage, your entertaining and all the rest of it."

"It will naturally be a long time," Miss Agnes said, "before we are out of mourning and can consider entertaining again."

"Of course," Ernest Wilburn agreed. "But even apart from these . . . unhappy circumstances, I fear you will have to curtail your usual hospitality. So far as I can judge from what I know of your father's estate—unless there are any assets of which we have no knowledge—it seems unlikely that you will be able to afford to remain in this house."

Miss Agnes stared at him incredulously.

"I don't think, Mr Wilburn, you can quite realize what you are saying. After all, 'The Cedars' is our family home. I am quite sure that Papa would never have countenanced our leaving it after all the care and money he spent on restoring it. That indeed would be callous and ungrateful. We should feel, in fact, that it amounted to a betrayal of dear Papa's memory. It would be almost irreverent. This is our own house, isn't it? I mean we can surely stay here without paying rent?"

"Well. . . . Yes and no. Let me try to explain, Miss Isit. 'The Cedars' is yours in the sense that you hold the title-deeds; but at the time when your father took possession of it, he found himself faced with the necessity of expensive repairs to make it habitable, and he hadn't, in fact, the money he needed available. So he mortgaged the property: in other words borrowed money on it. For some reason best known to himself he did not put the business in my hands: it was only the other day that I came to know of what had been done. But now we do know that he borrowed two thousand five hundred pounds at four per cent. The interest upon that loan is paid up to date. As you say, in such matters he was most punctilious. But, at the end of next quarter, you will have to pay the mortgagees—who are actually the Astill Estates Limited—the sum of twenty-five pounds: one fourth of the sum that is due to them annually. In other words 'The Cedars' will cost you the equivalent of a rent of a hundred a year."

Miss Agnes pursed her lips:

"I'm afraid, Mr. Wilburn, I am not very well versed in matters of this kind. But wouldn't it be much simpler and save us a great deal of trouble if we could pay off this debt—this mortgage, I think you called it—from the money Papa has left?"

"Indeed yes. Of course it would be. But here, I'm afraid, you find yourselves faced with another difficulty. When everything is settled, it looks as if you will have barely enough left to redeem the mortgage. In the meantime you must live—and you will need every penny you possess to do that even on the very modest scale which you will be forced to accept. You see, that isn't all either. If you continue to live in this house you will be liable for a number of other payments, such as rates and taxes, which you can't avoid; and frankly I don't see how you can possibly meet them in addition to the claims of the mortgagees."

Miss Agnes remained stonily silent. Miss Ellen sighed and shook her head. Wilburn saw there were tears in her eyes.

"If you will let me advise you," he said. . . .

Miss Agnes inclined her head. "Please go on, Mr. Wilburn."

"Well, the position is this. Apart from the house, which the existence of the mortgage makes a liability rather than an asset, sound well-selected investments should provide you with an income of rather less than two hundred pounds a year, which, after all, would be enough to live on, without any frills, if you rent a small house in an inexpensive neighbourhood. I've no doubt that I and my brother could find you a cottage somewhere in pleasant surroundings at a moderate rent."

"I should love to live in the country, Agnes," Miss Ellen said pleadingly.

Miss Agnes disregarded her: "Please go on, Mr. Wilburn," she said.

"As for 'The Cedars' . . . I hardly know what to advise. Of course you might sell it, but I hardly think the price it would fetch in the open market is likely to reach the sum for which it is mortgaged. On the whole I think it would be wiser to try to come to some agreement with the mortgagees, who, I imagine, might be interested in the land on which it stands because it happens to be surrounded by their property. In other words, I might possibly induce them—though this, of course, I can't promise—to take over the house and cancel the mortgage."

"And lose part of their money?" Miss Agnes was sharp enough, he could see, when she put her mind to it. "But that wouldn't be honourable, Mr. Wilburn, surely?"

Wilburn smiled. "My dear Miss Isit, you put it rather too harshly. In money matters, as in most other things, one is prepared to make up on the swings what one loses on the roundabouts, and sensible folk are ready to cut their losses if necessary. Half a loaf, they will say—or in this case approximately three-quarters—is a lot better than no bread. Like most other things in business, this becomes a matter of compromise."

"Papa never compromised in anything, Mr. Wilburn," Miss Agnes said sternly, "and I am positive that he would not wish my sister and myself to do so."

"But, you see—please forgive me for going on speaking in clichés—you can't possibly eat your cake and have it too. If you pay off the mortgage, you won't be able to live in the house. It's even worse than that. I'm afraid there's really no choice. You can't really afford to live in the house in any case. Whereas . . ." Wilburn smiled and continued persuasively. "Whereas, if you follow my plan: that is, allow me to approach the Astill Estates in the way I've suggested and find you a small inexpensive house in the outer suburbs or in the country, you would not merely have the satisfaction of feeling that you owed nobody anything, but might even be able to increase your very small capital by selling the greater part of the furniture with which this house is crowded. There is certainly far more of it than you could possibly use, and most of it would be out of place in a smaller house. You may not get very much money for it: this is an age of atrocious taste in which good things are not appreciated; but in your present position every little bit helps, and we ought to make the most of our opportunities."

Ernest Wilburn paused. The silence which followed his speech was discouraging if not ominous. The moment had obviously come for another of his 'little jokes'; but, remembering their effect on the Colonel, he had a feeling that the Miss Isits might take him too literally and, in any case, were unlikely to be amused. He fell back on another stock attitude which he had usually found effective with lady clients of a certain age: a bluff, avuncular benevolence tinged with a sort of caressive gallantry—the attitude, in short, of a kindly man of the world who counted it a privilege to help and shield them from the rough-and-tumble of circumstances with which they could not be expected to deal. This was usually accompanied by a reassuring pat on the shoulder or pressure of the hand; but the rigidity of Miss Agnes's shoulders and the inaccessibility of her hands, which were folded in her lap, deterred him from using this gesture.

"The best thing you can do," he went on, "is not to worry your heads about anything for the present. Just leave everything to me. You can rely on my promise to do all that I can to make the best of a rather intricate job. Don't get anxious if you don't hear from me for a day or two. The affair is complicated and will have to be handled with a good deal of tact—particularly that part of it which concerns the mortgage. Of course I shall consult you and secure your approval before I commit you to any important step. I'll look round again in a week or so and report progress on what I have done. In the meantime, if you should find yourselves in need of advice—or even of ready money, please don't hesitate to call on me for either."

He rose, smiling, well pleased with himself. On the whole, he felt, his tactics had gone down fairly well. Miss Ellen, at any rate, had responded to them correctly. As he spoke he had been pleased to see the obvious signs of relief and gratitude in her face. It was flushed with a mild glow of excitement, and the eagerness with which she hung on his words was flattering to his self-esteem. The stress of this emotional crisis had actually brought this subdued creature to life and made her seem more physically attractive than he had imagined her, with a kind of soft faded prettiness that added to his protective benevolence a tinge of genuine sentiment and made him feel unexpectedly tender towards her. One couldn't confidently feel tender towards Miss Agnes—though, indeed, the same influence of emotional strain had enhanced the formal beauty which he had always recognized—not so much as that of a sentient human being as of a work of art. In that shadowy drawing-room, against the background of old gilt furniture, it had found a setting that art could hardly have bettered. Its lighting was perfect; a cold gleam from the smoke-shrouded sky defining, with a just balance of light and shade, the classical regularity of every clear-chiselled feature: the curve of the smooth, pale forehead beneath the sweep of jetty hair, above eyebrows black as a firm, swift stroke of charcoal; the nose—too emphatic perhaps yet, none the less, nobly modelled; the faintly-smiling mouth, its short upper lip brushed with a dusky bloom, the lower lip full and (was it possibly?) sensuous. In this lighting and in repose, it was, Ernest Wilburn decided, a proud, an exquisite mouth. If it had belonged to anyone but Miss Agnes, he would have wanted to kiss it; but even as this strange desire flickered through his mind, he became aware of a disquieting quality in that faint smile. Was it bitterness? Was it irony? Was it scorn? He could not tell. He only knew, in his bones, that there was something in it that boded ill for his sense of triumph and satisfaction, and that the sooner he escaped from it the better he would be pleased. He began to make hurried adieus.

"Well now, if you will excuse me, Miss Isit . . ." he said.

"One moment, please, Mr. Wilburn."

"Most certainly. As long as you like."

"I shall not keep you long. I have listened most carefully to all you have said, and I am afraid we cannot agree with a word of it. It is our plain duty, as I see it, and as I'm certain Papa would see it, to pay his debts to the full. I would sooner die of starvation, and so would my sister, than take any advantage of the people who lent Papa money on this house, or let them lose anything by reason of our misfortunes. If there is enough money available, the mortgage must be redeemed. If there isn't—well, then we must go on paying them interest until we are able to redeem it. Have I made that quite clear?"

Ernest Wilburn assented feebly.

"And now, as to the house itself: I feel it is equally our duty, as Papa's daughters, to go on living here if we possibly can. You probably don't realize how deeply he was attached to it, and how we share his attachment. After all, it has been the home of our family for more than a century."

"Quite, quite. I entirely sympathize with your feelings.

They are perfectly right and natural. I've merely been trying to explain that it may not—and probably won't—be possible for you to live here, and to suggest the most practical alternative."

Miss Agnes smiled proudly, almost patronizingly.

"Do you really think, Mr. Wilburn, that I and my sister are as helpless as all that? Do you think that Papa could ever have countenanced our taking the line of least resistance in the way you suggest? I can see no reason on earth why we should not be able, between us, to earn our living and keep the position to which Papa's rank entitles us. After all, we are not without accomplishments, Mr. Wilburn, nor are we afraid or ashamed to make use of them. And I am thankful to say," she added, with a challenging air, "that we are both of us young and healthy."

Ernest Wilburn could do no more than agree, rather lamely, and assure her that he admired their spirit. He left 'The Cedars' that afternoon feeling slightly snubbed. He had forgotten, as he reflected afterwards, the hereditary implications of Colonel Isit's obstinate head. And, oddly enough, it had not previously occurred to him that either of the Miss Isits was young. He had never till that moment thought of Miss Agnes as a human being. And that was one of the biggest mistakes he ever made in his life.

6

ON THAT wave of rebellious pride the idea of 'The Cedars Preparatory Academy' was conceived in Miss Agnes's mind. The school itself struggled into existence after an interval of more than six weeks, during which the Miss Isits put their chaotic affairs—not exactly in order—but in a state that appeared presentable to the eyes of outsiders.

This process began, as Wilburn had suggested, with a sale of surplus belongings; but this did not mean that

'The Cedars' was exposed to the violations of a vulgar invasion. No posters, affixed to the long brick wall that shielded its privacy, proclaimed the date of a Public Auction. The announcement was made in the form of an invitation printed in copperplate and distributed by letter-post to a selected list of possible purchasers, who were informed that, in winding up the estate of the late Colonel Isit, R.E., C.I.E., the Misses Isit were prepared to dispose of a small part of their property, including a few choice examples of Regency furniture; several sets of old china; a pneumatic-tyred tricycle; a Victoria Carriage, by Mulliner, and a stylish-moving chestnut riding or driving mare named Rowena, fourteen hands high, complete with a set of harness furnished with silver, and two Indian riding-saddles—all of which could be viewed, by appointment only, on two specified days.

Most of the people who had been invited came, in due course, to 'The Cedars'; some, who had not enjoyed the privilege of Colonel Isit's acquaintance, out of sheer curiosity; others, who knew the Miss Isits socially, from a mingled desire to help them and possibly, at the same time, to pick up an odd bargain. They were received by Miss Ellen: Miss Agnes, under the stress of a natural emotion, having retired to a darkened room with one of the devastating sick headaches to which she was subject. The pieces of furniture selected for sale had been moved by the joint exertions of the Miss Isits, the groom, and the domestic staff, who were now all 'under notice', into the dining-room on the ground floor, which had been cleared to receive them, and which the prospective buyers were only allowed to enter one at a time in Miss Ellen's presence, the remainder dismally keeping the tiger company in the atmosphere of a dentist's waiting-room. From the strangers' point of view this arrangement was not a success. They objected, not unreasonably, to being kept 'hanging about', and the 'choice examples' of furniture, when finally revealed, hardly seemed to justify their long wait in the frozen drawing-room. Lady Astill, who had to wait half an hour for her turn, described them as 'junk'. As for picking up bargains, it soon became clear that nothing would be given away. Miss Agnes, before she collapsed, had ticketed every article with a price inspired by affection rather than reason; and the vulgar few who attempted to beat Miss Ellen down were rebuffed with a frigid refusal which, in spite of its politeness, made them feel they had been 'put in their places'.

"You'd have thought," Lady Astill complained to Ernest Wilburn afterwards, "the woman was doing me a favour—*me*, mind!—in allowing me even to look at her furniture, let alone buy it. I shouldn't have gone near the place if Joe hadn't told me they were down on their luck and it would be kind to give them a lift. There honestly wasn't a single thing on view that I'd have been seen dead with, except that old tiger-skin, which we might have put down in front of the billiard-room fireplace. When I told her I wouldn't mind giving her a couple of pounds for that, and she could send it round in the morning, you'ld have thought I'd insulted her, she went that red in the face. 'I don't think you quite understand, Lady Astill,' she said. 'It was a man-eater shot by my father at the risk of his life in Moogly Meringapatam!'—or some such place! Well, honestly, if they're as badly off as Joe says, I do think they might cut out these high-and-mighty airs when people like Joe and me, who don't know them from Adam, go out of their way to be kind. They tell me the little one who showed me round—what's her name? Ellen?—is the better of the two. Well, if that's so, all I can say is I'm glad I never set eyes on the other one! You'ld think by the way she behaved they were titled people like me, and I was a nobody. It's time they learnt this is North Bromwich, not Moogly Meringapatam. In my opinion they're asking for what they'll get."

They got rather more, in fact, than might have been expected; for the legend of their misfortunes had been widely circulated in Alvaston, and North Bromwich folk, though hard-fisted, are also warm-hearted. Ernest Wilburn himself, in an access of generosity, bought a number of 'pieces' for which he had neither room nor use.

The Victoria Carriage, by Mulliner, remained unsold; but the 'stylish-moving chestnut', on which Colonel Isit had ridden in leisurely stateliness through the suburban streets, was bought, in his cups, by a local butcher, a crony of the groom's, and was to be seen, thenceforth, clattering through the same streets and mounted by a boy in a blue-striped overall, carrying baskets of beef and mutton. Rowena's descent in the scale of respectability was a great grief to the Miss Isits: they would much rather she had been sold to a gentleman—even a gentleman-farmer—as she deserved. Horses, like elephants, were discriminating animals, and could always tell by instinct the difference between the seats of gentlefolk and 'other people'. The Colonel had said she had a mouth like velvet, and, though he always wore spurs, had never used them; but the butcher's boy carried a stick, and used it freely. The sight of Rowena, already grown shaggy and unkempt, swinging into the drive which she had once been used to enter and leave so decorously, with this pimply young yahoo in the blue-striped overall on her back, affected the Miss Isits so deeply that they felt forced to change their butcher—which was a pretty scurvy way, as he told the groom, of rewarding him for relieving them of a horse he wouldn't have given a quid for if he had been sober. Not that their custom mattered all that much!

It mattered increasingly little. Of course there were no more dinner parties. Miss Ellen, who was naturally plump, had a normal appetite which, in their days of plenty, she had dared to indulge within the bounds of propriety; but now that Papa was gone, dear Agnes continually insisted on the need for economy, and set such an example in the control of hers, which had always been pernickety, that Miss Ellen was shamed into a similar abstemiousness for fear of appearing greedy—consoling herself with the thought that it was all to the good of her figure, and that conditions would almost certainly become less stringent when the school-fees began to roll in.

Miss Ellen looked forward to their experiment enormously. For one thing, unlike Agnes, she had always had a wistful adoration for children, and failing any of her own, was eager for the chance of mothering other people's. It was to be called, as I have said, 'The Cedars Preparatory Academy,' though Miss Agnes did not at first specify for what her prospective pupils were to be prepared. The project, in fact, was deliberately kept rather dark. It was not even advertised as the sale had been, by circulars; and nothing so blatantly commercial as a brass plate denoted the change in the condition of 'The Cedars'. Only through a few carefully-selected mouths, the whisper went round in Alvaston, that the Miss Isits, being no longer engrossed in the care of their Papa, and having time on their hands, might condescend to grant a few highly-favoured girls the privilege of profiting at second-hand from the unique educational advantages they had enjoyed. 'The Cedars' would certainly not be a 'school' in the ordinary sense of the word—any more than the Miss Isits were professional schoolteachers. Its atmosphere would be that of a home life rich in the culture which was, alas, so rare in North Bromwich; its aims formative rather than didactic; and its pupils, while unconsciously assimilating the reflected glories of Rome and Paris (to say nothing of Moogly Meringapatam), and cleansing their speech of the unfortunate Midland accent, would be able to learn music, ballroom dancing, deportment, embroidery, elocution, and two modern languages—all those graces and accomplishments, in short, which would fit them to take their place in Polite Society—if the chance ever came their way. Only children from the very nicest families in Alvaston would be accepted, and—though the Miss Isits were shy of mentioning money—their parents would naturally be expected to pay considerably larger fees than those demanded by ordinary professional establishments which had nothing to offer but bare scholastic instruction, and made no pretence of equipping their pupils for Life.

At first sight Miss Agnes's project appeared hazardous. Many things were against it—not the least of which was the position of 'The Cedars' itself in the heart of an unsavoury slum, and the social exclusiveness of the Miss Isits, which had alienated the majority of those ordinary people on whose goodwill their success depended. Yet, oddly enough, 'The Cedars Preparatory Academy' went off with a flying start. In the fortunate period which immediately preceded the Boer War, North Bromwich was bloated with 'new money', whose owners were so naïve as to believe that the more a thing cost and the harder it was to come by, the more desirable it must be. And they were not only rich and naïve but also snobbish, deeply anxious that their children should not perpetuate the stigma of provincialism on which they affected to pride themselves; and though they might laugh at the Miss Isits' 'airs and graces', they were genuinely impressed by them. Thus 'The Cedars Preparatory Academy' had an undeniable *cachet*, and became, for the moment, so fashionable that the Miss Isits were in the happy position of being able to refuse a number of applicants for their tuition: which seemed to prove, of itself, how desirable it must be, and enabled them to pick and choose. They even began to regret the impulse of panic which had persuaded them to dismiss the groom and sell Rowena. Equitation would have made a desirable addition to the Academy's curriculum, and they would have been able, had they but known it, to keep their victoria on the road, and remain 'carriage-folk'. Now, alas, it was too late. It would never do for them to be seen behind a horse that was known to have been ridden by a butcher boy. Perhaps, later on. . . .

In the meantime they both worked like beavers and throve on it. This was probably the first period in their lives in which they had been fully employed. Miss Agnes, naturally, was the controlling intelligence. She had always had 'a wonderful head for figures' and had been accustomed for years to balance her household accounts to the halfpenny.

As the chief arbitress of elegance she also gave lessons in Deportment, of which she was a living example, Elocution, Italian and French, while Miss Ellen taught Music,

Ballroom dancing and Embroidery. Partly from their desire that the Academy should not seem like an ordinary commercial school, and partly out of respect for their father's memory, they made hardly any modifications in the interior arrangements of 'The Cedars'. While Miss Agnes took classes in Colonel Isit's library, which was also her office, Miss Ellen pushed back the furniture and rolled up the tiger-skin to conduct dancing-lessons in the drawing-room, or guided hesitant fingers over the yellow ivories of the silk-pleated Broadwood through the tinkling intricacies of *The Robin's Return* and *The Merry Peasant.* When Miss Agnes had 'one of her headaches', Miss Ellen took on the Elocution classes, and 'put expression' into her pupils' recitations in selected passages from *The Idylls of the King;* but Agnes would not allow her to give lessons in Deportment, for the teaching of which her physique did not qualify her; and though, in her youth, she had acquired a smattering of schoolgirl French, her accent was of a kind that made Miss Agnes refuse to let her make use of it.

So, for two or three years, to the mingled delight and scorn of their working-class neighbours, a procession of prim little girls from Alvaston was daily engulfed in the frigid gloom of 'The Cedars' front-hall, which always smelt faintly of damp stone and cooking vegetables, and emerged, some hours later, with their manners, accents and bearing, subtly improved by mere contact with the Miss Isits' formative influence. They all liked Miss Ellen, who was kindly and natural and found no difficulty in unbending; and they were all afraid of Miss Agnes. In winter they all suffered from chilblains, which Miss Ellen dressed with Tincture of Arnica in the privacy of a dark cloak-room made terrible by the presence of no less than six pairs of the Colonel's riding-boots, set upright in a row, like the pipes of an organ, and always kept polished, as if he were still alive. The interior of 'The Cedars' was usually several degrees colder than the air outside, because Miss Agnes's Spartan principles decreed that no fires should ever be lighted before the First of December or after the

Fifteenth of March. It wasn't so bad for the Miss Isits, who always wore Kashmir shawls and woollen mittens; but when it came to music-lessons, the keys of the piano were like slabs of ice, and it took more than a Mazurka or a set of Quadrilles to warm one's feet, since Miss Ellen was really hurt if one didn't tread lightly. In summer they were permitted to 'play', during the recess, on the lawn that surrounded the one remaining cedar at the back of the house; but even that wasn't much fun when one was aware, all the time, of the tall figure of Miss Agnes in her black sateen apron surveying one's frolics from the library window and deploring one's lack of deportment. And the garden of 'The Cedars', with its cat-scrabbled beds of sour and hungry soil, in which nothing but lean flag-irises ever throve, was not gracious and green, like the gardens of Alvaston, but resembled the yard of a prison, overlooked by the sooty windows of the Enville Road's back-to-backs, and surrounded by a sentinel chevaux-de-frise of factory chimneys whose trailing smoke made the air acrid and bleared the sky.

Education, however polite, was not very gay at 'The Cedars'. For, to tell the truth, in spite of their initial success, the Miss Isits were no more 'cut out' for school-mistresses than was the house itself suitable for use as a school. At the moment when they embarked on their venture they had had the field to themselves; but by the end of the third year, when its novelty was beginning to wear off, a rival establishment of a more ambitious nature was set up, a genuine 'finishing school' combined with the newly-fashionable kindergarten, in a large country house called 'Alvaston Manor' which had stood empty for several years in the middle of a well-wooded park with ornamental waters, in which young ladies could learn to swim, and equipped with a riding-stable of docile saddle-horses on which they would actually 'ride to hounds'. Its principal was a stylish, modern young woman, a product of Roedean and Girton, and the staff included a number of foreign mistresses who taught music and languages. As a further recommendation, if any were needed, it was learnt that a number of the 'boarders' came from London and that they included two daughters of a peer, who were 'Ladies in their own right'. Furthermore, its fees were enormous.

It was not long before the Miss Isits, acclimatized to rough weather as they were, felt the draught, though they had no desire, as they said, to compete with anything so flashy as Alvaston Manor; and 'The Cedars' received its *coup de grâce* from an epidemic of diphtheria and scarlet fever which broke out in North Bromwich about that time and raged furiously, as might have been expected, in the slums of Enville Lane. It would be a crime, parents said, to let their children so much as sniff the air of that polluted quarter. Many of them were probably glad of the excuse for removing them from an establishment that had ceased to be in the mode.

The Miss Isits fell upon evil times, and sustained them heroically. How dark was the struggle that went on within the scabrous, soot-blackened stucco of 'The Cedars', which was gradually reverting to its former aspect of neglected decrepitude and abandonment, not even Ernest Wilburn, who was nearer, perhaps, to their confidence than anyone else, was allowed to guess. They still 'kept up appearances': that is to say, they continued to be 'at home' on Second Thursdays and gave tea to their ever-narrowing circle of friends. On these social occasions Miss Agnes, in her black satin, was as dignified, and Miss Ellen, in her chiffon, as gay as ever they had been in their prime; though an acute observer might have noticed that both were thinner and that the dainty specialities, which had made their tea-parties famous, no longer appeared so abundantly or in so great a variety on the triple-tiered bamboo cake-stand, and that even the bread-and-butter was spread more thinly. The parlour-maid, in starched apron and streamered cap, no longer carried in the Benares brass tea-tray, and the brew in the green Rockingham teapot no longer steamed with the authentic bouquet of a specially imported Dharjeeling. The Miss Isits' domestic staff had, in fact, been reduced to one maid-of-all-work who, for love of Miss Ellen, had consented to 'stay on' at a diminished wage, but who could neither make dainty cakes nor be trusted to wash up fine porcelain—with the result that Miss Ellen had to do both. Furthermore, an acute observer might have discerned—not that the room was colder and darker (it could hardly have been that) but that it somehow seemed larger and emptier, and that, in fact, certain familiar objects of art and pieces of furniture had mysteriously disappeared. The great ivory elephant, for instance, no longer dominated the lintel of Napoleon's tomb; and his family, which had straggled so bravely along the length of the mantelpiece, were now huddled together, as though they were frightened or felt the cold, in the place he had formerly occupied. One only dared notice these gaps, as it were, surreptitiously and with a sense of indelicacy; for Miss Agnes's fine eyes, which were as dark and brilliant as ever, had a way of following one's glances and reading one's thoughts, and if they caught either straying she would quickly round them up, like a wise sheep-dog mustering an unruly flock, by alluding to the dinner-party Papa had given the Viceroy at Moogly Meringapatam (if that was its name) in 1890, or the scent of heaped freesias on the stalls at the Ponte Vecchio—neither of which the unfortunate straggler had ever seen or smelt. By such devices (if indeed the dignity of her presence were not sufficient) Miss Agnes was able to remind her visitors that they were enjoying the hospitality, however restricted, of one who had moved in exalted circles and knew the world—and that their material wealth, which was the only advantage over her that any of them could boast, was of small importance in comparison with these imponderables.

When school hours were over, the sisters were left alone with the cockroaches in the echoing house. Not wholly alone. The loss of Rowena had been compensated by the acquisition of two new pets. One, an Aberdeen terrier named Stewart, had been presented to Miss Agnes by one of her pupils whose parents wanted to get rid of him. He was a dour, self-centred little dog, with a strong smell, a bored, blinking expression, and an uncertain temper, the result of insufficient exercise. What appealed to Miss Agnes was his single-minded devotion. He was a one-woman dog, who refused to take interest in anyone but herself. His low black shape followed her tall black figure about wherever she went, like a witch's familiar, from morning to night. He was ready to snarl and bare his teeth at anyone who approached her, and slept on the hot-water bottle at the foot of her bed.

Miss Ellen, in secret, had done her utmost to purchase this morose little creature's regard by tempting him with scraps, which he gobbled greedily, but which tried his digestion and worsened his temper without improving their relations. She didn't resent Stewart's dislike of herself nearly so much as his invincible hostility towards the centre of her own affections, a small tabby cat, an unwanted denizen of the neighbouring slum, which, lured by the milkman every morning, had finally decided to attach itself to the house. Miss Agnes had objected strongly to the creature's presence, and shooed it away whenever she saw it.

"We cannot allow ourselves to be pestered by stray cats," she declared. "Nobody knows where it comes from, and it's probably infested with vermin. It would be a nice thing if it gave the children ringworm or mange. Besides, it may have kittens."

"I'm sure it won't," Miss Ellen said. "I can tell by the shape of its head."

"Well, Stewart dislikes it, and, after all, he was here first."

"I think it's a sweet little cat," Ellen said, "and so intelligent."

"How *can* you say that, Ellen? No cats are intelligent. They've no room for brains in their snakey heads, have they, Stewart?"

Miss Ellen concurred with her lips, but hardened her heart. Though she rarely showed it, she had inherited her own share of the family obstinacy. From the moment when she had first set eyes on its lank little ribs and christened it Waifie, this small creature had found a refuge in her empty heart, and it would have taken a greater power than Agnes's or Stewart's spite to eject it. Though she would have loved to own a dog of her own, she really liked cats better. Whatever their sex—and until the first batch of kittens arrived she had no idea of Waifie's—they were so much more gentle and ladylike and unobtrusive. Moreover, Waifie didn't, like Stewart, reject her advances; and if its affections were bestowed less demonstratively, she believed they were deeper. She continued to tempt her kitten—for it *was* hers—into the house, where it displayed an uncanny virtuosity in avoiding the attentions of Agnes and Stewart, stealing through the dark hall and passages like an evanescent shadow that mysteriously materialized at Miss Ellen's side whenever she was alone, and vanished, as swiftly, at the approaching swish of Miss Agnes's skirts or the patter of Stewart's paws. And, little by little, in spite of Miss Agnes's reiterated expressions of annoyance and Stewart's unmannerly assaults, Waifie established herself as the fourth living member of the household, and finally, by sheer persistence, asserted her right to sit blinking and purring contentedly on Miss Ellen's lap, which was much warmer, as she knew quite well, than the position which Stewart arrogated to himself on the tiger-skin in front of the fire. Miss Ellen found a strange comfort, too, in the proximity of this tiny warm fragment of life. To her, Waifie was not merely beautiful, but also the sole living creature to whom she felt drawn with a protective tenderness. No other passion, save her secret religious emotions, so melted her heart.

These were still, of course, her sweetest consolation, however Agnes might sneer at them. Though the degraded Rowena continued to canter past the gates of 'The Cedars', carrying the luscious Sunday saddles and sirloins that they could no longer afford, and the moths to make havoc with the upholstery of the abandoned victoria, the Miss Isits still went on foot, in opposite directions, at least twice every Sunday, to their respective places of worship:

Miss Agnes to the New Meeting, where she sat alone in the pew which members of the family had occupied for more than a century, Miss Ellen to mingle with the less distinguished congregation of St. Jude's. Each, in her own way, was deeply religious; and each, no doubt, found her own kind of satisfaction in these observances: Miss Agnes as the proud martyr defying adversity; Miss Ellen as the devout suppliant, humbly awaiting a miracle.

They certainly had need for such mystical consolations; for beneath their pathetic attempts to 'keep up appearances' they were in a bad way. During the whole of their last year at 'The Cedars', during which their earnings from the school had dwindled to next to nothing, they were practically living on the starvation-line. After all, there was a limit to the quantity of movable property which they could realize, and the dealers whom they approached surreptitiously often put a contemptuous value on articles which they could not bring themselves to relinquish without a pang. Little by little 'The Cedars' was stripped of most of the things they valued—the porcelain, the Persian rugs, the Colonel's pair of shot-guns and the very rifle with which he had killed the tiger.

A deeper humiliation awaited them when, after long searchings of conscience, they decided to sell his dress-clothes. The performance of this bitter sacrifice fell, as usual, on Miss Ellen, who carried them, after dark, to a shop, half pawnbroker's and half old-clothes dealer's, which she had noticed in a sordid street at the back of St. Jude's. Here, in a gas-lit cupboard that stank of soiled clothes, a greasy young man, wearing diamond rings, had examined them with dirty fingers.

"It's a beautiful material, isn't it?" Miss Ellen said timidly.

"The stuff's all right," he admitted, "but look at the length!"

He held them up one by one at arm's length contemptuously. Miss Ellen shuddered. It was almost as if he were displaying the fragments of the Colonel's dismembered corpse.

"What's more, only look at the cut of them! It's enough to make a cat laugh. We aren't dealers in fancy-dress, you know. This is a clothes-shop not a museum."

"I am sure they were made by a first-class military tailor in Savile Row."

"Yes, but *when* were they made? That's the point."

He examined the tailor's label within the breast pocket, and Miss Ellen blushed with shame, for she feared that the label would bear Papa's name and give away the anonymity she had gone to such lengths to preserve. The young man laughed scornfully.

"There! What did I tell you? June 1884 . . . More than twenty years old. We don't reckon to handle antiques except in the way of joolry."

Miss Ellen had a quick inspiration. Steeling herself to a tremendous sacrifice she slipped off her ring.

"Would this be worth much?"

The young man stuck a magnifying-glass in his eye and examined it.

"Where did you get this from?" he asked sharply.

"It was bought in India."

"H'm, I thought as much. You see there's no proper carat-mark, though I suppose it's gold."

"Oh, I'm certain it's gold," said Miss Ellen, "and the stone is quite perfect, isn't it?"

"It's all right, but it's only a garnet, you know, and the colour is nothing special."

"How much would it be worth?"

"I could do you one better than this for fifteen shillings."

"Oh, dear . . ."

"Look here, miss. Let's say a quid for the two suits and the ring together."

"Oh, no. I don't think I could accept that," Miss Ellen said.

"Well, I'll make it twenty-three bob, then; and, mind you, that's robbing myself. It's just that I'ld like to do business."

"You see, I don't really want to sell the ring. It has a sentimental value for me."

"Oh well, I know nothing about that. There's my offer: you can take it or leave it. It's all one to me."

Miss Ellen packed up the suits and carried them home again. She was almost thankful to find that her sister had staggered into bed with one of the headaches that usually overcame her in moments of anxiety, and was too deeply prostrated to enquire or to care about the results of her mission. Miss Ellen stole down to the kitchen and made her a cup of tea, and poached a dubious egg for her own meagre supper. She was thankful that circumstances had thwarted that momentary impulse to sell her ring. She knew she could never have forgiven herself if she had parted with it. She was almost glad, indeed, that the young man had offered so little for the dress-suits; for she could not rid her mind of that vision of Papa's dismembered body appearing suspended, piece by piece, in the gas-light. When she had eaten her egg she had a sudden desire to play the piano. There was nothing so soothing as soft music, such as Mendelssohn's *Songs without Words*, when one felt restless. "I might just as well play while I can," she thought, "for sooner or later it will have to be sold." But now that most of the Persian rugs and half the furniture had gone from the drawing-room, the notes of the old Broadwood rang out like those of a concert-grand, and, if poor Agnes heard the faintest twang while her head was still aching, it would drive her nearly crazy. In any case it was almost too late and would be extravagant to light a fire in the drawing-room; so she hung the suits up again in the cupboard from which she had taken them, and returned to the kitchen to fill the hot-water bottle which was the greatest source of sensual pleasure in her life. She looked everywhere for it in vain. Of course Agnes had taken it: when she had one of her heads she always needed three: one at her feet, another on her stomach, and a third under the nape of her neck. Miss Ellen sighed, and stared hopelessly at the cockroaches scurrying under the sink. Then she went on tiptoe upstairs, knelt and said her prayers, put on her vaselined cotton gloves, and slid cautiously into bed, like a bather who shrinks from the shock of an icy plunge.

In those winter days, the state of her hands, in which she had always taken such pride, was a great distress to her. It wasn't only the chilblains (though these were sufficiently disfiguring) but their sandpaper roughness, and the cracks and chaps that would never heal as the result of her having to do all the housework and washing-up in hard water. Though most houses in North Bromwich enjoyed the soft 'Welsh water', which came from the artificial lakes in the Garon valley, 'The Cedars' still depended for its supply on the well Abraham Isit had sunk in the Keuper sandstone. Every day that water had to be pumped to the cistern that gurgled in the attics until it ran over: four hundred and thirty strokes of the pump every single day. How well she knew it! And the awful injustice was that one had to pay water-rates just the same as if they were using the City's supply. When Papa was alive, it had been part of the coachman's duty to do the pumping; and when he had gone, one of the maids had done it under protest; it was the main reason, she believed, why they had found it so difficult to 'keep' their servants. But now there was no maid at all, the pumping had fallen upon her. Of course Agnes had offered to pump on alternate days: she was always ready to sacrifice herself to her high sense of duty; but extra exertions of that kind could be relied on to give her a headache; in spite of her queenly physique she wasn't as strong as she looked; so Miss Ellen, of course, had undertaken it, along with the cooking and other household duties of the more strenuous sort. As for the cooking, she really enjoyed it. It always gave one a mild sense of triumph to produce something out of nothing, and the products of a lady's hand were daintier and more delicate than those of a professional cook's. Miss Ellen did not mind hard work, even though she had not been born to it; and her sister was much better qualified to act as a manager and adviser than to do manual tasks. Yet often, about the time when she reached the two-hundredth stroke of the pump, Miss Ellen had thought how lovely it would have been if their duty to Papa had permitted them to take Mr. Wilburn's advice and rent a small house equipped with luxuries, such as water from the mains and gas and electric light, instead of wasting her strength and time on the trimming of oil-lamps and the carrying and shovelling of coal and the breathless job of pumping well-water to the top of this cold, cold house, so draughty and so enormous. Wasn't it rather a monstrous price, she sometimes thought, to pay for their pride? It was almost a consolation to think—though she knew this was wicked—that, the way things were going, this slavery to an ideal would some day have to come to an end. Then she felt the stealthy pressure of Waifie's pads through the counterpane and heard a plaintive 'miaow', and put out her gloved hand to stroke the sleek fur, rather cautiously, for Waifie sometimes brought a dead mouse to bed with her. It was strange that so many mice could scrape together a living from the crumbs in 'The Cedars'.

7

HEAVEN only knew how or when it would all have ended but for a fortunate chance that, on a February morning in the following year, took Ernest Wilburn to London in pursuit of a water-colour drawing, attributed to Crome the elder, which was to be sold at Christie's that day. The North Bromwich express had been held up by fog on the outskirts of London; and as he waited impatiently for the line to be cleared he found himself staring, without any purpose, at a copy of the day's *Times*, which he had read during the journey, then discarded and placed, with his hat, cane and gloves, on the seat beside him. There, from the upper third of the 'Personal' column, the familiar word 'Isit' met his eyes and thrust itself into his bemused mind.

"This is very odd," he said to himself. "I must be dreaming." For he could have sworn that, for want of anything better to do, he had read every word on the page. Retrieving the paper, he read the paragraph:

> ISIT: Will Major Arthur Isit, R.E., last heard of in India, or any person knowing his whereabouts, please communicate with Messrs. Marx and Verona, Solicitors, Lombard Street, E.C.

"Very odd indeed," he repeated, as he cut out the advertisement and slid it into his card-case. The names of his legal colleagues were unknown to him. They sounded foreign and shady, and, important though it was, he didn't much like their address. Most of the firms with whom Wilburn and Wilburn had business occupied chambers in the neighbourhood of the Inns of Court.

From Euston he drove straight to Christie's and inspected the drawing. The rare attribution was probably just, but the work didn't appeal to his taste. It seemed as though his day's journey to London had been wasted until, having lunched at his club with a bottle of Jesuiten-garten Auslese of the incomparable '93 vintage, he suddenly remembered the newspaper cutting and decided to investigate its origins. He drove down to the City in a hansom cab, sent up his card, and was immediately received by the partner whose name was Verona, but who looked as if it might have been Marx.

"I saw your advertisement in *The Times* this morning," he said.

"It was the third insertion," Mr. Verona said regretfully.

"I'm sorry that neither I nor anyone in my office noticed it before. Fortunately I'm in a position to give you all the information you want. Major Isit—or rather Colonel Isit—was a client of mine."

"Good, good. Then you can tell me where to find him?" Mr. Verona said eagerly.

"Unfortunately that is beyond me."

"Ah. He is no longer your client?"

"He died four or five years ago."

"Ha, ha, ha! Very good. Therefore you do not know his address. Ha, ha! Very good indeed!"

"But I shall be pleased to give you particulars of his heirs, if that's what you want. He had two unmarried daughters, for whom I still act."

"Good, good. That is just what I do want—or rather not I but my correspondents in Naples, Esposito and Gennaro. It treats of an estate, an inheritance, of a certain —excuse one moment while I confirm—a certain deceased Mr. Owen Vowg-han. Is that how you pronounce?"

"No, not Vowg-han: Vaughan. Of course. A Vaughan of Tregoyd. A lineal descendant of King Cadwallader."

"Is that so? He was of antique race?"

"Of an antiquity that you might almost call mythological. My two clients, by the way, are the late Colonel Isit's sole heirs. Is the estate considerable?"

Mr. Verona pursed his lips and oscillated both palms horizontally like the fins of a fish.

"Considerable enough. Wait . . . I hold here the documents. There are valuta, bank-deposits and securities, Italian Government five per cent rentes, of a total of roughly four hundred thousand lire. That is an income of twenty thousand a year: call it eight hundred pounds."

"That is a handsome fortune."

"A fortune more handsome in my country, believe me, than in England. There is also a villa, with its contents, surrounded by vines and olives, at Monfalcone."

"I'm afraid I don't know where that is."

Mr. Verona appeared to be shocked by his colleague's ignorance.

"On the Gulf of Salerno, not very far south of Naples."

"That sounds most attractive."

"Attractive? Monfalcone? Believe me, it is exquisite! Such sun, such light, such fruits, such good wine! The grapes grow on the mineral."

Wilburn smiled: That was exactly, he thought, what most Italian wines tasted like. He said:

"Thank you very much, Mr. Verona. I will get my

clients' authority to act for them in the matter and then communicate with you. You shall hear from me shortly."

"Good, good. Very good. I was abandoning all hopes of tracing them. Remember also that if there is any question, when the inheritance is settled, of the Miss Isits—a fantastic name, isn't it?—desiring to realize the property, I shall be pleased to charge myself with the affair, through my correspondents, for a modest commission—and to recognize the value of your services in the introduction. You think they will sell?" he added, rather eagerly.

"Upon my soul, I haven't the faintest idea," Ernest Wilburn said.

Yet, whirling home in the two-hour train to North Bromwich, and pondering on this incredible turn of fortune, he couldn't help fancying that the Miss Isits probably wouldn't. They would have had quite enough experience, he imagined, of life in North Bromwich. As he travelled home that evening, his senses lulled by the unbroken rhythm of the train, his inward eye was enraptured by a strange vision of a mountain-side, silvery with olive-groves, falling to a lazuline sea. There, ledged on the face of the mountain, he saw a long, pillared pergola, bordered by cypress pyramids and wreathed with serpentine vines, and ending in a belvedere, where, serenely posed against the luminous sky, stood a woman in whose classical profile he was surprised to recognize the features of Miss Agnes Isit—a picture that was no longer a Vandyck, but rather one of those miniature landscapes that gleam, with an enamelled radiance, through the mediæval arches of the Venetian masters of the fifteenth century, Bellini or Tintoretto. The impression was so powerful that when the snow-sprinkled train thundered in beneath the sooty span of the station-roof at North Bromwich and woke him with a jolt, his mind was still aglow with a singular sensation of abounding warmth and light, and his nostrils still smelt—was it myrtle or rosemary?

8

In due course the particulars Mr. Verona had promised arrived, and Ernest Wilburn, being satisfied with his enquiries, lost no time in carrying the astonishing news to the Miss Isits. The mission was one that pleased his romantic imagination. He already partook of the pleasure and excitement he knew to be in store for them. Occasions such as this did something to atone for the customary drabness of one whose main task was conveyancing. Having announced his projected visit mysteriously, he arrived at the front door of 'The Cedars' on a dank February evening, when Enville Lane appeared at its incomparable worst. As he waited beneath the dripping portico (for the bell-wires were broken, and he was forced to hammer with the door-knocker) he was touched by the dramatic contrast between those sodden, sooty surroundings and the vista of warmth and light which it would be his privilege to open before his clients' eyes. Miss Agnes, with Stewart vociferously hostile at her heels, grudgingly opened the door, and that contrast was reinforced. It was a year or more since he had set eyes on her; and though she welcomed him with her usual majesty and showed pleasure when she saw who he was, he was shocked by the change in her. It was not that she looked older—works of art, such as she, were ageless—but somehow she seemed to have shrunk. The picture was in need of cleaning, if not of restoration.

"I have brought you good news," he said.

"They say 'no news is good news'," she told him, "and that is the sort to which we are generally accustomed, Mr. Wilburn. Come here, Stewart! You must not go out. It's not bedtime yet."

"Only wait and see," Wilburn said. "Your sister must hear it, too."

They entered the drawing-room, the Aberdeen trotting reluctantly behind them and sniffling at Wilburn's calves.

Miss Ellen was sitting in a straight-backed chair on the draughtier side of the fireplace, the tabby cat nodding asleep on her lap with a slip of pink tongue protruding. Wilburn thought she looked happier and better-fed than her sister.

"You'll excuse me rising, won't you?" she said. "My little cat's fast asleep."

There seemed to be only two chairs left out of the number which had formerly overcrowded the room. Miss Agnes sank with dignity into the one that was empty, facing Miss Ellen, and graciously directed Wilburn to the fireward compartment of the sociable settee, while Stewart sat bolt upright in the middle of the hearth with his back to him, completely absorbing the rays of the fire.

"Mr. Wilburn says he is bringing us good news, Ellen," Miss Agnes said distantly. "Now, perhaps, we may hear what it is."

"Very well. I think I remember you once telling me you had an uncle."

"Yes . . . my mother's brother, Ludovic. She was a Vaughan of Tregoyd. An extremely ancient family. But Papa didn't like him; so there must have been something very unpleasant about him, for Papa was most liberal-minded and charitable towards other people's failings. Uncle Ludovic was in the army to begin with, of course; but I'm afraid he was what Papa always called an idler. He sold the family estate, which should have been ours, and went to live abroad. There must have been some reason for his doing that."

"Well, he may possibly have preferred it, you know. He lived in Italy, at a place called Monfalcone, on the Gulf of Salerno."

"I have never been south of Rome," Miss Agnes said. "The Romans consider the southern Italians an indolent people and most insanitary."

"He died there, a couple of months ago."

"Oh, poor man!" Miss Ellen exclaimed.

"Indeed?" Miss Agnes said, with a glance of withering

contempt at her sister's conventional comment. "Stewart! Stop scratching this instant!"

"The point," Wilburn continued, "so far as you are concerned, is that your uncle died intestate, and that by the Italian law of inheritance his property becomes yours."

He paused to see the effect of this announcement. He saw Miss Ellen's face aglow with excitement, her lips parted, as though eager to inhale the rest of the news. Not a sign of emotion showed itself on that of Miss Agnes—unless it were a slight heightening of colour which could hardly have been due to the moribund fire.

"Is this property . . . considerable?" she said at last.

"Very considerable. I must congratulate you; and I do so most heartily. Upon my word you deserve it, both of you."

"Will there be sufficient to pay off Papa's mortgage on 'The Cedars'?" Miss Agnes said.

Wilburn smiled. "Yes, indeed; and a great deal more."

"Then that must be done at once."

"Oh, Agnes, what a relief that would be!" Miss Ellen cried, picking up the bewildered Waifie and hugging her passionately. "Do tell us more, Mr. Wilburn."

"Well, there's rather a lot to tell you. There is a house—a villa, I should say—called the Castello Inglese, surrounded by a small quantity of land, mostly vineyard and olive-grove."

"I have never seen an olive-grove," Miss Ellen sighed.

"I have seen hundreds of acres of olive-groves in Tuscany, Ellen," Miss Agnes said. "The olive, in my opinion, is a stunted and much over-rated tree."

"In addition to the villa," Wilburn continued, "there is a good deal of money. I think you will be probably able to count on an income of between eight hundred pounds and a thousand a year."

Miss Ellen gasped: "Oh . . . !" and Miss Agnes blinked momentarily, as though the sum dazzled her. Then she quickly recovered herself.

"In that case, Mr. Wilburn," she said, "I see no reason

why we should not attempt to re-purchase our family home at Tregoyd. That, I'm sure, is what Papa would have wished."

Miss Ellen's face fell so piteously that Wilburn felt sorry for her. Her mind shrank, no doubt, at the labour and anxiety involved in the prospect of taking over and furnishing another deserted mansion.

"I wonder, Mr. Wilburn," she said, "if this house—the villa, I mean, has water laid on?"

"Really, Ellen," Miss Agnes broke in, "I don't think such matters as that are of any importance. We have no intention of living there."

"If you asked my advice," Wilburn said, "as you haven't done, I should urge you most strongly not to do anything precipitate. The great thing, the thing that gives me most satisfaction, is that you won't have to worry about your finances in future. Even if you should ultimately decide to try to re-purchase Tregoyd, I think it would be wiser, from every point of view, for you to go and have a look at your Italian property. There may be a number of formalities which can only be dealt with satisfactorily on the spot, in consultation with your uncle's lawyers; and I think it would do you both a world of good to make a break—even a temporary break—with the past. After all, the villa is yours; and though you may not want to live in it, there's no reason on earth why you shouldn't winter there. I must say I envy you your luck in being able to afford it. North Bromwich isn't exactly a health resort at this time of the year!"

Agnes nodded. "There may well be something in what you say, Mr. Wilburn. It is many years since I was last in Italy; and of course in my case the language presents no difficulty. If you really consider our presence is required, we will think the matter over and let you know what we decide."

She rose from her straight-backed chair and offered him her mittened hand in token of dismissal. The Queen of Sheba herself could not have bettered the majesty of the gesture.

"We are extremely grateful," she said, "for what you have done. Good-bye . . . Will you see Mr. Wilburn to the door, Ellen?"

Miss Ellen preceded him into the cavern of the icy hall. He was glad to find himself alone with her, for he felt tenderly towards her and thought she had been rather needlessly snubbed. He took her thin arm in the darkness (he would never have dared to touch Miss Agnes's arm) and found it surprisingly soft and warm.

"Well, what do you think of all this, Miss Ellen?" he whispered.

"Oh, I think it's quite wonderful, Mr. Wilburn," she said. "In fact I can't get over it. There's only one thing . . ."

"Yes?"

"Do you know if the Customs Authorities allow cats in Italy?"

"I'm afraid I don't. But I believe that on the continent generally, they're not nearly so strict about letting in animals as we are here."

"Oh, that's most encouraging. Thank you so much."

"Not at all. I do hope you will do your best to persuade your sister to take my advice. You both of you need a change."

"Persuade Agnes? Oh, Mr. Wilburn, if only you knew!"

A month later, on March the seventh, the Miss Isits shut up 'The Cedars' and set out for Italy, with the intention of staying at Monfalcone till the beginning of June.

PART TWO

I

Of those diabolical winds whose malice afflicts the shores of the Mediterranean from October to March—the grey Mistral that strips the cringing palms of Provence; the Tramontana, whose Alpine draught blanches the marble palaces of Genoa; the hot-throated Scirocco that parches and ravens Sicily; the gusty Gregale of Malta—of all these there is none that can compare in sustained malignity with the Libeccio, the fierce South Wester of Southern Italy. This boisterous devil had been raging for two days out of its allotted three on the late afternoon when the Miss Isits, travel-stained and bewildered, were shot out into the midst of a band of brigands, thinly disguised as porters, on to the platform of the Central Station at Naples.

After a journey so lengthy as this, in a packed second-class carriage, it was only to be expected that Miss Agnes should have been bowled over by an attack of migraine. Up till this moment her knowledge of elegant French and Italian had succeeded in steering themselves, their baggage and their live-stock through the bottle-necks of two frontiers and a thousand miles of unfriendly territory; but by now hunger and lack of sleep, combined with the distress of an attack which was nearing its climax, had robbed her brain of volition and her tongue of speech. Even had she been able to speak, her language, which was that of Dante, could hardly have been understood by the pack of human wolves that now beset them with uncouth cries and gesticulations, and snatched at their hand-luggage as they staggered light-headed towards the rear of the train where their registered baggage had been dumped; Miss Agnes determinedly dragging the reluctant Stewart past a series of iron posts that supported the station roof, Miss Ellen desperately protecting the damp basket in which Waifie was imprisoned by hugging it to her breast. When they reached their luggage at last, Miss Agnes collapsed with dignity on her cabin-trunk, and Miss Ellen sat down beside her, while the porters gathered round them in a circle, yelping and grinning, like wolves waiting for their natural prey.

"What are these dreadful creatures saying?" Miss Ellen asked.

"I neither know nor care," Miss Agnes answered wearily. "I suppose their language must be some kind of patois."

"But what are you going to do?"

"*Do?* Wait here and take no notice of them till somebody comes who can speak Italian."

At that moment the clamour broke out again, as a resplendent figure advancing scattered the throng to right and left like a lordly pike dispersing a shoal of minnows. Miss Ellen's heart rose at the sight of his gold-braided cap and uniform, which surely betokened authority, though Stewart, who disliked the smell of him, growled and tugged at his lead. After a quick glance at the Miss Isits' flat-heeled shoes, he swept off his cap and displayed a smile of gold teeth. Miss Ellen too smiled and nodded; it was the least return she could make for such a courtly gesture; but Miss Agnes stared at him coldly.

"Ah . . . Americane," he said.

"We are nothing of the sort," Miss Agnes snapped. "We are English."

With an expressive gesture he waved the distinction aside. "It is the same thing, Signora. If you are English you are going to Capri, of course. The boat sails tomorrow morning, if the tempest permits. It is a terrible sea. Now I take you to the hotel. Very good hotel; very good beds. English kitchen: roas' beef. *Hotel Splendide.*" He pointed to the ribbon on his cap.

"We are *not* going to Capri," Miss Agnes answered firmly, "and we are not going to any hotel. We are going to Monfalcone."

"Monfalcone? Sure! You are going to-morrow morning. Impossible to-night. It is thirty-forty kilometres. Too much wind; too much rain; very dark. You understand?"

"I understand perfectly," Agnes said in her best Italian. "But, as I have told you, we are going to Monfalcone."

"Ah . . . the Signora speak Italian? *Brava . . . Bravissima!* Then I explain."

He burst into a spate of rapid speech reinforced by gesticulations to which the circle of wolves responded with approving yelps and grins.

Miss Agnes emerged undaunted.

"I repeat: we are going to Monfalcone," she said. "Kindly procure me a carriage."

"Very well, very well," the porter of the *Hotel Splendide* replied irritably. "I will do all the possible; but I warn you it will be expensive—very expensive."

He selected a couple of stalwart ruffians who immediately grabbed at the luggage on which the Miss Isits were sitting and swung it to their shoulders, while the remainder of the crowd melted away.

"I myself will charge myself with the puppy," he said majestically, snatching the lead from Agnes's hand before she could protest. But Stewart thought otherwise. He had not only suffered forty-eight hours of purgatory but also, at the end, had been dragged willy-nilly past a series of iron posts of a unique and desirable odour. With a snarl he fixed his teeth in the trousers of the hotel-porter, who dropped the lead with a yelp.

"Ah . . . A bulldog!" he said. "This is certainly the English bulldog."

"Leave him to me," Agnes said without pity. "He objects to foreigners." If she had added: 'And so do I,' she could not have made her attitude more plain.

The two porters, in spite of their burden, had broken into a run. The Miss Isits straggled after them, as fast as their trembling legs would permit, along a dirty platform of an unconscionable length, the hotel-porter shepherding them with the nonchalance of a man-of-war that has captured a rich prize. They waited for another half-hour, during which the officials of the municipal *douane* suspiciously ferreted among their winter underwear in search, as their escort explained, of wine and cheese. Finally they passed out of the station into a court-yard, where the drivers of a number of rickety carriages, resembling Rowena's moth-eaten victoria, disputed for their possession. The porter of the *Hotel Splendide* waved these aside, explaining that the Signore needed a two-horsed carriage. Miss Agnes, exhausted and too giddy to stand any longer, subsided once more on one of the cabin-trunks with the muddy paws of the offended Stewart befouling her lap. Around them the Libeccio swept in fierce gusts, and rain fell without ceasing. Though the air that surrounded them was undeniably warm, they might just as well have been in North Bromwich, Miss Ellen thought. She was so faint with hunger by now that she couldn't help asking Agnes if she thought they could get a sandwich.

"I couldn't eat anything, thank you; and I don't know the Italian for sandwich anyway," Agnes said bleakly. "Indeed I doubt if there *are* such things in Italy. When we get to the villa, you can have a cup of cocoa."

It had begun to look as if they would never get there, when, all of a sudden, a phantasmal two-horse cab crept slowly out of the windy darkness and drew up beside them. At the suggestion that he should drive them to Monfalcone, the coachman expressed indignation. After a protracted and vociferous argument which lasted five minutes and in which both disputants appeared to be tearing their emotions to shreds, their escort announced that, as a special favour, they could be transported to Monfalcone for a hundred and fifty lire.

"Tell him that that is ridiculous," Agnes said firmly. "That is seven pounds; more than the second-class railway fare from London to Naples. If he won't be reasonable you had much better send him away and call another carriage. You know perfectly well you can always beat them down."

The hotel-porter shrugged his shoulders and re-opened

the argument, in which the cabman illogically explained that he had a wife and nine children and that his horses were hungry and old and as tired as himself. At last, having shouted himself dumb, and with a gesture of unfathomable resignation, he climbed down from his seat and opened the dripping sheet, that had once been waterproof, which covered the seat of his carriage.

"He says he will take you for a hundred lire and a present for himself," the porter said, "but he wants the money in advance."

Agnes handed him four sovereigns from her purse, dislodged the reluctant Stewart, and climbed under the hood, while the two porters hoisted the luggage on to the driving-seat. The springs sagged beneath the weight of them.

"This is not a very nice carriage," she said.

The hotel-porter laughed out loud and translated her remark into Neapolitan. He, at any rate, realized the humour of the situation. Like most members of an old civilization, he enjoyed the ridiculous *naïveté* of the Anglo-Saxon. His attitude was almost fatherly as he tucked the Miss Isits in.

"Now there are the porters to pay," he reminded them.

"How much?" Miss Agnes asked cautiously.

"Eh . . . They have waited a long time," he said, "and they are very poor men."

"I don't see what that has to do with it," Miss Agnes said. "Will a lira each be sufficient?"

"You should give them five lire between them."

"That is more than two shillings apiece."

"But only regard the hour and the weather, Signora!"

Agnes sighed—she was too weak to argue, and reluctantly disgorged five small silver coins. It was hard for her to depart from the established habit of parsimony.

"And then, there is myself . . ."

He looked, Ellen thought, far too grand to accept a tip of mere silver, and appeared shocked, if not offended, when Miss Agnes, with brutal directness, asked him how much he expected.

"That is for you to say, Signora," he said. "You will give what you wish."

He got—the supply of smaller change failing—considerably more than she wished: a gold half-sovereign which evidently satisfied him, for he bowed the Miss Isits off with a superb repertory of gestures.

"When the Signore return to Naples," he said, "they will stay at the *Hotel Splendide*, and I will conduct them to Pompeii, Erculaneum and Vesuvius."

Agnes, however, declined to commit herself so far as that; and, lacking a reply, he gave the signal to start. The driver immediately lashed up his horses and the carriage leapt forward into the windswept darkness with a velocity which suggested that the poor beasts imagined he was taking them home. By this time Miss Agnes, having shot her last bolt, was in a state of blanched collapse. She lay back on the musty cushions, with closed eyes, while the flimsy *carrozza*, buffeted by terrifying gusts as it bounced and skidded over the slimy setts, pursued its furious way southward. For all she knew of that part of the journey she might as well have been dead; but Miss Ellen, her wits sharpened by fasting and want of sleep, felt more than usually alive and awake. Though the carriage often seemed to be on the point of overturning, its rapid movement exhilarated her, recalling, with an added fillip of actual danger, the vicarious excitement she had experienced when, as a girl, she had read the account of the chariot-race in *Ben Hur*. It was exactly as though she was taking part in that breathless struggle. On either side of the street, without any regard for the rule of the road as she and Rowena had known it, a string of carriages similar to their own appeared to be racing furiously in opposite directions, passing and repassing one another, the drivers brutally lashing their teams and urging them on with agonized cries. Though she was sorry for the poor horses and glad that Agnes was too far gone to see what they suffered, Miss Ellen felt passionately anxious that their own chariot should win; her heart leapt with pride when they passed a competitor; and all the time, as they whirled along, she was conscious of the strangeness and, as it seemed to her, the brilliancy of the shops that lined the long street on either side and the people who thronged the pavements. They were not like the ill-lighted shops of North Bromwich, which hid their wares jealously behind steam-bleared windows. Their interiors lay wide open to the street, encouraging inspection, and their goods overflowed the pavement with splashes of opulent colour. There were terraced cafés too, with striped awnings, where, in spite of the weather, people sat at small tables reading their papers and sipping aperitifs; and the smell of these streets tickled her nostrils with all sorts of exotic and stimulating savours, far more varied and interesting than Enville Lane's uniform odour of stale beer and fried fish and scented shag tobacco. Yet the prime significance of all these new sensual excitements was this: that she was freed, at last, from a life of commonplace drudgery. She had emerged, without realizing the process of transformation, into a brave new world. She was 'abroad': she was actually in Italy! Never again would she have to remain dumb when Agnes talked of her travels. She could hear herself beginning in a nonchalant voice: "When I was driving through Naples last year . . ." or casually mentioning "that little street—you *must* know the one I mean—that leads from the Pincio to the Ponte Vecchio." She wished, impulsively, that Agnes had been sufficiently conscious to share her enthusiasm, and was tempted to beg her to open her eyes, if only for a moment; but, on second thoughts, she wasn't quite sure how Agnes would 'take' such an inroad on her sufferings. On the whole, better not . . .

By this time, indeed, the shop-fronts and café-terraces had become fewer and shone less brightly; the fury of the chariot-race, for lack of competitors, had abated, and the pace of the horses slackened to a leisurely trot. The rain too had ceased, though the south-west wind still blew in malicious gusts. They had left the newer and more pretentious streets of the city behind and now threaded its meaner fringes, passing between houses that seemed to be mouldering into ruins. Then the last street-lamp fell behind, and the surface of the road, which had been uneven enough before, became even rougher, the ramshackle carriage lurching from rut to rut or floundering through puddles of muddy water. It was now pitch-dark but for the flame of the carriage-lamp which dappled with a flickering beam, like that of a corpse-light, endless walls faced with crumbling mortar on either side of the road. Miss Ellen became oppressed by a sense of confinement from which there was no escape. The mood of exhilaration failed her, and her imaginations were suddenly tinged with fears that recalled vague stories of kidnappings and banditti which she had heard in her youth. Even the driver's silence disquieted her. They had been rash, she felt, to trust themselves to the mercy of this sinister foreigner who, for all she knew, might be driving them and their belongings to some haunt of drunken brigands lost in the depths of a lonely countryside, where they would be robbed, gagged, and held for ransom—or even worse! In comparison with this nightmare no-man's-land, the slums of North Bromwich, which she had always avoided, now seemed homely and sane and safe.

Still the carriage jogged on and on. Once or twice she was gladdened and reassured by the lighted streets of a small town or village, through which the coachman whipped up his horses and renewed his wild cries, as though he were anxious to leave them behind as quickly as possible. Then once more she was engulfed in the darkness of open fields which the beam of the carriage-lamp could not penetrate. There were few signs of life on this road which seemed to lead nowhere, save occasionally a frightened dog (or was it a wolf?) whose green pupils suddenly flashed through the darkness and vanished, an uncouth, hooded human figure that shouted and stumbled away, or the sleepy driver of a mule-cart, immense and garishly painted, that swerved into the ditch—if there were a ditch—to avoid them, with whom the cabman exchanged a torrent of unintelligible abuse.

After an hour or two even these rare apparitions

ceased. They had reached, it appeared, a zone lonelier and even more terrifying: the foothills of a range of mountains which the road climbed in endless gyrations between walls of bare forest. It was narrow and stony now as the bed of a torrent and grew steeper with every turn, and its increasing wildness convinced Miss Ellen more than ever either that they were the victims of some black conspiracy, the end of which could only be guessed at, or that the driver had lost his way and was ashamed to admit it. She sustained these torments of the imagination and listened to Stewart's snores until she felt that unless she shouted or wept she would certainly go mad. Finally, when she could bear them no longer alone and in silence, she spoke to her sister.

Miss Agnes and Stewart awoke together with a jump and sat bolt upright.

"What's the matter, Ellen?" she cried. "Why did you poke me like that? What time is it? Where are we? Have we arrived?"

Miss Ellen apologized: "I'm so sorry: I was frightened."

"Frightened? Frightened of *what?*"

"We've been wandering about for hours and don't seem to be getting anywhere. I'm positive this horrible man doesn't know where he's going."

"What nonsense! He knows he's taking us to Monfalcone."

"I wish you'ld make certain."

Miss Agnes jabbed the driver in the small of the back with her umbrella—he, too, awoke with a start—and addressed him deliberately in literary Italian to which he replied with a spate of dialect that sounded to Ellen most impolite.

"Speak more slowly," Agnes commanded.

The driver replied more excitedly and even faster.

"For heaven's sake don't make him angry," Miss Ellen pleaded.

"He says," Miss Agnes replied, "or I *think* he says, that we have to cross the mountain before we reach Monfalcone. He says God made the mountains; it isn't his fault; and that it will take two more hours because the horses are tired and the road is so steep. Now, perhaps, you are satisfied."

"Poor creatures!" Miss Ellen said. "And the luggage is so heavy too. Don't you think it would be kinder to them if we got out and walked up this hill while the driver leads them—that is," she added quickly, "if your head's not too bad?"

"My head has cleared now, I'm thankful to say, after that nice long sleep. I think it would be an excellent idea to stretch our legs and ease the horses. I expect Stewart would like a run too. Come along then, Stewart!"

They dismounted—though the driver declined to do anything so foolish—and the horses, astonished by a relief that was too welcome to be believable, took heart and moved forward so quickly that they soon left the Miss Isits behind. The carriage-lamp danced out of sight round a new turn in the road. It was so dark in the thick of the chestnut woods that Miss Ellen could not see a yard in front of her.

"Oh, do be quick, Agnes!" she cried, "or we shall never catch up with him."

"Stewart must take his own time," Miss Agnes said. "You can't hurry them."

Stewart was not merely taking his time but was entranced and excited at that moment by a variety of strange scents such as he had never encountered on the pavements of North Bromwich. Suddenly, without any warning, he gave a hysterical yelp, snatched the lead from Miss Agnes's limp hand, and plunged in full cry down the brushwood slope into the depths of the forest.

"He has probably smelt a wolf," his mistress said calmly. "Brave little dog!"

For Miss Ellen that didn't improve matters. At that moment she would have given her eyes to find herself back in North Bromwich, shivering in front of the fire at 'The Cedars', with Waifie warm in her lap. The thought of poor Waifie helplessly imprisoned in her sodden basket and being driven away from her, perhaps for ever, by that horrible foreigner who was so cruel to his horses, only increased her distress.

"Oh, what can we do?" she cried.

"Wait here till Stewart comes back."

"But supposing he loses his way?"

"He won't. Aberdeens have wonderful noses," Miss Agnes said.

They had waited for more than ten minutes before Stewart reappeared—or rather announced his return by a series of yaps that implied his impatience at their lagging behind.

"What did I tell you?" Agnes said. "They *know*. Don't stand there gaping. Come along, now. Pull yourself together."

They must have stumbled for more than a mile up-hill in the dark before the light of the stationary carriage-lamp assuaged Miss Ellen's fears. She crawled in breathlessly, groping for Waifie's basket which had slipped to the floor. She picked it up tenderly and hugged it to her. With a little worse luck it might have been jolted into the road.

They had reached, in fact, the top of the pass, and the air that seeped down from the icy mountain summits was even colder than that which chilled the hall of 'The Cedars' in winter; and the Miss Isits, prepared to enjoy a sub-tropical climate, had discarded their woollen underwear. Miss Agnes picked Stewart up and folded her arms about him in place of the sealskin coat which now lay packed with moth-balls along with the tiger-skin in the attic at 'The Cedars'; but Waifie's basket unfortunately gave no such warmth or protection, and Miss Ellen froze till her teeth began to chatter.

"What's the matter with you now?" Agnes asked contemptuously. "Still frightened?"

"Oh no, I'm quite all right now, thank you," Ellen replied, "though it *is* rather chilly, isn't it?"

"That must be your imagination," Agnes said firmly. "We're in Southern Italy. It can be a great deal colder than this, I'm quite sure, in Kashmir, but I never heard dear Papa even mention it. You would be a great deal wiser and happier, Ellen," she went on, "if you did as I do. Whenever I find myself in the least inclined to complain or facing difficulties, I always ask myself: 'What would Papa have done?'—and the answer is never in doubt."

"Yes, indeed: I'm sure you're quite right, Agnes," Miss Ellen sighed. "But I do hope that the servants will have had your letters and prepared some supper and aired the house—I mean the villa—for us."

"That," said Agnes, "is what I call meeting trouble half-way, as you always do. If they haven't—well, then we shall have to camp out, as Papa did hundreds of times in the Himalayas."

"You're always so hopeful, aren't you?" Miss Ellen said. "And I do believe it's actually getting a little warmer."

As indeed it was. For more than an hour, almost imperceptibly, they had been descending the southern slope of the mountain massif into a zone of invisible olives and figs and vines. The wind, too, had fallen completely; the fierce gusts no longer troubled the tepid air, and that air itself had grown heavy with warm odours—the aroma of myrtle and rosemary that breathed from the brushwood which clothed the rocky slopes on either side, and occasionally a more poignant perfume of orange-blossoms stealing across their path from walled gardens where the trees sheltered beneath mats of woven straw. Then the stars came out to illumine a tumbled countryside so silvered with olive-groves that it seemed the moon was shining, and lights blinked from the balconies of white-washed farms or from under pergolas of chestnut wreathed in stark vines. The landscape the stars revealed was not merely gentle but kindly; and the air, which grew softer with every mile of their descent, seemed to warm Miss Ellen's heart no less than her frozen body. The white homesteads became more frequent; they clustered together to form the fringe of a village, from the midst of which rose the dome of a campanile covered with bright yellow porcelain tiles and surmounted by a cross, the sight of which brought a prayer of thanksgiving to Miss Ellen's lips. Then the driver whipped up his horses to a final effort, and the carriage swung, almost gaily, into a little piazza surrounded on three sides by tall shops and houses, and on the fourth wide open to a beach where the ground-swell raised by the fallen gale spumed and pounded on shelving sands.

"Oh, Agnes!" Miss Ellen blurted out. "I can smell the sea!"

Miss Agnes sniffed. "I can only smell garlic and fish," she murmured.

The driver stood up in front. He cracked his whip and waved it with a gesture of triumph.

"Monfalcone!" he cried.

"This is Monfalcone," Agnes translated with a more refined accent, but without showing any inclination to get out. "We had better stay where we are until we see if any of the staff have come to meet us."

It was evident that the whole village of Monfalcone Marina had turned out to meet the Miss Isits. From the first moment when the cracks of the whip, the crunching of wheels and the clatter of hooves echoed through it, the little piazza had broken into life, like a kicked ant-heap. Scores of children, some of whom had obviously been put to bed, appeared from dark-arched alleys and danced about them; women suddenly thrust wide the windows of upper storeys and leant over on their balconies shouting to their neighbours below and on the opposite side of the square; shopkeepers and customers crowded the doors of groceries and vegetable shops; a squat round-spectacled clerical figure in a soutane emerged from the door of the church; from the steps of the town-hall two armed policemen in three-cornered hats and dark cloaks lined with scarlet descended, with the intention, as Miss Ellen thought, of protecting them from the crowd. They did nothing of the sort, but stood by, with superb indifference, while the remainder of the crowd pressed round them like bees swarming about a queen. Some of the bolder children pulled faces and others spat. One small ragged boy would have clambered into the carriage had not Stewart leapt up snarling and showing his teeth.

"Inglese . . ." this horrid child bawled hoarsely. "Castello Inglese!"

"They evidently expect us and know who we are," Ellen thought, "but they're not very polite. Everybody seems to shout in Italy." Miss Agnes, protected by Stewart, stared straight in front of her with queenly disdain. They appeared to be getting no further, and the coachman was beginning to show signs of bewildered impatience, when the crowd broke apart, like the waters of the Red Sea divided for the passage of the children of Israel, to make way for a figure of importance, who, Miss Ellen decided, must surely at least be the mayor. He was a floridly handsome man, of between thirty and forty, in a black double-breasted coat, cut tightly at the waist, and striped cashmere trousers. His moustaches were carefully curled, his eyes bold and lustrous, and he wore a straw hat, carefully set acant, which he swept from his head with one hand, while, with the other, he seized the importunate child by the scruff of the neck and cast him aside as though he were an unmannerly dog.

"Good evening, Signorine," he said in a rich melodious voice with an American intonation. "Good evening and welcome."

Miss Agnes bowed and returned his salutation in Italian. "We desire to go to the Castello Inglese if you will have the goodness to direct the coachman," she explained.

"Sure, sure. . . . I get you. I come to take you there. I am one of the house. I am Salvatore, your butler. I think of everything. This is all your baggage?" He seemed rather humiliated by the fact that there wasn't more of it. "Very well. I myself will take another hack and lead the way. This is Monfalcone Marina. Your villa is two kilometre from here, up the hill."

He bowed again and replaced his hat, then spoke in commanding tones to the coachman, who answered him vehemently. For a moment—to the delight of the crowd—

they stood shouting at one another and gesticulating. Then he turned to Miss Agnes and took off his hat again.

"Excuse me, Signorina," he said respectfully. "This man says he has only been hired as far as Monfalcone Marina. If he take you up to the Castello Inglese you gotta pay more. He is a Neapolitan coachman. Very low people. But have no thought of it. I see to everything and pay what is just, no more, when we are arrived."

He raised his hand; and there, as by a miracle, stood a one-horse carriage even shabbier than theirs.

"What a nice man!" Ellen whispered.

"Hush! He may hear you. Remember he understands English."

"But he *is* a nice man; so helpful and so . . . superior. I feel we can trust him."

"It is a mistake to trust anyone in a strange country," Miss Agnes said.

They started and drove on in silence. In the carriage ahead they could see their new butler, lolling back magnificently, his straw-hat still poised at the same rakish angle.

"What did he say his name was?" Miss Ellen asked at last.

"Who? The butler? Salvatore."

"Salvatore. I must try to remember it."

"It means 'Saviour'," Miss Agnes said.

"That's rather appropriate: he *did* save us, didn't he?"

Agnes only grunted in reply. They drove on in silence again, slowly climbing the steep hill-side through intoxicating wafts of orange-blossom. Suddenly Miss Agnes became aware that her sister was laughing.

"What's the matter now?" she said irritably: she was always irritable after one of her headaches.

"Well, really, I hardly like to say. . . . Such an odd idea. Do you know, Salvatore reminds me of Mr. Dench?"

When she had spoken she marvelled at her own courage. It must have been because she was so relieved and light-headed. Never before, in twenty-five years, had she dared to utter the name of Agnes's suitor. She could almost feel her sister blushing beside her in the dark.

"I think you must have taken leave of your senses," she said angrily. "This man is only a domestic servant—and a foreigner at that." She was silent for a moment, then added: "Still, it may be an advantage to have a man about the house."

2

THE GENERAL impression of their arrival at the Castello Inglese remained strangely blurred in Miss Ellen's mind, though some disconnected details stood out in it with the clarity which invests certain incidents of one's childhood—as the result, no doubt, of the lack of sleep and food which had rendered some parts of her brain unusually sensitive while others were confused. During the last two hundred yards they had been compelled to stumble on foot over a stony track that wound through an olive-grove, emerging, at length, on a wide terrace paved with tiles, prolonged by a vine-entangled pergola and backed by a huge house whose many arched windows, all of them lighted, gave the impression of an enormous lantern specially lit to celebrate their arrival. A high loggia, vaulted like the crypt of a cathedral, enshrined the main entrance to the house, where Salvatore, who had preceded them with a lantern, flung open the door to disclose a vast entrance-hall, floored with green-glazed encaustic which made it resemble a swimming-bath, where the remainder of their uncle's household staff awaited them in attitudes of expectant humility.

Salvatore, who evidently knew the correct procedure, presented them one by one. There was Carolina, the cook, a small, wizened old woman with flat eyes, like a snake's, the cramped indistinguishable features of a marmoset, and a top-knot of grey hair transfixed by a tortoise-shell comb, who made so deep an obeisance when she bowed to kiss their hands that Miss Agnes had to stoop to accommodate her. This custom of hand-kissing, which was new to Miss Ellen, embarrassed her: she felt she should have washed or at least wiped her travel-grimed fingers before she submitted to it, though Carolina's face was probably even dirtier. Miss Agnes, on the other hand, sustained the proceeding with a queenly nonchalance, as though she had been accustomed to having her hands kissed every day of her life. The insanitary process was repeated by two slatternly, lovely, bold-eyed girls, with brightly-coloured handkerchiefs on their heads, whose names Miss Ellen could not attempt to remember, and by a bald-headed rustic hobgoblin, even more simian than Carolina, whom Salvatore introduced as Antonino, the gardener. All of them nodded and smiled and welcomed their new mistresses with an exaggerated profuseness which Salvatore cut short by inviting the Miss Isits to accompany him up the marble stairs to their bedrooms.

This proceeding which, on the part of a man, would certainly have struck Miss Ellen as indelicate in any other circumstances, appeared perfectly natural in these. He turned down the sheets of their beds and thrust in his hands to assure them that they were warm and well-aired. He even went to the trouble of indicating the local and general sanitary provisions of the villa, displaying, with a smile of friendly pride, Miss Ellen's personal domestic chinaware, and flicking a speck of dust from it with a napkin which had mysteriously appeared on his arm.

Miss Ellen could not feel quite sure that it wasn't the same napkin which, half an hour later, he carried on the same arm when, spick and span in a white cotton coat, he waited on them at the dinner-table; but it would have been churlish, she thought, to entertain such a suspicion of a man whose solicitude had already smoothed away so many of their difficulties, whose eyes were so quick to anticipate their wants and his hands so deft to supply them as, moving with the quietness of a bare-footed Indian over the tiled floor of the salone he filled their goblets with the deep crimson wine of Monfalcone.

Miss Ellen jibbed at this. Her experience of wines had

been discouragingly limited to the chilled, astringent claret her father had served on formal occasions at 'The Cedars'; and she was so light-headed already that she dreaded the effect of strong liquor on an empty stomach. Miss Agnes, however, accepted it with approval.

"You had better not refuse the wine, Ellen," she said. "It is generally considered unsafe to drink water abroad. Is the water good here, Salvatore?"

"Yes, yes, plenty of very good water, Signorina. It comes from the roof. But the wine is much better for the stomach." He spoke like a wise physician prescribing a dietary. "This is a famous wine, the wine of the Castello Inglese. The girls make with their feet."

Miss Ellen shuddered inwardly at the picture, but felt it would be unkind to check his enthusiasm. She was extremely thirsty, and the wine, which had an agreeable flavour, seemed innocent enough. Its taste was so pleasing that she did not protest when Salvatore refilled her glass, though its effect, which was insidious and cumulative, accounted, no doubt, for the air of unreality which from that moment, transformed her circumstances into those of an Arabian Night. Never, in all those meagre years at 'The Cedars', had she eaten with such an unguarded—an almost unladylike—appetite. Every dish appeared to her more picturesque and delicious than the last—from the amber consommé, in which tiny green peas were floating, and the chicken, served with rice and a bitter green salad and dressed with velvet sauce, to the sweet which Salvatore announced as a *Suppa Inglese* though it was neither English nor Soup, but nothing less than a rather soppy trifle. Miss Ellen, careless of Agnes's possible disapproval, devoured every course voraciously, and was aware, as she ate, of an unaccustomed, intoxicating brilliance in all her surroundings: in the great height and extent of the salone, from whose vaulted roof swung a Moorish lantern glazed with ruby and emerald; in the arabesque patterns in blue and gold of the tiles on the floor; of the chestnut refectory table at which she was sitting, from whose polished surface the crystal and silver and a bowl full of feathery mimosa were reflected as in a dark pool; above all, in the reassuring presence of Salvatore, so respectful and silent in his movements and yet so protective—that was the only word for it—in his concern for their comfort. And it wasn't as if, she thought, he were not a manly man. On the contrary.

She had no idea how long the meal lasted, though, at the end of it, she became conscious of Agnes severely informing her that she had better go to bed. It was at this moment that her conscience reminded her of poor Waifie, whom, in the pressure of so many excitements, she had left in her basket. This, oddly enough, did not appear tragic but moved her to laughter.

"I must put the cat out first, Agnes," she said, rather thickly. "Only imagine: I've left her upstairs."

"Stewart needs a run too," said Agnes.

"Do not give it a thought, Signorine. I will think of the dear little animals. I will think of everything. Have no fear."

With an extraordinary combination of grace and agility, Salvatore passed up the stairs.

"How obliging he is!" Miss Ellen exclaimed.

"No doubt he regards it as his duty," Agnes replied. "He appears, I must say, to be a well-trained servant; but we must not be blind to the fact that new brooms sweep clean. And I expect he realizes that he is in a good place."

"Still, no English butler . . ." Miss Ellen began, but refrained from finishing her protest as she saw Salvatore re-entering with Stewart's lead in one hand and the bedraggled Waifie tucked under his other arm.

"You see we make friends already," he said with a smile too disarming to seem familiar. "Now I put them out to perform their little duty. After, I bring them upstairs. Is that true?"

"You had better tell Carolina or one of the girls to bring them," Miss Agnes said.

Salvatore shrugged his broad shoulders and bowed.

"Then I say buona notte, Signorine, e buon' riposo."

The next thing Miss Ellen remembered distinctly was being in bed, a huge wrought-iron bed with linen sheets of coarse texture, and hearing the door-hinges creak as Waifie was thrust inside. She didn't remember undressing or putting out the light. After that there was silence save for a rasping click which signified that Miss Agnes was locking her bedroom door. Miss Ellen was too comfortable and drowsy to think of locking hers.

She slept. . . . How she slept! When she woke, bars of golden radiance shed by the louvres of the Persian shutters dappled the floor at her bedside. But it was not the light that had wakened her; it was a tap on the door which she had heard in her sleep. The tap was repeated.

"Come in!" she said cheerfully; then gasped with a sudden 'Oh!' and pulled the sheet up to her chin—for the person who had tapped on the door was not, as she had expected, one of the maidservants, but Salvatore. He had changed his white cotton coat for one of grey alpaca; his chestnut moustaches were carefully brushed and curled, his cheeks clean-shaven and ruddy, his hair newly oiled. On his upturned hand he balanced a breakfast tray.

"You sleep well, Signorina Elena?" he said, as he put down the tray on a table at her left hand. "It is a magnificent morning. Full sun. The Libeccio is finished. Now I open the persians."

He folded back the shutters and a flood of light entered the room. It displayed, to Miss Ellen's shame, the clothes she had carelessly laid aside overnight and an untidy dressing-table littered with hairpins and other oddments of her toilet. It must also, she hurriedly reflected, display her own sleep-tousled self.

If anyone had told her on the morning when she left 'The Cedars' that, within three days, she would be seen in bed by a man, she would have been indignant. Yet here it was, actually happening; and after her first gasp of surprise, she was not so much shocked as amused that she, Ellen Isit, of all people, should find herself so little embarrassed in such unbelievable circumstances. That was what foreign travel did for one: it broadened the mind. She was none the less thankful to know that the night-dress she had selected for the journey and was now wearing was a 'sensible' garment, made of a self-coloured flannelette and cut high at the neck.

Salvatore apparently took the unusual proceeding as a matter of course. When he had let in the light he began to tidy the room with the matter-of-fact air of a capable housemaid, rolling up Miss Ellen's corsets and turning her black cotton stockings inside out when he had shaken them at the window. There was no sign of distaste in his good-humoured face or in his eyes, whose irises, now, as the sunlight caught them, she saw were of the tawny colour of his moustache, with hot flecks of amber or gold in them. When he had finished his tidying he came and stood by the bed.

"You like the breakfast?" he asked her.

It was delicious, she assured him, and the tray was so daintily laid. The coarse earthenware coffee-pot and milk-jug, the crisp rolls, the pale slab of butter, together with a jar of dark honey and a green-glazed plate piled with a pyramid of oranges and tangerines newly picked from the tree with leaves on their stalks, made a picture it seemed almost wrong to derange.

"The honey is our own," Salvatore said. "It is honey of the chestnut-tree that Antonio make from bees, and the milk is of goat. Now I give you a bath, Signorina?"

At this—though she need not have taken his English so literally—Miss Ellen blushingly demurred. How would her sister, she asked herself, have reacted to such a suggestion? Till that moment, oddly enough, she had forgotten Agnes's existence. "I think *I* would rather take in the other breakfast-tray, Salvatore," she said.

"I have already knocked; but the door is shut with a key. I think the Signorina still sleep."

"Then we had better not disturb her. She often sleeps heavily after one of her headaches, and in any case she prefers her breakfast downstairs. Please leave a little of that milk in the saucer for Waifie, and then I think I'll get up."

She waited until the door was securely closed behind him. Then, barefooted on the sun-warmed tiles, she cautiously approached the window. The bland air and the morning sun were so exhilarating that she felt she would like to run or leap like a ballerina, but, emboldened though she was by her encounter with Salvatore, the fear of being seen on the balcony in her night-dress deterred her. There was no need thus to risk her modesty. From within the room she could command one of the least paintable and most overpainted 'views' in Europe: *Monfalcone, from the Terrace of the Castello Inglese*, which, together with its companion-piece, *The Old Capri Fisherman*, was to become the subject of the world's most popular picture-postcard.

It is all very well to sniff at this view and call it hackneyed. There are few works of art, even the greatest, whose splendours do not pall with excessive familiarity; and in the case of Monfalcone it must be admitted that the supernal craftsman has moulded his forms and laid on his colours with an almost theatrical abandonment, seeking immediate and shattering effect rather than a mature satisfaction. Yet this view of Monfalcone remains a masterpiece, and the virginal eyes with which Miss Ellen beheld it that morning had been denied acquaintance with any such beauty as this before. They saw the vast cup which torrents and landslides have scoured out of the seaward face of the Apennine limestone choked and over-spread with a glistening sea of olives, tossed, here and there, into a foam of sunlit peach and almond-blossom. As they swept down through three thousand feet from the fleece of bare chestnut-woods etched against the blue sky, to the russet roofs of Monfalcone Marina, its golden dome shining in the sun, and the calm sea whose surface shimmered with the silken sheen of a tropical butterfly's wings, they could see how the downward drift of olives embowered the luminous shapes of innumerable white-walled homesteads, each set like a pearl in its dark matrix of orange-plot and girt with its garth of emerald-green winter-wheat and tawny terraces of tilth bloomed with grey-green beans and lupins. Islands floated, like clouds becalmed, on the peacock sea: the rocky Siren Islets, so near that it seemed as if an outstretched hand might touch them; and far beyond these, in the distance, where the hues of unfathomable air and water commingled, so subtly that one could not guess where sea ended or sky began, loomed the grey ghost of Capri, its barren cliffs laced with snowy fringes of foam, its white villas reflecting the light of the morning sun.

Nor were Miss Ellen's eyes alone enchanted: her other senses shared in her sight's acuteness. That thin mountain air, from which she derived an intoxication more delicate perhaps but no less pleasant than that produced by the Castello Inglese wine, was the vehicle of strange odours—not merely of the perfume of orange-blossom nor yet the warm ambience of myrtle and rosemary or the aromatic scents of the *macchia* whose hot wafts pervade the hill-sides of Monfalcone when broom-pods snap and lizards bask in the sun, but the sweetish fumes of milk-blue charcoal-smoke rising from innumerable hearths, including that of the kitchen of the Castello Inglese, where Carolina was already preparing the midday meal.

Her ears too were enraptured with unfamiliar sounds. On the first morning after a spell of foul weather, when the Libeccio has blown itself out, the folk of Monfalcone had returned to their labours renewed and refreshed. While the men tilled their terraces, ankle-deep in the powdery soil that had been sweetened by rain, or tied trailers of vines to their trellises with shoots of green myrtle; while the women stooped, gathering herbage for their cows with curved sickles, or dreamily watched their tethered goats pasture; while the barefooted girls picked their way in deliberate procession between the grey rocks, with baskets of building stones or manure balanced on their heads—all that hidden world of the olive-groves of Monfalcone quickened with babbles of gossip and laughter and brief snatches of song, like a woodland awakening at dawn in the prime of spring. The songs of Monfalcone do not sound beautiful to a Northern ear, nor can its voices be called melodious; yet, at a distance, as Miss Ellen heard them, they seemed gay and innocent, as tender and spontaneous as birdsong; and their plaintive Grecian modes, enriched with unexpected trills and turns and roulades, suggested not so much echoes of an ancient culture that has degenerated as improvisations inspired by the birth of a new one, simple enough to be hopeful—an instinctive expression of exuberant life.

For a long time Miss Ellen stood entranced at her window, gazing, sniffing and listening. Suddenly, far below, in the golden campanile of Monfalcone Marina, church-bells clanged—not with the sober persuasiveness of English suburban church-bells; but with harsh insistence, as though they were summoning people to catch the last train to heaven, or alternatively as if a madman had been unloosed in the belfry. Was it Sunday? Miss Ellen wondered. She had lost all count of the days, though it seemed to her that it ought to be Monday. If it were Sunday people wouldn't be working in the olives. If it were Sunday, she really ought to unpack her best dress and find out at once from Salvatore if there was an Anglican church in Monfalcone, as in most civilized places abroad. That was one of the ways in which she was going to score over Agnes, who certainly couldn't expect to find a Unitarian Chapel in a Catholic country. The bells clanged in an access of excited urgency; then their clatter abruptly ceased. Though she had no means of telling the hour, it appeared to be unlikely that she would be able to dress in time for the morning service, and having breakfasted so greedily she couldn't, in any case, participate in the Blessed Sacrament. On the whole, Miss Ellen decided, the best thing she could do was to get dressed quickly and explore the villa and its garden before Agnes awoke.

After the gloom of her little back-bedroom at 'The Cedars', which had faced north, where, even on a midsummer morning, she could hardly see to 'do her hair' properly, the brightness of this airy and spacious chamber was a delight. There was, moreover, an enormous pier-glass in which, as she slipped her night-dress down from her shoulders, she was able—and at first faintly shocked—to see herself reflected from head to toe. Such a thing had not happened since she was a schoolgirl; yet, from what she remembered, it seemed to hei that she had not greatly changed. Of course her figure had 'set' and filled out a little; but apart from her face, which was certainly no longer a girl's, her body looked lither and younger than she could have imagined. What a wonderful thing it was, she told herself, to let air and sunlight play on her skin like this; what a delicious sense of freedom it gave one; how wildly, how sweetly it stirred the blood! Miss Ellen smiled at herself in the glass; she stood on her toes and lifted her arms like a dancer preparing for a pirouette. With her unbound hair (and, of course, a leopard skin) she could imagine herself in the role of a leaping Mænad, or some white nymph threading the olive-groves with a satyr in pursuit; but in the midst of this rapture there came to her a vision of Agnes sleeping off her 'head', marble-cold and virginal, in the adjoining room, and with it the memory of what Agnes had said to her only a few hours before: "I always ask myself what Papa would have thought . . ." She hardly dared to imagine what Papa—or Agnes, indeed—would have thought of her now.

Miss Ellen laughed. This was the second time she had recently caught herself laughing at inappropriate thoughts. This time her laugh was the outward sign of an inward and unconscious emancipation. Without being able (or even wishing) to discover the cause, she perceived that her attitude towards life, if not her nature, had changed overnight. She felt as one of those scrawny irises that still languished in the sour, cat-scrabbled garden at 'The Cedars' might have done, if some benevolent magic had suddenly transplanted it into the rich volcanic soil of Monfalcone; its shrunken rhizomes swelling, a stream of warm sap rising into its shabby leaves. In this expansive moment she didn't care twopence what Agnes—or even what dear Papa—would have thought of her. She had discovered—and in a degree more intense than ever before—her capacity for relaxation and physical enjoyment, and was—wickedly, maybe—resolved to exploit this delicious mood as far as she could before Agnes, or her own conscience, or merely Fate, 'nipped it in the bud'.

Eager and excited as she was, she determined not to hurry over her toilet, to which she gave more than her usual care, and even, as a concrete symbol of change and revolt, altered the dressing of her hair, which in North Bromwich she had worn screwed up into an uncompromising 'bun' on the top of her head, by dividing it with a new parting at the side and letting it fall more loosely, unconfined by anything but a blue ribbon which matched her eyes. When she was a girl she had often been told she had pretty hair, but since then—and particularly after her 'disappointment'—she had never taken the trouble to show it to advantage. The result surprised and pleased her: her hair, released from the torment of an unnatural constriction, appeared not only more plentiful but also more lustrous.

Then she deliberately selected her flimsiest summer frock, the white muslin with black spots she had only worn in the tropics on the voyage from India and later at one or two garden-parties when they first came to Alvaston, and after a final satisfied glance at herself in the long mirror, picked up Waifie, hurried downstairs, and stepped out into the sun on the terrace.

Here new marvels awaited her; not merely in another view of the superb expanse she had seen from her bedroom window, but beauties nearer and more intimate. Apart from the terrace itself, on which a row of bulging earthenware jars, each capacious enough to conceal one of the Forty Thieves, were topped by scarlet geraniums, the white arches of the loggia, festooned with magenta bracts of bougainvillæa, and the stone-pillared pergola from which hung the pale tassels of wisteria, still in bud, the garden of the Castello Inglese was no formal pleasance. It looked as if old Antonino was either too ancient, too lazy, or perhaps too wise, to attempt to control or even to direct single-handed a profligate fertility that was beyond his powers. As a result of this, though the mind of man had doubtless announced the theme, Nature herself, with triumphant zest, had amplified and elaborated it in the manner of a Passacaglia, occasionally dominating it with a bold counterpoint of her own beneath whose exuberance the man-made intentions of colour and even of form were transformed or lost. Thus, the stark pillars which had been planned to support clambering vines and wisteria were already wreathed to their capitols in garlands and trusses of ivy; the crumbling parapet was covered with emerald mosses or stained with lichens, and every cranny in the masonry occupied by stone-crops and toadflax, wild stock or valerian; while the flag-irises, now in full bloom, which had been planted to border the long walk under the pergola, had overflowed their beds and spread over the falling slope as though by the force of gravity, in a cascade that spent its imperial purples and blues in a drift of self-sown oxalis, whose sheets of pale green and gold competed with blood-red orchises, spires of asphodel and deep-glowing anemones for the possession of every particle of earth Antonino's mattock had left undisturbed. It was almost as if this opulent Nature of the South, impatient of the limits of man's chromatic imagination, had snatched the design from his hands and decided to show him with what greater daring the resources of living colour might be employed, deriding all his preconceived conventions and reconciling the most hazardous contrasts by sheer breadth and bravura.

Small wonder that Miss Ellen's eyes, conditioned by the smoky monotones of North Bromwich, or, at the most, by the vertical suns of the tropics, which flatten all colour by their strength, were so dazzled that day that she could not 'take in' any detail, but was merely transported by a display that was almost too lavish to be believed. She tried to put her impressions into adequate words, but could get no further than deciding that it was 'as beautiful as a dream' and 'a veritable fairyland', both of which descriptions seemed hardly to do it justice. Then she suddenly realized, for the first time, that this paradise was actually hers—or half hers, at any rate; that these beauties were, and would be, a tangible, personal possession so long as she lived. This was even more startling and inconceivable. It made her feel giddy. Probably she had made herself giddy by going out hatless into the noonday sun. In India, at that hour, she would certainly have worn a topee.

"I think," she told herself, "it would be wiser to go into the house."

It seemed an enormous house, though, in fact, it was probably smaller than 'The Cedars'. Its apparent size and impressiveness arose from the fact that the building, unlike the rectangular block of 'The Cedars', lacked depth, being lodged on a narrow shelf cut into the hill-side, over which it sprawled, east and west, for thirty or forty yards. There was no 'back' to it; Carolina's kitchen and the servants' quarters enjoyed the same generous quantity of light and air and the same style of architecture as the owner's apartments. It had not, like 'The Cedars', been planned as a whole, but had evidently been constructed and expanded haphazard and by degrees to suit the occupants' fancies, resources or desires, and in accordance with the physical conditions imposed by the lie of the land. Yet the effect of the whole was harmonious, and, like that of the garden, owed as much to the exigences of nature as to the mind of man. It had grown rather than been built. It was actually a part of the mountain-side. The very stone of which its walls were constructed had been blasted and quarried out of the rock and re-arranged, as it were, within a few feet of their matrix; and no sooner was this arbitrary displacement completed than the same exuberant green life which had transformed the garden had conspired to obliterate every discordant sign of change and had reclaimed the building as a part of the natural landscape, and given it the appearance of always having been there.

It appeared large to Miss Ellen, too, because the rooms were so lofty and bright and airy. In a clime where sun was abundant its builders seemed to have been more eager to enjoy the blessing of light than those who had built

'The Cedars' in a region where sunlight was rare. The imposing staircase hall through which they had passed to the salone overnight occupied the whole height of the building, and was as full of light as the entrance-hall at 'The Cedars' had been gloomy. As she re-entered it Miss Ellen reflected that these two were the only rooms she had seen as yet on the ground floor. On her right were two folding doors of dark oiled chestnut which obviously must lead to another important chamber. Preceded by Waifie, with tail erect and the mangled remains of a blue-green lizard in her mouth, she opened one door and entered.

The room, to her surprise, was an artist's studio: the kind of room of which she had often dreamed. It was long and even larger than the salone, lighted by three tall, round-arched windows thrown open to air and sun. In one corner, at the end of the room, stood a dais supporting an easel; in the other a concert-grand piano. This was a richer source of potential delight than she had ever hoped to possess, and the sight of it made her regret that she had not packed her 'music': it would be the height of joy to sit there alone, out of Agnes's hearing, and play such a magnificent instrument to her heart's content. The floor was tiled, like the entrance-hall, with sea-green encaustic, and strewn with Persian rugs which, together with a number of cushioned divans, gave the studio an air of oriental luxury: it seemed a pity that they had not brought the Buddhas in various materials which had survived their misfortunes, to complete the picture. There were several shelves of books which she looked forward to reading. Since Papa died she had never had time to read anything. She examined them eagerly, while Waifie, curled up on a divan, crunched the remains of her lizard, which was zoologically allied—and therefore the next best thing—to a bird. Miss Ellen discovered a row of musty Tauchnitz and a number of novels in French, with which she looked forward to improving her knowledge of that language, together with—had she but known it!—a considerable library of pornography, including a set of Burton's Arabian Nights, which seemed to her most appropriate to their surroundings.

Next she examined the pictures on the walls. They were not the kind of pictures to which she was accustomed: the steel engravings of military scenes and celebrities with a sprinkling of Landseer animals which had infested the downstairs rooms at 'The Cedars'. Apart from the landscapes, which seemed to her 'modern' and crude, they were not, indeed, the kind of pictures which, in spite of her recent experiences, her maidenly modesty could accept without a blush. She could hardly feel comfortable in their presence, she felt certain that Agnes would expel them from the room. It would be tactful and kind, she thought, if she could get Salvatore to remove them before Agnes set eyes on them. It was clear that Papa, as usual, had been right. Captain Vaughan, their benefactor, had most certainly not been a 'nice' man. The large picture on the easel was covered by a curtain of crimson velvet. It would probably be as embarrassing as the rest, if not more so; but since she was there and alone Miss Ellen could not resist the temptation of taking a peep at it. As she touched the velvet it fell from the frame revealing a male—an extremely male nude of generous proportions. It was the portrait of a young man, a handsome young man admittedly, leaning negligently against one of the pillars of the pergola against a background of shimmering sea, with craftily-smiling eyes and lips and a wreath of vine-leaves on his head. It was a mischievous, provocative smile, she thought; yet the features—and particularly the eyes—seemed oddly familiar. Where had she seen it before? A voice startled her.

"You like, Signorina?"

Salvatore, who had stolen up silently in his rope-soled shoes, was standing behind her. When she failed to answer, he laughed an amused, caressing laugh.

"It is I, Signorina. The Capitano—Don Ludovico, as we called him, painted it many years ago. He always say it is his best picture. It pleases you? No?"

Miss Ellen pulled herself together rapidly. She felt

this was not a question that should have been asked.

"The curtain slipped down," she lied, "when I was arranging it. You had better put it on again. Is my sister awake yet?"

"The Signorina Agnes takes breakfast," Salvatore replied, still admiring his own presentment with satisfaction and with his head on one side. "She ask where you are just now. I say: in the garden."

"I must go to her at once," Miss Ellen said desperately. "Where is she?"

"In the salone, Signorina. On the opposite side of the hall."

She retreated precipitately, forgetting all about Waifie, and entered the salone to find Agnes sitting alone in state at the head of the refectory table. She was wearing black satin—it must have been Sunday after all—and her appearance in that setting would certainly have satisfied Ernest Wilburn, though his favourite living Vandyck had now been transformed into a Goya. It was reasonable to expect that three nights in the train culminating in the agonies of a crashing sick-headache would have left her limp and subdued, but Miss Agnes looked neither. She, no less than Miss Ellen, appeared to have been revived and stimulated by the Monfalcone air. Her straight back was —if that were possible—straighter and stiffer than ever; her fine eyes gleamed more brightly if not more imperiously; and her marble-pale face, with its cameo-clear precision of line, was slightly flushed over the cheek-bones, as if it had come alive in the night. Moreover, she was apparently making a hearty breakfast.

"Ah, there you are, Ellen," she said. "I was told that you had gone out. I felt hungry, and so I ordered some bacon and eggs. I am delighted to hear from Salvatore, the butler, that our Uncle Ludovic never abandoned his English breakfast. I must confess he has gone up in my estimation. After all, blood will tell. You had better join me."

Miss Ellen timidly admitted that she had already breakfasted upstairs.

"What? In bed? I'm surprised at you, Ellen. Papa would never have countenanced anything so slovenly. Have you no self-respect?"

Miss Ellen murmured something about doing in Rome as Rome did.

"You should have known better," Miss Agnes said severely. "It is our duty as Englishwomen to set an example and not to succumb to these lax foreign ways. And what on earth, may I ask, do you think you've done to your hair?"

Miss Ellen said she had just felt like doing it differently.

"Doing it differently, indeed! Remember, you are not a young girl. You have merely made yourself look ridiculous. If you don't take care, we shall have you going native."

Miss Ellen blushed with unwonted anger. It was on the tip of her tongue, for the first time in her life, to tell Agnes to mind her own business, and to shock her still further by boasting that a man had brought in her breakfast. By an effort of will she held back the unseemly words and said nothing, consoling herself with the reflection that before very long poor Agnes would really get something to be shocked about. Agnes had much better reserve her indignation, she thought, for the moment when she found herself confronted by Uncle Ludovic's picture of Salvatore!

3

Miss Ellen was not privileged to witness this dramatic scene, nor yet its sequel, in which the Castello Inglese was completely cleansed of her Uncle Ludovic's pictures. Whether Agnes expelled them with her own hands, or gave orders to Salvatore for their removal, she knew no more than what had happened to a number of 'curious' books which disappeared simultaneously from the studio shelves. Though they were joint owners of the villa, Agnes left no doubt as to which of them was the predominant partner. The air of Monfalcone, which, in Ellen's case, had had a subtly relaxing effect, produced, in Miss Agnes, an increasing moral stringency, releasing, at the same time, a torrent of energy. There was no likelihood of *her* going native or pandering to any foreign laxities. She had assumed, as a right no less than a duty, the White Woman's Burden and carried it forward without regard for the corns she trod on, being determined to make the Castello Inglese the stronghold (and, at the worst, the last ditch) of Anglo-Saxon order and decency.

Thus while Miss Ellen continued to stray, bemused and enchanted, through a paradise rich in unfamiliar sensual experiences each more exciting than the last, enjoying, at the same time, the unwonted delights of leisure and irresponsibility, Miss Agnes proceeded to organize the establishment more or less on the lines of an English country-house in the strictest period of the Victorian era, and brought to the task the administrative capacity which had undoubtedly made her Papa a pest to his superiors no less than his subordinates in India. In the timeless air of Monfalcone, where one day is neither better nor worse than the next, she decreed that everything should be done on the tick of time; in that blessed clime, where mankind is normally as easy-going as nature, she insisted on discipline and, strange to say, imposed it. It was as though the energies unused during more than half a lifetime had found their natural vent. The blood of Empire Builders ran in her veins, and within the limits of her new domain she proceeded to build one.

There was no more coffee and rolls upstairs in the morning. A gong sounded punctually at nine o'clock, and an English breakfast was formally served in the salone. At nine-thirty precisely Agnes went to inspect the kitchen, which her uncle had never entered in his life, and interviewed Carolina to whom she gave orders for the meals that were to be served during the day—in which neither onions nor garlic nor oil must be used. At this ceremony the younger girls, Maria and Assunta, assisted and were examined for any signs of slovenliness or uncleanliness and allotted their duties for the day. If such things had existed in the shops of Monfalcone she would doubtless have put them forthwith into uniform with starched aprons and caps with streamers. Fortunately for them, Monfalcone didn't run to such elegancies. Next, at ten, in the loggia, she interviewed Antonino the gardener, and gave him instructions, which he neither understood nor had the least intention of fulfilling, on the culture of English vegetables. At ten-thirty Salvatore awaited her in the salone, produced his accounts, and reported on things in general, like a sergeant-major attending his commanding officer in the regimental orderly-room.

Salvatore's accounts gave Miss Agnes's precise mind a good deal of trouble. They were scribbled, illegibly, on odd scraps of paper, in a manner that made exact reckonings almost impossible. They were also immense. It seemed odd to her that, in a country where living was supposed to be cheap, it should cost so much to feed a household of seven. In spite of his patient and apparently frank explanations, she found it hard to believe that she wasn't being 'done'. She particularly disliked his constant reminders that, in Don Ludovico's day, the accuracy of his accounts had never been questioned or their details examined, and resented even more his manner of humouring her with a sort of amused tolerance which suggested, in spite of his deference, that she was a tiresome old woman and that her niggling over such trifles was beneath the dignity of a real lady. Most of all she detested his masculine way of sweeping her questions aside with the patronizing assurance that she need give these matters no further thought and that he would see to everything.

"*Non dubitare*, Signorina. . . . Have no doubt," he would say.

But Miss Agnes had her doubts: If she was Captain Vaughan's niece, she was also Colonel Isit's daughter, and no evasions, however charming, could satisfy them.

"Next week," she decreed, in her best Italian—she had 'nipped in the bud' his habit of speaking English, which implied a familiar equality between them which she could not countenance—"next week I shall accompany you every day to the shops and superintend your purchases. It is not," she explained, not very convincingly, "that I doubt your honesty, Salvatore; but I find your accounts rather puzzling and would prefer to look into everything myself."

Salvatore shrugged his broad shoulders and smiled. That was, of course, as the Signorina wished. It was the same by him. He was always at her service.

So next Monday morning, while Miss Ellen continued to wander through her newly-discovered paradise like an enchanted child, the piazza of Monfalcone Marina was treated to the spectacle of the new owner of the Castello Inglese descending, dressed to the nines, to do her shopping, followed, at decorous intervals, by Salvatore, equally elegant in his (or Captain Vaughan's) black coat and striped trousers and his straw hat set acant, and the giggling Assunta, with an empty basket on her head.

The descent was much hotter and longer and steeper and stonier than Miss Agnes had imagined. By the time she reached the Marina her feet were swollen and bruised within her elastic-sided boots; but her sense of duty fortified her in this discomfort, and the shopkeepers, despite their difficulty in understanding her, seemed not merely obliging and polite but delighted to see her. When she failed to make herself understood, Salvatore tactfully intervened. It was clear that they regarded him with respect and consideration. When they demanded outrageous prices for their wares, he came to her rescue, haggling over small coins with a vehemence which, on her part, would have seemed undignified, until she had to stop him.

Assunta stood waiting submissively with her basket to pick up their purchases, though several times Miss Agnes caught her exchanging bold smiles and provocative glances and rude remarks with young men who should have known better. Then, heavily-laden, the procession re-climbed the hill. For six days in succession Miss Agnes added to the gaiety of the Marina by providing this spectacle; and throughout them Salvatore maintained his attitude of long-suffering patience and respectful politeness. He did not even take off his black coat when they toiled up the stony path, and never presumed to speak unless Miss Agnes addressed him. On the seventh, when she totted up the accounts, she found they amounted to half as much again as Salvatore, unwatched, had spent in the preceding week.

This result was humiliating; but Salvatore, with admirable restraint, did not take advantage of it—as was natural enough, since the more the Miss Isits spent, the larger would be his commission. But Miss Agnes was shaken. Perhaps, after all, she had misjudged him; and though her pride would not allow her to show it, she could not help feeling herself at a disadvantage.

"We have spent more this week than last, Salvatore," she told him.

He showed no surprise.

"Eh! The Signorina is a foreigner."

Miss Agnes broke into indignant English:

"Is that any reason why I should be fleeced?" she demanded.

"Fleeced? I not understand. Ah, you want to say 'stung'. It is like this. The people at the Marina are poor people, and they know that the Signorina is rich, very rich and generous like Don Ludovico, so they say to themselves: 'Here is a foreigner who understands properly nothing and eats bacon for breakfast and meat every day. What difference will one soldo, two soldi—a lira, maybe—make to one who holds money, much money in the pocket, and a beautiful property such as the Castello Inglese? But when they see me, Signorina, come to make the shopping, they say: 'This is no fool of a foreigner. Here is one who has been in America and understands everything, and so cannot be stung! He is faithful also to his Signorine, who give him full confidence. Very well, then. We make the just prices.' "

"But that, Salvatore," Miss Agnes maintained, "is not honest."

"Ah, honesty, honesty," Salvatore sighed: "that is

quite another thing. First of all, Signorina, one must live. So what is one to do?"

What, indeed, was one to do with such crooked reasoning? The unwelcome fact was that next week, when she allowed Salvatore to do his shopping alone, the household expenses returned to their normal high level. He had won his point by allowing her have her own way, and Miss Agnes was reluctantly compelled to let him get away with it. It was her duty, no doubt, to instruct him in those moral principles to which he was blind, just as it was equally her duty to prevail on Assunta not to flash her black eyes at every young man she saw, and to teach her to make useful articles. But, by this time, spring was nearing its zenith in Monfalcone: during the last few weeks, the blossom of peach and almond had fallen to leave the trees fledged with pale green; the following snowdrifts of cherry-bloom had melted and vanished as rapidly; and soon, amid clusters of bronzy leaves, the fruit swelled and grew ripe and red as Assunta's lips, and the laden branches became the haunt of mischievous orioles that chuckled and whistled to one another with gay, defiant notes—and before Antonino could stoop to pick up his gun, were off and away, in a flash of gold, to some other, unguarded orchard. The cicalas, too, had crept out of their winter crannies: they zizzed all day in the forest of olives whose tops had grown pale with ivory bloom until it seemed as if the whole landscape seethed and simmered with heat. Spring had passed—in a breath, in a night—and summer had come. It was too hot in the morning now for Miss Agnes to face the prospect of trudging down to the shops at the Marina and toiling home again. She had been used to a tropical climate; but this was different. The heat of Monfalcone was not like the crushing heat of the plains of India, to which sensible white women, such as herself surrendered, knowing that it was useless to fight. To her shame, she confessed that she had no desire to struggle. This Italian sun was no pitiless enemy, but rather a wise and kindly friend who gently whispered that any excess of energy was not only undesirable but also unprofitable;

so Miss Agnes, without in the least abrogating her principles, refrained from the discomfort entailed by practising them. Though still convinced in the back of her mind, that Salvatore defrauded her systematically, she was prepared to believe that he would prevent other people from doing the like: if anyone's nest was going to be lined, it would be his—with, just possibly, an occasional odd feather for Carolina. As she had remarked on the night of their arrival at Monfalcone, it *was* a great comfort to have a man about the house—particularly a man so untiring and capable and unfailingly respectful as Salvatore. His attentions gave her an opportunity—if not an excuse—for relaxing. It is possible that her long struggle in North Bromwich had exhausted her more than she realized, and that she was beginning to feel her age.

While Miss Agnes nibbled the lotus with suspicion, Miss Ellen gobbled it as unguardedly as she had gulped down the insidious vintage of Monfalcone, and relaxed without a qualm. She had always liked being lazy, though she had never before been permitted to indulge that liking. She did not suffer from the reaction which made Agnes feel (if she did not show) her age. It was true that, reckoned in terms of time, Miss Ellen's age was only five years less than her sister's; but the period which separated them was one of crucial years, and she had always been disproportionately young in spirit. When Miss Agnes's body wilted in the summer heat, hers luxuriated, and her energies, physical and mental, began to unfold and expand. She was, in fact—though nobody who had known her in North Bromwich would have guessed it—a Child of Nature, and for this reason the more adaptable to the exuberant landscape and climate of Monfalcone, and the more acceptable to its denizens—who like herself, lived close to the earth.

She had quickly and easily made friends with all those of them with whom she came in contact: with old Antonino, unhurriedly sapping his garden from dawn to sunset, and with that wizened witch Carolina producing miraculous dishes from a larder that looked like a dust-bin, no less than with Assunta and Maria, the two laughing girls. That was one of the things that appealed to her most about these southern people, so simple and yet so shrewd, so impulsive and yet so immemorially wise: they were always laughing—even when they grumbled they could laugh. And there had not been much room or occasion for laughter in Miss Ellen's life. Even when the joke was against herself she shared in it, for their laughter was friendly.

She was also by nature loquacious and sociable; and these qualities, combined with her lack of self-consciousness and an aptitude for 'languages' which her sister had suppressed, enabled her, as she picked up a smattering of dialect words, many of which were improper, to satisfy her curiosity about a multitude of things which Miss Agnes either accepted without scrutiny as a regrettable matter of course or considered it beneath her dignity to explore. Thus, while Miss Agnes wrote letters to lawyers or checked her accounts or sat fanning herself in the sea-green studio or under the shade of the loggia, her mind brooding on the decorous past or on her plans for the future, which included the erection of a marble memorial for Papa and a second rehabilitation of 'The Cedars', Miss Ellen plunged headlong into a present that was sufficient unto its fantastic self, dismissing from her thoughts the fateful day when, in the ordinary course of events, they would return to the chill realities of North Bromwich.

She explored not only the garden and vineyards and olive-groves of the Castello Inglese, but strayed far afield through the adjoining peasant properties where nobody turned her back or scowled at her. There were no notices warning trespassers that they would be prosecuted. She drank wine from the subterranean cellars of little farms under the budding trellises of vine from which the grapes that made it had been picked. She gossiped with old women tending their goats and young women suckling babies from their brown breasts. She chattered with young men, bronzed and stripped to the waist, who looked up inquiringly when they heard her step or saw the flash of her muslin dress shining through the olives: during her short stay in Monfalcone she had considerably extended her knowledge of human anatomy. Nearer home she listened to old Antonino's innocent dissertations on the physiology of his livestock, and encouraged Assunta and Maria to discuss their love-affairs, to the outspoken details of which she listened breathlessly. "You will shock the Signorina," old Carolina reproved them. But Miss Ellen was not shocked in the least. She was merely learning.

The only member of the household, indeed, with whom she had not established such terms of frank intimacy was Salvatore. That was a pity, she thought: he was such a manly man, and she had admired him so much and looked forward to being friends with him. Yet somehow the basis of that friendship, which she had felt so safe and so natural on the very first morning when he had brought up her breakfast, seemed now less secure. Perhaps the embarrassing incident of the picture had had something to do with it. After that she could, naturally, never help feeling shy of him, particularly when they were alone. This was as much beyond her power to control as a chemical reaction: He had the power of making her turn pink, like blue litmus in contact with an acid. Her throat reddened, her pulses fluttered, under the influence of his bold, dark eyes. She had always thought of them as 'dark'—but in reality they were tawny, resembling in colour, brown sherry or Papa's dry Madeira: but when the sun lit their hot flecks they became oddly inhuman—more like the eyes of a wild animal—a tiger, perhaps—than a man's.

It seemed that she was not alone in feeling awkward and blushing beneath Salvatore's gaze. She had noticed the same phenomenon in Assunta, who took cover in the darkest corner of the kitchen to escape from it, and always seemed restless and apprehensive in his presence—like a rabbit that had smelt a stoat. That was just how Miss Ellen felt. It wasn't that Salvatore's glance was possessive, nor yet that he was unduly familiar or took any liberty. It was simply that when he came near her—and sometimes, quite unintentionally no doubt, he came very near—she became aware, above the more obvious odours of tobacco and hair-oil and garlic, of a more subtle, essentially male emanation which instantly put her on her guard and brought into play an instinctive mechanism of self-protection. Against what? She couldn't imagine. Yet there, however unreasonably, it was . . .

She had experienced this strange reaction to a frightening degree when, one morning in May, they had met in the remotest part of the olive-groves. She had slept badly the night before. This was the season of the spring migration of quails from Africa, and over all the seaward slopes of Monfalcone the peasants had set up nets suspended on tall chestnut-poles to catch the birds in their flight. To induce the quails to fly low and alight they used decoys, imprisoned in wicker cages, whose eyes they had put out in order to make them utter a cry of distress which, Antonino had told her, resembled their mating-call. When she heard this Ellen had protested against quail-nets being set up in the garden of the Castello Inglese; but Agnes, whom she had expected to be more sympathetic, had scoffed at her scruples. Such had been the custom of the country, she said, for thousands of years; it was as natural for the Monfalconesi to reap this warm-blooded harvest as to pick their olives or grapes, and a foreigner who protested against this cruelty on humanitarian grounds would be thought interfering and ridiculous. It was much less cruel to net quails than to torture lizards as Waifie did. Besides which, she liked quails. Papa had always shot them in India.

Still Miss Ellen could not get over the horror of this pitiful hecatomb. During that sleepless, moonlit night, the monotonous, stuttering cry of Salvatore's blinded decoys had kept her awake. She had determined, as soon as it was light, to get up and release them—though whether that would mend matters much was rather doubtful: they would probably be snapped up at once by the peregrine falcons swooping down from the cliffs of limestone.

The sun had just scaled the ridge of mountains to eastward and was gilding the motionless tops of the olive-groves when Miss Ellen, determined but unkempt and tousled with her sleepless vigil, slipped out of the house on her mission of mercy. But by now the blind quails had stopped calling, and she couldn't find them. There was no sound of bird voices in the groves but the shrill challenge of the chaffinches, the muted chuckle of siskins flitting to and fro in the olives, and occasionally a rich burst of song from the nightingales which, in Monfalcone, preferred to sing by day. After searching for the cages in vain, Miss Ellen decided to give up her quest. She sat down on a stone, disheartened rather than consoled by the dispassionate loveliness of a scene that hid so much cruelty. It was at this moment that Salvatore appeared.

He had risen before dawn to go 'hunting' as he called it, and looked very different from the decorous figure, curled, oiled and blackcoated, whose suave presence lent such an air of dignity to the Castello Inglese and to Miss Agnes's progress to and from the Marina. He was wearing patched trousers and a ragged cotton shirt unfastened at the neck. His sanguine face shone with sweat, and the stubble on his cheeks was of the same colour as the tawny growth that shagged his torso and showed through the tears in his shirt and its open neck. His hair, too, was not tidily brushed back from his brow as usual. It appeared to grow low on the forehead, like a Highland bull's, over his eyes, whose fire-flecked amber shone through its unruly fringe. Though he was heavily built and broad-shouldered, he was slim in the hips, and his movements, as he climbed the terraces, were swift and easy. They gave the impression of being those of an immensely powerful but agile creature, full of the joy of well-being and radiant with rude health. Over the right shoulder he carried a single-barrelled hammer gun, that looked like a child's toy; from his left hand there swung a string of dead quails and other small birds with their claws tied together by string. Both of his hands were sticky with blood and feathers, and there was another smear of blood on his brow, where he had wiped off the sweat. When he saw Miss Ellen he smiled, revealing a row of teeth whose whiteness and regularity a pretty woman might have envied. He approached and sat down on the stone beside her, so near that she could feel the heat of his body. He threw the trussed corpses carelessly on the ground and pointed with a blood-stained finger.

"Quails . . ." he said. "You like, Signorina?"

Miss Ellen edged away from him, as far as the size of the stone would allow her. Salvatore followed her and came even closer, as though he supposed she was studying his convenience.

"You like?" he repeated.

"Poor little creatures," she said. "I don't like the horrible way you entice them into the nets. Carolina says you put out their eyes."

He smiled lazily. "Why not, Signorina? If you do not blind them they are stupid birds and would be of no use; but when they are blinded they cry all night; and those that fly over the sea and hear them calling, they say to themselves: This is corking good luck: here are females; now we have a good time! It is natural. You don't think?"

Miss Ellen shivered. As he spoke he had picked up the bundle of quails; he was smoothing their mottled plumage with his blood-stained fingers caressingly. It reminded her of Waifie's manner of gloating over a mouse she had killed, giving it gentle pats with her paws and pushing it away from her in the hope that it might struggle to escape and give her the chance of pouncing on it again.

"I think that only makes it more cruel," she said in a shaky voice.

He laughed. "Cruel? I don't understand. These are not Christians but animals. Only twice a year quails come here, and we gotta be quick and catch them how we can before the falcons have them. They are good to eat—very good—you soon see, Signorina—with basil beside them."

"But it's not only quails you kill," Miss Ellen said. "What are those other poor little birds?"

Salvatore took up the bundle of feathers and prodded it. "These are *tordi*, what you call trush, and this is the nightingale."

"A nightingale? Oh, but you shouldn't have shot that, Salvatore!"

"The Signorina is right," he agreed. "He is small and his meat is not worth the shot and powder, which cost much in these days. One needs a dozen like him to make it worth while. Unfortunately, I only saw one. But he will go in with the trushes and make you a nice soup for supper. Perhaps I shoot more to-morrow."

"I would much rather hear them singing," Miss Ellen said.

"Hear them singing?" He gazed at her with a quizzical smile, as though he found the idea both novel and entertaining. "You like to hear the birds sing, Signorina? See then what I will do: I will make Antonino catch them with lime and with traps and put them in a cage on the terrace, if the Signorina Agnes permits. Then you shall see and hear them all day."

"Oh, please don't do that," Miss Ellen entreated him. "I'm afraid you don't understand. I don't like birds in cages. I like them to fly about and sing and enjoy themselves."

Salvatore shrugged his broad shoulders. He gave her up.

"The Signorina is very romantic and sentimental," he said, "just like an American. All foreigners are much the same: a little as children. For me this is curious. They never grow old. Now the girl of Monfalcone, she is quite different. At fifteen she become a woman. At seventeen, maybe, she marry and have many children, one every year. Then she soon grow fat as the pig or lean as the anchovy, one or other; and then, at thirty"—his face showed disgust—"she is finish: no good any more for a man—only fit to work in the campagna or cook maccheronis. But the English are different, and I have seen the same thing in Nuova York in America. Their faces, perhaps, are changed; but their bodies and legs remain young and, what we say, appetizing. It is a pure marvel. the difference. You, Signorina, for example—speaking with respect—are old enough, and not to say beautiful, though one must say very simpatica; but when I see the feet, and not the face, I say to myself: 'There goes a young girl.' And to tell the truth I think you are grown more young every day since you come here. You feel that way? Don Ludovico, the captain, say it is the Monfalcone air that is too strong for foreigners. Many times we see curious things happen that make us laugh, I can tell you!"

Miss Ellen rose hurriedly without any comment. It was not merely the double-edged nature of Salvatore's compliments (if compliments they were) but their personal drift that disturbed her. She knew she had shapely ankles, and, in secret, took pride in them; but it wasn't for a man-servant—even 'speaking with respect'—to mention them, much less to look at them. She could hardly believe that he would have dared to do either with Agnes, who would no doubt have had the presence of mind to rise the moment he sat down near her. As usual, Agnes had been right: one couldn't, if one were a lady, afford to be natural or friendly with foreigners. For all their apparent respect, the veneer was thin; they could not understand the social distinctions in whose shelter English ladies were bred.

"It must nearly be time for breakfast," Miss Ellen said.

Salvatore glanced at the sky. "It is not more than eight. We have yet an hour, Signorina. But I, too, must shave the beard and prepare myself for the table." He picked up the quails and shouldered his gun. "With the Signorina's permission," he said, "I will now accompany her."

"Please don't trouble," Miss Ellen protested.

"It is nothing. A pleasure. I follow," he said with a caressing smile and a bow that might almost have been ironical.

Without answer she set off hurriedly in the direction of the house, hoping, all the time, that her speed might rid her of his company, conscious too, all the time, of his eyes, which she could not see, but which she felt as acutely as though they had power to penetrate the clothes she was wearing, appraising, approving, rejecting the figure beneath them. The faster she went, the nearer, the more potent they seemed. She was panting as well as blushing now. What would Agnes have done? Turned, no doubt, and told him witheringly that he wasn't wanted. But Miss Ellen had neither her sister's composure nor her courage. That would merely have made a 'scene' which she knew she couldn't have carried off. And to have made a scene would have been equivalent to admitting that she was frightened.

She was frightened in earnest now. Though she knew it was quite ridiculous, she was losing her head, tripping over the stones of the rocky path with no thought but a frantic desire to escape—not so much (and this surely was odd) from the man who was following her as from the garlanded youth of her Uncle Ludovico's picture, whose image she had never yet been able to expel from the depths of her mind. She broke into a run; but Salvatore's long stride kept pace with her. Finally, hardly knowing what she did, she forsook the path and made a bee-line up-hill for the house, scrambling over the walls of rough stone that retained the tilled terraces. As she surmounted the last of these, her foot slipped and she fell. In an instant Salvatore was beside her. His brown hands closed on her arms; he raised her to her feet.

"Permit, Signorina," he said, as he lifted her bodily, and as easily as if he had picked up a fallen child.

"Oh, thank you," she gasped.

"You are not hurt, signorina?"

"No, no . . . I don't think so. It was silly. My foot must have slipped."

As she stood there, smoothing her dusty skirt, something told her she was being watched and she raised her eyes to see Agnes standing in her long night-dress at the bedroom window, surveying her with an expression of cold anger and disgust on her pallid face. It was her duty, Miss Ellen felt, to explain this uncomely scene; but before she could find appropriate words the tall figure of Agnes had turned away and disappeared from the window. Salvatore was laughing softly.

"The Signorina see us," he said. "I think she is not too much pleased."

Miss Ellen did not answer him. She scuttled into the house and up to her room where she lay on the unmade bed, confused, hot and still panting. Gradually recovering, she came to see with what lack of proportion and balance she had behaved. There was no reason on earth why she should have taken fright and fled frantically from a man whom nothing but the speed of her flight had forced to pursue her, who had merely offered politely to keep her company on her way home. The trouble was that when once she had started to run she couldn't stop. It was true that the fantastic incident, which was all her own fault, had ended in a situation that was, to say the least, humiliating and might be considered compromising—as was suggested indeed by Salvatore's associating her with himself by the use of the word 'us' and the expression on Agnes's face. But that was all nonsense. She wasn't, heaven knew, a frivolous girl, but a middle-aged woman (who didn't quite look her age) with a reputation, not undeserved, she hoped, for seriousness and propriety. She would have the right, if Agnes referred to the unfortunate scene, to decline to discuss it, or even—though this was hardly conceivable—tell her to mind her own business. There was nothing in her conduct for which she considered herself answerable to Agnes. Though her sister persisted in treating Salvatore as her private property and spent hours closeted with him every morning in mysterious consultations, he was as much her servant as Agnes's, since she paid half his wages. For the first time in her life she was able to feel that she and her sister met on an equal footing. Though she had consented, by mere force of habit, to allow Agnes to act as the senior partner in their joint affairs, this concession by no means implied the right to look down on her figuratively or to spy on her movements. When she heard the breakfast gong boom in the hall she went down determined to stand by her rights and maintain her dignity whatever Agnes might say.

The strange thing was, Agnes said nothing. That is not to say that this breakfast was a comfortable meal. She sat at the head of the table with a rigidity and erectness more devastating, by comparison with Miss Ellen's exaggerated affectation of ease, than usual. Her features were intensely constricted, and pale as a carving of ivory, and this unnatural pallor not only enhanced their classical perfection of line but also—as Ellen had observed before in moments of pain or emotional stress—their resemblance to Papa's, so that the ghost of Colonel Isit, mysteriously re-embodied, appeared to dominate and haunt the breakfast-table. Miss Ellen had come down determined to show her contempt for the ticklish situation and brazen it out by making a more than usually hearty meal. Miss Agnes ate nothing. She sipped a cup of weak tea with awful deliberation, as though it were hemlock and the drinking of it a ritual sacrifice, while the untouched bacon and eggs went cold and gelatinous on her plate. Miss Ellen at first affected to enjoy hers, but the silence made her aware that she was eating noisily and that Agnes was not merely watching her with disgust but listening. The poison from Agnes's tea-cup infected them. She began to feel rather sick. Perhaps she had eaten too greedily; perhaps, without knowing it, she had strained herself when she fell. With the eggs half finished, she laid down her knife and fork. Salvatore ceremoniously picked up the plate and carried it away. He offered her fruit. She refused it, shaking her head. For some reason, hard to divine, her courage had left her and she couldn't speak to him; but when she raised her eyes from the empty plate she could see him—a very different figure now from the sanguine, unshaven, satyr of the olive-groves: just an admirably well-mannered and competent man-servant, moving quietly to and fro in his grey alpaca coat as though nothing whatever had happened that could perturb him. Under Agnes's scrutiny she watched him out of the corner of her eyes. Was it possible, she asked herself, that, beneath his customary decorum, his mien was even a little more jaunty than usual? Was it conceivable that the faint tremor of his eyelid which she noticed, was a wink—and intended for herself? She hoped not—and yet the speculation encouraged her. With a concentration of effort she forced herself to break the oppressive silence.

"Are you not well, Agnes?" she enquired, in a trembling voice.

"Why do you ask that?" Miss Agnes said coldly.

"Well, you haven't eaten much breakfast, have you?" Miss Ellen said. "I was afraid the heat might be starting one of your heads."

Agnes gave a short laugh. "I never felt better in my life. I am glad to say that the heat has no effect on *me*," she added pointedly. Then she changed her tone: "Salvatore!"

Salvatore slewed round on his heels with an ingratiating smirk:

"Signorina?"

"Please go into the studio before you clear the table. I have something I wish to say to you."

"Certainly, Signorina."

He opened the double doors of the salone and stood aside at attention while Miss Agnes passed through with a measured stateliness, looking neither to left nor right. Stewart followed, trotting at her heels, with a bored, disdainful air, emitting an offensive growl as he passed Salvatore's ankles. The doors closed discreetly behind them.

4

STEWART had never settled down at the Castello Inglese like the more adaptable Waifie, who asked little more of life than warmth, sunshine, milk, and occasionally a small fish which Salvatore kindly brought up for her from the Marina. In the daytime, when she wasn't asleep or eating, she could play with lizards and sharpen her claws on the chestnut poles of the pergola. At night she no longer slept on Miss Ellen's bed, as the cold of North Bromwich had forced her to do, but received visitors with superb aloofness in the garden. The surrounding properties swarmed with lank, brindled tomcats, invisible by day, which converged and congregated on the terrace of the Castello Inglese, eager for a moonlit glimpse of this exotic tabby beauty whose fame had soon travelled as far as the Marina. Miss Ellen thought it must be lovely for Waifie to be sought by so many followers, so long as they didn't infect her with fleas or mange; but Miss Agnes objected to their agonized serenades—not only because they kept her awake but also because her delicacy was revolted by the thought of such goings-on right under her bedroom window.

"I wish you would keep the disgusting creature shut up," she said. "If I had thought she was going to behave like this I should never have consented to your bringing her here. I know only too well what will happen next," she added darkly.

It happened surprisingly soon. But then, time passed so quickly at Monfalcone. They were so adorable that Miss Ellen decided to keep the strongest, a tortoise-shell. Miss Agnes, as soon as she heard of them, decreed that Salvatore should drown the lot; but Stewart anticipated the judicial murder by smelling out Waifie's hiding-place and devouring the whole litter. Miss Ellen was furious, for poor Waifie as much as for herself. She carried the mangled tortoise-shell kitten into the salone with tears in her eyes and showed it to Agnes.

"Well, what do you expect?" Miss Agnes said callously. "Stewart hates cats, don't you, Stewart? And so do I, for that matter. I'm surprised that you grudge the poor little dog his natural pleasures and proclivities."

"I think he's unnatural and horrible," Miss Ellen said passionately.

Natural or unnatural, this savage crime was the only pleasure poor Stewart had succeeded in indulging since he was transported to Italy. He detested Monfalcone and everything about it—particularly his jailer, Salvatore, into whose malicious power his mistress had betrayed him. He hated the strange farinaceous food Carolina prepared for him, because it tasted of garlic and made him grow fat and gave him dyspepsia. He hated the heat. He hated the rural surroundings, in which not so much as one bit-bucket or scrap of gutter-garbage was smellable. He hated the village no less. In this uncivilized place the infrequent street-lamps were not set on convenient posts, but attached to the angles of houses or slung on cables overhead; the streets, too, were made hideous and unfriendly by ill-bred curs, half pointer, half lurcher, much bigger and stronger than he, who despised and disliked his short legs and stiff coat as abnormalities, and, whatever their sex, resented his polite investigations with snarls and bared teeth. In his private domain there were no sporting amenities: in more than three months he had not sniffed a single wild rabbit: all the rabbits of Monfalcone were safely kept in wire cages, and the only other chaseable animals in which he was interested were the goats, who had horns with which to defend themselves. He might just as well have been a prisoner on a desert island. No wonder his dour, self-centred little mind grew bored and morose and ill-tempered! The only diversion indeed which this bitter exile provided was the tame pastime of sitting behind the wrought-iron gates of the Castello Inglese, yapping or growling defiance at the strings of supercilious mules that went jingling by, dashing forth to snap at the calves of passing children, which were providentially bare, or fiercely challenging the arrival of any visitor.

Apart from Salvatore's mother, a wrinkled old woman swathed in dense layers of skirt and petticoat which made her invulnerable, who arrived, at least once a day, carrying an empty basket, and departed, an hour or two later, with a strong smell of wine (which Stewart disliked) and the same basket mysteriously swollen, there were few visitors to be challenged. Though the news of the Miss Isits' arrival and detailed accounts of their installation had been broadcast in the form of a 'running commentary' through the kitchens of all their villas, the members of the foreign colony seemed to be in no hurry to call. Miss Ellen was at first disappointed by this. She liked the excitement and chatter of tea-parties, and had looked forward to frequenting a cosmopolitan society more broad-minded than the official circles in which she had moved in India, and more cultured and amusing than the suburban families of North Bromwich. Miss Agnes, too, had been hurt, though she wouldn't show it, by a lack of common courtesy as it was understood among gentlefolk. It was only after tactful inquiries from Salvatore, on whom she relied increasingly for guidance and information, that she learnt that few of the foreign gentlemen and even fewer ladies had been in the habit of visiting the Castello Inglese in Don Ludovico's time. This only confirmed those suspicions, darkly hinted at by Papa and more lately fortified by the contents of the studio, that Captain Vaughan had lived 'under a cloud' and had stayed abroad for reasons that were anything but creditable.

"It shows," she declared, "that Uncle Ludovic was not a nice man; and though there is no reason why we should be made to suffer from his reputation, I can quite understand people hesitating to call at a house that has a bad name until they have found out what we are like."

"Don't you think they might come and see for themselves?" Miss Ellen asked.

"Well . . . Yes and no. I think they are well advised not to take steps in the dark and risk becoming socially involved with people whose acquaintance they might regret. That applies to us equally, Ellen. The society of places abroad is extremely mixed, as I've warned you already. Many women who could not be accepted at home are received in such places, I believe, without question. Of course, if we intended to stay here any length of time, I should find out from the British Consul in Naples the names of people we might safely know. Now we are only birds of passage; but I shall certainly take that precaution if we ever come here again."

"If we ever come here again?" Miss Ellen repeated.

"You are forgetting 'The Cedars', Ellen," Miss Agnes said reprovingly.

She wasn't forgetting 'The Cedars'. Could she ever forget the dank reaches of Enville Lane, the bare, cat-scrabbled garden, the sepulchral chill of the hall and drawing-room, the four hundred and thirty strokes of the pump every day? Yet, for all the beauty and light and spaciousness of her existence at Monfalcone, her sociable soul did crave the solace of human companionship (Agnes's was hardly human) and the fringes—she had rarely penetrated deeper—of family life. Agnes, alas, was so self-contained and self-sufficient that such things didn't matter to her; but it was hard for Miss Ellen, whose personal resources were more limited, to spend all her time talking to Waifie, who couldn't answer, or gossiping in the kitchen: an innocent pastime on which her sister frowned. She was not even able to talk with Salvatore, who, at least, understood what she said. Since the unhappy incident in the garden, which had never been mentioned, Agnes hardly ever allowed him out of her sight.

Still, she did yearn for friends or even casual acquaintances outside the narrow, closed circle of the Castello Inglese. In her first days at Monfalcone, when she was exploring the Marina, she had often caught sight of people of both sexes dressed in robust boots and tweeds, who must surely be English, and had even heard English spoken by others who sat lazily chatting and sipping vermouth under the awnings of the café-terraces down by the quay. Once or twice she had been moved by a rash desire to accost them and introduce herself, or to make some enquiry that would lead to acquaintance; but the shadow of Agnes's certain disapproval had always deterred her in the end. No lady, she knew, could possibly speak to strangers; and no lady alone, or even escorted by a gentleman, could set foot in 'licensed premises' without losing caste. Later on, at the end of April, when the trusses of wisteria loosened their lilac panicles and drenched the air of the piazza with their provocative scent, a whole multitude of middle-aged spinsters, who could only be English, hatched out like frail may-flies whirled on the wafts of perfume, alighting to set up their easels at every street corner and perpetuate their romantic emotions in hasty and not very convincing blobs of lilac water-colour, until the crowds of pestering children drove them back to the hotels and boarding-houses from which they had so boldly emerged. But by the middle of June, when the heat began in earnest, these pallid ephemerids had been blown away and vanished like the wisteria-bloom, and only the hard core of permanent foreign residents remained, more uncompromisingly English than ever in homespuns and 'sensible' shoes. By this time they had become aware of Miss Ellen's lonely figure, and occasionally condescended to stare at her when she passed; but their stares were still inquisitive rather than friendly. She wondered if they guessed who she was.

Miss Ellen need not have wondered: they knew perfectly well who she was. Every movement she and her sister had made since their arrival, their habits, their food (including Agnes's bacon and eggs), their finances, their clothes—all these had been minutely registered and discussed by the foreign colony of Monfalcone. There were a number of reasons why none of its members had called. The first was sheer laziness. At the time when they arrived, at the beginning of March, it had been generally decided that it would be fairer to give the Miss Isits a chance of 'settling in' before they were disturbed by callers; but by the middle of June it was far too hot to think of toiling up-hill to the Castello Inglese; and it was learnt from the fountain-head of information, the omniscient Salvatore, that his Signorine did not intend to make a long stay, but might be expected to return to 'their English estate', as he grandly put it, as soon as cooler weather made railway travelling comfortable, so calling on them would be a waste of time and energy. Other considerations were involved. The foreign colony of Monfalcone consisted of two layers: an inner, firmly exclusive set of long-established residents, strictly vowed to maintain the standards of respectability, and an outer, more loosely constructed and morally unstable, of folk generally speaking less well-to-do and less respectable, composed of those who vaguely called themselves 'artists'—which was enough in itself to condemn them—and a fringe of mere loafers and hangers-on, who for various reasons, none of them creditable, had succumbed to the amusing indolence of Monfalcone and decided they might as well live there as anywhere else. The former, who were respected by the villagers not because of their morals but because they consumed large quantities of firewood at a high price and paid their bills regularly, were conscious of the shady reputation of Captain Vaughan's house and chary of entering it until they were sure his relatives were 'all right': the latter, who had been Don Ludovico's friends and boon companions, had been equally discouraged by Salvatore's account of the Miss Isits—and particularly of Miss Agnes—and had decided that their society would probably not be amusing and that their peculiarities were better viewed from a distance. So the Miss Isits, isolated on their Ararat by the waters of two conflicting inhibitions, got the worst of both worlds, and not so much as a sprig of olive from either.

Their first visitor, who, strictly speaking, belonged to neither, though he frequented both, was certainly no dove: a handsome, white-maned, elderly gentleman named Ronald Sanctuary, whom Miss Ellen had often noticed and secretly admired at the Marina. Ronnie Sanctuary was accepted by all the 'nice people' of the foreign colony, partly because he had charming manners and was one of its oldest inhabitants, but even more because he 'knew everybody' and happened to be heir-presumptive to the ninth Earl of Chadminster—a relationship which gave him the local courtesy-title of 'Baronino' and had enabled him to live on credit in Monfalcone for half a lifetime. He was, in fact, rather a wicked old man, though his lurid reputation was now somewhat dimmed by the patina of advancing years. He was equally acceptable to the undesirables because, being a genuine aristocrat, he wasn't a snob, and, as a needy man of the world, understood the ways of Bohemians. He had been for years a crony of Don Ludovico's, and now braved Stewart's growls and teeth, not because he particularly desired to make his friend's nieces' acquaintance but because he wanted to borrow a book which he knew Captain Vaughan had possessed.

At the moment of his arrival both the Miss Isits were taking their siesta, Miss Agnes upstairs in her bedroom, Miss Ellen in the studio. The clang of the bell at the gate, and Stewart's furious barking, awoke her. A moment later she heard steps and the sound of Salvatore's voice on the terrace. Then the doors of the studio were flung open and the two figures appeared.

"Barone Santuario," Salvatore announced ceremoniously, gave Stewart a vicious sideways kick, and then vanished, closing the door behind him.

Miss Ellen slithered from the divan and hurriedly arranging her skirt stammered a few words of salutation in her halting Italian. Ronnie Sanctuary bowed and smiled, and answered in English.

"You must really excuse me," he said. "Salvatore showed me in without tellin' me you were restin'. Very naughty of him. Let me explain. My name's Sanctuary, and I'm an old friend of your uncle, Captain Vaughan. I have been meanin' to pay my respects for some time, but you know all the streets of Monfalcone are paved with good intentions; and in any case I thought it would be kinder to wait till you were settled in. Do tell me if I'm bein' a nuisance. . . ."

Miss Ellen said "Not at all", and begged him to sit down. She was immediately impressed—as who was not? —by his charming manners and cultivated speech. She wondered, at first, if she hadn't better call Agnes: it was unusual for a maiden lady to receive male callers alone; but this one was so obviously a gentleman, quite apart from his age, that she felt herself safe with him. She was also secretly pleased to think that she had the privilege of receiving their very first caller unembarrassed by Agnes's presence. She hoped Agnes would go on sleeping until the visitor had gone. Ronnie Sanctuary proceeded to talk easily and charmingly about nothing in particular, occasionally glancing at the denuded bookshelves in search of the book that he wanted, a translation of the *Satyricon.*

"I thought I had better not procrastinate," he explained. "I understand from Salvatore that you may soon be hurryin' away from us."

"You know Salvatore well, I suppose?" Miss Ellen asked.

"Salvatore?" Ronnie Sanctuary's faunish lips were wreathed in a cunning smile. "Well, yes, indeed. Known him ever since he was a boy—for some years before poor Ludo . . . adopted him. And a remarkably good-lookin' boy he was, quite remarkably good-lookin'. A delightful head: the image of the young Tiberius. As a matter of fact it was I who suggested poor Ludo's usin' him as a model. It's a pity you never saw him when he was younger. Ludo painted a portrait of him once, the best thing he ever did. Used to stand on that easel. By the way, what's happened to the pictures?"

"I think my sister has put them somewhere else."

"Well, I can't say I blame her. Poor Ludo was a charmin' fellow, perfectly charmin'; but he wasn't a good painter by a long way, you know, oh no, he wasn't a good painter. To tell you the truth, I'm a bit surprised that Salvatore stayed on with you. He must have done pretty well for himself, I imagine. Poor Ludo was always generous. He could afford it. And during his last years, when his health was failin' and he lost the use of his legs, I'm afraid he was completely under Salvatore's thumb. Indeed, I don't think I'm givin' away any secret when I tell you our young friend expected to have the house left to him when poor Ludo died."

"This house? Do you mean bequeathed to him in Uncle Ludovic's will?"

"I can't vouch for it, of course, and poor Ludo himself never mentioned it to me. He grew so touchy latterly that even I found it hard not to quarrel with him. Still you needn't be surprised, my dear lady, it wouldn't be the first example of a legacy like that in the case of a lonely bachelor with no family of his own. After all, Salvatore had given poor Ludo the best years of his life. No doubt the will came as a great shock to him."

Mr. Sanctuary chuckled as though he found the idea of Salvatore's disappointment a joke. When he smiled his curly mouth went up at the corners and showed a mouthful of small regular teeth that were probably his own. Miss Ellen found him delightful but rather mischievous. She had never met any man who made her feel so much at ease or so little shy. To sit talking with him was just like gossiping with a shrewd, handsome, worldly old lady who had outlived all her own emotions and settled down to enjoy the comedy provided by other people's with a humorous detachment that in no way abated her curiosity. If it were not so humorous, Mr. Sanctuary's detachment might have been cruel. As it was, she found its novelty engaging, and its naughtiness as innocent as a child's.

"You see," he went on, "Salvatore probably regards this house as his own in any case. The land on which I persuaded poor Ludo to build it originally belonged to his family, who probably owned it for hundreds of years. The people here are very odd about land. Though they sell their land to foreigners who build villas on it and pay them quite well for it, they never think of it as being anything but theirs. And of course they're quite right. The foreigners come and go; but it usually comes back to the Monfalconesi in the end. There are very few old foreign families in Monfalcone, though there are lots of old villas that have been turned into farm-houses. That's what would have happened to the Castello Inglese if poor Ludo hadn't changed his mind. As it is, I'm delighted to say, having made your acquaintance, our young friend will have to wait a little longer. It won't do him any harm. How long did you say you were stayin' here?"

"That depends entirely on my sister," Miss Ellen said. "She is not very strong . . ."

"You don't say so? She doesn't look delicate."

"You've seen her?"

"My dear young lady"—Ellen blushed at the compliment—"you must never imagine that anyone can appear at the Marina more than once without being seen by everybody! I've seen yourself and your sister several times. I should hate to embarrass you by telling you to your face what I thought of *you*, but your sister struck me as a woman of enormous distinction—quite extraordinary, if an old man may say so. And remember, in the remote age when I was an impressionable, gay young man about town, such distinction was much commoner, alas, than it is in these days. A most strikin' profile . . ."

Ellen sighed. "If only you could have seen her fifteen years ago!"

"Unfortunately I didn't. Otherwise I mightn't have been the crabbed old bachelor you see before you."

"You may be a bachelor; but I'm sure you don't look the least crabbed or old," Miss Ellen protested ingenuously.

Mr. Sanctuary preened himself and pulled up his neatly-creased trousers to contemplate with satisfaction his silk-socked ankle and patent leather shoe.

"Not too old to be flattered by a charmin' young woman, perhaps," he said with the curly smile that showed all his small teeth like a skeleton's. "But let us be serious. You're not leavin' us just yet, thank heaven. How long have you been here?"

"We came here in March . . . I think."

"In March? Dear, dear, how time flies! Four months. This is serious. Extremely serious." He wagged his white head and pursed his mobile lips. "It's a pity nobody warned you about Monfalcone. If you've stayed here four months, there'll probably be no hope for you. Take myself for example. I came here for luncheon—just for luncheon!—and I've stayed for life."

"I shouldn't mind that at all," Ellen laughed.

Mr. Sanctuary sighed. "Then your case, I'm afraid, is already incurable, my dear lady. And it's not only that . . ."

"*Do* tell me," Miss Ellen begged like an excited child. It was extraordinary how gay and coquettish he made her feel.

"Well, I think you should know," Mr. Sanctuary continued, solemnly waving a manicured finger; "I think you should know that the air of Monfalcone has curious effects—particularly on conventional people."

"Oh, *I'm* not a bit conventional," Miss Ellen assured him.

Mr. Sanctuary disregarded the interruption.

"Its action is also insidious," he went on didactically, "like that of the Monfalcone wine—which I sincerely hope you'll avoid if you have any tendency to rheumatism. But that's by the way. A friend of mine, who is a chemist, once explained to me that it resembles the action of a minute quantity of some chemical substance dropped into a saturated solution of the same salt. The solution suddenly solidifies and turns to crystal. And that is exactly what happens to human beings in Monfalcone. If they stay here long enough they become what they really are."

"But I *know* what I am," Miss Ellen broke in.

"Oh no, you don't," Mr. Sanctuary said snappily. "You can't possibly know till you've tried. We are none of us, unfortunately, what we seem. Take your uncle, for example. When the poor feller came here first he was a perfectly ordinary soldier; but by the time he died . . . well, the less said about it the better. We northerners, you know, are rather like icebergs: the greater part of our nature is submerged and invisible. We're perfectly safe as long as we're attached to the polar ice-cap; but when we break away and float into warmer waters and begin to melt—that's the time when we become dangerous to navigation."

Miss Ellen laughed. "But surely," she said, "you can't imagine that people like my sister and I are ever likely to become dangerous to . . . to navigation?"

"You never can tell," Mr. Sanctuary said. "You never can tell. Anyway, don't forget that I've warned you. Now I think I had better 'remove the inconvenience', as we say in Italy. I'm afraid I've disturbed your siesta most inconsiderately. Please don't trouble to see me off. I know the house well . . ." He hesitated. "Oh, by the way, that reminds me: there's a little book of your uncle's I wanted to borrow: a translation of Petronius. It used to be over here."

He moved mincingly to the bookshelf. "How very strange! It's not in its usual place."

"My sister's been re-arranging the books," Miss Ellen said hurriedly. "It's quite possible she may have taken it up to her bedroom."

"The *Satyricon*? Really, really . . . That would be very odd bedside readin' for a maiden lady!" Mr. Sanctuary chuckled. "However, the book isn't here," he went on, "so I'll say *au revoir*." And Miss Ellen laughed too, though she did not understand the cause of his mirth. "When I say that, I mean it," he added gallantly.

Miss Ellen held out her hand. Mr. Sanctuary bent over it and kissed it; and before she could recover from the delightful shock, he was gone.

"What a delightfully old-world courtliness!" Miss Ellen thought. Though he spoke with such a cultured accent, it was hard to believe he was English: his manners owed their polish to his having lived so long in the best cosmopolitan society. Salvatore had called him 'Barone'—she couldn't guess why, and yet the title of nobility suited him: he was so completely *ancien régime* she could easily have imagined his going to the guillotine with a smile on his lips, like a *marquis* (or was it *marquise?*) in *A Tale of Two Cities*, which she must certainly re-read. And how clever and well-informed he was, too! Those sparkling allusions to the science of chemistry and the behaviour of icebergs were certainly signs of a lively and cultured mind such as one would rarely have met in Moogly Meringapatam—and hardly ever in North Bromwich. He had said so much in so short a time that she could hardly begin to remember everything. The part about Salvatore's expectations was what vulgar people (and why shouldn't one be vulgar for once?) would call an eye-opener. It revealed Salvatore in quite a new light, and might explain a number of things in his attitude that had puzzled her. Considering his disappointment, he had behaved remarkably well. She supposed she ought to pass on this information to Agnes; but, on second thoughts, perhaps she had better keep it to herself: Agnes would condemn her at once for listening to gossip.

The part of the interview which had impressed her most deeply was Mr. Sanctuary's dissertation on the properties of the Monfalcone air. Though no doubt he had exaggerated, with the mischievous intention of shocking or teasing her, there was certainly some truth in his contention that it altered people—or rather made them become what they really were. Though she wouldn't have liked to admit it to anyone, she could confirm, from personal experience, not so much, indeed, that she was physically changed—though she did feel younger, and his compliments suggested that she must look so—as that her thoughts and feelings (if not her behaviour) had been freed from their self-imposed restrictions. Was she herself, Ellen Isit, potentially a melting iceberg? Though novel, the idea was not wholly unattractive; but it made her laugh to think what would have happened if Mr. Sanctuary had dared to suggest such a thing to Agnes, whose moral temperature was much lower than her own. The main bulk of *her* nature was certainly 'under water'. If that ever started to melt, it would indeed be dangerous! But of course that was out of the question. When Mr. Sanctuary maintained that 'you never could tell', he didn't know Agnes.

These wild speculations were interrupted by the sound of the dry cough which invariably signified her sister's approach. The door opened, and Agnes entered, followed by Stewart, sniffing the air, as though he suspected that Mr. Sanctuary was still there in hiding. Agnes's inquiring eyes swept the studio just as suspiciously, lighting at once on the disordered divan on which Miss Ellen had been resting, and the chair which still bore the impression of Mr. Sanctuary's hind-quarters. She pointedly re-arranged the covers of the one and punched the cushions of the other.

"I thought I heard voices," she said. "Has anyone been here?"

"Yes," Miss Ellen admitted. "A Mr. Sanctuary has called. I didn't like to disturb you while you were resting."

"The bell and Stewart's barking had already disturbed me. You should have told me at once. Who is this Mr. Sanctuary?"

"He told me he was an old friend of Uncle Ludovic's."

Agnes sniffed. "That is hardly a recommendation, is it?"

"Well, he seemed to me a friendly harmless person. Salvatore showed him in without any warning. I was actually asleep when he came."

"Salvatore should have known better. I shall have to explain to him that it is unusual for English ladies to receive gentlemen visitors behind closed doors."

"He was quite an old man . . ."

"His age is beside the point. If you were forced to receive him alone—and you needn't have done so—you should have taken him out on the loggia. What did he want?"

Ellen hesitated. It would be unwise, she felt, to mention the book which Mr. Sanctuary had wanted to borrow.

"I think it was merely a social call," she said prudently. "He just happened to be passing, and looked in on the chance of finding us in. He said he was sorry to miss you, and looked forward to seeing you when he called again. I'm sure you'll like him, Agnes. He's certainly a gentleman."

"That is a thing I prefer to judge for myself," Agnes said.

5

AMONG the outer circle of Monfalcone society Ronnie Sanctuary had a roaring success with a fantasia based on his otherwise unprofitable visit to the Castello Inglese and his interview with 'the old trout', as he called Miss Ellen. To the inner circle he gave an assurance that the Miss Isits were not in the least like their Uncle Ludovic, on the strength of which nearly all the best people decided to call. The cabmen of the Marina made hay under the fierce sun of August by driving them, one after another, up the mountain road. A tray to receive callers' cards was placed on the marble table in the hall.

Miss Agnes was not to be caught napping by visitors again; she took her siesta fully dressed to receive them, and slept—if she slept at all—like Stewart, with one eye open. As a further precaution she instructed Salvatore to give her a brief report on the standing and moral reputation of all visitors before they were allowed to enter the house, and welcomed them, if approved, not in the studio, whose air was still contaminated by memories of Captain Vaughan, but in the salone, whose furniture and dimensions gave it the character of a state-apartment. Occasionally her sister was permitted to be present as lady-in-waiting.

Miss Ellen found all the new visitors delightful. One could never have guessed what a wealth and variety of human charm had lain hidden in Monfalcone: Miss Agnes declined to accept them at their face value until she had made further inquiries. Any person who had habitually visited the Castello Inglese in Captain Vaughan's time—such as Mr. Sanctuary—was summarily eliminated. Those who survived this acid test, were assayed by her own observations and the evidence of Salvatore, on whose judgment she relied in this matter, as in most others, though Miss Ellen noticed a certain sameness in the standards by which he judged them.

"Tell me, who and what is this Miss Murphy, Salvatore?" she asked.

"I think you not like her much, Signorina," he answered decidedly. "She is an artist, and very poor, who live alone in a studio at the Marina of one room only, and paint pictures that foreigners buy—I cannot say why unless for charity. Also, she has many cats."

"I told you I thought she looked kind, Agnes," Miss Ellen said. "That was why Stewart would keep sniffing at her."

"Well, *I* thought she looked blowsy and grubby," Agnes declared, "and the cats confirm it. She was also much too effusive. However, I suppose you had better return her call, Ellen——. One must not be discourteous—but I think our acquaintance should end there. I am not at all sure she isn't an American," she added, in the precise tone with which she might have said: 'I'm not sure she isn't a typhoid-carrier.' "Now tell me about Miss Spettigue, Salvatore."

"Oh, the Signora Spettigue: I am sure you like *her*, Signorina. She is very rich and has many servants: a real Signora who never consider expense or looks at a bill. Many times she has attempted me to go to her as butler with high wages before you come here."

"Any why didn't you?" Agnes asked.

Salvatore appeared to be shocked. "Am I not attached to the Castello Inglese?" he said with dignity. "There is also loyalty."

Agnes smiled with satisfaction, but Ellen bit her lip: she was longing to let Agnes know what Ronnie Sanctuary had told her.

"And Mrs. Hamilton-Gough?"

Salvatore spread his hands, as though the problem of describing Mrs. Hamilton-Gough were too much for him.

"That is difficult, Signorina," he said. "But I think perhaps you like. I cannot say. It is possible that she has more money than one sees—but she is very *avara*—what you say stingy. It is a magnificent house, the 'Villa Minerva', but a mouse could not find to eat there, and the servants are always more hungry than the mice. I think she lives on a pension, because she change a cheque every month of the same amount at the grocer and count every centesimo."

"Has she a husband?"

"I think. But that also is a mystery. They say he is Indian."

"An Indian? Impossible!" Agnes declared.

"You have not quite understood, Signorina. I do not wish to say he is black, but an official—an officer—who has made service in India."

Agnes pricked up her ears. "In that case I am sorry I didn't see her when she left her cards; but if she had any connection with India, I will return her call myself. You had better order a gharri for to-morrow afternoon, Salvatore, and I will visit the 'Villa Minerva' while the Signorina Elena calls on Miss Murphy's cats at the Marina."

They jogged down the hill the next afternoon in a crackling heat. The shiny seat of the little carriage broiled them like a salamander, and though the red striped awning tempered the sunlight overhead, the glare from the white road beneath beat up in their faces, and gusts of hot air, heavily laden with the composite smell of the horse and its driver, were wafted to meet them as they descended into the crucible of the Marina. Miss Ellen was lightly clad in her summer muslin and had secretly left off her stays: but Miss Agnes's corsets were tightly laced beneath her black satin, and she had only consented at the last moment to discard the ostrich-feather boa, bought in Port Said, which was part of her formal plumage. Fortunately for Miss Ellen, Agnes's throat was too rigidly encased in a 'neck' supported by whalebones for her to be able to turn her head sideways and notice the liberties her sister had allowed her figure, though her downward glance soon perceived that Ellen was not wearing gloves.

"If you like we'll turn back and I'll get some," Miss Ellen said.

"Now that we've come so far downhill it would hardly be fair to the horse. It's quite possible, judging by what I saw of her, that Miss Murphy won't notice."

"I don't think I could have got them on: it's so terribly hot."

"One would think, by the way you complain, you had never lived in India. At Moogly the temperature was up in the nineties for weeks on end, but Papa never modified his uniform in any respect."

If it wasn't as hot as Moogly Meringapatam, that station must have resembled the threshold of hell. Six brazen weeks had sucked every drop of moisture out of the cracked soil of Monfalcone: the air within that great cup of stone quivered like that of a lime-kiln: even the leaves of the prickly-pears appeared wilted with drought. Half-way down the hill and up the increasing scale of heat, the carriage stopped at the gates of the 'Villa Minerva'.

"I think I'll drive up to the house," Agnes said. "I don't want to get my skirt dusty. You need do no more than leave cards on Miss Murphy, and if you are quick you will be able to wait for me here—unless," she added, "you prefer to walk home."

The carriage swerved into the drive and Miss Ellen proceeded down-hill. In the village itself there was not a breath of air, though the houses that shadowed the narrow, malodorous streets took some of the sun. The little piazza lay mute and crushed beneath a ponderable heat. Its shops were empty, the café-terraces deserted; the shutters of every upper storey closed. No semblance of life was visible save one or two of the yellow-blotched pointer curs that Stewart loathed, which lay panting against the walls, occasionally nibbling at a flea or snapping at flies. There was apparently nobody from whom Miss Ellen could discover the way to Miss Murphy's studio except one small boy lying face-downward on the steps of the church. Miss Ellen prodded him awake with her parasol and made her inquiries. The child stared at her blankly. Then she had an inspiration: "The Signorina who has many cats."

"Ah . . . *La madre dei gatti*."

He scrambled to his feet and ran. Miss Ellen pursued him over the beach, where the tired sea, smooth as glass, spread with a flap and an almost inaudible hiss over sparkling sand through which her feet ploughed up to the ankles. The bare-footed child, outpacing her, knocked at the door of a pink-washed building, which looked like a disused sail-loft, crouched under the cliff. As Miss Ellen floundered towards it, the door opened, as though pulled by an invisible hand, to receive her. She entered, timidly.

For some moments her pupils, pinched by the glare of sea and sand, could not accommodate to the darkness of the interior. Gradually she became aware of a large pink object, vaguely human in outline, like an unfinished piece of primitive sculpture, stretched on a divan and surrounded by an arabesque of moving shadows which eventually defined themselves as cats. There must have been more than a dozen, of various colours, shapes and sizes: cats leaping, cats slinking, cats rolling and arching their backs, appearing, fading, vanishing, in every direction. Then a soft southern voice cooed: "Well, now, isn't this a perfectly lovely surprise"; and the large pink object, which now resolved itself into the figure of Miss Murphy overflowing a *crêpe-de-chine* wrap, rose from the divan like a corpse emerging from its tomb at the resurrection. Miss Murphy appeared to be less embarrassed by her apparel—or the lack of it—than her visitor.

"I was just resting after my bathe," she explained. "Sit down, honey, and I'll make you a cup of real English tea—that is if there's any left. You see, the trouble is, I can never find anything."

That wasn't, Miss Ellen thought, surprising. Now that her eyes had become accustomed to the light, Miss Murphy's studio revealed a confusion that must have been due to years of neglect. The converted sail-loft, in which the fishermen of the Marina had once kept nets and canvas, was now so cluttered with accumulations of junk—from the frayed rugs on the floor to the cobwebbed beams of the roof—that it resembled a second-hand furniture store in a slum. Apart from the central clearing occupied by the divan, there was no foot of its cubic capacity which did not appear to have been silted-up with the detritus of Miss Murphy's haphazard existence; piles of papers and books that had slithered to the floor; stacks of dusty canvases; cooking-utensils, tableware, cardboard boxes, clothes, biscuit-tins—all indiscriminately mingled in a breccia of empty paint-tubes. It must actually have been quite a spacious studio—and yet there was no room left in it (appropriately, Miss Ellen thought) to swing a cat, or for any creature larger or less sinuous than a cat to move about in. Miss Murphy, in spite of her bulk, seemed quite at home. Tenderly dislodging an immense ginger tomcat from a pile of paint-streaked overalls on which he lay dreaming, she dived deep into a welter of wreckage and dredged up a small tin of tea, which she proceeded to brew in a kettle over a spirit-lamp, talking all the time, as though to herself, in her dreamy Kentucky voice.

"Yes, this certainly is a perfect surprise," she said. "Do you know, honey, I never expected you'ld come to see me? If I hadn't just happened to hear that you'd brought your sweet little cat all the way from England, I should never have dared to call; but when I heard that, I said to myself: 'Virginia, these Miss Isits must certainly be lovely women——' and I do declare I simply couldn't resist it. I don't expect the tea will be what you fancy, honey: it must have been in the can a good many years, and there's no milk or sugar. I never take it myself, except when I feel out of sorts; but I know what you all are."

Her tea, in fact, tasted like a decoction of musty straw laced with methylated spirits; but Miss Ellen, gulping it down as a matter of honour, declared it was delicious. As she sat heroically sipping it, in embarrassing proximity to the abundant figure of Miss Murphy, which in its generous curves resembled a plump, pink fondant, she began to feel pleasantly sleepy. Perhaps this was partly the effect of the heat: it was even more the result of Miss Murphy's voice, which resembled the crooning of doves in a summer woodland or the murmur of flowing water, its modulations floating, as it were, above the rhythmical plash of tired waves on the sand outside, and muffled (as was everything else in the studio) by immemorial dust.

It was odd, Miss Ellen thought, that so gentle, so soothing a voice, should proceed from that ample shape—if 'shape' were a word that could be correctly applied to Miss Murphy. Yet, as she examined her hostess less shyly, the quality of the sound began to seem less incongruous. Miss Murphy must certainly once have been a 'lovely' woman—in Miss Ellen's rather than in her own sense of the word. How long since, it was hard to guess. Though she was probably well advanced in middle-age, her freckled face showed no wrinkles and her abundant auburn pigtails no streak of grey. She had wide-set pale blue eyes of an appealing innocence, and her childlike mouth accorded with the simplicity of her speech. Even if Miss Ellen had wanted to stop her talking, she wouldn't have had the heart to do so; it was obviously a pleasure so rich and so rarely gratified. During the next two hours she learnt all there was to be known about Miss Murphy's history.

She had first come to Monfalcone more than thirty years ago, as the winner of a two-year travelling scholarship from a College of Art in Kentucky. A well-to-do 'class-mate', who remained anonymous, had travelled with her from Baltimore to Naples. There they had heard Monfalcone mentioned as a small place less frequented and less expensive than Sorrento or Capri; and, like the Miss Isits, had made a bee-line for it with all their belongings.

"You see, honey," Miss Murphy explained, "the very first day we arrived, and went down to the beach from the pension to bathe, my friend said to me: 'Why, Virginia, what a cute little shack; I guess we ought to hire it and have it made over. We can undress there, without being stared at, when we want to bathe, and other times you can use it to do your painting. Let's go to the realtor and see.' Well, of course, it wasn't for hire; so what do you think? My friend just bought it outright for two hundred dollars. First of all we just used it as a bathing-hut, like I said; but later on we put in a few carpets and a couple of divans and set up housekeeping. It was a lovely adventure for both of us too. You see my friend had always been used to a luxurious home-life, and enjoyed the novelty; and I—well, of course I'd fallen in love with the place, and just couldn't get over it because everything was so different. Then, one day, my friend said to me: 'See here, Virginia, this is all very well for you and your painting, but I reckon I've had enough of the simple life with nothing to do and nobody but you to talk to. What's the good of having money to spend if there's nothing to spend it on? I came all this way to see Europe, and so did you, and we haven't yet done so much as one single cathedral or ruined castle or picture-gallery. It's time we began to move on and go some place else, so I've gotten us railroad tickets for Rome and Florence. You've no call to worry about money: I've plenty for both.'"

"But how lovely!" Miss Ellen cried.

Miss Murphy sighed. "Yes, wasn't it? But I couldn't possibly go with her."

"But why on earth not?"

"Well, you see, I'd just started painting a picture of the Marina. It's up there somewhere," she pointed vaguely to the canvases stacked on the rafters—"but even if I could find it, I don't think it's worth showing to you: you see I never finished it. And I couldn't leave the cats."

"But surely . . ." Miss Ellen began.

"Well, now, what a disappointment! I felt sure you would be sympathetic. There were only two of them then; but they'd made their home here, and it was just too dreadful to think of them finding the place all shut up. My friend was quite rough about it. 'Look here, Virginia Murphy,' she said, 'if you think more of those darned animals than of me, your best friend, I tell you straight, I'm through with you! What's more, I give you fair warning: if you stay on like this you'll get the way you won't be able to move for the rest of your life.'" Miss Murphy laughed softly. "And the odd thing is, you know, she was perfectly right; I've never left Monfalcone from that day to this. Why should I?"

Miss Ellen endeavoured to find an answer; but apparently none was needed.

"After all, why should I? I've everything here that a person like me could possibly want: a good roof, rent-free, over my head—I ought to have told you that my friend gave me the title-deeds of the studio in spite of her having been so raw with me; a climate that's better than any I've ever known at home, and nothing to hurry or worry about. If there was one thing I never could bear it was being hurried. I guess I was just born lazy, you know: it must be the Irish blood in me."

"But surely it isn't quite so simple as that," Miss Ellen protested. "You can't live on nothing, can you?"

Miss Murphy chuckled softly: "I'll say you can't. Yet, you know, Miss Isit—I do wish you'ld tell me your other name, honey, I hate formality—it's much easier than you might think. When I began to get near the end of my poor little dollars, after two or three years, I said to myself: 'Virginia, my girl, you're for home.' It was all very well to say that, honey, but how could I get there? I hadn't the fare to Naples, let alone to America. So I thought: 'Well, what will be will be,' and it certainly was. Did you notice those fleshy ice-plants that clamber over the cliff? Mesembryanthemums, they call them. Well, they haven't any roots to speak of, and even if they had, the roots have no soil to spread in; yet they seem to keep on growing fat just the same. A gentleman-friend once told me they live on air; and I guess that's what I've done, or pretty near it. If you don't mind waiting, something's sure to turn up; and if it comes to the worst you can always sell a picture. Not that I like doing that, mind. I always feel as if the pictures one's painted were part of one's self:

it's as bad as having a tooth drawn. But when nice visitors come to stay at the pension and hear there's an American artist living all alone in this cute little studio, they often come wanting to buy one as a souvenir of Monfalcone, and they won't be contented without one, so what can I do? I just have to let them go. It's a good thing I painted so many when first I came here, but there aren't many left now, thank goodness."

"Do you mean you've given up painting?" Miss Ellen inquired.

"Well, you can't paint pictures without buying paints, can you, honey?" Miss Murphy answered reprovingly, "and you can't buy paints without sending an order to Naples, which means writing a letter and sending the money and all that; and then folks are so careless you can't be sure you'll get what you've ordered. It's much easier to wait till some artist who's staying here gives you some as a present."

"But you can't count on them doing that?"

"Oh, I don't *count* on anything, honey. It's much better not to."

"But how do you manage to live in the meantime?"

Miss Murphy laughed softly, as though she found the question ridiculous.

"Well, I'm not exactly wasting away, am I, honey? If you'd lived as long as I have in Monfalcone you wouldn't ask. You know what the Bible says about not one sparrow. Well, I guess I must be like that. Just when things look their worst something's bound to turn up, and the people here are so kind and warm-hearted, you'ld never believe it, when once they get used to you and know you're not grasping."

"Of course you must speak Italian fluently?"

Miss Murphy laughed. "Not a dozen words, honey. You see I never had any brains for languages. But that makes no difference. I guess they generally understand what I want, which is all that matters. On and off I must have owed hundreds of lire at the piazza, but nobody's ever bothered me about money. They know that I pay when I can. Why, in summer I can very near live on the fruit folks send me: they've far more than they want, so why shouldn't I? And in winter they bring me dried figs and honey and beans and lentils, and flasks of oil and wine—though I much prefer water. Then the fishermen often bring me fish for my cats, and there's generally enough for me too. There's nothing I really have to buy except bread, and I make that myself from the grain an old woman gives me. It's much easier to live here, when once people like you, than any place else—though I sometimes do wish they wouldn't bring me so many kittens. They just leave them on the doorstep, you know," she added reflectively.

Miss Ellen was silent. "Do you know," she said at last, "you remind me of something Mr. Sanctuary told me the other day. I expect you know him much better than I do."

Miss Murphy shook her head.

"But you must. He's been here for more than thirty years."

Miss Murphy sighed. "I'm afraid I don't know any foreigners."

"Well, he said that people who stay long in Monfalcone always become what they really are. I believe he's right."

"Yes, I dare say he is. I certainly know I should just hate being anyway different from what I am. But then, I don't suppose I ever have been."

Miss Ellen gazed at her wide blue innocent eyes. No doubt, by the accepted standards of human conduct, Miss Murphy was nothing but a parasite and a sponger on the benevolence of a society to which she contributed nothing. Yet somehow, in spite of her prejudices, this neither shocked nor offended her. Ordinary standards of life were not applicable to Monfalcone. She regarded her rather as a strange transatlantic seed that had floated away from its natural habitat and, caught in the grip of some mysterious current, had been washed up and taken root in this friendly, alien shore. It was a waste of sympathy to feel sorry for Miss Murphy, for Miss Murphy was clearly not in the least sorry for herself. But she did feel an overpowering desire to be kind to her. The most practical and obvious help she could give would be to offer her services in clearing out this Augean studio; but that, she felt, might quite possibly be resented, for Miss Murphy evidently preferred it to remain as it was. Finally, with anxious trepidation, she mildly suggested that Miss Murphy might be persuaded to sell her a picture.

Miss Murphy's eyes widened; her childlike mouth quivered:

"Oh, honey, I do think that's mean of you," she said reproachfully. "Just when I thought you and me were going to be real friends."

"But I should simply love to possess one," Miss Ellen protested. "Just some little thing to remind me of Monfalcone when we go home."

Miss Murphy's eyes brightened. "Do you really mean that, honey? Then I'll tell you what I'll do. I'm going to *give* you one."

"Oh, but you mustn't do that!" Miss Ellen protested.

In vain . . . Before she had finished the sentence Miss Murphy's pink shape had disappeared into the backwoods of lumber and dragged out a ladder, which she hoisted and propped against the rafters on the roof. The rungs buckled beneath her weight as she slowly ascended, revealing an alarming expanse of pink thigh.

"Oh, do be careful," Miss Ellen entreated. "I'm sure that ladder's not safe."

"It never was safe, honey," Miss Murphy answered serenely, "but the rungs haven't broken yet, so why should they now? Well, I do declare—would you believe it?—here they are, after all! Four beauties—and one's a tortoise-shell. Did you ever! I've been wondering for the last week where on earth she had hidden them. Get up on a chair, honey—no, not that one: it's got a leg broken—and I'll hand you them down."

Miss Murphy stooped sideways. The ladder slewed sideways, too. For one moment she appeared to be swinging in air like some monstrous pantomime-fairy in pale pink tights. Then she righted herself by a lurch in the opposite direction, and Miss Ellen received in her outstretched hands a litter of kittens.

"Well, isn't that just lovely?" Miss Murphy purred, almost as if she were their mother. "Now wait while I find your picture."

She rummaged in the darkness of the roof, dislodging a cloud of dust; then descended uncertainly with four or five cobwebbed canvases hugged to her bosom.

"I'ld like you to have this one," she said, selecting the largest, an enormous painting of a vine-wreathed pergola with a demure ginger cat in the foreground. "That's my dear little Jefferson, the first kitten I ever had."

"I don't really think you ought to deprive yourself of such a large picture as that," Miss Ellen said weakly.

Miss Murphy looked hurt. "Now don't be mean, honey. It's one of my very best. I want you to have it, and that ought to be enough for you." It was much more than enough, Miss Ellen thought, as Miss Murphy thrust the cobwebbed monstrosity into her hands. "Now is there anything else I can give you?" she murmured reflectively. "What about one of those kittens? You shall choose the one you like best."

"They're all so delightful," Miss Ellen said defensively, "that I couldn't possibly choose."

"In that case you'd better take two, honey," Miss Murphy said.

The sun was descending, though she could hardly believe it, when, half an hour later, Miss Ellen escaped, trudging through the hot sand with two wriggling kittens clutched in one hand and the picture dangling from the other. Miss Murphy, statuesquely draped in her wrapper like a figure of Demeter, stood filling the door of the studio, and watched her out of sight with a vague, benevolent smile. Miss Ellen was far too much encumbered to wave good-bye; yet she, too, smiled to herself as she went—not because she was pleased with her presents, all of which she would have gladly renounced, but because—in spite of the dusty confusion of Miss Murphy's studio and the all-too-embarrassing results of her generosity—she still felt the soothing effects of her company and her surroundings. Indeed, though the strict principles in which she had been schooled would not allow her to approve of Miss Murphy's irresponsibility, though no daughter of Colonel Isit (and, even more, no sister of Agnes) could conceivably condone her indolence or consider such a disordered existence as anything but immoral and reprehensible—though she didn't envy Miss Murphy, and most certainly couldn't imagine herself accepting such a manner of life without pangs of conscience, yet, in spite of all, there was something in this slovenly Nirvana that appealed to that side of her nature which had emerged in Monfalcone. Miss Murphy herself, for all her moral defects, was so obviously good. And so obviously happy, too. When she came to think of it, Miss Ellen felt she had never experienced the radiance of positive goodness and happiness in such a strong degree. It was comforting to feel that this source of spiritual warmth would now be available to her. In spite of their dissimilarities of nature, breeding and outlook, Miss Ellen's heart glowed to think that she had at last found a friend. She had never before had a friend. . . .

As she approached the house, panting beneath the weight of her various burdens, she was surprised to hear the sound of male laughter proceeding from the salone. This distraction was all to the good: it enabled her to convey Miss Murphy's presents in secret to her room, where she hid the picture under the bed and shut the two kittens in Waifie's travelling-basket. Was it possible, she wondered, that Agnes had brought home a visitor? In that case, she supposed, she ought really to tidy herself; but her anxiety not to miss such a novel excitement, together with the new courage inspired by Miss Murphy's bold disregard of appearances, impelled her to go down as she was.

Disappointment awaited her: the only occupants of the salone were Agnes and Salvatore. At the click of the latch they stopped talking, and she entered in silence—a silence that seemed so constrained that she wondered if they had been talking about herself. Whatever the subject of their conversation might have been, she felt like an intruder. Salvatore immediately busied himself in laying the dinner-table, but the flush on Agnes's cheeks betrayed excitement; and though she compressed her lips to their normal severity her fine eyes were lit with an unusual brilliance. It was years, Ellen thought, since she had seen her looking so handsome or so young. "Well, was your call satisfactory?" she asked. "Did you like Mrs. Hamilton-Gough?"

"Extremely satisfactory. I was most agreeably surprised. As Salvatore said, she is a lady. But the name is pronounced 'Guff', not 'Goff'. You must be careful to remember that, Ellen. People are sensitive about the pronunciation of their names, particularly when they are hyphened, as hers is. Mrs. Hamilton-Gough is a very superior woman. She has lived a great part of her life in India; so, naturally, we had a great deal in common. In fact it was quite extraordinary that we never happened to meet. She also, unfortunately, deserves our sympathy."

"Why?" Ellen asked innocently.

"Her husband. It appears he was in the Woods and Forests and held quite an important position when he retired. But when Mrs. Hamilton-Gough settled in Monfalcone because of her mother's health—the old lady is ninety—the wretched man selfishly refused to join her, and—would you believe it?—only allows her three-fifths of his pension to live on! No wonder she finds it difficult to keep up a big villa like that."

"Why need she keep up a big villa?" Miss Ellen asked innocently.

"Why, to put her things in, of course—and her mother's and her married sister's as well."

"Oh, you didn't mention her sister."

"I wasn't allowed to see her. In fact she sees nobody except by appointment. There is some mystery—but I gather she has never got over the shock of her husband leaving her."

"What? Has her husband left her too?" Miss Ellen giggled. "It seems to run in the family, doesn't it?"

"It is nothing to laugh about, Ellen. I cannot imagine a situation more painful for both of them, and one can't but admire the dignity which they both show. Not one word of complaint."

"What does she look like? I mean Mrs. Hamilton-Gough?"

"That's beside the point; but, as I've told you already, she looks unmistakably like an English lady and behaves like one. I was happy to meet her, and still more happy to hear her opinions of the rest of the foreign colony. It is most fortunate, it appears, that we haven't committed ourselves to knowing any of them; there would seem to be only four or five houses which we can possibly visit. The remainder are, evidently, without any exception, most undesirable. The Italians, on the whole, are much more respectable. According to Mrs. Hamilton-Gough there are among them a few old titled families who keep themselves apart from the foreign riff-raff."

"Did she mention Miss Murphy?" Ellen asked eagerly.

"She did not; but I made a point of inquiring about her. Of course Mrs. Hamilton-Gough doesn't know her personally—she knows nobody at the Marina—but from what she has heard there appears to be considerable doubt about this woman's sources of income, and she was shocked by her impertinence in calling on us. The worst is suspected."

Miss Ellen laughed. "Poor thing! What a shame! Oh Agnes, I wish you could see her!"

"You forget, I have seen her once. We have returned her call, as I suppose we were bound to by common courtesy; and that, fortunately, is enough. I ought to have told you that I met Mr. Sanctuary at the 'Villa Minerva'."

"I'm surprised at that. He was a friend of Uncle Ludovic's."

"He was extremely kind to your Uncle Ludovic during his last illness, Ellen, but that is a very different thing from having been friends with him. No doubt Uncle

Ludovic had a better side to his nature; and, as you suggest, I could hardly have met Mr. Sanctuary in that house if there had been anything against him. Incidentally, I gather he is a cousin of Lord Chadminster, and I must say I found him charming. Salvatore confirms my opinion."

"You've always told me we oughtn't to be guided by what servants say."

Miss Agnes flushed and looked round quickly, to see if Salvatore was still in the room. He had gone.

"I think such a reminder is most uncalled-for, Ellen," she said. "I have seen a great deal more of Salvatore than you, as is only natural, and let me tell you that I do not regard him as a servant in the ordinary sense of the word, and that he has never for one moment presumed on the confidence I place in him. His position in this house is more like that of a land-agent—a calling that no gentleman need be ashamed to pursue—than that of a domestic. I think the moment has come when I can tell you something that I thought it better not to mention before. It is this: when I came to pay him his first month's wages, together with any arrears or expenses that might have occurred between the time of Uncle Ludovic's death and our coming here, he flatly refused to take anything. He said—and I quite believe him—that he found it a pleasure to serve us. I must confess that put me in an awkward position; but I could see at once that he'ld have been hurt if I'd pressed the matter. As you heard him say the other afternoon, he is attached to the house. He has great personal pride as well as a natural delicacy. I had recognized this from the first, but it was only by chance—I forget just how it happened—that he innocently let slip the fact that his ancestors, the Ferraros, were once the biggest landowners in Monfalcone. Ah yes, I remember: he showed me their coat-of-arms over the door of that large house at the Marina which is still called the 'Palazzo Ferraro'. He told me that the title—they were Counts—had lapsed several hundred years ago. What is more, it may surprise you to hear that the land this house is built on actually belonged to them. You have only to go out with him shopping, as I have done, to see how the people respect him. And I think we should do the same. People who have come down in the world through no fault of their own and never complain of it should not be despised."

"But I assure you I don't despise him, Agnes," Miss Ellen protested. "Only, you see . . . Well, the very first day we came here I remember your telling me that we ought to be cautious with foreigners."

"Let me remind you, Ellen, that *we* are the foreigners here. Italy is not a British possession like India. We have to remember that here we are *not* the Ruling Race, and that Southern Italians are particularly sensitive. Whatever else we are, we must not be insular. As Mrs. Hamilton-Gough pointed out, that is just as bad for our prestige as the lax behaviour of so many Anglo-Saxon visitors which gives us all a bad name. That is one of the reasons why she has always kept to herself and made a particular point of maintaining social relations with the local aristocracy. I hope I may have the pleasure of meeting some of them next Thursday. I should have told you, we are invited to dine at the 'Villa Minerva'."

"To dine? Why, we've nothing to wear, Agnes."

"You have your black lace, and I my brocade."

"But you're still in mourning."

"I have decided," Miss Agnes said, "to come out of it. After all the step had to be taken sooner or later, I suppose, and this is a good opportunity. I warned Mrs. Hamilton-Gough that your Italian was poor—she complimented me on mine, by the way—so she had promised to seat you by somebody who speaks English."

6

MISS ELLEN anticipated the dinner-party with misgivings. Agnes was always at ease in the best society, but she doubted if she herself could rise to the standards set by Mrs. Hamilton-Gough. She would much rather have been going to take tea again with Virginia Murphy—as she fully intended to do on the first opportunity—at the risk of being loaded with more presents. The problem of concealing the kittens had already given her sufficient embarrassment, until Stewart, who had been sniffing suspiciously at her bedroom door for several days, solved it by smelling them out and indulging his repressed lust for blood by a massacre. As for the painting, which was far too large to be got rid of in any other way, she had managed to slip it into the narrow space between a tall Florentine wardrobe and the wall, where she felt certain that Assunta's perfunctory broom would not discover it.

In the meantime she got out her black lace dress and tried it on—none too soon, for she found that the waistband had shrunk, or, more probably, that her waist had expanded as the result of greed, laziness, and the highly farinaceous diet which Carolina provided. The chest, too, seemed narrower than it used to be, and accentuated her bust to a degree which Agnes would certainly consider indelicate, though, but for her fear of this, she would have felt rather proud of it. As it was, she curbed her appetite for several days. But that made no difference; so she brazenly let it go, and decided to conceal her figure with a tinselly Assiut scarf which had been haggled over, like Agnes's ostrich-feather boa, at Port Said.

The result, surveyed in the long glass, pleased her enormously; it was so dashing that she doubted if she could live up to it, yet almost insignificant compared with that of Agnes as she appeared in the salone on the evening of the party. Agnes, too, had put on flesh since her arrival at Monfalcone. Though she had not been forced to 'let out' the famous brocade, her figure was no longer bony, and the gold tissue displayed its tall elegance to the greatest advantage. She had 'come out' of mourning so far as to put on her jewels, including a paste tiara and a pair of ornamental ear-rings whose shining length accentuated the slenderness of her neck and the lustre of her dark hair.

Miss Ellen was not alone in being impressed by this regal

spectacle. When she reached the salone, she found Salvatore surveying it with his head on one side and with a smile that showed obvious pride and satisfaction in the credit it gave to the establishment, and vicariously to himself. He stood gazing at Miss Agnes, spreading his hands, and shaking his head as though words failed him.

"Excuse if I speak," he said at last; "but truly the Signorina is magnificent. Now all Monfalcone shall see! But wait—there is one thing wanting!"

With the triumphant gesture of a conjurer extracting a rabbit from his hat, he produced a bouquet of orange-blossom, which he had evidently prepared beforehand, and presented it, with a courtly obeisance, to Agnes, who received it as nonchalantly as though such attentions were an everyday matter and no more than her due.

"Thank you, Salvatore," she said quietly. "That was very thoughtful of you. Now I think we had better go. We must not be late."

They drove down to the 'Villa Minerva' through a warm darkness that was spangled with fireflies and sweetened by the perfume of the orange-blossom bouquet. Salvatore, his glossy hair equally perfumed, sat on the box at the driver's side: he had accompanied them as a matter of course, to add to the dignity of their arrival by his attendance, and to hand them out of the cab. There was no getting away from it, Miss Ellen reflected: he *was* a superior man. Only imagine an English manservant presenting his employer with a bouquet! Such a thing was unthinkable. Yet how naturally, how gracefully, Salvatore had done it! There was no trace of false servility in the compliment, no flavour of presumption. Nor was the charming gesture unvirile: that indeed was an accusation that could never have been brought against him! No, the manner of his gift had been as correct as Agnes's reception of it—each defining, without underlining, the social differences which separated them. It would have been even more tactful, of course, if Salvatore had prepared a second bouquet for herself; but quite possibly his neglecting to do so showed an even subtler refinement of tact, by emphasizing Agnes's position as the head of the household. If he had given her flowers as well, Agnes might have been jealous; and on the whole she felt thankful that he hadn't, for she wouldn't have known how to thank him or even what to do with them.

These reflections were cut short by their arrival at the lighted portico of the 'Villa Minerva'. Salvatore leapt down from the box with agility and assisted Miss Agnes to alight. When Miss Ellen followed her, he turned and ceremoniously took her gloved hand. As he did so, he pressed it. Miss Ellen blushed violently—not so much because she was shocked, as because Agnes's eyes were on her. She wondered if he had pressed Agnes's too . . .

She was still blushing when Mrs. Hamilton-Gough received them and welcomed them in a deep bass voice which terrified her. From the first moment she did not find it difficult to understand why Mr. Hamilton-Gough had considered his freedom worth three-fifths of his pension. His wife was a gaunt, sallow, angular woman, even taller than Agnes, with long, bony, bangled wrists and a crushing handshake which made Miss Ellen wince. She had small, dark eyes which glared at her from behind gold-rimmed pince-nez as though she loathed her at sight. And for the best of reasons: not only was she wearing a copy of Miss Ellen's black lace frock, which had been bought off the peg in Whiteway and Laidlaw's store at Bombay, but also an identical, though slightly more tarnished, Assiut shawl. But whereas the frock fitted Miss Ellen's figure rather too tightly, it drooped from the angular shape of Mrs. Hamilton-Gough like shreds from a scare-crow. With one look at it, in which scorn was mingled with disgust, she bundled the Miss Isits, almost as if she were ashamed to be seen with them, into a small inner room which Miss Ellen felt certain she had seen before. The walls were decorated with numerous trophies of the Woods and Forests; there was even, she noticed, a tiger-skin on the floor, in the middle of which a stout, monocled, red-faced gentleman in a dinner-jacket and cummerbund, with a Kitchener moustache, stood gazing with strained intensity at Ronnie Sanctuary, who had evidently been murmuring something under his breath.

Mrs. Hamilton-Gough introduced him to Ellen as Mr. Potter, then abruptly left her alone with him, dragging Agnes and Mr. Sanctuary away with her into the outer room. Mr. Potter stared after them anxiously, as though he would gladly have followed, then resigned himself to Miss Ellen's company.

"I'm sorry," he said in a brassy level tone without any modulation. "Didn't quite catch your name, I'm afraid."

Miss Ellen said: "Isit."

Mr. Potter glared at her through his monocle, the less ferocious eye suspiciously following Mrs. Hamilton-Gough's retreat. "I beg your pardon," he said. "Our hostess's voice is generally on the loud side, I must admit; but she's inclined to mumble, and unfortunately of late my hearing is somewhat defective."

Miss Ellen, raising her voice, repeated: "Isit."

"I've just told you it is," Mr. Potter answered brusquely, "and I can't very well converse with you, can I, unless I know how to address you."

"My name's Ellen Isit. Castello Inglese," Miss Ellen shouted.

"H'm . . . So that's actually your name? Uncommonly confusing, isn't it? Oh, yes, now I know where I am; I've heard something about you. A nice house, the Castello Inglese. Belonged to that fellow Vaughan. Your cousin or uncle, wasn't he? Yes, Ludovic Vaughan. Not much in my line, I must say. Never could get on with artists. Un-English, aren't they? Are you staying here long?"

"I really don't know," Ellen told him. "So far my sister has made no definite plans."

"But she *ought* to have made definite plans, you know. Really she ought. That's what's wrong with this place. Everything here is indefinite. Nobody ever makes any plans—and if they do, they change them. Take this dinner-party, for instance. It's like everything else. You know what I mean?"

Miss Ellen timidly admitted that she didn't exactly.

"Well, you ought to, then," Mr. Potter declared severely. "How many people do you suppose our hostess has asked to dinner? Ten or twelve, I'll be bound. At what time were we invited to dine? Eight o'clock precisely. Now it's thirteen and a half minutes, and how many guests have arrived? You and me and your sister and Sanctuary. And why, if you please? Because we're English, and all the rest are her blessed Italians—people without any sense of time or responsibility. That is why the Roman Empire declined and fell. In the meantime, what happens? Will the dinner be spoilt?" Mr. Potter's eye fixed her savagely. "The answer is 'yes'. Does that matter? Not in the least. Take my word for it, there's no such thing as eatable food in this country, and if there were the cooks would ruin it. I've lived here for fifteen years, so I ought to know. Is that right or isn't it?"

Mr. Potter, with a lift of one eyebrow, released his monocle, which fell with a glassy tinkle against his starched shirt-front.

"If it's as bad as all that," Miss Ellen said, "I wonder how you have managed to live here so long."

"You do? Then I'll tell you. By refusing to truckle and putting my foot down firmly. That's the only kind of treatment they understand. If you ever visit my house, as I hope you will, you will be able to realize what determination can do. When my sister left it me, fifteen years ago, it was no different from any other villa—ridiculous word, by the way!—in Monfalcone. You know what I mean? All cluttered with olives and myrtles and prickly pears and vines running rampant everywhere, and cracked pots full of rubbish littered all over the place. No order. No system. Untidy. Thoroughly un-English in short. But I soon changed all that, though it cost me a pretty penny, I don't mind confessing."

"I'm sure it did. What did you do?"

"Do? The only thing possible. Knocked down every tree within twenty yards of the house and levelled the terraces. Got my cousin in Surbiton to send me a plan of his garden and laid it out ship-shape and Bristol fashion; brick-edged paths, and a croquet-lawn, and planted-out borders and so on, and arches of rustic woodwork instead of the plaster pergola. Got some packets of seeds sent from England too, and raised them. Some of the plants that you'ld like to see there by rights don't do any too well unless you're firm with them. Lack of water in summer. But can you change the climate? The answer is 'no'. Can you make an Italian gardener understand what you want in plain English? Not a bit of it. What is the answer then? Do it yourself. Result? A real bit of old England. There's even a flagstaff to run up the Union Jack on St. George's Day. Come and see for yourself. Apart from the beastly mountains you might almost imagine yourself in Bournemouth or Devonshire."

"But if that's what you want," Miss Ellen suggested, "why not live in Bournemouth or Devonshire?"

Mr. Potter re-fixed his monocle deliberately and glared at her with shocked surprise.

"Because I don't own a house in England, my good lady, and I *do* own one here. Do I regret it? A thousand times 'no'. England is not, by all accounts, what it was when I was younger. Never has been the same, I'm told, since the Boer War, what with Lloyd George and all that. No more respect for the sturdy individual, and too many restrictions and tarradiddles and taxes. Much better keep the flag flying out of their reach. Am I right?"

"Well, I expect you know best," Miss Ellen said.

"The answer is 'yes', and I do," Mr. Potter replied with an emphasis which denoted that the subject was closed. He raised his hand to his ear. "I seem to hear voices. To judge by the clatter, it would seem that foreigners have arrived." He looked at his watch. "Only thirty-two minutes late. That is better than usual. Allow me."

He stood aside, inviting Miss Ellen to precede him. A large number of strangers had invaded the outer room and were being pounced on by Mrs. Hamilton-Gough, who introduced them loudly, one by one, to Agnes. Miss Ellen could not catch their names: but each appeared to be prefaced by some title of nobility. As a sample of Southern Aristocracy they disappointed her. The most important, a grizzled, unshaven old gentleman, whom her hostess addressed as 'Prince', was a slightly more dignified version of the cabman who had driven them down that evening; and an effusive, large-bosomed lady, whom Mrs. Hamilton-Gough called 'Marchesa', closely resembled the woman who kept the salt-and-tobacco shop at the Marina. Not one of them, she saw, could hold a candle to Agnes, whose majestic head, surmounted by the flashing tiara, towered over them as superbly as the crest of a bird of paradise among a flock of daws. She did feel, none the less, that it was rather shabby of Mrs. Hamilton-Gough not to introduce her; for she had never met a prince or a marchioness before. This deliberate slight, no doubt, was the result of the unfortunate similarity of their dresses. It made her question the genuineness of her hostess's gentility: a real lady, she felt, would have risen above such a comic coincidence. At any rate, she knew better than to push herself forward.

She could not have done so in any case; for, at that moment, dinner was announced, and the whole company surged into the dining-room like a herd of hungry swine besieging their feeding-trough. She found herself placed between Mr. Potter and Ronnie Sanctuary, who greeted her with a familiar nod and a quick flash of his tiny teeth, and started to eat his soup peacefully without taking any more notice of her. Mr. Potter, having cleared his throat, as it were, for action, inhaled his noisily, like a bad eight feathering their oars. Loud snatches of speech in at least three languages dizzied Miss Ellen's ears. The guests, with the exception of her neighbours and herself, all seemed to be talking and eating at once. Judged by Carolina's standards of cooking the dinner was awful: an exact replica of the standard meal which had been served at 'The Cedars' on formal occasions in Colonel Isit's time—with the fortunate exception of the wine, which was potent and plentiful and lacked the familiar acridity of her father's chilled claret. Miss Ellen, abandoned by her companions, drank it down greedily to salve her humiliation, and soon felt more (or rather, less) like herself. Mr. Potter continued to eat stolidly, like a fireman stoking a furnace, while Mr. Sanctuary picked daintily at the indifferent food, and listened, with a leer on his curly lips, to a number of jokes which Miss Ellen could not understand. At last she could bear her isolation no longer.

"Mr. Sanctuary, I don't think you're very polite," she said. "Aren't you going to speak to me?"

Mr. Sanctuary screwed up his eyes and peered at her with a mocking smile.

"My dear . . . young . . . lady," he said effusively. "Upon my word, I apologize. To tell the truth I have been struck dumb by beholding your sister's triumph. She's positively scintillatin'. If she goes on wipin' our hostess's eye like this she won't be forgiven, and you'll never be asked here again. Not that that matters much. The most borin' house and the very worst food in the whole of Monfalcone."

"If you feel like that," Ellen said, "I'm surprised that you come here."

"Half a dinner is better than none, dear lady, and the wine is excellent, though Mrs. H.-G. doesn't know it. What is more, I happened to know that *you'd* been invited," he added mischievously.

"I'm positive that had nothing to do with it," Miss Ellen said. "Until I forced you to speak to me you had no more idea I was here than my other neighbour. I wish you'ld tell me about him."

"The worthy Potter? A pure grotesque, dear lady, a pure grotesque."

"Poor man! How unkind you are."

"Not at all. It is a natural phenomenon. He has lived in Monfalcone for fifteen years. If you stay here as long as that, you'll certainly become as grotesque as all the rest of us. Only, of course, you won't *know* you're grotesque. We never do—such is the kindly dispensation of Providence—but you will extract considerable pleasure, as I do, from observing the others."

"Do you know, Mr. Sanctuary, I'm beginning to believe you're rather a wicked old gentleman," Miss Ellen said.

Mr. Sanctuary wriggled with delight.

"Old? Alas, you are right: I am not so young as I was. A gentleman? Well, let us hope so, though that isn't important. Wicked? That is a word you'll have to forget if you become, as I'm sure you will, a permanent member of Monfalcone society. Good and evil do not concern us. We merely ask if people are bores or amusin'. Now our friend on your left is a bore of the deadliest variety; but he has cultivated his natural defects to such a masterly degree that he's become even more amusin' than he is borin', and when he blows up with apoplexy or goes clean off his head, as the poor feller probably will, we shall miss him bitterly. You may feel all this sounds rather complicated, I'm afraid; but you'll come to it—oh yes, you'll come to it. Why, you've begun to expand already."

Miss Ellen cast a nervous glance downward at her corsage, on which Mr. Sanctuary's eye appeared to be fixed, and wrapped her shawl closer.

"From all that you tell me," she said, "one would imagine that there wasn't a single sane person in Monfalcone. Is everyone queer?"

"Let us rather say, every foreigner. The Italians are sane enough. You see they've lived so long in the Monfalcone air that they're immunized—like Mithridates, you know"—Miss Ellen didn't—"who took graduated doses of hemlock and arsenic daily, just to protect himself, and died happily of old age. Speaking of which, by the way, most mediæval Italians, from the Borgias downwards, were poisoners; but everyone—particularly their wives—got so used to it that poison went out of fashion. Occasionally the mode is revived. Only look at the face of that crafty old villain on our hostess's right. Are you surprised that he's outlived three wives, and all of them wealthy?"

Miss Ellen gasped. "Isn't he Prince Something-or-other?"

"The Principe di Roccapalumba."

"Is he *really* a prince? I've never seen one before."

"Don't take the principality too seriously. They're three-a-penny in Naples. Counts and Marquises are a penny a dozen. If you'ld happen to like one of your own, it could be arranged—though it would be easier if you were American."

"But this one is genuine?"

"Undoubtedly. The Roccapalumbas have had time to acquire some of the worst blood in Europe. They're an extremely ancient family."

"Like the Ferraros?"

Mr. Sanctuary looked puzzled. "Which Ferraros do you mean?"

"The Counts of Monfalcone. Salvatore's family."

"My dear lady, what on earth are you talking about? So far as I know there have never been any Conti di Monfalcone. Salvatore's family are like all the rest of the Monfalconesi, peasant-proprietors: humble folk, and tolerably honest as far as they go, which is not saying much. How did you get this quite fantastic idea into your head? Never heard such nonsense!"

"Of course it was long before your time," Miss Ellen explained. "The title became extinct more than two hundred years ago; but you can still see the house the family lived in at the Marina; it's the one with the coat-of-arms over the gateway. You must know the one I mean?"

"But perfectly. That's the old Municipio—the Town Hall, as you'ld call it. The arms over the gateway are those of the Bourbons, which for some reason or other—pure laziness in all probability—have not been removed. Who told you all this?"

"Salvatore himself told my sister. In confidence. I probably shouldn't have mentioned it. Are you sure it's not true?"

"Quite positively. It's sheer moonshine. The fellow's a *scugnizzo*—a charmin' guttersnipe."

Miss Ellen hesitated. "Mightn't it possibly be true

without your knowing it? He does look like an aristocrat, doesn't he?"

"Most certainly. Nearly all Southern Italians do—unless they *are* aristocrats." Mr. Sanctuary smiled meditatively. "I find this extremely interestin'." He puckered his eyes, regarding the distant figure of Miss Agnes and stroking his chin. "Very interestin' . . . It would seem that our youthful Tiberius has been romancin'. Now *why?*"

"Well, he *is* a romantic figure, isn't he?" Miss Ellen sighed.

"That was poor Ludo's opinion," Mr. Sanctuary replied with a wolfish grin. "I must confess I don't share it: I happen to have known Salvatore since he was a boy, and have followed his career with interest. Let me, for once, be serious, Miss Isit, and teach you something for the good of your soul. There is no such thing in this world as a romantic Italian. If you will get that into your head and keep it there you may be saved quite a lot of trouble. I'm not jokin'. I mean it. Now, alas, I fear, we must suspend this delightful flirtation. Our preposterous hostess's eye commands me to do my unwelcome duty to my other neighbour. Be kind to poor Potter: he may not be with us for long."

Mr. Potter was redder than ever in the face and breathing heavily as the result of his labours. Before Miss Ellen could rouse him from the stupor of repletion, Mrs. Hamilton-Gough had risen, given the ladies the signal to retire, and begun to shepherd them from the dining-room in strict order of precedence.

Miss Ellen, naturally, came last. In spite of the effects of the wine, which had temporarily heartened her, she felt terribly 'out of it' amid this concourse of women, to none of whom she had been introduced and not a word of whose rapid speech she could understand. Modestly detaching herself from the crowd, she sat down in a corner alone and resigned herself to admiring the virtuosity with which her sister entertained the Principe di Roccapalumba and his third wife. Ronnie Sanctuary had been right. Agnes was positively scintillating. Never, in all her life, had Miss Ellen felt so proud of her. Yet together with her frank, unenvious admiration and pride, there was mingled, this evening, another, unusual emotion, strangely akin to pity. There was something a little tragic and fateful in Agnes's brilliance—resembling that of some fragile, tinselled ephemerid spinning to its death in the rays of the setting sun. For all the distinction of feature, the energy of spirit, the consciousness of social success, which lifted her so shiningly above this shabby aristocratic company—and particularly above the gaunt, envious figure of Mrs. Hamilton-Gough—she was, in fact, a lonely woman, poised insecurely, as it were, upon the very brink of a disappointed old age. In the article of Agnes's triumph, Miss Ellen's heart bled for her, and tears filled her eyes.

She suppressed these determinedly. It occurred to her that this melting mood was probably the result of the heat and the insidious Monfalcone wine, of which she had undoubtedly drunk too much. But though she could explain, it was beyond her power to dispel it. In this, as in most other things, she differed from Agnes: she was not made for high society. As the evening dragged on, she would have given anything to escape from the lights and the noise—to be falling asleep in her comfortable bed at the Castello Inglese with Waifie purring beside her . . .

It was past midnight before the party broke up. Salvatore was waiting at the door to hand them into their carriage, as smiling and attentive as ever. The mere sight of that friendly, familiar figure, filled Miss Ellen with relief and removed all the doubts Mr. Sanctuary's suggestions had implanted in her mind. She experienced a quick, passionate revulsion in Salvatore's favour. What if he had been romancing a little when he spoke of his family? Aristocracy was a great deal more than a matter of birth; and, so far as appearances went, he showed far more signs of it than any of the faded nobility the snobbishness of Mrs. Hamilton-Gough could collect. Why, in any case, should she trust the word of that wicked old man any more than his?

Agnes, too, seemed pleased to see him, and answered him gaily when he inquired if they had had a nice evening. She even laughed happily and made no attempt to correct him when he told her, ingenuously excusing himself, the flattering remarks he had heard about her appearance from what he called the 'persons of the service.' In North Bromwich Agnes would not have considered it seemly to listen for a moment to what servants had said; but Salvatore made such things sound so natural and friendly. It was a great pleasure for him, he explained, to hear his own Signorina praised.

Agnes still glowed with communicable excitement, though Ellen was almost asleep, when the cab crunched up to the entrance of the Castello Inglese. Ellen noticed that, as they passed through the hall, she looked at herself in the glass. Ascending the stairs, she said pensively:

"Did you notice that tiger-skin of Mrs. Hamilton-Gough's, Ellen? It is not nearly so fine a specimen as the one Papa shot at Moogly. I have been thinking it might be quite a good idea to ask Mr. Wilburn to have it sent out to us. It would look remarkably well in the salone. Don't you think so?"

Miss Ellen hesitated.

"Of course, it would look lovely," she said. "But surely it's hardly worth while going to so much trouble for the sake of having it here until we go home?"

"I'm sure Salvatore would be dreadfully disappointed if we left Monfalcone before the wine and the oil were finished; and by the time that is over it will be nearing the end of October. Considering everything, I think we had better decide to stay here for the winter. The Prince tells me that November and December are delightful months. Good night, dear. Sleep well. You look rather tired."

She bent down and kissed her. Once more, as she entered the bedroom, Miss Ellen felt like crying. It was the first time Agnes had kissed her since they were girls.

7

AGNES's success at the 'Villa Minerva' threw wide open to her every door in Monfalcone that could be entered with propriety. The Italians, though by no means averse to dining out, usually restricted the entertainment they offered to coffee or vermouth; but the members of the foreign colony vied with one another in the elaborateness of the dinner-parties they gave in honour of the Miss Isits. Miss Agnes might almost be said to have 'broken' rather than 'gone' out of mourning. It soon became clear that her brocade, which the sea air had tarnished, could neither sustain her dignity nor the stress of the social programme, and that she would have to replenish her wardrobe, though it was decided that Miss Ellen's 'black lace', being less affected by climatic change, need neither be added to nor replaced.

The result was a two-day shopping expedition to Naples. Salvatore accompanied them, as a matter of course, in the capacity of courier and bodyguard. When first the idea was broached, Miss Ellen had felt his presence unnecessary in view of Agnes's mastery of the Italian language: it seemed to her rather odd that two maiden ladies should travel with a young—or a not so very young—man, and she wondered what Ronnie Sanctuary would think of it. But Miss Agnes insisted. The experience of their confused arrival at Naples had distressed her more than she chose to admit; and, however unconventional the arrangement might seem, it was justified by the event.

The expedition proved to be a charmingly light-hearted adventure. Salvatore, who had replaced his butler's uniform by one of Captain Vaughan's Savile Row suits, looked so distinguished that he outshone every other man they met on the journey. If, as Miss Agnes had always maintained, he knew his place, he was also, and proudly, aware of theirs. He would not, for instance, allow them to stay at the *Hotel Splendide*, which Agnes, remembering the porter's recommendation, had selected. It was no sort of place, he said, for ladies of their quality. He took them, instead, to a more pretentious establishment at Santa Lucia, the hall-porter of which, he said, was a distant cousin of his own, and established them in a suite with a private bathroom and a view of the bay, which seemed to Miss Ellen much too grand for them.

"Are you sure we can afford to stay in a place like this?" she asked timidly.

Agnes laughed. She had laughed much more often and easily lately.

"We are not so poor as all that, after all," she said. "And in any case Salvatore has arranged special terms through his cousin."

Salvatore, in fact, arranged everything. He secured a brand-new *carrozza* with a spanking pair, which was much smarter than Papa's victoria had ever been. He sat on the box, and gave the driver directions. Under his tutelage they no longer found Naples a predatory and terrifying city. His company was a *laissez-passer* through the crowds of touts and beggars that infested it. There were no more ugly hagglings or disputes about money. Cabmen, porters, everyone seemed glad to accept what he offered. When Miss Agnes suggested that he should carry her purse, he refused it with his usual phrase:

"*Non dubitare* . . . Do not doubt, Signorina: I think of everything. I keep the account, as I always did for Don Ludovico, and when we go home you pay what is owed. You not trust me?"

How could they do anything but trust him? He was not merely capable, but knowledgeable in the most surprising directions. He took them, for example, to the very court-dressmaker's in the Toledo which the Marchesa had mentioned to Agnes as being the smartest in Naples. It was unusual, Miss Ellen thought, that he should come inside with them and assist Miss Agnes in the choice of the gowns that were displayed. But Agnes did not resent this or find it odd. "You will always get better attention from female shop-assistants," she said, "if you have a man with you, and though my Italian is more than adequate for ordinary social uses, these Neapolitans speak in such a slovenly manner that I can't always understand them. Besides which, Salvatore knows just what is worn in Monfalcone, and I have discovered he is naturally gifted with excellent taste."

Miss Ellen was not so sure about that. Salvatore's tastes seemed to her to lean towards the flamboyant, and the dresses he appeared to admire were certainly not such as she would have chosen for Agnes or herself. But Agnes apparently needed no persuasions in that direction. After hiding herself for years in her severe brocade and her modest black satins, she seemed determined to draw attention to her rediscovered charms by a reckless exploitation of colour combined with barbaric adornment. Though she asked Ellen's opinion, she showed no inclination to take it.

"How do you like this?" she asked, appearing in a flame-coloured evening dress profusely embroidered with silver. "Madame says it would need no alteration at all: it might have been made for me."

"Of course it's extremely striking," Miss Ellen said. "But don't you think it's a wee bit young for you?" Agnes flushed with annoyance. "I mean . . . well, I think it would look rather out of place in North Bromwich with such a low neck."

Agnes kicked the draped skirt aside contemptuously and turned her back on her.

"What do you think, Salvatore?" she asked in Italian.

Salvatore lowered his spread hands in a gesture of humility.

"Who am I to judge? But if I am permitted to speak, Signorina, I would say, with respect, that I find it magnificent. The Signorina resembles a queen."

"Then I will take this as well as the other two," Agnes said. "The gold tissue which you called a 'robe de style', and the ivory satin."

"What? All three?" Miss Ellen goggled.

Agnes did not answer her. "I think that will be sufficient, madame," she said. "Please make out the account.

I am afraid I shall have to ask you to accept a cheque, if you can trust me for so large a sum."

Salvatore appeared to be shocked by her crudeness in mentioning money.

"Excuse, Signorina," he said. "This is for me. I think of all that. My cousin at the desk, he pay everything. *Non dubitare.*"

They drove back to the hotel in a frigid silence by which it was intended that Ellen should suffer for her lapse from tact. In the afternoon Salvatore arranged to take them for a drive. He bought them water-ices on a vine-shadowed terrace overlooking Posilippo—to Miss Ellen's dismay, for she had been warned, by Agnes herself, that the Neapolitan water-supply was not reliable. It seemed preferable, however, to run the risk of contracting typhoid rather than that of again upsetting her sister, whose glacial mood, by this time, had fortunately begun to thaw. Indeed it was difficult for either of them to feel constrained in Salvatore's care-free company. He was just like a happy schoolboy, Miss Ellen thought, so natural, so gay and so lively, yet always so discreet, so much in the background. He seemed determined to make them share his holiday mood, and even prevailed on the mandoline-players attached to the restaurant to accompany him—if the Signorina would excuse it?—in a Neapolitan song. He had a light, melodious, flexible tenor voice, with deep masculine tones in it, and sang with a passionate wealth of gesture which Miss Ellen found moving. When he had finished, the chief musician wrung his hand and congratulated him, and Agnes suggested giving him a handsome tip which Salvatore insisted on halving. The loyalty with which he protected their pockets was quite wonderful, Miss Ellen thought.

That evening they dined in the hotel and Agnes wore her new dress. The head-waiter attended them personally, making swift falcon-swoops on their table again and again. He hoped the *menu* pleased them. It was choicer than that which was being served to the other guests and had been specially ordered for them by Signor Ferraro. If they preferred anything else he would have it prepared immediately. Salvatore had also ordered the wine: a full-flavoured and slightly fizzy Gragnano which, as usual, went straight to Miss Ellen's head. When she stepped unsteadily into the lift and was snatched upstairs to their room like a lamb in an eagle's talons, she felt that, in spite of the morning's unfortunate contretemps, she had spent one of the most exciting days of her life. But they were both of them too tired to make use of the bath which Signor Ferraro had so kindly provided at their expense.

Next morning an expurgated edition of Salvatore, who, as less innocent eyes might have guessed had made a night of it, escorted them in silence on the long drive home to Monfalcone; and that very week the series of parties which Miss Ellen described to herself as a 'whirl of gaieties' began. They were not, in fact, as gay as all that; but they were extremely correct, and Miss Agnes, wearing her new gowns in rotation, achieved a success that almost justified the cost of their two-day flutter in Naples—which amounted to more than the sisters had spent on themselves during the whole of their sojourn in North Bromwich. Though she gasped at the bill and concealed it from Ellen, she neither grudged paying it nor reproved Salvatore. With their income assured, she felt there was no need to save, and took Salvatore's extravagance as a token of the importance he attached to 'his Signorine', as he possessively called them.

One of the major events of their programme was a middle-day Sunday dinner provided by Mr. Potter in defiance of the August heat. When he asked them to share 'his humble meal', they had no idea what they were in for: a roast leg of mutton, preceded by ox-tail soup and followed by a suet pudding. This was not for him, he went out of his way to explain, an unusual bill of fare, but one which he had taught his cook to prepare as a matter of routine every Sunday since he had settled in Monfalcone, as a protest against the foreign kickshaws he was forced to put up with during the rest of the week. At first he had found great difficulty in procuring mutton, which, it appeared, the Southern Italians did not eat; but, refusing to be beaten by local ignorance or prejudice, he had eventually arranged for a *gigot*, as these people insisted on calling it, to be sent every week from Naples by parcel post. The result, though a triumph of faith and ingenuity, was not appetizing; for parcel posts—like everything else in this wretched country—were unreliable, especially in summer; and the taste of the skinny joint, which was like venison basted with lanoline, was imperfectly disguised by the strawberry jam which their host served in place of red-currant jelly, and made both the Miss Isits feel squeamish. Mr. Potter, however, to judge by the noise he made, found nothing amiss, and fell on the suet pudding which followed it with such gusto that Miss Ellen became anxious lest the catastrophe which Mr. Sanctuary had prophesied should overtake him before they escaped.

When they had eaten, Mr. Potter dragged them both out into the blinding sun to show them his garden and the flagpole on which, in their honour, he had hoisted the Union Jack. The result of his conquest of nature resembled a patch of desert carefully preserved in the heart of an oasis, for no native vegetation had been permitted to survive, and most of his northern exotics, deprived of the meanest measure of moisture or shade, lay wilted in swathes about a few leggy, forlorn survivors.

"At the moment my garden is not at its best," Mr. Potter confessed. "The cisterns have unfortunately run dry, and I am consequently short of water. Can we hope for rain to revive it? The answer is 'no'. Can I build more capacious cisterns? For years I have found the cost of cement and labour prohibitive. Are we daunted? Not on your life! Why? Because we are English! If you will do me the honour of sharing my Sunday dinner again in some three months' time, when the climate becomes more reasonable, I may even be able to supplement the joint with a home-grown boiled cabbage. Brussels Sprouts and Cottager's Kale, I am sorry to say, do not flourish here as they should. They have failed me twelve seasons running, but that does not mean that I have abandoned hope. On the contrary. What is my horticultural motto? Never say die! But they do."

In defiance of the blistering heat and of his plethoric condition, which was aggravated that day by a stiff shirt with a throttling starched collar, a frock-coat and spats, Mr. Potter insisted on accompanying the Miss Isits to their carriage at the foot of the hill, and rebuffed Miss Agnes's invitation to take a siesta.

"What? Lie down in the afternoon? Never done such a thing in my life! Poor look-out for the world if we Englishmen took to slovenly habits like that! This is the time of the day when I always take my exercise. Why? Because it sets an example. Will the natives follow it? The answer is 'no'."

At parting, Mr. Potter presented them with a bundle of old *Daily Telegraphs* and copies of a local weekly published in Stony Stratford.

"Thought you'ld like to glance through them," he panted. "You need not send them back. My weekly tonic. I read them through twice every Sunday. That is how I keep in touch with civilization. Why don't I read the Italian newspapers, like Sanctuary? For two reasons. First of all, because I can't: the language the Bible was written in is good enough for me. In the second place even if I could, there's nothing in them worth reading; they don't even give you the result of the Derby or the Boat Race! I've often twitted poor Sanctuary on the subject—in a kindly way, mind, I shouldn't like to upset him. He takes no care of himself, and is beginning to show his age. I have a feeling the poor old feller may not be with us for long."

Miss Agnes, surprisingly, approved of Mr. Potter, whose eccentricities probably appealed to the Empire-Building streak in her constitution.

"He may not be exactly an intellectual," she declared, "nor even so well-connected as Mr. Sanctuary; but I will say this for him: he doesn't pretend to be anything that he isn't. I respect him not only for that but also because—as

Mrs. Hamilton-Gough assures me—there has never been the least breath of scandal attached to his name. I'm sure he has a Heart of Gold."

In that torrid season, the Miss Isits found their new social life fatiguing; and even when September came in, the heat showed no signs of abatement. It grew so fierce that even Miss Agnes's fey energy began to falter. There was no escaping it. From the moment when the sun soared above the mountain ranges to eastward until it plunged like a molten cannon-ball into the steamy sea, the vast crucible of limestone in which Monfalcone sweltered was brimmed with a still, devitalized air that quivered with direct and reflected heat. The sun was no longer a gay, inspiriting friend but a merciless enemy. The land cracked and gaped beneath it, like the blackened lips of a desert castaway dying of thirst, cloven by huge fissures from which one might almost expect the scorching breath of earth's central fires to issue. Yet, unlike Mr. Potter's exotics, the native vegetation of Monfalcone throve and even exulted in invisible sources of moisture. Figs ripened profusely; the blood-red pulp swelled till it split their skins; peaches flushed or grew tawny-golden on every tree; from every vine grapes hung in tight clusters of amber or purple. Miss Ellen, who had never seen such delicacies outside a fruiterer's shop, indulged her appetite recklessly, and paid for it by a bout of colic which put an end to her social activities for three days. Miss Agnes, more prudent in this as in everything, was unsympathetic and said she deserved to suffer for making a pig of herself; but Miss Ellen thought it was worth it—more particularly as the attack coincided with the arrival of a lion-throated *scirocco* which, laden with clouds of Libyan dust, fell greedily on the blanched olive-groves and sucked the last dregs of vitality out of the fainting air. While such a devilish wind was abroad, one might just as well stay in one's bed—or rather on it.

In the second week of September the weather broke: one breathless night the aching sky suddenly cracked like a hammer-smitten cauldron. Its clangorous reverberations rocked and rolled to and fro overhead in echoes beaten back from the crests of the mountains. The air, which had grown dense and dark, was split by forked flashes, and the starless sky remained livid all night with summer-lightning that whitened and waned without ceasing. In the brief intervals between the crashes of thunder an uncanny silence brooded on the Castello Inglese, as though its very stones were bracing themselves to meet the next assault of sound; and the creatures within it lay waiting too: Carolina and the two maids muttering prayers and fingering their beads beneath the kitchen table; the Miss Isits, by no means unnerved but none the less physically shaken, in their virginal beds. Miss Ellen had the unperturbed Waifie for company, her fur crackling with electricity when she stroked it. Miss Agnes, next door, had a harder task in comforting Stewart, who lay shrunken and trembling, his small eyes blank with terror, emitting a yap of frightened defiance at each clap of thunder. After two hours of continuous bombardment the storm reached its climax in a salvo full overhead. Simultaneously a flash of violet light filled the room, and the house shuddered so violently to its rocky foundations that Miss Ellen felt sure the chimneys must have been struck, and was almost surprised to find herself still alive. In the tingling silence that followed, broken only by Waifie's contented purring and the beating of her own fluttered heart, she heard stealthy steps in the passage outside her room and a tap on Miss Agnes's bedroom door.

"What is it?" she heard Agnes call sharply. "What is it? Who's there?"

Salvatore's voice answered in a hoarse whisper:

"It is I, Signorina. Excuse—but I am come to inquire if the Signorina is frightened. This is only to say I am here. I will open the door if the Signorina wishes for company."

Then she heard Agnes speak in soft intimate tones that seemed strangely unlike her. "Thank you, Salvatore," she said tenderly. "It was extremely kind of you—and like you—to think of me. But I'm not frightened of thunder, not in the very least. You had better go back to bed."

Salvatore laughed: "The Signorina is very courageous. I had thought that perhaps she would like me to close the shutters . . ."

Miss Ellen, straining her ears, could hear no more. The rest of their colloquy—if indeed it continued—was lost in the roar of rain that sluiced down from the sky as fiercely as if, at that moment, all the waters that had been sucked up into cloud from sea and land by the heat of summer were descending simultaneously. The sound of this deluge drowned the peals and rumbles of retreating thunder. It was momentarily even more terrifying than these, being directed, as it seemed, with a more particular, more pitiless spite. It beat on the flat roof and the terraces of the Castello Inglese like drumfire; it thrashed the closed windows so violently that it seemed to Miss Ellen the glass would surely be splintered; and soon, above the splash and gurgle of spouting gutters and the continuous rustling roar that swelled from myriads of helpless leaves in the olive-groves, a new sound arose: the hoarse bourdon of new-born torrents of storm-water that poured and foamed from the peaks and bastions of limestone, plunging downward through every parched channel and gully to reach the sea. In a moment the mountains, for so long crushed and dumb under the tyranny of heat, had found their voice; and that voice was wild and terrible.

It was also, Miss Ellen found, exhilarating. For all her sensations of awe and tremulous excitement, she was conscious of a strange physical relief, as though some tension which had strained her body without her being fully aware of it had been suddenly released. More than that: she was assailed by an impulse ungoverned by reason to take a more personal part in this elemental riot. She wanted to feel the rain as well as to hear it. She felt she would like to throw wide the windows, to strip off her night-dress and walk forth naked into the storm-tormented darkness. The knowledge that Salvatore was about and Agnes awake deterred her from such a gross lapse from modesty. Yet the wild desire was too strong to be resisted. With a fluttering heart she left her bed, cautiously opened one window, stepped out on the balcony, and stood with the rain beating down on her. She spread wide her arms and threw back her head to receive it. It fell on her burning eyelids; it filled her mouth; its delicious coolness and moisture assuaged the drought of her body, which craved them as fiercely as the cracked earth of the olive-groves. In that rite of surrender she discovered a physical ecstasy as rich and passionate as any her spirit had found in religious experience; it was as though she shared in a sacrament of which not only human kind but all other living things were partaking. She stood there, rapt and excited, until she was soaked to the skin, until it seemed as if every pore in her body had drunk its fill. Then, cleansed, refreshed, and sublimely contented with the result of this secret and scandalous adventure in paganism, she took off her clinging night-dress and relapsed on her bed, where she lay like a Bacchante forspent and fell into a deep and gentle sleep.

When Miss Ellen awoke next morning, the memory of what she had done seemed irrational and extravagant. If she had not found herself lying naked and seen, on the floor, her sodden discarded night-dress, she would have supposed she had been dreaming. This was not the sort of behaviour that Agnes—or even she herself—could have countenanced. She felt more than ever convinced that there must be something in what Mr. Sanctuary had said; that the air of Monfalcone had a mysterious quality which produced curious effects in the nature of those that breathed it. Had she, in fact, already become just a tiny bit crazy, like the rest of them, without knowing it? Was she, too, becoming a grotesque? And after all, did it matter so very much, if this process of transformation involved the delightful rebirth of youth and joy in living, the sense of sheer physical relief and lightness of heart which thrilled her now? If both she and Agnes were changing, as they seemed to be, it would be no great loss to either of them or to anyone else, for that matter!

In that night, the whole atmosphere of Monfalcone had changed. The oppression that had weighed on the valley for weeks had lifted and vanished on the wings of the storm that was now spending its spite forty miles away in the Abruzzi. Though millions of gallons of water had poured down to the sea and muddied the shallows offshore, gleaming pools that lay caught on the terraces still mirrored the sky, so that the smoke of the olive-groves seemed to be shot with silver. The substance of sky itself was no longer opaque but crystalline: the sun shone through it as through a dome of sapphire, its rays dancing back reflected from every spangle of rain that still clung to the myriads of stiff leaves, so that the whole landscape that stretched from the towers and pinnacles of rock still silvered with moisture to the red roofs of Monfalcone and its golden dome, seemed to be set in a matrix glistening with crystals of quartz, and to sparkle as though these pinpoints of light were alive. She was to feel the results of this miracle of violent lustration more keenly when, later in the day, she set off down the hill to the Marina to visit Miss Murphy, whom the burden of heat had compelled her to neglect. The rocky mule-track had been scoured so clean by the flood that every stone in it appeared to have been newly polished; the limewashed walls of gardens and cottages, though they still showed patches of damp, looked as clean as white linen dried by wind and sun; the narrow streets were no longer defiled by dust and ordure—every particle of unsavoury refuse had been swept from their surface into the sea; the very air of the alleys appeared to have been cleansed and freshened: it had a sweetness of its own, characteristic, and comparable in its own way to the incense of the surrounding gardens and olive-groves, which was the grateful odour of damp earth and ripening fruits. Even the sands over which the wrack of the flood had been poured appeared unsullied. Even Miss Murphy's studio, its windows now flung wide open, smelt as if it had been spring-cleaned.

"The fall is the time of year I love best, honey," Miss Murphy said. "The day after the first rain comes in September makes you almost glad of the heat that has gone before. It's just like being born again, like you'd been made over. And say, don't the cats love it too! They're twice as full of pep as they've been through weeks. Can you guess what I did last night? You'll never believe. I sure couldn't resist it. When the rain began—it was quite dark, you know, except for the lightning in the sky, and I knew for certain that none of the folks down here would be out to see me, they re that scared of thunder—I took off my wrap and went out into it, just as I was!"

"But my dear," Miss Ellen cried. "That's exactly what I did! Only I wasn't as brave as you: I kept on my nightie."

"Well now, isn't that utterly marvellous? It only shows! Didn't I always declare that you and me were twin spurrits? What a pity, now, we couldn't have done it together!"

Miss Ellen was not so sure about that. She felt that the ecstasy she had achieved was essentially personal and private, and couldn't quite see herself advancing stark-naked over the sands hand in hand with Miss Murphy. She was even a trifle distressed, on second thoughts, by the unanimity of their reactions. Was Ronnie Sanctuary right? Could this be the beginning? Was she fated, thanks to the Monfalcone air, to go the same way as Miss Murphy? She changed the subject at once, and began to tell her friend—she still counted her as that—of the expedition to Naples and their social adventures. At the mention of Salvatore she noticed a blurring—no more than the faintest cloud—in Miss Murphy's blue eyes.

"You know who I mean?" she asked.

"Sure I do," Miss Murphy replied. "Salvatore Ferraro. I've known him ever since he was a little brown imp running naked over the sands outside my studio."

"I can see you dislike him."

"I don't dislike anyone, honey. But I hope you and your darling sister will take care not to be too free with him."

Miss Ellen laughed uneasily. "What do you mean?"

"He was a naughty boy, honey; and I'm afraid he's a wicked young man. I wouldn't like to blame him, mind: I guess it's not all his own fault. When he was no more than a lad he got mixed up with bad men—what you might call undesirables—and they certainly spoilt him. One of them—an American gentleman, I'm sorry to say—took him out to New Haven, Connecticut, and said he intended to send him to school at Yale; but I guess Salvatore soon quit, if he ever went there. When he came back this side, he lived for some years in Naples; and I have heard them say that he had something to do with the Camorra, if you know what that means."

"I don't," said Miss Ellen, wide-eyed.

"Well . . . it's something not very nice, honey: the same as what we call hoodlums; and though Captain Vaughan took him back again in his house and smartened him up a lot, he hasn't lived that down. They still call him the *Camorrista*, you know."

"I think that's a shame," Miss Ellen said. "It's just 'Give a dog a bad name and hang him'. If he weren't honest, I'm certain that Agnes would have discovered it. And he has such beautiful manners," she added regretfully.

"Oh, yes, I'm sure he has," Miss Murphy sighed. "They all have, you know: that's the worst of it. But it wouldn't be fair to you as a friend—as a vurry dear friend —if I didn't tell you that the folks down here are scared of him. Particularly the young girls. He's well known as terrible Don Juan."

"That doesn't surprise me," Miss Ellen said. "I expect they run after him."

"I dare say they do, honey. Girls are quite different here from America. But whichever does the running it comes to the same thing, doesn't it?"

"I'm sure he'll improve under Agnes's influence," Miss Ellen said cheerfully. "We ought to feel sorry for him. Only think of it! I don't suppose he has ever known a good woman before."

Miss Murphy sighed heavily and shook her head.

"Well, you never know, do you? I guess it's our duty as Christians to hope for the best, as I always do. Now tell me about the kittens."

Miss Ellen prevaricated—not so much because she felt that Miss Murphy would be hurt to hear of their fate as because she feared that if she admitted the truth she would immediately be presented with two more from that inexhaustible reservoir. With a decisive farewell, far too swift for Miss Murphy's leisurely processes of thought to keep pace with her, she managed to escape unembarrassed by any presents while her hostess was still rummaging in the debris in search of something to give her.

Though it was against all her principles to listen to gossip, even when it came to her from such innocent lips as Miss Murphy's, she was a little perturbed by what she had heard about Salvatore. It seemed a thousand pities that he had thrown away the advantage of a good education offered to him by his generous American friend. If he had taken his degree at Yale, his natural endowments would have made him quite undistinguishable from a gentleman. In that case, on the other hand, he would certainly never have accepted employment as their butler, and she could not conceive of their living at the Castello Inglese without him; so, though it seemed hard on him, from her own selfish point of view, it was all to the good.

She was more deeply troubled by Miss Murphy's dark hints as to his manner of life in Naples. She did not know what 'Camorra' meant, and the word 'hoodlum' said little more to her. Yet it was reasonable to suppose that a young man so high-spirited and vital as Salvatore must have 'had his fling' and quite possibly 'sowed his wild oats'. The less said or thought about these, the better. As to Miss Murphy's suggestion that he was still a Don Juan and dangerous to young women, she could well believe it. She had never in her life met a man whose presence radiated charm and virility to such an embarrassing degree. She was even a little thrilled vicariously —though she supposed she ought not to be—by the thought of his conquests, which a woman of her own age or Agnes's could dwell on, if she so wished, with immunity and detachment and without any emotional risk to herself. She liked men to be men; and so long as he served them faithfully and did not permit his amours to disturb the smooth domestic tenour of the Castello Inglese, they were no business of hers, and even less of Miss Murphy's. It did strike her, however, that if she had been confronted with a situation of this kind in North Bromwich, only a few months ago, she would have regarded it more seriously and probably have been equally indignant and shocked. This change in her attitude was no more than a token of her emancipation, perhaps a result, as Mr. Sanctuary would mischievously have suggested, of the Monfalcone air. It rejoiced her to feel that already her mind had broadened, as became a woman of the world. Her heart was even tinged with a mild regret that she had not come to Monfalcone when she was younger; though on the whole, perhaps, it was just as well that she hadn't. . . .

On one thing, at least, she was firmly decided: that it would be beneath her dignity—and also ill-advised—to 'pass on' to Agnes any of the tittle-tattle she had heard about Salvatore from Miss Murphy and old Mr. Sanctuary. She had a feeling that Agnes might show less tolerance than herself, and, quite possibly, take him to task. If these tales were not true, Salvatore would be justified in resenting her interference: if they were, Agnes would probably hate her for having told them. In either case, she would have made an enemy of him for life—and, according to Virginia Murphy, a dangerous enemy. For all that, she would keep her eyes open.

8

If Miss Ellen had kept them tight-shut, she could hardly have failed to notice an appreciable increase of tension in the atmosphere of the Castello Inglese during the next few weeks. It was the season of the *vendemmia*, the vintage, which, in modern days, has replaced and combined the numerous fertility-festivals of the ancients. At this time, when the major labours of the year are over and the last crops have come to fruition, in an air that is neither too hot nor too cold for the highest degree of physical enjoyment, the peasants of Monfalcone have, from years immemorial, abandoned themselves to the gay recklessness that accompanied their ancestors' Saturnalia.

The *vendemmia* at the Castello Inglese was a comparatively modest affair; for its vineyards only covered a small acreage, and the establishment was not equipped with modern machinery. Its wine was made in the ancient way, by trampling the juicy clusters in vats or tubs. Every hand and foot on the estate had a share in the making, which was supposed to ensure good luck for all those who took part in it during the following year. Miss Agnes would have preferred to send her grapes to a neighbouring press, but yielded at length to the persuasions of Salvatore, who declared that these old-fashioned and (as it seemed to her) insanitary methods of wine-making largely accounted for the acknowledged excellence of the Castello Inglese wine.

"If they put in the presses," he explained, "the wine it taste bitter—what you call tart, because it break all the stones you call pips; but with the feet in the tub of wood, the stones are not broken. Besides, all the old men they say it is better fortune. You see what will come!"

"I think it is most disgusting," Miss Agnes said, "and I insist on your keeping old Antonino out of the tub in any case."

"Then the poor old man lose his luck for a year. That is not too kind, Signorina."

"I'm surprised that anyone of your intelligence should be so foolish as to take any notice of superstitions of that kind, Salvatore. A man like you, who has been in America!"

Salvatore smiled. "In America also," he said, "I have stir the Christmas pudding for luck. I think: 'What is the difference?' "

"I'm quite sure you didn't stir it with your feet," Miss Agnes replied, "though, of course, I have never been in America. However," she sighed, "if you really think the old method is better, I suppose you will have to have your own way. But before they begin, you must provide every one of them with a scrubbing brush and some soap and see that they're used."

"Soap? In the wine? Oh, but that would spoil it! Such a thing has never been done in my life, Signorina."

"Well, you're going to do it now," Miss Agnes said firmly. "They say that what the eye doesn't see the heart doesn't grieve over, and I shall take care that mine do not witness this revolting procedure."

Miss Agnes's abstention in spite of all his persuasions—which seemed, indeed, to Miss Ellen, a trifle half-hearted—added considerably to the gaiety of the *vendemmia*, on which her presence would have fallen as a blight. Miss Ellen enjoyed every moment of it, from the golden dawns in which she went down with her basket, to the evenings, even more richly gilded by sunset, when, on the terrace outside the kitchen, the girls tucked up their skirts and the men their trousers to tread out the grapes. Not only the household of the Castello Inglese were engaged in the vintage. It was a communal harvest; and as soon as Salvatore had decided that the grapes were ready he had called in a number of pickers from the neighbouring properties to help. His choice of helpers bore testimony to the æsthetic taste which Miss Agnes had remarked in him. They were all young girls, and most of them decidedly pretty, though none, Miss Ellen decided, were more dazzling than their own Assunta, whose figure, she noticed, had developed amazingly during the summer, and whose soft cheeks showed the hue and bloom of a ripening peach. In the freedom of the vineyards and the air of this licensed festival, Assunta appeared to have shed the timidity which had made Miss Ellen feel sorry for her when she was cornered by Salvatore's hot gaze in old Carolina's kitchen. She seemed confidently aware of her beauty and grace of movement, boldly flashing her lustrous eyes and her brilliant teeth at every man who came near her, irrespective of age, with an immodesty which, but for the naturalness of her abandon, would have seemed forward and unbecoming. What a wonderful thing it must be, Miss Ellen thought, to be lovely and young and know it! Was it surprising that more than once she fancied she caught Salvatore's eyes drawn in Assunta's direction? Why shouldn't they, indeed? It pleased her romantic mind to imagine that this might be the beginning of something 'between them'. Of course, in a way, Salvatore was a little too old, and much too good for her; but then love always laughed at such differences (provided there was nobody to nip it in the bud) and the prospect of watching the development of a simple romance between two such charming people—a union of Salvatore's magnificent virility with Assunta's youthful grace—would enrich the sterile atmosphere of the Castello Inglese with an emotional interest. She could already see herself making exquisite little clothes for the baby. She could see them coming hand in hand, rather shyly, to ask her to be its godmother—though probably that privilege would be reserved for Agnes. Quite improperly, since Agnes was still a Unitarian. By evening Assunta's baby had become so real to her that she began to regard it as—very nearly—her own.

The favour of Salvatore's burning glances, indeed was widely distributed that day between his bevy of beauties. He was stimulated by their propinquity and the licensed intimacies of the *vendemmia* to the top of his form. He had never, indeed, looked more handsome, Miss Ellen thought, than now, moving among them with the possessive pride of a pasha inspecting his harem—or, perhaps, of a tall antlered stag passing to and fro amid a herd of submissive hinds. Together with the uniform of his domestic calling he had shed every trace of formality, without abating in the least his physical prepotence. That, indeed, was more evident than usual. Against the gleaming white of his shirt (Miss Ellen had always noticed with pleasure that his linen, even when it was threadbare, was clean) the skin of his strong throat, his fine features, his sinewy arms, showed the darkness as well as the firmness of bronze. In movement, his grace—though of a different and less self-conscious quality—vied with that of Assunta; and, combined with this grace—unexpectedly in a man of his years who led a sedentary life—he had a suppleness which compelled her admiration. There was nothing soft about him. It was a joy to watch the abounding strength and ease with which he lifted the heavily-laden baskets of grapes and swung them, with an action every separate movement of which would have given a sculptor delight, to the heads of the girls who carried them to be heaped on the terrace with the deliberate rhythm of figures moving in a Grecian frieze. He was as light-hearted as he was indefatigable. From time to time, as he worked, he would break into song, and the other pickers, though far less melodiously, would join him, with a spontaneity which made Miss Ellen think of the golden orioles which had pillaged the ripening cherries in May. If she could have mastered the words and the tunes, Miss Ellen would have sung too, for she envied them the delight they must surely find in giving voice to a physical exaltation which she herself experienced but was unable to express. Her dumbness made her feel it all the more deeply. In this common toil of the ripened vineyards she felt she was partaking of a pagan sacrament as intensely satisfying as that solitary rite in which she had celebrated the coming of the rain. It was a dazed ecstasy in which her normal perceptions of time and self and place disappeared. This was not Monfalcone, nor was she Ellen Isit. She had become a mere disembodied phantom of joy in a new dimension her life had never entered, save, perhaps, in the unconscious serenity of earliest childhood.

For three days, drugged with sun and toil, she laboured in the vineyards, attaining, through the absorption of a mechanical task, this Nirvana of unthinking happiness which persisted, through sheer tiredness, during the hours when she slept. The work was harder than any she had done before. There seemed no end to the wealth of purple clusters that had to be stripped from the vines. On the fourth day, when the grapes lay piled in mounds on the terrace in an air already laden with the heady fragrance of must, she took part in the crowning ceremony of the festival, the treading out of the wine.

By this time they were all, including herself, light-headed with triumph, hunger and fatigue: it was almost as though the fumes of the must had unsteadied their senses and made their thoughts reel. Laughter and song broke out more easily than ever in this abandoned mood. They were so riotously noisy and happy, so unrestrained in their horseplay, that Miss Ellen began to feel anxious lest her sister should hear them and be shocked—as, indeed, she herself had been when she caught sight of her own figure reflected in the mirror in the hall: that of a sun-brown Mænad, with wild eyes and dishevelled hair, splashed and stained from head to foot with the juice of the grape. It was Salvatore who had insisted that, if only for the sake of the good luck it would bring herself and the household, she must take the lead in the treading. Directed by him, she had stepped gingerly and decorously into the vat and felt the flesh of the bursting grapes yield beneath her. The warm juice squelched between her toes and squirted over her legs and knees under the hem of her skirt, which she lifted as high as her diminished sense of modesty permitted. As she trampled, Salvatore encouraged her.

"Good, good, magnificent, Signorina Elena!" he cried. "You are what the American call 'good sport'. This is like the baptism. Now the Signorina is truly baptized of Monfalcone. This shall be the strongest wine that was ever made at the Castello Inglese. You see when you drink!" He nodded and laughed, and the others, laughing, applauded him. "The Signorina love the wine and drink much, like a good Monfalconese."

"I think that's enough," Miss Ellen panted shyly. "Can I get out?"

"Sure, sure. Like you wish. Now I take you."

Before Miss Ellen could protest—and even if there had been time she would probably not have protested—he had picked her up bodily and deposited her on the wine-splashed terrace.

"Now thou, Assunta!" he called.

As Assunta advanced with a careless, flashing smile, Salvatore caught her waist with both hands, swung her into the air, and held her there struggling half-heartedly. Then he lowered her body, gathering it to him, and kissed her fiercely on the mouth, again and again. Miss Ellen gasped: she was at once ashamed and transported. This, indeed, must be Love! Never, even on the stage, had she seen such a prolonged and passionate embrace. And they were not acting.

It was at this moment that the catastrophe which she had been dreading occurred. Unheeded by any of the laughing company, Miss Agnes had appeared on the terrace, with Stewart at her heels. She stood there, stock-still, her eyes fixed, to the exclusion of all else, on the shameful spectacle. Miss Ellen gazed at her sister in terror. The look in those eyes was not so much one of anger as of bitter scorn and hatred. Agnes's face was old and haggard and pale as death; but in the middle of her high forehead Miss Ellen could see the vertical bulge of a single livid vein. Once or twice in her life she had seen the same sign on her father's forehead: it had always been the presage of an outburst of uncontrolled rage. Her first instinct told her to warn the storm's unconscious victims.

"Salvatore . . . Salvatore!" she whispered. "The Signorina!"

Salvatore perfunctorily dumped the shrieking Assunta into the vat and slewed round, still smiling, to meet Agnes's terrible eyes. Miss Ellen saw the smile stiffen on his lips; saw him blink and draw back instinctively, like a man who suddenly finds himself faced by a cobra ready to strike. Then, quickly recovering himself, he accepted the challenge with a defiant gaiety.

"Ah. . . Our Signorina is come to honour the little festival!" he cried. "Welcome, welcome! Now finally we are all together."

Agnes made no answer. She did not even seem to hear him. She turned slowly, majestically, and walked back to the house, with Stewart, a picture of contemptuous boredom, mechanically following her. Once she swayed and put out her hand, as though seeking for some support; then went on, so unsteadily that Miss Ellen doubted if she would reach the steps of the loggia without falling, and ran after her calling: "Agnes, Agnes! Don't go away! We are having such fun . . ." But her sister waved her back with a feeble gesture of impatience and went on her way without speaking. Miss Ellen, entering the loggia, saw her tall figure staggering across the hall and clutching the iron banister-rail as she hurried upstairs. It would be useless, she knew, to pursue her. She stood barefooted in the loggia, with tears in her eyes, while she heard Agnes's bedroom door close, and then, with deliberate finality, the click of the lock.

With a sunken heart, she returned to the group on the terrace. They were as noisy and hilarious as ever. It seemed to her that Salvatore's laughter was even noisier, as though he were deliberately determined that it should reach Agnes's ears. Carolina had brought out a flask of wine and a plate full of *zeppoli*, sweet cakes of dough fried in oil. They were all eating and drinking voraciously and talking so fast, with their mouths full, that she could not understand what they said. Salvatore urged her to join them; but she couldn't, hungry as she was. The icy terror of Agnes's eyes still haunted her; she could not escape it; it had the effect of quelling her excitement and zest, and made her unable to share the others' abandonment. She felt suddenly, desperately lonely: a stranger, a foreigner, who had neither part nor lot in an exclusive rite to which she had only been admitted on sufferance. She had been a fool, of course, to imagine that she could identify herself with these people of different race and alien culture, with whose unfathomable instincts, thoughts and emotions she had nothing in common. For all their politeness and affectation of deference, she knew now that none of them cared a button for her or would be anything but relieved if—to use Mr. Sanctuary's phrase—she 'removed the inconvenience' of her unwanted company—as was bitterly proved by the fact that when, after watching them for a while, she stole away, not even Salvatore appeared to notice her going. At this moment she felt she would have been more at home in North Bromwich.

She went up to her bedroom and, making as little noise as she could for fear of disturbing Agnes, washed the stains of the vintage from her face, her arms and her legs and changed for dinner. She would not have been surprised if, on such an occasion, Carolina had forgotten to prepare any; but, oddly enough, at the accustomed hour, the gong sounded in the hall, and when she entered the salone, Salvatore was waiting, spick and span as usual in his white coat, and ready to serve it.

"The Signorina?" he asked. "You wait for her? No?"

"We had better not wait," Ellen said. "She is still in her room. I'm afraid she has one of her headaches."

"Then I put the soup on the tray with roast bread and carry upstairs?"

"I think you had much better leave her alone. She will be better to-morrow."

"Let us hope," Salvatore said politely—but not, as Miss Ellen felt, with much conviction.

She did not enjoy her meal, though Salvatore, as was his wont when they were alone, was friendly and talkative and more than usually attentive, filling her glass more often than was necessary. Miss Ellen, though the wine raised her spirits a little, did not feel like talking. When she had finished her dinner, she went out and sat on the terrace. The air still had a milky warmth, and a late-rising moon shed a radiance of silver over the falling olive-groves, casting inky shadows from the stripped vines on the tiles of the pergola. Since the coming of the rain the song of the cicalas had ceased, and night seemed strangely silent; but the abundance of moisture had encouraged the mosquitoes to breed in multitudes: the thin whine of their wings rose and waned in Miss Ellen's ears, and though she wrapped a rug round her ankles, their bites soon forced her to go indoors.

But that night she could not sleep. It was not so much that her brain was full of the day's excitements as that it was achingly empty. She was too tired even to think; so she lay awake hour after hour listening to the chime of the clock in the hall and the fine, indistinguishable sounds that wandered like the ghosts of dead leaves about the sleeping house. Once she thought she heard steps and sat up in bed; but when she strained her ears nothing more could be heard, and she supposed she had been dreaming. It must have been two o'clock in the morning—by now she had lost count of the time—when, still half asleep, she awoke to a subconscious conviction that something was happening in the corridor outside her room. Impelled by an unreasoning curiosity, she slipped out of bed, and a moment later found herself standing at the door and eagerly listening. There was not a sound to be heard, and, as she came to her senses, she reproached herself for her foolish imagination. Yet still, against reason, that intense curiosity troubled her. She knew that something that was mysterious and which concerned her was afoot. Her bemused consciousness demanded that she should find out what it was. With uncertain fingers she lifted the latch, pulled the door ajar, and peered into the corridor.

It lay flooded with moonlight reflected from the whitewashed walls and the polished tiles of the pavement, utterly silent and seemingly empty, as her reason had told her it would be. Yet she could not be satisfied: her inward conviction that there was something wrong or unusual compelled her to open the door wider and poke her head outside. On the opposite wall of the corridor she could see the three doors of the servants' bedrooms: nearest her own Salvatore's; next, that of the room which was occupied by Carolina and her niece Maria; at the far end, Assunta's. Outside the last of these, which was in shadow, she distinguished the motionless shape of a tall woman in a white nightgown, on her knees with her ear close to the keyhole. Though she could hardly believe her eyes, the identity of the eavesdropper was unmistakable. Miss Ellen drew back with a faint gasp of surprise and closed her door guiltily. As her hand left the latch, the key fell to the floor with a tinkle. Then she hurried back to bed and lay waiting for what would happen next. But nothing happened.

9

WHEN MISS ELLEN awoke next morning her head ached, and her dazed mind was so darkened by a sense of impending disaster that she almost wished she had died in her sleep. Nothing in all her life since that awful day when she had been told the news of her lover's death in Moogly had filled her heart with so deep a despair as the sight of Agnes's humiliation. The incident affected her strangely. Quite apart from the mingled shame and pity which she felt on her sister's behalf, she was distressed to think that, quite probably, Agnes had heard the tinkle of the falling key and knew she had been watched. If she had, their next meeting would be intolerably embarrassing. The most hopeful possibility was that Agnes, being even more overwrought and exhausted than herself, would not come down to breakfast, thus giving them both time to adjust their shattered emotions sufficiently to cope with the situation.

In this hope she was disappointed. At an early hour the sounds from the room next door informed her that her sister was rising as usual. Miss Ellen herself lingered over her toilet until she was certain that Agnes had gone downstairs: it would have been the most painful accident of all for them to have emerged simultaneously from their rooms and met, face to face, on the very scene of last night's catastrophe.

Yet when she entered the salone, five minutes late, she found Agnes not only sitting at the table eating her eggs and bacon but also, apparently, enjoying her breakfast more than usual. There was no sign in her eyes of the distress which still tortured Miss Ellen. On the contrary, her features were so rigidly composed and her manner was so self-possessed that Miss Ellen began to wonder if, after all, she had not been dreaming. The only visible token of any emotional stress in Agnes's face was the slight heightening of colour over the cheek-bones which it often showed on the morning after one of her 'heads'. Salvatore also was present, looking a trifle subdued, perhaps, but none the less smiling and eager to supply their needs. The only noticeable variation from the normal was that Agnes did not address him, though she was by no means silent, and even talked to Miss Ellen more than usual.

"I am not in the least surprised," she said, "that you are late for breakfast after having worked so hard at the vintage. It is a good thing that business is over."

"I enjoyed every moment of it," Miss Ellen said, not quite truthfully.

"No doubt. But it does disturb the routine of the house, and I shall be glad to get back to normal and take things in hand again. By the way, I have come to the conclusion that we are overstaffed. There really isn't enough work in this house, with only two in the family, for a man and three maids; so I have decided to dispense with one of them."

Miss Ellen asked: "Which?"

"Assunta, naturally. It would hardly be fair to separate Carolina from her niece. Maria is a nice, quiet girl in any case. I should be sorry to lose her. Assunta, on the other hand, is more suited, I feel, to the rough life of the fields, and is much the less cleanly of the two."

"Poor little thing!" Miss Ellen hesitated. "Well . . . I suppose you know best, Agnes."

As she spoke, Ellen caught a side glance at Salvatore. He had stopped on his way to the side-table with a pile of plates in one hand, and turned round, his mouth opened, as though he were going to speak. His forehead was flushed brick-red to the roots of his curling hair; his tawny eyes blazed with a murderous light such as she had never seen in them, and his handsome face had grown ugly with anger. Miss Ellen trembled, twisting her napkin nervously, in a silence charged with a high potential of violence like a momentary lull in a thunderstorm. It was no use his glaring at Agnes like that, she thought, for her sister's eyes were firmly fixed on her empty plate as though she were determined not to see him. Then, apparently, Salvatore thought better of it. He turned again on his heel, planked the plates down noisily on the sideboard, whipped his napkin over his arm, and made straight for the door.

"Salvatore!" Miss Agnes said calmly.

He answered mechanically, without facing her: "Si, Signorina? Commandi?"

"I suppose you will not be going to the vineyard this morning?"

"No, Signorina."

"In that case I shall want to see you as usual, in—let me see—half an hour's time, when I have spoken to Assunta. Do you hear me?"

"Si, Signorina."

He closed the door briskly, almost slamming it, and went out.

A smile quivered on Agnes's lips. Miss Ellen noticed that she hid it by using her napkin. She also saw that her breath came quickly and that the colour on her cheeks glowed in patches as she rose and turned her back.

"Do not forget this evening, Ellen," she said.

"This evening? What do you mean?"

"We are dining at Mrs. Spettigue's. It will be a big party, no doubt; and I think it is important we should both of us look our best. I shall wear my ivory satin."

For Miss Ellen the remainder of the day resembled a prolongation of her nightmare. Now that the excitement of the vintage was over, she felt herself at a loose end and could settle to nothing. She took out a book to read, but sat with it unopened on her lap, watching old Antonino removing the tubs of must, sweeping and swilling crushed grapes and stalks away from the juice-splashed terrace, whose stained and littered surface suggested the peculiar squalor of the floor of a tap-room on the morning after a bank holiday, or the scene of an orgy—which, indeed, it was. The house—that dear house which she had always found so friendly!—seemed eerily foreboding and lifeless, as though it shared the weight of her own emotional distress. Silent, too: she missed the brief, sudden outbursts of song which usually issued from the kitchen windows when the maids and Salvatore were busied about their morning work. At this moment, no doubt, Assunta was being dismissed. Miss Ellen could imagine the scene without seeing it: the tears, the entreaties, the protests—all equally unavailing against the cold iron of Agnes's will. She felt sorry for Assunta: the poor child was so full of life, such an incarnation of full-blooded youth and generous impulse, so poor a match for Agnes's grim maturity. She felt sorry—though rather less so—for Salvatore too. His frolics—even his kisses—seemed harmless enough when they were seen in proper proportion against the background of established customs which no foreigner had a right to judge. Even English girls were sometimes kissed under the mistletoe, though she never had been.

She pitied Salvatore even more (for by now the half-hour had passed) as she pictured him standing before Agnes's judgment-seat in the salone. She knew well how cutting Agnes's tongue could be—particularly when edged by a righteous indignation, though she felt sure he was much better able to take care of himself than poor little Assunta. After all, Agnes knew which side her bread was buttered, and was much too level-headed to allow her annoyance to deprive herself of a confidential servant the use of whose skill and efficiency was a prime condition of her life at the Castello Inglese. Miss Ellen was sorry she had not thought to place her deck-chair within earshot of the salone, though when she looked down the terrace she noticed that all the windows had been shut, so that she would probably have heard nothing, in any case, of what went on inside. Whatever they were talking about, the interview was lasting longer than usual. If it were over she would almost certainly have seen Salvatore pass on his way back to the kitchen, or at least heard his voice as he discussed it with Carolina.

She sat wondering so long that, as a consequence of her

sleepless night, she finally dozed off in her chair and slept until she was awakened by the boom of the gong for luncheon.

"Well, now I suppose I shall know the worst," she thought, as she passed through the hall and timidly entered the salone.

To her surprise Agnes was not there. Even more surprisingly, the table had been laid for one. That could only mean that Agnes, poor thing, had 'gone down' with another headache; it also implied that Mrs. Spettigue's grand dinner-party would be 'off'. As she stood looking at the half-empty table, Salvatore bustled in with a dish of her favourite food, *ravioli*, which Carolina only provided on special occasions. His face was still flushed, but not, this time, with anger, for his lips wore a jaunty smile. Was it possible, she wondered, that Agnes's onslaught had driven him to drink? She pointed to the single cover.

"The Signorina?" she said.

"The Signorina, she eat her luncheon upstairs. Maria carry it."

"Oh, what can be the matter? Is she ill, Salvatore?"

Salvatore laughed. "Ill? Not at all. She is very well. *Sta molto bene . . . benone.* She say I tell you she has not sleep too well through the night and must repose in bed this afternoon before she dress herself for the party. Eat well, Signorina—very good *ravioli* of buffalo-cheese, and plenty of wine. Then you go to bed just the same till the hour of tea-time. Always very late parties at the Signora Spettigue's. If you not rest you go to sleep before you come home. Very grand party, very diverting. The Signorina wear her white dress we buy in Naples, with the diamonds over the head."

"Are you perfectly sure she's all right?"

"*Non dubitare*, Signorina. I tell you already. Now eat well, before they grow cold."

Inspired by Salvatore's smiles, Miss Ellen devoured the double helping of *ravioli*, and drank so heartily that she almost found courage to ask him for his private account of Assunta's dismissal and his own interview with her sister;

but she forbore—partly out of a sentimental respect for his feelings, and partly because she had retained enough presence of mind to realize that it would be imprudent to 'go behind' Agnes's back.

It was evident—and also surprising—that in the matter of Assunta those feelings had not been deeply wounded. Perhaps, after all, her romantic imagination had overestimated the depth of his passion: perhaps, as Miss Murphy's reading of his character suggested, he had only been trifling with the poor girl's affections. As to his interview with Agnes, the problem was more mysterious. If they had quarrelled seriously, she would not have expected to find Salvatore in such a light-hearted mood: if they had parted in anger, Agnes certainly wouldn't have told him that she was going to wear her ivory satin and tiara that evening. Whatever had happened, it seemed that, in the end, Salvatore's combination of charm and tact had triumphed. If they had, she could only admire him the more. No other person—except Papa, whose methods, of course, were different—had ever been able to 'manage' Agnes before. In any case, it was a relief to know that the storm had passed over. So she left it at that, and, obeying Salvatore, went to bed and slept like a log.

She awoke to hear the clock in the hall chime seven, and to realize that, unless she started dressing immediately, she would be behind time. Remembering what Agnes had said, she took unusual care with her toilet and arrived downstairs out of breath to find her waiting. The morning's excitements, far from exhausting Agnes, had evidently done her good. Never in all Miss Ellen's experience had her beauty appeared more challenging or more brilliantly outshone her own dowdiness. The ivory satin *robe de style* had an artful simplicity of line and a perfection of cut that revealed the shape of Agnes's figure with a far subtler effect than the more flamboyant 'creations' of Salvatore's choice. It was that of a young woman: at a distance one would not have given her a day over thirty-five. Nor was that all. The lustre of her eyes and of her raven hair vied with that of the paste that sparkled in her tiara and the buckles of her shoes; while her consciousness of her own elegance gave her face an air of serenity, of happiness, of sweetness, of softness, which, even at her best, it had lacked for many years. Though she had never ceased to admire her, it seemed to Miss Ellen that the old epithets she had so often applied to her sister, such as 'queenly' or 'distinguished', were no longer adequate. There was a new element in her beauty which, obviously correct as the description was, she could only call 'virginal'.

"Oh, Agnes," she cried. "How lovely! You look like a bride."

Agnes laughed—and the laugh was neither defensive nor scornful.

"Well . . . I think the dress suits me," she said modestly. "If we had only thought of shortening it in time, you might have worn my brocade. Salvatore is already outside with the carriage, so we had better be starting."

Mrs. Spettigue's dinner party, for all their anticipations of grandeur, was not very different, apart from the elaborateness of the cooking and the addition of champagne, from the others the Miss Isits had attended. It could hardly have been otherwise; for the social material available in Monfalcone was limited. Most of the guests were old friends. Mr. Potter and Mr. Sanctuary were both there, smartened-up for the occasion. Mrs. Hamilton-Gough, in gold tissue that fitted her nowhere, surveyed Agnes's white satin with a sourly competitive eye, but appeared slightly reassured by the sight of Miss Ellen's black lace. The Principe doddered in, late and half-shaven as usual, with his surviving wife, followed by the stout Marchesa, in a figured cretonne which made her resemble a badly-upholstered arm-chair, and her husband, the Marquis, who looked what he was: a not very prosperous Neapolitan lawyer.

The only member of the company with whom Miss Ellen was not already more or less distantly acquainted, was her hostess. In Mrs. Spettigue's case she felt disinclined to agree with Salvatore's social judgement. For all the grandeur of her house and her party, she seemed to Miss Ellen a gross and vulgar woman, by whose side even Mrs. Hamilton-Gough appeared a paragon of refinement and good form. To begin with—and this novel spectacle shocked Miss Ellen deeply—Mrs. Spettigue's cheeks were plastered with a coating of crimson which looked as if it might have been splashed on by a scene-painter. This raddle was of a shade that clashed equally with those of her copper-dyed hair and a vermilion dress spangled with silver, whose bodice, hazardously confining a bosom even more voluminous than the Marchesa's, shook violently whenever she laughed (and she never spoke without laughing) releasing, with each gust, a carillon of tinkling sequins. The best that could be said for her vulgarity, Miss Ellen decided, was that it was good-natured and that she was aware of it. She was evidently on familiar terms with all her other guests—particularly the men, boisterously chaffing poor Mr. Sanctuary, who, in spite of his curly smile, looked like a piece of frail Dresden jostled by a pint pot of earthenware, and cracking jokes (which were probably risky, Miss Ellen thought) with Mr. Potter, whose face reddened so furiously whenever she spoke to him that it seemed on the point of bursting. Her voice had a moist, throaty quality, which gave the impression that she was gargling her words.

And yet Mrs. Spettigue was undeniably kind. She was the very first member of Monfalcone society who had ever gone out of her way to notice Miss Ellen, as she now did with an embarrassing effusiveness, at the same time almost pointedly, it appeared, neglecting Miss Agnes.

"Now, I won't have you standing in the background like that, Miss Isit," she said. "I expect you know everyone here, or, if you don't, you ought to. We don't worry about 'p's' or 'q's' in this house, I'm thankful to say. We prefer to enjoy ourselves. If you don't, it'll be your fault, not mine; and whatever you do, I promise to keep my eyes shut. We're all boys and girls together. You needn't be scared, dear. There's only one man here to-night who's really dangerous, and that's my old friend Charlie Potter. Ha-ha-ha! Do you hear what I say, Potter?"

Miss Ellen thought it most odd that she omitted the Mister.

Mr. Potter turned round: "What's that? What's that?" he demanded.

"I'm telling this nice girl here to beware of your wicked wiles."

"Wiles? . . . Wicked? . . . *Me?*" Mr. Potter's eyes goggled so fiercely that his monocle shot out. He bowed, as far as his starched collar would permit, over Miss Ellen's hand. "Miss Isit and I are old friends." He refixed his monocle and glared at her. "Old friends. . . . Is that true, Miss Isit? The answer is 'yes'. Are you frightened of me? Not a bit. Who is the person our hostess ought to have warned you against? Ronnie Sanctuary. The poor old boy's looking remarkably frail to-night, don't you notice the change in him? Failing rapidly, I'm afraid."

Mrs. Spettigue handed him off like a Rugby three-quarter running for the line. "Oh, come off it, Potter! Ronnie's tougher than you are," she said, "and not so fat. I'm ready to bet he'll outlive the lot of us. But let's be serious. You're going to sit on Miss Isit's right at the dinner table. Now isn't that nice for you? But you mustn't monopolize her."

"Why not?" Mr. Potter demanded gallantly.

"Because she's too young and innocent for a wicked old man like you," Mrs. Spettigue pushed him again and laughed so uproariously that Miss Ellen felt sure her sister's eyes would be drawn to them in disapproval—as indeed they were. "And also," their hostess went on with a wheezy roar which was the nearest her powerful voice could get to a whisper, "because I want her to entertain a distinguished visitor. Now don't be jealous, Potter, you won't have an outsider's chance with him. He's a bachelor with a title."

"Another of your shoddy Neapolitan dukes, I suppose," Mr. Potter said scornfully.

"Not at all. He's a knight, and as English as you and

me. To tell you the honest truth, I'm scared stiff of him. A professor, or something of that sort. I've no brains, have I, Potter?"

"The answer . . ." Mr. Potter began; but Mrs. Spettigue gave him no time to finish the sentence.

"As a matter of fact," she broke in, "I've never set eyes on him. I just happened to hear that a titled Englishman was staying down at the *pensione*, so of course I invited him; but I shouldn't be a bit surprised if he found us too easy-going—you know what I mean? That's why I've put him next to *you*, Miss Isit: I don't know if you *are*, but I'm sure you look far more brainy than me."

"If only you could have put him next to my sister . . ."

"No, no, that wouldn't do. I have to put someone who speaks good Italian next to the Principe, so she has to sit there. The new guest ought really to be next to the Marchesa. But she doesn't speak English at all, so that wouldn't do, either. It just comes to this, dear: you and I have got to share him and make the best of it. If he starts talking science or whatnot, I shall push him right on to you. Goodness gracious, this must be him! Don't run away, dear. Stay here, and I'll introduce you."

With a gust of unmeaning laughter that nearly blew them both off their feet and set all the sequins tinkling, Mrs. Spettigue pushed her bosom through the throng like the stem of an ice-breaker, and returned, a moment later, with an elderly, grey-haired gentleman in tow. He was a refined, a distinguished figure, Miss Ellen thought, with a pleasant, clean-shaven face and extremely well-cut clothes. Though somewhat bewildered by Mrs. Spettigue's boisterous reception he had the composure of a man who is sure of himself. As she saw him advancing, Miss Ellen was troubled by something familiar in his features which she could not define—unless it were a faint resemblance to Salvatore; but before she could search her memory for a more plausible explanation, her hostess was introducing him.

"Miss Isit, allow me to present Sir Benjamin Dench. That's right, isn't it?"

"Yes, indeed," the stranger replied. "But Miss Isit . . . Can it be possible?"

Miss Ellen laughed: "You can't really remember me. I'm Ellen Isit. I was only a girl when we met, with my hair down my back."

"Tied up with a black velvet bow. I remember you perfectly. Is your sister Agnes still . . . living?"

"That is she—over there, in white satin."

"Well, really. Upon my word! Most remarkable! She looks hardly a day older than when I last saw her—how many years ago?"

"I think we had better not count them," Miss Ellen said.

"No. You're right. Very much better let the sleeping years lie. I was doing some work at the time on malaria. Manson's papers had been published but Ross hadn't made his discoveries. I remember your father well, too. Of course he's retired. Is he still going strong? At my age one is chary of asking questions of that kind."

"He died, nearly five years ago."

"I'm sorry. . . . Your sister is married, of course?"

"No. . . . She never married."

"Dear, dear . . . what a pity." He hesitated. "Neither did I. What are you doing here?"

"We've been living here since the spring. Our uncle, my mother's brother, left us a house called the Castello Inglese. And you?"

"Oh, I'm a mere bird of passage, a tourist. I gave up my professorial chair a couple of years ago. English winters don't suit me, so I've simply been idling round in search of a place with a tolerable climate to settle in. I'm attracted by Monfalcone, I must confess. You and your sister have found it agreeable?"

"Agreeable? I think it's the most wonderful place in the world. But I'm not at all sure you would find it equally attractive to live in. There'ld be nothing for you to do here."

Sir Benjamin laughed. "That's precisely what attracts me most. I've worked very hard during the years we've agreed not to number, and the idea of doing nothing appeals to me."

"That's quite understandable, of course. What I really meant was . . . well . . . that it would be difficult for a man so . . . distinguished as you are to cut himself off from the world to which he's accustomed."

"Distinguished?" Sir Benjamin laughed. "You mean my poor little knighthood? That was the purest accident. It just happened that a royal visit coincided with my Vice-Chancellorship of the University. They had to knight somebody or other, and fell back on me."

"Still, you *are* Sir Benjamin," Miss Ellen said reprovingly.

"From the best of my recollection, I used to be 'Ben'. Don't you think, as old friends, we ought to return to it?"

During the dinner that followed, both Mrs. Spettigue and Mr. Potter were relieved of the duty of entertaining Sir Benjamin Dench and Miss Ellen, who found so much to talk about that they had neither time nor inclination to speak to their other neighbours. In spite of his rejection by Agnes, Sir Benjamin evidently remembered Moogly Meringapatam with a wistful affection. It was natural that both of them should avoid any direct allusion to that painful incident; yet Miss Ellen could not help noticing how, from time to time, Sir Benjamin took off his glasses and gazed, with a puzzled air, at her sister now launched upon brilliant flights of Dantesque Italian on the opposite side of the table. When he put them on again, he sighed and shook his head and said: "H'm . . ."

Miss Ellen was deeply moved by his obvious fascination, of which Agnes, engrossed by the Principe, seemed quite unconscious. In all probability she had not heard Sir Benjamin's name and had no idea that he was looking at her, though her outstanding brilliance that evening gave her the right to claim the admiration of every man in the room. What would happen, Miss Ellen wondered, when Ben Dench and she actually met? The situation was so full of dramatic possibilities that she could not resist the temptation of imagining its climax: a *scène à faire* in which

Agnes and her old lover, confronted, stood gazing at one another with tears in their eyes—all the mistakes and misunderstandings of the painful past forgotten or forgiven in one exquisite moment of reconciliation in which Heart spoke to Heart.

Indeed, her prophetic imagination leapt on so rapidly that by the time Mr. Potter was choking over the red mullet of the second course, her sister had ceased to be Miss Isit and had become Lady Dench. Though Miss Ellen could see herself illumined by the glory reflected from Agnes and hear herself referring casually, among strangers, to 'my sister, Lady Dench', the main source of these romantic fancies was neither snobbish nor personal; they sprang rather from an innocent and generous desire to witness the happy ending which would transform her sister into what she should always rightly have been: the princess of a fairy-tale in real life. Was it too late, was Agnes too old for a part in this transformation scene? The answer (as Mr. Potter would have said) was emphatically 'no'. One glance at her this evening, scintillating—that was Mr. Sanctuary's word!—in white satin at the Principe's side, was sufficient to confirm it beyond dispute. As for herself, in an unobtrusive way, she would do all she could to make that sweet dream come true.

With this subtle purpose in mind she endeavoured again to divert their conversation in the direction of Agnes. It would be just as well, for example, though perhaps hardly necessary, to let Sir Benjamin know that Agnes now possessed a substantial income and property of her own, and to insist, again, on the freedom of her life during the years in which they had lost sight of one another from the least hint of any romantic complication. But Sir Benjamin, apparently, was not having any of that. Though he encouraged her once or twice more by removing his glasses and furtively surveying Agnes with a glance that showed more curiosity than attraction, he was more interested, it seemed, in the excellent food (which, confessing a tendency to dyspepsia, he ate with caution), in the climate, social conditions and cost of living in

Monfalcone, and in the private history of Miss Ellen herself, who was so unused to anyone taking notice of her in preference to Agnes that she was almost too shy to answer his personal questions.

"You know, Ellen," he said—"you don't mind my calling you that, do you?—the mere fact of our meeting again and talking like this after so many years has a curiously pleasant and softening effect on one. It brings back the past so vividly and makes it so delightful that one begins to feel sentimental, which is odd for a white-haired old man like me."

"How can you call yourself old, Ben!" Miss Ellen protested. "You're different, of course, from what you were at Moogly; but you're still in the prime of life. I always think white hair is so distinguished; and you must confess you can look back on a wonderful career. It must be delightful to be able to rest on your laurels."

"Well, well. . . . I suppose a man is as old as he feels; and I must admit that I feel remarkably young this evening, and have done so, indeed, ever since I arrived at Monfalcone. It must be the air. *You* certainly seem to thrive on it. You've changed very little, you know, since I last saw you at Moogly, though your hair isn't down your back."

"What nonsense you talk, Ben! It isn't fair to flatter a middle-aged spinster like that. Now, if you were speaking of Agnes. . . . Only look at her!"

Sir Benjamin Dench showed no desire to do so.

"Yes, indeed, I admit she's remarkably well-preserved. She was always handsome. That hard, clear-cut type of woman often wears well."

"Agnes isn't hard in the least. How can you suggest it?"

"She's a great deal harder—and always was—than her little sister. Of course, you were only a child in those far-off days, but I've always remembered you; and when I look at you now . . ."

He did look at her fixedly. Yet, strangely enough, his scrutiny did not disconcert her or make her blush, like Salvatore's, though the colour of their eyes was the same.

Sir Benjamin's were friendly and honest and wise, Miss Ellen thought. Above all, they were kind. Even if the bouquets he offered her were old-fashioned and slightly faded—and what compliments made to a woman of her age were not?—they were at least more genuine than Ronnie Sanctuary's elaborate arrangements of immortelles, and their perfume, though faint, was sweet to her, while the smile that accompanied the gift had no trace of irony. It was a delight to meet a celebrity, whose services to his country had been appropriately honoured, and to find him so completely unspoilt, so unpretentious. Perhaps this was partly due to his having belonged to a profession which was notably humane, richly endowed with experience and understanding of human nature. And, after all, there were no friends like old friends: in their company one didn't have to defend or explain oneself.

Indeed, the more she thought of it, the more surely was she convinced that Destiny or Providence had brought Sir Benjamin Dench to Monfalcone with the deliberate intention of throwing him and Agnes together again in circumstances from which all the old impediments to their marriage had been removed. And what a delightful couple they would make: his stable nature and simple charm the perfect foil to Agnes's dignity!

"We must make plans at once," she said, "for you to come and see our house. I feel sure you'll love it. What about to-morrow afternoon?"

"That would have been delightful. Unfortunately it can't be done. I've booked my berth on the boat from Naples to Palermo, and shall have to leave here in the morning. After a month in Sicily I intend to go on to Egypt."

"Oh, but how disappointing! Why didn't we know you were here before?"

"That was just my bad luck. I had no idea you were living here, or, of course I should have called. Now that we've met, Monfalcone attracts me more than ever, and I shall certainly come here again in the spring on my way back from Egypt. In the meantime I wish you would keep a look-out for a modest villa suited to an elderly gentleman of moderate means. You see, for the first time in my life I am my own master and free to live where I like, and, as I've told you, I'm looking for a quiet home in some place with a decent climate and not too many social distractions. Will you do that for me?"

"Of course. . . . But I'm dreadfully sorry you're going," Miss Ellen said despondently. "What a shame you weren't sitting by Agnes! It would have been such fun for both of you. Why, I don't suppose she even knows you are here. I must try to catch her eye now, or somebody else is bound to get hold of her."

As she spoke, Miss Ellen launched an appealing glance in Agnes's direction. It was in vain. Her sister's eyes were staring in front of her. What was more, her face was no longer sweet or serene, but distorted and suffused by a flush of indignation. Her thin hands were clasped so tightly that her finger-tips had gone white, and a similar tensity stiffened her figure. Evidently something had angered her. Miss Ellen could not guess what. She had been so engrossed in the excitement of her encounter with Benjamin Dench that for the last half-hour she had neither heard nor seen what was happening at the table around her, being conscious of nothing in it but a clatter of tongues and cutlery regularly punctuated by Mrs. Spettigue's gusts of raucous laughter; but now there was no doubt that, unknown to her, something monstrous and unseemly had occurred. Her heart fluttered and fell. Wasn't it just like Fate, she asked herself, that this wonderful moment when everything seemed to be going so well, this romantic meeting deferred for so many years, should be ruined in this cruel fashion?

Though she still went on talking to her neighbour, all her thoughts were with Agnes. What could have upset her like this? Had Mrs. Spettigue shocked her modesty with some indecent word or tale that no lady could hear? Had the Principe insulted her with some dishonourable gesture or proposal? She could not imagine. She only knew that

Agnes was suffering acutely and longed to comfort her. At the moment when Mrs. Spettigue, with a final blast, upheaved her tinkling bust and rose from the table, Ellen forsook her companion and made a dart for her sister.

"What is it, Agnes?" she whispered. "Is there something the matter with you?"

"I'll tell you later. We're going home at once. I refuse to stay under this roof another moment."

"But Agnes darling, we *can't* go like that!" Miss Ellen pleaded.

"We are going immediately. I have told the servant to ask Salvatore to bring round the carriage."

"There's still time," Miss Ellen said. "I have such a surprise for you."

"I've had quite enough surprises to go on with," Agnes snapped.

"My neighbour at dinner . . ." Miss Ellen gasped inarticulately. "You didn't see who he was?"

"Of course not. You know I'm short-sighted."

"It was Benjamin Dench."

"*Who?*"

"Sir Benjamin Dench, dear. The one we knew at Moogly. He's longing to speak to you."

Agnes gave a harsh laugh: "*That* man? I'd forgotten his existence. Why should he want to see me, or I him? Come along now. The carriage is here. The servant is beckoning."

Miss Agnes clutched Ellen's arm. Her hand was icy.

"But we can't go without saying good-bye to our hostess, Agnes," Ellen protested.

"I have no wish to speak to that woman ever again."

She tugged Miss Ellen along rapidly under the bows of Mr. Potter, who jumped back with surprise as though he had been stung, while Mr. Sanctuary, from the distance, raked them with a long-range leer, and Sir Benjamin made a futile attempt to give chase as Ellen helplessly waved him good-bye from the drawing-room door. Salvatore was waiting to hand them into the carriage.

"The Signorine part early," he said, "at the hour

when the others begin. That is a pity."

"Tell him to drive straight home," Agnes said, without explanation.

"I *do* wish you'ld tell me, Agnes," Miss Ellen whispered.

"Please be quiet. Not before Salvatore."

They drove home in silence; Agnes burning with an indignation whose heat could almost be felt; Ellen consumed with regret for the frustration of her planned scene and impatient to know what had caused it. When they entered the salone, Salvatore, who was equally curious, seemed inclined to linger. Miss Agnes dismissed him, but had to speak twice before he went—which, as Miss Ellen noted, was unusual. As soon as the door closed behind him, Agnes spoke. It was clear that she was still suffering from a painful emotion, so exhausted that she had to sit down.

"That abominable woman!" she said.

"She's vulgar and noisy, of course," Ellen said, "but I must say she seemed kind—to me at any rate."

"To *you?* Naturally! She made a fuss of you, didn't she? That was only part of her plan to humiliate me, to take her revenge. In the early part of the evening she hardly spoke to me. Later on, when she'd whipped herself up with champagne, she let herself go and showed what was at the bottom of her filthy mind."

"Filthy, Agnes?"

"Yes, filthy! If I could think of a more horrible word for her I would use it."

"I can't understand . . ."

"Of course you can't. You've the mind of a child of ten." Agnes paused for a moment. "Do you remember what Salvatore told us about her—how she had tried to bribe him to leave us by offering him a fantastic wage to come to her? That, no doubt, was the root of her behaviour. Jealousy. Since she couldn't have him for herself she was determined to blacken his reputation in my eyes. She began by joking about it, in abominable taste, with Mr. Sanctuary; but I could see that every word was aimed at myself. Then she turned her foul tongue on me, and said she supposed I realized what everyone else in Monfalcone knew: that Salvatore was a man of the basest character: that he'd lived on the earnings of loose women in Naples; that the police still kept their eyes on him; that he was well known to have been involved in every kind of disgusting vice. Then she dragged Uncle Ludovic into it, and another man whose name I forget, an American, whom she said Salvatore had blackmailed so cruelly that he took his own life. Then she leered at me and burst out with one of those horrible laughs. 'I suppose,' she said, 'you two old girls think you're in love with him? It seems to run in the family, doesn't it?' That was what she said, though I'm sure I don't know what she meant by it."

"But how monstrous! . . . How *could* she?" Miss Ellen broke in with indignation. "Even to suggest that we . . ."

Incredibly, Agnes smiled. It was a strange, a horrible smile, Miss Ellen thought. Then she spoke more calmly, in a flat, exhausted voice: "There is nothing monstrous about it," she said. "That was the first time she spoke the truth. I do love Salvatore and he loves me. I am going to marry him."

"Oh, Agnes! Agnes!" Miss Ellen cried. "It's impossible. You must be mad."

"Impossible? Why impossible?"

"What . . . oh dear, dear, dear . . . oh, what would Papa have felt?"

Agnes laughed, with the strange harshness that Miss Ellen had heard in her voice before. She spoke with trembling lips, her whole face contorted.

"Papa is dead and buried," she said, "but I am alive—*alive*, really alive, for the first time in all my life."

"But . . . Oh, Agnes, I beg you to think before you do anything . . ."

Agnes pushed back her chair and rose towering above her with angry eyes.

"Will you hold your tongue, Ellen, and listen to me? I have thought till I'm sick of thinking. Now I've made up my mind. Don't stare at me in that stupid fashion.

I am not a young woman, I know, but I am not too old to have feelings . . . natural feelings—nor are you, for that matter; so you may as well stop pretending, as I have done. What have our lives been, yours and mine? Only think of them: all those barren, wasted years in India and North Bromwich when we gave up our youth to a selfish old man who thought so little of it and so much of himself that he squandered his money and left us to starve, for all he cared!"

"Agnes . . . Agnes, stop! I can't hear you speak of Papa like that!"

"Oh yes you can, and you will. There's no harm in you facing the truth for once in a way, Ellen. Starve . . . That is the word. We'd been starved before that. I've been starving for thirty-five years—for half a lifetime. And I didn't know it. Nobody ever told me. But I know what I was starving for now, Ellen. I was starving for love. I wanted a lover, a man: and at last, thank God! I've got one. Nothing, nothing in this world is going to take him away from me. Do you understand now?" Her voice quavered: "Oh, Ellen, Ellen, if you only, only knew how lonely I've been and how happy I am!"

She sank down in her chair and put her thin hands to her eyes as she broke into tears. Miss Ellen was crying too as she knelt beside her and gathered her in her arms to console her.

10

The marriage between Agnes Isit and Salvatore Ferraro was duly solemnized, a fortnight later, in the town hall of Monfalcone, after preliminary formalities at the British Consulate in Naples, but without any religious ceremony. Her sister's neglect to solicit the blessing of God on her union distressed Miss Ellen; for although, since their arrival in Monfalcone, she had been deprived of the ritual consolations of her religion (having been shocked on her one and only visit to the church with the golden cupola by its odour, which was not that of sanctity), she still believed that marriage was a sacrament and that a mere civil contract had no validity.

On a less serious plane, she was equally disappointed that this wedding, the first in the family, should have lacked the proper accompaniments of a train of bridesmaids, orange-blossom, *The Voice that Breathed o'er Eden*, and tears in the vestry; but indeed her mind was so numbed and bewildered by the rapidity and unexpectedness of the whole affair that she was hardly capable of indulging these regrets. The one thing that could console her for its unromantic nature was her ardent but not very confident hope that Agnes would be happy.

Agnes herself appeared to have no doubts about this. For all her deliberate rejection of conventional sentiment, she could not disguise an elation which Miss Ellen found harrowing. Her mood had the fateful effulgence of a candle-flame that flares before it dies down; beneath her affectation of matter-of-factness she was as excited and tremulous as a young girl, displaying, at the same time, an affectionate gentleness so foreign to her nature that Miss Ellen frequently found herself on the verge of tears.

Salvatore appeared no less elated than his prospective bride, though the quality of his elation differed from hers, being rather that of a man who had wagered a big stake and won—so surprisingly that he was still unable to grasp the extent of his winnings. Up till the very eve of the wedding he continued to perform his domestic duties, waiting on the Miss Isits at table as usual and conducting himself, in every respect, as though, until the ceremony was completed, he still regarded himself as their paid servant. It seemed rather odd to Miss Ellen that affianced lovers should behave with such constraint. No endearments ever passed between them in her presence; he still, out of habit no doubt, addressed Agnes as 'Signorina', and took his own meals in the kitchen with Carolina.

It was not until she was on the point of leaving for Naples

that Agnes made any reference to the domestic arrangements which would have to be made to meet their new condition.

"I am afraid," she said, "I shall have to ask you to change bedrooms with Salvatore on our return. As a matter of fact the one that he has been occupying is quite pleasant, and in summer actually cooler than yours."

For a moment Miss Ellen was stupefied. Her room, with its balcony open to wind and sun, commanding the superb sweep of the olive-groves from the mountain's crags to the sea, had grown dear to her; its wide vista, continually changing, yet ever new, had become one of the most precious sources of pleasure and consolation in her life at Monfalcone. Quite apart from this, she had a right to it. After all, the Castello Inglese was as much hers as Agnes's. She felt it her duty to rebel.

"Isn't it usual," she asked, "for married people to occupy the same bedroom?"

Agnes blushed. "Unfortunately, yes. Salvatore, however, prefers to sleep in a room of his own. I think it shows great delicacy on his part. Of course, when we come home," she went on, "a great many other things will have to be changed. Naturally, Salvatore will take his meals with us in the salone, and Maria will wait at table. Without him we shall find ourselves rather short-handed in the house, so we have decided to take back Assunta."

"Assunta? I thought you said . . ."

"It is on my conscience that I may have treated her a little harshly; but she will be none the worse for having learnt her lesson. She is flighty and thoughtless, but Salvatore assures me that her morals are all that they should be, and she knows the routine of the house so well that it seems a pity her training should be wasted."

"I'm glad you think that. I must say I always liked her. Is there anything else?"

"Well, yes . . . After thinking it over carefully, it seems to us only right and proper that newly-married people should enjoy a measure of privacy—that we ought to really keep a sitting-room to ourselves. A man always likes to feel he has a den of his own. So we've decided to use the studio."

"You mean . . ." Ellen halted. "Then I shan't be able to use the piano?"

"Oh, I never thought of that. Still, we shan't always be there. You will be able to play it sometimes, I expect. I've already told Carolina to change the bedrooms, so you'll have nothing to worry about." Her face lit up suddenly: "Ah, here's Salvatore. That means, I expect, that the carriage is waiting. Is the luggage all in?"

Salvatore smiled and nodded, without removing a black Neapolitan cigar from his teeth. "All ready," he said. "Now we go. Come along, Agnes."

For a moment Miss Ellen was shocked by the change in his manners. He did not draw back as usual, with a bow, to allow them to pass into the hall, but stalked on ahead, with a rapid, swaggering walk which seemed of itself to assert his new position. He was, Miss Ellen admitted to herself, beautifully dressed in a dove-grey flannel suit that had come, no doubt, from her Uncle Ludovic's inexhaustible wardrobe; but, oddly enough, it struck her that he looked less distinguished—much less, indeed, like a gentleman—in this than in the more formal black clothes he had adapted as a uniform. The light colour emphasized the redness and thickness of the back of his neck; and the suit, which had evidently been cut for a slighter figure, made him look grosser than she could have believed. It was a pity, she thought, that he had chosen to wear that large silver horn, an amulet protective against the evil eye, suspended from his watch-chain; and really Agnes should have told him that a gentleman should not keep on his hat in the house or wear it rakishly cocked on one side out-of-doors. She was even more shocked when, instead of waiting to hand her sister into the carriage, Salvatore got in first and sat down without paying her any attention, folding his arms and leaning back carelessly as he puffed at his cigar. Agnes was barely settled in and had not even time to arrange her skirt, before he gave the coachman the signal to start, and the two-horse carriage leapt forward, nearly jolting her out of her seat.

Miss Ellen stood at the gate with the bored Stewart at her side and watched it jog down the hill. It seemed, for a while, as if Agnes were not even going to wave her good-bye; but, at the turn in the winding road, she looked back and raised her gloved hand. At a distance her face seemed to Miss Ellen unnaturally small and pale and fragile—particularly in comparison with the back-view of Salvatore's bull-neck. When Agnes turned it again and spoke to Salvatore, who answered her with an impatient jerk of the head, tears of love and compassion dimmed Miss Ellen's eyes. She felt as though her sister were being carried away from her, perhaps for ever, into a future shadowed by omens of indefinite doom. Suppressing her tears, which Stewart regarded with slightly puzzled contempt, she herself turned away and went blindly upstairs to her room—that room which, in a week's time, would be hers no longer—and threw herself down on her bed to have a good cry.

No longer constrained by the presence of Agnes and Salvatore, the tension of the Castello Inglese immediately relaxed. Monfalcone had never appeared more lovely that in this October weather; its hill-sides dyed with the crimson of turning vine-leaves, the groves thronged, and musical with the faint songs of the earliest olive-pickers. Maria, together with Assunta, who had returned to the house as though nothing had happened, on the evening following the honeymooners' departure, sang all day in the kitchen, more shrilly than they would have dared had Agnes been there. It was evident that nobody regarded Miss Ellen as a person of any importance. All her meals were hurriedly prepared, badly cooked, and served late by Maria, who didn't even trouble to make herself tidy.

Miss Ellen didn't mind that. She even found it a relief not to be always on her best behaviour, to share in the relaxation of a discipline which she had occasionally found irksome. But she did miss Agnes more than she could have imagined. This was actually the first time they had been separated since they were girls, and, try as she would, she couldn't forget that last pathetic glimpse she had caught of her when she turned in the vanishing carriage and waved her hand. She tried to console herself with an orgy of music; but the blight of an imminent farewell to her piano shadowed this too, and not even Mendelssohn could conjure away her dark mood; so, for most of the time, she sat out on the terrace, lazily watching Waifie's pursuit of the remaining lizards, which had changed the emerald greens of spring for the dun hues of autumn, and had already grown sluggish with the approach of hibernation. On that high terrace she did not hear—and perhaps it was just as well—even the faintest echoes of the roar of ribald laughter with which the comedy of Agnes's wedding convulsed Monfalcone.

It was not, indeed, until, bored with her own company beyond bearing, Miss Ellen decided to take profit from Agnes's absence by having a nice long chat with Miss Murphy, that she even became aware of it. She walked down to the Marina early, intending to spend the whole day with her friend. It was a delicious morning of bright sunshine, with no more than a hint of autumnal chill in the air moving down from the mountains, which invigorated her and made her feel on good terms with herself and the world. Many of the village folk recognized her and smiled at her as she passed; and this pleased her, for it showed that she was no longer regarded as a stranger but known and accepted. At this hour of the morning the little piazza was thronged with the first of the new season's tourists and members of the foreign colony bent on foraging—for the vegetable-boat from Sorrento had just come in, and a large catch of fish had been landed. Miss Ellen enjoyed the colour and movement of the bustling crowd. She looked forward to exchanging greetings with many acquaintances and, probably receiving congratulations on Agnes's marriage. Mr. Sanctuary would almost certainly be in evidence, as would Mr. Potter, who always came down at eleven o'clock to the post office to pick up his *Daily Telegraph* an hour in advance of the delivery.

The first person she recognized in the distance was Mrs. Hamilton-Gough, striding across the piazza in ill-cut Harris tweeds after having changed her husband's monthly cheque at the grocer's. Miss Ellen didn't like Mrs. Hamilton-Gough, who had been rather rude to her on their first meeting; but her heart was so gay and overflowing with charity this morning that she smiled when she saw her and saluted her, as she drew nearer, with a wave of the hand. Mrs. Hamilton-Gough stalked on, without returning her salute. Miss Ellen, remembering that she wore pince-nez, concluded that she was short-sighted and had not seen her; so she ran after her and wished her a friendly good-day.

"Isn't this a perfect morning?" she said.

Mrs. Hamilton-Gough turned momentarily and looked right through her, then stalked on without answering. Miss Ellen blushed with annoyance to realize that she had been cut dead.

She was still confused and angered by this deliberate slight when she saw Mr. Potter emerge from the post office with his newspaper under his arm. When he recognized Miss Ellen, his face suddenly turned the colour of a bougainvillæa; he tore off the wrapper hurriedly, opened the paper and appeared to be deeply engrossed in its contents as he walked away. The smile of welcome faded from Miss Ellen's face. She was almost certain that Mr. Potter had seen her, and instinctively shrank from incurring a second rebuff. But here, thank heaven, sauntering past the café-terraces and surveying their occupants with a quizzical smile, was her oldest friend, Ronnie Sanctuary, who, at least, could be counted on to behave like a gentleman. Determining to risk the encounter, Miss Ellen accosted him.

"Good morning, Mr. Sanctuary," she said. "What a perfect day!"

Ronnie Sanctuary greeted her with his curly smile, which seemed to have more than its usual mocking devilry.

"Well, well," he said. "So it's you!" He took her arm

playfully. "What is the latest news of the happy couple?" he whispered.

"They've gone to Naples for a week."

"Ah . . . So the young dog returns to his . . . let us rather say to the scene of his earlier triumphs. I must thank your sister for enlivening this dreary scene with such a pretty piece of comedy." He gripped her arm tighter and leered. "Don't forget what I told you about the danger of melting icebergs and the Monfalcone air." He chuckled obscenely. "Better watch your step, dear lady, before it's too late. Your turn may come next. Oh yes, your turn may come next. This sort of thing is infectious. You never can tell."

"Don't you . . . don't you think they'll be happy?" Miss Ellen asked anxiously.

Ronnie Sanctuary grinned, showing all his tiny teeth.

"Happy? *What* a question to ask about any marriage! Your sister, presumably, has already got what she wanted, and our youthful Tiberius will certainly get what *he* wants—which is something quite different, by the way. The disparity of age, which some people find shockin' and others amusin', will be no obstacle to *that*. The only regret in my mind is that poor old Ludo isn't alive to see it. Now that would have been comic if you like!"

He minced away, chuckling to himself like an elderly faun, and Miss Ellen, perplexed by his merriment, went on her way to Miss Murphy's studio. There, at least, she was sure of not being mocked at.

"You've heard the news about Agnes, Virginia?" she asked.

"Yes, I've heard the news, honey."

"What do you think of it?"

"Me? Oh, *I* never think about anything. Haven't for years. Thinking does no good, anyway, does it?—so why bother about it?"

"Do you suppose they'll be happy?"

"That depends what they want, honey. I'm perfectly happy because I want nothing, you see. I don't even *want* to be happy, and that's why it comes to me."

"If only I could be certain that he will be kind to her. Of course, I know you don't like Salvatore, from what you said to me."

Miss Murphy looked hurt.

"Didn't I tell you before that I don't dislike anyone, honey? It isn't worth while. It may do them harm and it doesn't do you any good. Much better take things and people just as they come, like the weather. You can't *do* anything about it—so what's the use trying?"

"You haven't answered my question, Virginia."

"What was that, honey?"

"Will Salvatore be kind to her?"

Miss Murphy winced, as though she disliked being cornered.

"He'll have to be, won't he, if he's to get all he wants?"

"You don't think he's in love with her, then?"

Miss Murphy blushed. "I know nothing about things of that kind. You see I was never in love myself, so I simply don't understand them. I'ld really much rather we talked about something else. How is your dear little cat and the kittens I gave you?"

It was all very peaceful and soothing, Miss Ellen thought; yet somehow, that day, her mind refused to surrender to the suave influence of Miss Murphy's company which, at the moment, she found almost irritating. She was still smarting from the 'cut' administered by Mrs. Hamilton-Gough, and even more subtly disturbed by the defection of Mr. Potter and Mr. Sanctuary's mocking smiles. Her brain, in which the first instinctive horror and fear of Agnes's marriage had been stunned by its sheer suddenness, was coming to life and beginning to realize the implications which her generous delight in Agnes's obvious (if pitiful) happiness had obscured. It became clear that the world of Monfalcone regarded her sister's marriage either as a social catastrophe, in whose shame she herself was involved, or as what was far worse and more wounding—an extravagant joke. She could put up with the scorn of Mrs. Hamilton-Gough and Mr. Potter's cowardice; she could even steel herself against Mr. Sanctuary's mischievous smiles. What perturbed and then distressed her was a growing conviction that Agnes—Agnes of all people!—had made a ghastly, an irreparable mistake. She was not afraid for herself—past misfortune had proved her own toughness and capacity for taking the rough with the smooth. But Agnes's case was different. She was the tenderer plant: nobody had ever made a more cruel mistake than Ben Dench when he had said she was hard: though her nature seemed diamond-like, it was as brittle as glass; she was actually much the more sensitive, as was proved by the fact that the very least upset gave her a headache.

When she looked back on their joint history, Miss Ellen realized that—though Agnes, by the undisputed right of her age and superior grace and intellect, had always directed their lives by 'taking the lead' and 'making decisions'—it was herself, the younger and plainer, who had done most of the less agreeable work and dealt with unpleasant emergencies. All her life, she was thankful and proud to say, she had been Agnes's protector no less than her slave, without Agnes's knowing it—almost without knowing it herself till this day. And now, in an emergency which should have called for her greatest powers, in the duty of protecting her sister, as people said, 'from herself', she had utterly failed. Her consciousness of this lapse made her miserable. If anything 'went wrong'—as her fainting spirits assured her it would—the fault would be hers.

In this guilt-burdened mood Miss Ellen awaited the return of Signor and Signora Ferraro from Naples, half expecting, when first she saw Agnes, to notice a tragic change. In the event, she had never seen her sister look brighter or better. Though they arrived an hour late, and Carolina's dinner was spoilt, she showed no signs of irritation nor of an approaching headache, though from the account she gave of their sight-seeing and shopping activities Miss Ellen would have expected her to be on the verge of a collapse. Salvatore, too, appeared to have enjoyed himself, though he did look as though he had been eating and drinking too much. It seemed odd to see him sitting at the head of the dinner-table, with Agnes at his right hand and her on the left, and Maria timidly waiting on them, instead of himself in a double-breasted black coat with a napkin over his arm. All through the meal he kept up a running fire of jokes and questions in dialect with Maria, rarely speaking to Agnes, though, when he did, he addressed her as 'darling', and occasionally offered her tender morsels from his own plate.

When she saw him do this Miss Ellen shivered. She could hardly believe that Agnes would not resent it. But apparently she didn't. Nor, for that matter, did she appear to be disturbed by other defects in his table manners—such as his cramming his mouth with maccheroni, which he washed down with wine, and more than once blatantly using his fork as a toothpick—to say nothing of punctuating the meal with a series of hearty eructations, Agnes's acceptance of which seemed to Miss Ellen to prove that Love was not only blind but deaf.

He drank a great deal of wine, she noticed, and shouted to Maria for more whenever his glass was empty. As a result of this, towards the end of dinner, he became talkative and demonstrative, twitting Agnes on her lack of appetite and encouraging her to eat by patting her face and pinching her ear, and once, with a more surprising lack of decorum, leaning over to put his arm round her waist and giving her a smacking kiss. Though she protested at this and went red, Agnes didn't seem really to mind it. Salvatore had kept her glass filled as well as his own. Perhaps that explained her insensitiveness. Or was it merely her loyalty to her husband that allowed her to condone these painful solecisms? In that case, Ellen thought, Agnes might find some difficulty in 'keeping it up' when the novelty of her condition wore off.

When he had finished the meal with a glass of brandy, which had never before been served at the Miss Isits' table, Salvatore undid the top button of his trousers and lit a Neapolitan cigar.

"As it's our first evening," Agnes suggested, "I think it would be nice for Ellen to sit with us in the studio."

Salvatore laughed. "To sit with us? I do not wish to sit. Now I go to the piazza."

"Must you go there this evening, dear? Isn't it rather late?"

"No, no. It is not too late. You not understand, Agnes. My friends know I come home and expect me. It is my duty to entertain."

Agnes sighed. "You won't stay there too long, dear, will you?" she said. "I think you had better take your overcoat. The air is quite chilly to-night."

"That is nothing . . . I think of everything," Salvatore told her. "It is better you not await me. One sees you are tired."

"Very well." Agnes said regretfully. "I will not stay up. But when you come home you can knock at my door. I may still be awake."

"*Non dubitare*, Signorina . . ."

" . . . *Signorina?*" Agnes reproached him.

"I should say 'Signora'. La Signora Ferraro . . . You think that sound very nice?" He kissed her playfully. "That is to keep you contented, my little one, until I come home. Then I kiss you again . . . ha? Why not I kiss Elena too? Is she not now my *cognata?*"

The two sisters spent the rest of the evening shivering together in the studio. Agnes was right. Already the night air was appreciably colder, but the physical chill of the room was nothing to that of its spiritual atmosphere. Was it possible, Miss Ellen wondered, that Agnes had been jealous of Salvatore's brotherly kiss, or was it that she felt secretly humiliated by his going to the piazza and leaving her on their first evening at home?

These questions were difficult to answer. Miss Ellen could only realize, and regret, that something had happened to Agnes which made them seem like strangers rather than sisters. The widening of the gulf that now separated them might merely be due to the fact that Agnes had become a married woman, the initiate of mysterious rites in which she had neither the privilege nor the desire to share, the receptacle of awful secrets the mere knowledge of which was sufficient to alter their relationship. Whatever the cause might be, there could be no doubt whatever that Agnes had changed. Even when she spoke casually of their adventures in Naples, she did so as if these belonged to a world of experience in which Ellen could have neither part nor understanding. After trying in vain for an hour that seemed endless to make conversation, Ellen decided to go to bed.

"I think you should come too, Agnes," she said. "You must be fagged after your drive. If you overtire yourself it may give you a headache."

"I have not had a sign of one since we went away, and I'm not a bit tired."

"You're not going to sit up for him, Agnes?"

"I shall do what I think best. Good night, Ellen."

Miss Ellen went up to her new room. This would be her first night in it, for she had hung on to her beloved view as long as she could. It was a small and gloomy chamber, its single window overshadowed at the back by the cliff against which the Castello Inglese was built. Though she threw the window wide-open it seemed to admit little air, and such air as there was had a dank, devitalized quality. Furthermore, the springs of the bed had sagged in the middle beneath Salvatore's weight, so that she felt as cramped and uncomfortable as though she were lying in a hammock. It filled her with misery to think that this machine of torture would be her resting-place for the rest of her life at the Castello Inglese. It seemed to her like hours before she could get to sleep.

She was wakened in what must surely have been the middle of the night by a sudden commotion: fierce barking, followed by muttered curses and the sound of dull blows. For a moment the startled voice of Agnes rose above the uproar; then a door slammed violently, and after that all was still. By this time she was wide awake and found herself laughing. That had been Stewart, defying Salvatore to enter his mistress's room!

She struck a match and looked at her watch. It was half-past one. "Poor Stewart!" she thought . . . "Poor Agnes!"

II

THAT 'brave little dog', too long deprived by Carolina of his natural carnivorous diet, had avenged himself on his ancient enemy by drawing blood from the left leg. Salvatore made much more fuss than he need have done, Ellen thought, over such a trivial injury, being terrified, as Agnes told her, of hydrophobia. While the scratch was healing he set about the plans he had conceived in his new quality of a landed proprietor. There was no doubt that he took his position seriously and was determined to make it clear. One of the first things he did was to send Assunta down to the Marina for a pot of paint, and to add to the marble plaque that bore the name of the Castello Inglese the words *Proprietà Ferraro*. Although she agreed with Agnes's enthusiastic opinion that the lettering was beautifully done and confirmed, if that were needed, his artistic taste, Miss Ellen was not quite sure that she approved of this addition. After all, the new description was hardly accurate, since the house and the property were half hers. However, in Agnes's present mood of entranced adoration, she felt it would not be wise to press her own point of view.

It soon became plain, indeed, that Salvatore's talent for management which he had previously exercised as Agnes's agent would now be displayed on his own responsibility. Neither Agnes nor her uncle before her had realized the productive potentialities of the estate. She had money, yes; but money was a thing of which nobody could mind having more. The sustaining walls of the terraces, over which the wild flowers of Monfalcone had sprawled in such profusion, had been allowed to subside and disintegrate from sheer neglect, with the consequent loss of a large area of cultivable ground. The olives, also, had been left for too long to go their own way, and must be lopped and pruned heroically if they were to produce a full harvest of oil, which, as he said poetically, was 'the gold of Monfalcone'. It was obvious that old Antonino's leisurely labours could not accomplish a quarter of these reforms in the remainder of his lifetime.

"That old man is too weak and too lazy, Agnes," Salvatore said. "Now I tell him to go."

"But he's worked here for so many years, dear," Agnes pleaded.

"Worked? I tell you that is not the word. He has eat his paunch full every day, and taken the payment. There is another thing: he is of a bad race—*mala razza*—who are never friend to my family."

"Poor old man! I'm quite sure he has never done *you* any harm. Do you think, at his age, he'll be able to get other employment?"

Salvatore laughed. "That is his affair. I guess he not starve. He has sons and daughters. Now I send him away and find a young man who is strong to work under my eyes. I see to everything, Agnes. *Non dubitare* . . ."

Next morning the strong young man reported for duty. His name was Francesco, and, according to Carolina, he was Salvatore's first cousin.

"Now I shall have to take care of my little Maria," she complained. "One Ferraro was bad enough, but two . . . *Mamma mia!*"

Still, as Salvatore had said, Francesco was strong. He set to work instantly on uprooting the drifts of iris and asphodel with a destructive efficiency that rivalled Mr. Potter's. By the time the terraces nearest to the house had been stripped bare of every blade of green, the olives were ready for picking and the second main harvest of the Castello Inglese began. Once more the bevy of beauties whom Salvatore had chosen to help in the vintage descended on the groves.

"I should have liked to assist with the olive-picking, particularly after having missed the *vendemmia*," Agnes said; "but Salvatore thinks I should find it too fatiguing, and won't allow me."

That wasn't at all surprising, Miss Ellen thought. Marriage had made little difference to Salvatore's manners with young women. Indeed, they were bolder than ever, and not even the blindness of love could have prevented Agnes, had she been present, from noticing the freedom of his attitude towards Assunta, whom he pursued without making any attempt to disguise their mutual attraction. That, however, Miss Ellen decided, was no business of hers. At this season the custom of the country evidently sanctioned behaviour that seemed strange, if not improper, to northern eyes; and for herself she enjoyed the olive-picking even more than the vintage. Though the sun shone clear and bright, its heat was no longer oppressive, and the great valley of Monfalcone, reddened now with the death of the vine, seemed more flagrantly beautiful than ever before.

It was a blessing, perhaps, that her day-long labours in the olive-groves made her so tired; for, except on those evenings when Salvatore smartened himself up to play cards with his boon-companions at the Marina, and Agnes was glad of her company, she found herself banished from the studio; and it was much more pleasant to snuggle into bed with Waifie than to sit all alone in the dreary salone, which, now that the days were shortening and the nights growing colder, seemed almost as comfortless as the drawing-room at 'The Cedars'.

The rare evenings when she was invited to share the warmth of the studio fire with them were hardly more cheerful. Agnes, no doubt, asked nothing more than the pleasure she derived from her husband's presence; but Miss Ellen did not find their company entertaining. Without being hypercritical she found it increasingly difficult to imagine what Agnes could 'see in him'. Though his attitude was still tolerably (and tolerantly) polite to both of them, surely Agnes, blind as she was, must realize that Salvatore's manners—which had once been his principal asset—were steadily deteriorating? As her butler he had taken great pains with his personal appearance: no matter how late or how hard he had worked on the land during the afternoon, the hour of dinner had always found him kempt and clean-shaven—a picture, as she and Ellen had agreed, of spruceness and elegance. As her husband and the acknowledged head of the household—a station in which smartness would have been even more justified—he did not seem to regard his appearance as a matter of importance. He no longer shaved himself, but was shaved, once or twice a week at the most, in the barber's shop at the Marina, which was the nearest approach to a social club in Monfalcone. Except on those evenings when he had planned to visit the village and had togged himself up accordingly, he sat down to dine in his soiled working clothes, unkempt and even unwashed.

In other ways the character of the evening meal, which had always been something of a ceremony, was now changed. It was no longer served at a fixed hour, but earlier or later according to the time when Salvatore was ready for it. The food Carolina prepared tasted different too, for the taboo Agnes had laid on the use of onions and garlic had been summarily lifted, and the dishes she served to suit the Miss Isits' exotic palates were replaced by the more robust native dietary of Monfalcone which, healthy as it may have been, was a tax on their delicate digestions. Nor was that all. On the evening of Agnes's return from her honeymoon, Miss Ellen had been embarrassed and distressed—for her sister's sake more than for her own—by Salvatore's table-manners. Now, freed from the inhibitions imposed by his holiday clothes, the grossness of his appetite and the greed with which he gobbled his food disgusted her. She was shocked even more—and indeed 'didn't know where to look'—when, at the end of the meal, flushed with wine, he unbuttoned his waistcoat and trousers, lolling back in his chair while he picked his teeth methodically and bandied improper jokes with the giggling Assunta who, within a week, had been brought in to wait at table instead of little Maria. It was a mercy, Miss Ellen thought, that Agnes's knowledge of

Italian did not embrace the rude dialect of Monfalcone, though, even without understanding it, she might reasonably have resented the noisy familiarity of their conversation.

The rare evenings she spent in the studio after dinner were even more trying. By this time, as a rule, Salvatore was either excited or fuddled. In the first case he was inclined to be embarrassingly affectionate—not only to his wife, but, occasionally, to Miss Ellen herself. In the second he would sit with a scowl on his handsome face, which had coarsened so much, she thought, during the last few months, silently chewing one of the black cigars whose reek made her head ache, and methodically spitting into the fire or a big brass cuspidor—the principal trophy of his American travels, of which he was inordinately proud. Though his aim was frequently faulty, this did not appear to trouble him. When he had finished his cigar, he lay back in his chair and snored.

Was it merely her pride, Miss Ellen wondered, that prevented Agnes from showing the disapproval, if not the disgust, she must surely have felt? Did that benevolent serenity conceal a profound disillusionment? On the whole, she was inclined to think it did not. Incredible though it might seem, she believed that Agnes was still ferociously in love with her husband: not merely prepared but contented to accept him as he was—willing, too, to relinquish for his sake her own high standards of refinement, and to forgo, without regret, the social privileges her station had previously assured her.

Though she never mentioned these, there could be no doubt that Agnes realized the extent of her sacrifice. There were no more invitations to dinner-parties. Mrs. Hamilton-Gough's stony 'cut' at the Marina had defined the change in their social position as clearly as Mr. Potter's blushing evasion. Ronnie Sanctuary was now the only member of the Monfalcone society who had the courage to defy its edicts by visiting the Castello Inglese. He dropped in, as he was passing, fairly frequently, and made himself at home as 'an old friend of the house', treating Salvatore as an equal and displaying his usual quizzical courtesy towards his wife and his sister-in-law. Miss Ellen, more wary for once than Agnes, who looked upon Mr. Sanctuary as a loyal friend, could not persuade herself to take his politeness at its face value. He came there, she believed, either in search of what he could get—such as a meal on days when no more agreeable hospitality offered itself, or out of sheer mischievous curiosity—to spy out the land and glean new material for the exercise of his wit in politer circles. In either case his visits were not unprofitable; for he invariably arrived with an empty shopping-basket which his old friend Salvatore obligingly filled with bottles of wine, while his exclusive news of the Signora Ferraro's comical infatuation and the oddness of the whole situation at the Castello Inglese was worth several dinner invitations a week to him.

What disquieted Miss Ellen far more than their almost complete social isolation or Agnes's entranced acquiescence in Salvatore's vulgarities and the progressive deterioration of their standards of life towards his own level, which was that of a Monfalcone peasant, was the dictatorship he imposed on the conduct of the establishment. The dismissal of old Antonino and the reinstatement of Assunta were only a beginning. The next victim was Stewart, whom, after that first savage attack, he banished from Agnes's bedroom to a dungeon at the back of the house. After Stewart came Carolina and little Maria, both of whom disappeared at a moment's notice in a tempest of protests and tears which Agnes was not permitted to hear.

"That old woman," Salvatore explained, "she been here too long. She belong to the same bad family as Antonino. Many times I have told Don Ludovico how much she rob him, but his heart was too gentle: I think he liked being robbed. But I am not gentle and have the eyes open too. I see what goes out of the house to feed her family, and I put a stop. Now I look for an honest woman and find her. *Non dubitare.*"

He did not have to look far; for his mother was waiting

on the doorstep with a sister of his cousin Francesco within five minutes of old Carolina's departure.

"My mother is very kind, Agnes," he said. "She has heard this moment that Carolina is going, and says she will charge herself with the kitchen without payment until we find somebody else. She is very good cook, my mother. You see!" He smacked his lips. "Now we eat in the real manner of Monfalcone. In a month you get fat."

"Won't it be rather awkward, having your mother in the house, darling?" Agnes mildly suggested.

"Awkward? What you mean 'awkward'?"

"I mean . . . well, your eating in the salone and her in the kitchen."

Salvatore laughed. "That is nothing. She is my mother, yes; but she is an ignorant woman and not understand too much how Signore eat, so it is much better she stay where she cook. Now I go to hire the house where she live in the village."

"Wouldn't it be rather rash to let it if she's only coming here temporarily?"

Salvatore winked: "Who knows? Perhaps she like living here and consent to be permanent. Then we save money as well as eat better. Is not that what is called good business?"

There was no doubt as to Salvatore's business capacity. For the moment when he insisted on taking her financial affairs in hand, as he did as a matter of course, Agnes was surprised and delighted to notice the enormous reduction in the household expenses. Now that his mother consumed on the premises the large quantities of food she had previously taken away, the cost of living at the Castello Inglese had become negligible and she found money accumulating in her bank. Salvatore himself was proud to take credit for all these savings and boasted of his part in them. In his unmarried days, he had been careless of what Agnes spent and had even—as during their shopping expedition to Naples—encouraged her to be extravagant and to 'make a fine figure', as he called it. Now he jealously watched every farthing that went out of the house. At that time, again, he had gained her respect by refusing to handle her money. Now he took good care that she had no money to handle, and assumed complete control of all her finances, conducting them with a shrewdness that she could only admire.

"I have always known," she told Ellen, "that Salvatore was a remarkable man; but I must confess his grip on affairs astonishes me. There is nothing superficial about it. His mind goes straight to the roots of everything and will not be satisfied until he understands it. Only this morning, for instance, he asked for a copy of Uncle Ludovic's will, with the terms of which he had not been exactly acquainted. He was under the impression that everything had been left to *me*. Then the other day, when I happened to speak quite casually of the North Bromwich property, he showed an equal interest and asked me all kinds of intelligent questions about it. He was quite distressed when I told him 'The Cedars' was not let. There is hardly a thing of that kind in which he does not appear to be interested: he wanted, for instance, to know all about the English law of inheritance, which apparently is different from the Italian and, as he thinks, is in some ways less fair."

"Less fair? In what way?" Miss Ellen enquired.

"Well, in England, you see, a man who has a grudge against his wife can leave her practically penniless, and vice versa; while in Italy, unless they have children, the bulk of the property goes to the surviving partner. That seems to me only right. After all, in God's eyes, they are one."

"Yes, I see," said Miss Ellen. "But what about unmarried people?"

"Oh, in that case, I believe, the property is divided among their surviving relatives. You and I have none; we are actually the last of the Isits; so, if you should die first, your share would pass on to me. But I really don't know," Agnes continued brightly, "why we should dwell on such gloomy subjects. We are a healthy, long-lived family, and you are the younger. Still, it is a great satisfaction for me to know that, in the end, Salvatore will regain at least part of the Ferraros' ancient property. I don't want to influence you, Ellen, but I do think it might save a lot of confusion if you made a will."

Miss Ellen laughed. "I don't see any need for that, Agnes. After all, I'm much younger than you, and I don't feel the least bit like dying just yet."

"Well, you never know," Agnes said darkly.

"Such a thing has never entered my mind. If I did make a will, I shouldn't know whom to leave my share to . . . unless there is such a thing as a charity connected with cats."

"Cats? Really, Ellen, I never heard such nonsense! Of course the obvious person is Salvatore."

"Salvatore's nothing to me, Agnes."

"He is your brother-in-law and my husband. What have you against him?"

"Nothing . . . except that I hardly know him."

Agnes frowned. "This only confirms what I've long suspected. You've never appreciated his qualities or realized how much we owe him. I have often thought—indeed I can't help thinking—what a shame it is that a man of his calibre, so strictly candid and straight as well as so capable, should have been denied the educational advantages which he deserves. If he had been given a chance I believe he might well have become a great mathematician or lawyer—or possibly a banker. You know I have always prided myself on the possession of a certain clearness and exactness of mind, which I inherited, no doubt, from Papa; but when it comes to figures Salvatore makes me feel a mere muddler. He sees everything at a glance and never, never forgets. It is a most exceptional gift." She sighed. "If only he and I had happened to meet twenty years ago!"

"In that case," Ellen said with unconscious cruelty, "he would have been a boy in his teens."

Agnes blushed. "Even so," she said coldly, "I might have helped him and influenced him, if only as a friend.

Do you know, he has told me that I am the first real friend he has ever had?"

"There was Uncle Ludovic . . . and the man who took him to America.'

"Those were neither good nor helpful influences, I'm afraid. Salvatore is extremely reticent about both of them; and, of course, I respect the delicacy of his feelings and ask no questions. It is enough, and more than enough, for me that after such a wasteful and troubled boyhood and youth he has at last found true happiness and that I have been privileged to share it."

Miss Ellen wondered . . . On the surface, at any rate, Agnes showed no signs of discontent with her doubtful bargain. Physically she was in better condition than Ellen had ever known her, suffering rarely if ever from the devastating attacks of migraine that had made her life a purgatory. Her temper, too, was more equable and her appetite had improved. Though the cooking of Salvatore's mother tried her digestion, she was putting on flesh: a change on which Salvatore frequently commented with satisfaction. As for him, Miss Ellen had no reason to suspect that he wasn't equally contented, though it would have been difficult for her to divine the secret thoughts of a man who habitually concealed his feelings beneath the smiling mask which seemed common to all his compatriots.

He certainly had every reason to be pleased with himself. He had married a wife superior in station and wealth to any he could reasonably have hoped for: a woman who not only loved him with uncritical devotion but had also made his future secure and given him, along with her love, a large share of the two things he most coveted: landed property and sufficient means with which to develop it. Efficiently as he had served them as their butler—and nobody could dispute the virtuosity he had displayed in that rôle—his tastes were not really domestic: he was a peasant, a man of the soil, the hot volcanic soil of Monfalcone to which he belonged. Though he could wear his domestic uniform as to the manner born and match it with the courteous attentiveness of the perfect manservant, he had always been happier and more himself when he went out with his gun at dawn to shoot quail and woodcock, or toiled, stripped to the waist, in the vineyards or under the olives. To this natural bent, which had been thwarted throughout most of his life, there was now added the pride of possession. There was plenty of scope for his skill and energy as a husbandman in the long-neglected acres of the Castello Inglese, and he gave of both to the full.

The results, though no doubt economically sound, were a grief to Miss Ellen, who saw the flowery wilderness which she loved gradually changing and finally vanishing beneath her eyes. The destruction of the great drifts of naturalized irises, whose flowering she had looked forward to seeing in the spring, was only a beginning. Within a few months the lines of the wayward terraces had been straightened, their crumbling walls restored with new-quarried stone. The forest of gnarled olive-trees, on whose billowy roof she had looked down every day from the beloved balcony that was no longer hers, had been so ruthlessly lopped that it seemed to her unlikely that the mutilated stumps could survive—their large boughs sawn up for firewood and the feathery crowns tied in bundles and carried down to the Marina to fire the limekilns or feed the baker's oven. She resented this desecration of all she had loved, not only for the loss of beauty but also because, in the back of her mind, she couldn't forget that half of it, at least, was her own, and felt that she was entitled to some say as to what was done with it. She even went so far as to raise a mild but unavailing protest with Agnes. "It isn't as if we depended on the land for our living, is it?" she said.

"I am surprised—I might almost say shocked," Agnes replied, "that you should have mentioned this. It is a matter in which you and I are totally ignorant and Salvatore is an expert. If you had thought for a moment you would have realized that you ought to be grateful rather than critical. Salvatore has already improved your property—if you insist on regarding it in that light—out of all recognition. Instead of being a liability, on which we were forced to spend money for labour unprofitably year after year, it is about to become an asset. What is more, I think it is only fair to my husband that you should remember that he is working his fingers to the bone, day in and day out—you can see for yourself how tired he is when he comes in at night!—without being paid a penny for all he is doing. If it comes to that you will find yourself far better off when he has finished all he intends to do than when he began."

"Those old olive trees were so lovely, Agnes," Miss Ellen said. "When I had my own room—I mean Salvatore's—I used to watch them for hours. Sometimes they were like plumes of smoke drifting down to the sea; and sometimes, when the wind blew, they all turned silver."

Agnes sniffed.

"I have never considered the olive an attractive tree, as I told you long ago. But, apart from that, I know Salvatore would be deeply hurt if you even suggested that you were not delighted with everything he had done. It has all been worked out on a plan which we have considered together. Every penny we save on the house—and you would be astonished, if you took the trouble to find out, how much we are saving—goes back into the land to pay for materials and labour. For the moment, of course, we shall not see any startling returns; we may even have to draw on our capital, as I have done already; but in three or four years' time, when the place is in order, it will not merely have covered our present expenditure but show a handsome profit for which you may well be grateful. When we do reach that point, Salvatore proposes buying more land to extend the estate: there is another sadly-neglected property that marches with ours on the west and which formerly, I understand, belonged to the Ferraros. I for one cannot blame Salvatore for such a natural ambition. Of course, if you wish to make difficulties and keep your own income separate from ours, no doubt something can be arranged; you could write to

Ernest Wilburn and ask his advice; but I must warn you that, if you did, my poor Salvatore would be deeply and justifiably pained by your lack of trust in him. To say nothing of myself."

"But Agnes, of course I wouldn't dream of doing anything like that," Miss Ellen protested. "You know I've no use for the money. I hardly ever spend a penny. I simply don't understand it."

"That is fairly obvious, I think," Agnes answered acidly. "In those circumstances don't you think you would be well-advised to leave matters of this kind to people who do?"

"Please let's say no more about it," Miss Ellen pleaded. "I only felt . . ."

"Other people have feelings too, Ellen."

They left it at that, and Salvatore pursued his ruthless way. Perhaps it was something more than mere love of the soil—more even than natural acquisitiveness or pride in possession—that drove him thus to transform the Castello Inglese. He came, as Miss Murphy had said, from one of the humblest families in Monfalcone, a family of peasant-proprietors who had lost their land. In his ragged childhood he had borne and resented the stigma of bitter poverty, from which he had escaped by forming associations that, however profitable to himself, were distasteful to his fellow-villagers. The rumours of his activities in Naples and his connections with the *camorra* had further blackened a name that was already shady, and the only respect he enjoyed was that accorded to a man who was known to be violent and unscrupulous and, once thwarted, might become dangerous. Though, apart from his amorous adventures, he had finally settled down to a fairly respectable life at the Castello Inglese, the unsavouriness of his reputation had not been forgotten, and he was still regarded with general dislike and suspicion.

His marriage with Agnes Isit gave him the opportunity of overcoming these prejudices. The fact that neither he nor his wife was 'accepted' by the foreign colony did not trouble him in the least: after all, these people were merely outsiders—in the contemptuous phrase of his countrymen 'quails that pass'. But he did respect—and even fear—the judgement of his own people; and the possession of Agnes's money enabled him to distribute favours so substantial that, in their own interest, they would be compelled to modify its harshness.

From the beginning he was shrewd enough to realize that his new wealth and power could not be expected to influence in his favour the more solid inhabitants of the village who had properties of their own; but, besides these, the commune of Monfalcone contained many families such as his which, through sloth, incompetence, or the exactions of usurers, had lost their possessions and lived on the verge of starvation. It was to these that he knew his lavishness would appeal. If once he could make them dependent on him, as the largest and most generous employer of labour in Monfalcone, the remainder, whose approval he coveted, would be forced to come into line and acknowledge his position as a power in the land.

From the day when he found himself master of the Miss Isits' income and capital, Salvatore pursued this design of personal rehabilitation. He was a gambler by nature; yet behind his passion for gaming there was a core of hard-headed self-interest, a Latin realism, which tempered his extravagance even at its most lavish. His desire to assert and enjoy the power his wife's fortune provided, and to shine in the eyes of those who had previously despised him, were agreeable by-products, as it were, of his main design—which was the accumulation of money and land that would assure him a comfortable and prosperous old age during the years in which he might reasonably expect to survive her.

Thus the changes which he made in the economy of the Castello Inglese, and which so deeply distressed poor Miss Ellen, served three purposes, providing him at the same time with an outlet for his abundant energies, which had been wasted in the boring routine of a menial occupation, the prospect of increasing affluence, and the opportunity of flattering his opinion of himself.

No doubt Salvatore was as happy as Agnes was in his happiness. During the whole of that autumn he showed himself indefatigable; rising at dawn to go out on the land and set his gangs of labourers at work; wielding axe and pick and shovel with the best of them, and regaining thereby a great part of the magnificent physique which years of sedentary living had sapped and softened; laughing and joking good-humouredly with the men who worked beside him, and chaffing the bevies of pretty girls whom he had chosen to carry stones for the walls and earth for the terraces—and to provide him, as Miss Ellen unwillingly suspected, with means of private diversion.

Though she hated the results of their labours, she often went down into the olive-groves to watch the gang at work, while she listened to their chatter and singing. She longed to identify herself with these jolly, care-free folk, so much livelier and more natural, she thought, than the silent labourers she remembered seeing at work beneath a leaden sky in the dun English fields on the outskirts of North Bromwich: men who moved about their job sluggishly, as though their very spirits were burdened with the clay that clodded their boots, whose faces looked grim and sullen and even hostile. It was the enlivening influence of warmth and light which made these Italians so different, and gave Salvatore's gang the air of a family party in which he himself took the part of a benevolent host. He was still, she noticed, a little too free with the younger girls, unnecessarily so indeed for a married man; yet his fun was probably quite innocent and paternal, and there was no doubt that they rather threw themselves at him, as seemed natural enough, considering their thoughtless age and his obvious attractiveness.

There was one girl in particular—a younger sister of Assunta—who appeared to be quite blatantly flaunting her charms. As she watched her, Miss Ellen couldn't help remembering the hot season of the *vendemmia* (could it be only three months ago?) when she had imagined that Salvatore and Assunta were in love and would probably make a match of it, which would, in fact, have been much more suitable than his marriage with Agnes; and this memory, in turn, reminded her that she rarely now set eyes on Assunta, who had been relegated to the kitchen to help Salvatore's mother and replaced in the dining-room by Francesco's sister, Angelina. Miss Ellen did not know why this change had been made. Perhaps Agnes, recalling that painful scene on the terrace, had insisted on it—if she were able to insist on anything that didn't accord with her husband's inclinations. And now that she came to think of it, entranced by this young girl's vivid reincarnation of her sister's charms, she suddenly remembered how Assunta, during the last few weeks, had looked sullen and saddened and not in the very least like the brilliant creature of the vintage. Was it possible, she wondered, that Assunta had had hopes of Salvatore which Agnes (unconsciously, of course) had nipped in the bud? Was she still eating her heart out for him? That indeed would be tragic and pitiful—but how, oh how, like Life! She sighed to herself and decided that it would be kind and womanly to find out what was really the matter with Assunta and, if possible, to console her. The thought of this poor child's bitter disappointment disquieted her feelings so deeply that she stole away from Salvatore's jolly family party and went up to the kitchen to find her and have a word with her. This would be a propitious moment, for it was the hour at which Agnes, accompanied by the exiled Stewart, retired to her bedroom and took her siesta.

It was unusual for Miss Ellen to enter the kitchen of the Castello Inglese. Agnes preferred to manage all the domestic arrangements and disapproved of anyone but herself even talking with the servants, since such conversations, innocent though they might seem, were a common source of gossip, and every word spoken in them quickly found its way to the village. The kitchen itself was not an inviting place: it was dark and ill-ventilated and generally pervaded by the dust and fumes of charcoal mingled with odours of cooking in which, since old Carolina's departure, stale cabbage and garlic preponderated. In Carolina's time it had been dirty, as judged by the standards Miss Ellen had maintained in the kitchen at 'The Cedars': under the management—or mismanagement—of Salvatore's mother, who was not merely unmethodical but even unclean in her person, it had become a positive pigsty. Miss Ellen had often wondered how Agnes, whose eyes and nose were so sensitive, could tolerate a welter of disorder and filth which would have disgraced the meanest hovels in the slums of the Marina, though, of course, it was difficult for her to reprimand her own mother-in-law, and Salvatore, who spent hours in the midst of it, apparently found nothing amiss. She approached the door cautiously and tapped on it, calling Assunta. Nobody answered: from within she heard a babble of high-pitched female voices speaking in dialect so fast that she could hardly distinguish a word. She pushed open the door and poked in her head.

"Are you there, Assunta?" she called.

The excited babble ceased abruptly. Three figures defined themselves in the smoke: Salvatore's mother, Francesco's sister, Angelina, and a handsome dark girl, of the same physical type as Assunta, whom she imagined to be a visitor from the village—probably another of the vast and predatory family of Ferraro. The old woman glared at her venomously. She was not merely dirty but hideous, with a toothless mouth and bleary, encrusted eyes. It was hard to believe that this foul misshapen hag could have produced such a paragon of manly beauty as Salvatore.

"Assunta is not here," she said.

"Will you tell me where I can find her?"

"Who knows? She is gone, and does not come back again."

"Do you mean she has left—that she's been sent away?"

The old woman laughed evilly: "I know nothing about it. You had better ask the Signora."

Agnes did not appear in the salone at tea-time that afternoon, but remained in her bedroom till dinner. From her silence and her forbidding manner, it was evident that something unpleasant had occurred; her eyes looked red and swollen, as though she had been crying—though that was unlikely, Miss Ellen thought, for, however much she was upset, Agnes never cried. Salvatore, on the other hand, appeared to be in excellent spirits, eating loudly and heartily, and joking, with a blatancy that smacked of bravado, with the new, dark girl, who clumsily waited at table. Miss Ellen waited till they had finished dinner and the stranger had gone out of the room before she dared ask her question.

"Assunta has left our service," Agnes said coldly. "I dismissed her this morning."

"But why? What has she done to deserve that?"

Agnes sighed wearily. "I suppose you will have to know sooner or later," she said. "Some brute of a man has betrayed her."

"Oh dear, what a shame! Do you know who he is?"

Agnes did not answer. Slowly turning her head she fixed her eyes full on Salvatore. They had lost their light; they were no longer commanding and challenging, but hurt and reproachful and quite unutterably sad. Salvatore blinked, as though her gaze disquieted him; then quickly recovered himself. He rose and patted her cheek playfully. He laughed.

"Why you look at me like that, Agnes? What must I do about it? Am I to keep my eyes on all these young girls day and night and see that no man come near them? That would be what you call a full-time job for a man who is already much occupied. This is nothing to be so serious. It has happened before. And—who knows?—perhaps it will happen again. Now I go to the village and talk to that old man about the new property. He still think he is clever and ask too much, but I guess we shall buy it dirt-cheap before I finish, because I find out he is pressed for debts and must have the money."

It was rarely now that he resigned himself to spending the hours after dinner alone with Agnes in the studio or to remaining with her for more than a few moments except at mealtimes. Though he was usually tired out at the end of the working day, the symptoms of his fatigue took the form of an increasing restlessness. It was no longer enough for him to sit smoking and spitting until, drowsy with repletion, he dozed and began to snore. And though often, in sudden bursts of talkative enthusiasm, he would enlarge, for ten minutes at a time, on his grandiose plans for the future, he now seemed incapable of discussing them calmly with Agnes, listening—and even sometimes deferring—to her advice, but made decisions and acted on them without consulting her, and showed impatience at the least hint of criticism.

"See here," he would say, angrily, "this thing is not for women to understand: I am a man, and I know what I do."

In these days he did not even think it necessary to add the familiar: "*Non dubitare!*"

Often, indeed, it seemed to Miss Ellen that Agnes irritated him. More than once she had caught his eye examining her sister, feature by feature, with the oddest of looks: his heavy brows knitted, as though the mind behind them were puzzled to think how on earth he came to be married to this elderly foreigner. At other times she surprised a look in them which was more difficult to interpret: the fixed stare of a caged or cornered wild animal, full of suspicion and hatred. Then, suddenly, he would jump up, as though he could bear the sight of her no longer, and make a dash for the door. Agnes herself, providentially, appeared to be quite unaware of anything sinister or unusual in her husband's conduct. Whatever he said or did, she never showed the least ruffling of temper. It was evident that she continued to adore him with a tender pride in which the protective and the possessive were mingled.

Miss Ellen could only admire this almost military loyalty, which (along with her head for figures) Agnes had inherited, no doubt, from Papa, and found her devotion as beautiful as it was pathetic. It only proved, she thought, what a wonderful thing true love must be: that a woman so strong-minded and independent, a woman whom many people had even called 'hard', should be capable of such self-effacement and gentleness. Yet, while she admired her, Miss Ellen's heart often ached for her—particularly on those evenings when, without even making the excuse of visiting the village on business, Salvatore left Agnes stranded in the studio alone with the miserable Stewart, and lurched off to the malodorous kitchen to sit gossiping and laughing with his mother and Francesco's sister, Angelina, whom she already suspected of being anything but an angel. First Assunta, then Angelina . . . In her inmost mind she was prepared to bet who the next victim —or aspirant to his favours—would be. It was odd how his fancy always turned towards dark women. Even Agnes was dark. Miss Ellen felt thankful, on the whole, that she herself was fair.

On these painful occasions she often wondered why the deserted Agnes did not invite her to share the warmth of the olive-wood fire in the studio, as would have been only natural and sisterly. This was only another example, she supposed, of her sister's pride, denoting a tacit refusal to confess that she was either neglected or lonely, and, again, of her characteristic spirit of independence: if she couldn't have Salvatore with her, she preferred to have nobody.

She certainly had Salvatore less and less frequently as autumn declined into winter, with long periods of torrential rain and boisterous gales that raged without bate for a week on end and rocked the whole house, for all its protective cliffs, like a ship at sea. During these wild weeks it was impossible for him to expend his energies on the sodden land. The wind beat so fiercely from the south, occasionally veering west or backing to eastward, that one couldn't even open the doors to step out on the terrace without gusts rushing in and blowing the furniture about; every chimney in the Castello Inglese smoked; shutters were torn away from their fastenings and the windows behind them seemed on the point of being blown in.

It was miserable enough for all of them: the kitchen-folk cowering over their charcoal braziers in the light of a flickering oil-wick; Agnes huddled with Stewart close to the studio-fire, her eyes smarting with wood-smoke; Miss Ellen spending most of the time in her back bedroom, which, though fireless, was warmer than the smoky salone, being small and sheltered from the wind. Even the window-panes of the salone were bleared with a mist of salt blown up from the roaring beaches a thousand feet below, where Miss Murphy's studio, no doubt, lay marooned and sheeted in flying spray. But if the rest of the household were equally weather-bound their condition was not so distressing as Salvatore's. Devoid of any resources such as they enjoyed—for he had nothing to do in the house and would not—or could not—read, he prowled through the long corridors, pacing restlessly to and fro, like a hungry tiger in a menagerie. He looked so sullen and ill-tempered at meal-times that it came as a relief when, one day, he announced his intention of going to Naples. It was significant, Miss Ellen thought, that this time he did not invite Agnes to accompany him, though she did not resent the omission.

"It is only natural," she said, "that a manly man such as Salvatore should sometimes desire the society of other men."

Though this was not her interpretation of his probable motives, Miss Ellen was tactfully silent.

By the end of December, winter had come in earnest. Though the northerly wind brought clear skies and periods of sunshine, the air that seeped down from the mountains' ridges was icy, and their higher slopes, between the stark chestnut-woods, lay whitened with patches of snow. The Castello Inglese, with its high vaulted roofs and tiled floors, resembled an ice-house. It was impossible to keep warm inside it; and outside, though the sun shone brightly, it seemed equally impossible to find shelter from the wind. Miss Ellen could not help envying Sir Benjamin Dench in Egypt. Even Agnes, whose principles forbade her to complain of the weather, found it hard to discover excuses for this Southern Italian Winter, which had neither the crisp stimulation of an Alpine zone nor the temperance which deluded northerners attribute to the Mediterranean.

Salvatore, accustomed to the climate's extremes and expecting discomfort, suffered less than his wife or her sister. His visit to Naples, whatever its object, had brought back his lost spirits. So long as he could go out with his gun and the soil was dry enough to be tilled, he had no cause for complaint. His negotiations with his neighbour were drawing to a satisfactory close, and the new land was paid for by the sale of a block of Captain Vaughan's governmental securities. He came in one evening brandishing the title-deeds triumphantly.

"Now the land is ours, Agnes," he boasted, "as far as you can see. Next I turn this old fellow out and make the cottage fit to rent to some foreigner."

Agnes glowed with approval. "I think that is an admirable idea. It would be nice to have European—I mean Anglo-Saxon—neighbours, wouldn't it, Ellen?"

Miss Ellen looked up from her sewing.

"Yes, indeed; and I believe I can find a good tenant," she said.

"*You* can find a good tenant? Not a friend of Miss Murphy's, I hope?"

"No . . . The poor thing has no friends except me, I'm afraid."

"How can you possibly think of anyone suitable? The only person we know in Monfalcone is Mr. Sanctuary, and he hasn't been near us for more than a month." (As was true enough—Ronnie Sanctuary having deserted them from the moment when his tales about the Castello Inglese ceased to be 'news'.)

"I had a post-card the other day," Miss Ellen said, "from a friend in Egypt who asked me some time ago to find him an inexpensive house in Monfalcone. It was . . . well, as a matter of fact, it was Sir Benjamin Dench."

"*Sir Benjamin Dench?*" Agnes blushed. "Really, Ellen," she said, "I think that would be most unsuitable: more unsuitable, indeed, to-day than ever before."

Salvatore laughed. "What is the matter, Agnes? What you go red like that for? Who is this Sir Dench?"

"He is a man we knew slightly in India, many years

ago: but I have no wish to renew the acquaintance," Agnes said firmly.

Miss Ellen flared up: "I think that is most unfair, Agnes. Sir Benjamin is a distinguished scientist and an extremely nice man."

"If he has plenty of money, he is a nice man all right," Salvatore said.

12

So THE winter passed. It was early in March, when the hill-sides were sprinkled with peach-blossom and the terraces, sown with wheat, spread a corduroy of malachite beneath the grey-green olives, that Agnes fell ill.

For some weeks before this she had been, as she admitted later, a little 'out of sorts'; but it was not her way to complain of trifling discomforts, and up to then she had both felt and looked remarkably well. Her face had recently shown more colour than usual; and Miss Ellen, who had always regretted her habitual pallor as the only flaw in her complexion, had rejoiced to think that marriage 'suited her'.

Agnes had suffered, of course, from a certain amount of chronic dyspepsia: the natural consequence of her mother-in-law's cooking. But so had they all—and none more, to judge by the outward and audible signs of it, than Salvatore himself. For all that, she had been freer than Miss Ellen ever remembered from her principal thorn in the flesh; those paroxysmal headaches which had been the bane of both their lives. She was therefore the more surprised when, on a spring morning, whose sheer loveliness made it seem ridiculous for anyone to be ill, she heard, from the room in which Agnes slept, the unmistakable sounds of violent sickness.

At first she took it for granted that the old malady had returned, though this symptom generally manifested itself at the end of an attack, and Agnes, appearing, as her principles compelled her, at the breakfast-table, denied this, irritably declaring that her head had never been clearer. If this were a bilious attack, it was certainly one of an unusual type. Miss Ellen examined her anxiously. More than once, during breakfast, Agnes turned deathly pale; she shivered and complained of the cold, though the morning was balmy.

"There is nothing whatever to worry about," she maintained; "but I think, all the same, I had better go back to bed and stay there till luncheon with a hot-water bottle. Above all things, don't tell Salvatore. He has quite enough to worry about without being disturbed by this little upset."

Miss Ellen, left to herself, began to wonder. She had no exact knowledge of physiology; but sickness, so early in the day, might be significant. Was it possible . . .? There were, of course, the biblical precedents of Sara, the wife of Abraham, and Elizabeth, the mother of John the Baptist, and, as the Gospel according to St. Luke informed her, with God nothing should be impossible. Yet she could not help feeling that the age of such miracles was past; and as Agnes's sickness continued during the day, with increasing chilliness and prostration, she dismissed this hopeful theory of its cause. Salvatore, who came in for luncheon, treated the matter even more lightly than Agnes.

"This is the stomach," he said. "It is well known that all foreigners are weak in the stomach. My mother will make Agnes a cup of camomile to soothe; then she sleep, and to-morrow she will be better. *Non dubitare.*"

"Don't you think we should send for a doctor?" Miss Ellen asked.

"A doctor? I tell you, this is a thing of nothing! Many people of Monfalcone suffer from the stomach at the beginning of the spring. Don Ludovico, he was the same, as I remember well. You like to waste money?"

Agnes herself turned down the suggestion with equal scorn.

"I have never consulted a doctor in my life," she declared, "and I've no intention of doing so now, just because I've eaten something that has disagreed with me. I refuse to have any foreigner examining me and poking me about. Besides which, Salvatore assures me that the doctor in Monfalcone is a fraud and knows far less about trivial ailments like this than his mother. She may be uneducated, though that is through no fault of her own, but she is full of the wisdom of experience. I sincerely hope you are not going to lose your head, Ellen."

Miss Ellen reluctantly left it at that. She knew it was no good attempting to argue with Agnes in her present condition of exhausted irritability. And the attack, to her great relief, cleared up in three days, though the weakness that followed it kept Agnes in bed for a week.

"What did I tell you?" she said triumphantly. "Perhaps now you will realize that it is foolish to worry over trifles? Salvatore, as usual, was right."

"All the same," Ellen said, "I think you should take a tonic. You may feel quite all right, but you do look terribly washed-out."

"It is natural to me to have a pale complexion. Vivid colouring, in my case, is never a sign of good health, as you ought to know by this time. All I need now is rest and fresh air and a simple diet—and not to have people continually going about with long faces and worrying as you do. In this you might take a lesson from Salvatore. That is one of the things I have always admired in him. He never fusses. His cheerfulness is a tonic in itself."

For a week Agnes sat on the terrace in her chaise-longue which Salvatore carried out every morning. It was the one, he said (not very tactfully, Miss Ellen thought), which Don Ludovico had used during his last illness. But his patience was admirable, and his smiling good humour never failed, though Agnes's weakness made her exacting and irritable. It was extraordinary that a man so roughly brought-up should be so light-handed and gentle. Of course, as Miss Ellen reflected, he had had long experience of nursing poor Uncle Ludovic and was used to the vagaries of invalids; yet, in these days, he showed a tenderness of which she could hardly have believed a man capable. She felt herself deeply indebted to him, not only for the delicate tact with which he had handled Agnes in her more provoking moods, but also for the sunny equability of temperament, the unfailing optimism, which made him such a Tower of Strength. She could not imagine what she would have done if, in these harassing circumstances, she had been left alone in a foreign land to 'manage' Agnes herself. Agnes had spoken more truth than she knew when she had said, long ago, what a comfort it was to have a man about the house.

Yet, for all the delicious airs of the Monfalcone spring and for all Salvatore's assiduous tenderness, it soon became clear to Miss Ellen that her sister was not 'picking-up'. She was, in fact, 'going back'. It was all very well for Agnes to assert that her complexion was naturally pallid. The pallor which Miss Ellen noticed now was of a different quality from that which, combined with her jet-black hair, had given her face its somewhat haggard distinction: it was yellowish and opaque, resembling the keys of the old Broadwood piano in the drawing-room at 'The Cedars' as she remembered them, dimly illumined by the sickly subaqueous light that struggled through the smoke-bleared windows which faced Enville Lane.

It seemed to her also that Agnes's finely-cut features, which discriminating people invariably admired, were becoming more pronounced—particularly her nose, which had always been slightly prominent. All the bony structure of the face was accentuated—more especially the cavities of the orbits, from whose shadowy depths those magnificent eyes, which, by contrast with the general shrinkage of the facial tissues, appeared even larger and finer, burned with a brightness, a watchfulness that was frightening in its intensity. Frightening or frightened? By no word that she spoke did Agnes betray any fear. Fear was not in her nature. Yet her features, for all their composure, showed an unspoken—perhaps an unconscious—anxiety.

She was also losing the flesh she had 'put on' in the first three months of her married life. That was hardly surprising. Since the three days' bout of sickness her stomach had remained queasy. Her appetite had never returned, and even the soft foods which Salvatore instructed his mother to prepare seemed to give her discomfort, if not actual pain. When Miss Ellen anxiously commented on her thinness Agnes resented it.

"There you go, fussing again! I prefer to be thin," she said irritably. "All the Isits are naturally spare and sinewy. Remember Papa. In the late sixties he had a beautiful figure, as slim as a boy's. *You* are the only member of the family who has ever been unbecomingly plump. You must have inherited that from the Vaughans. And, as I've always said, you eat too much anyway."

"You've never been nearly so thin as you're getting now."

"You seem to forget I've been ill and am not yet fully recovered. Nor am I so young as I was. I wish you would leave me alone, Ellen. There will be plenty of time for you to start worrying about me when I begin to worry about myself."

Yet Miss Ellen continued to worry and could not disguise it. In the beginning Salvatore's cheery equanimity had sustained her spirits. Now she could not persuade herself that he wasn't treating the case too lightly. After he had carried Agnes downstairs and settled her in her chaise-longue after breakfast, he hurried away to the newly-bought property and rarely returned before sunset, when he burst into the house overflowing with bluff high spirits and demonstrative affection.

"Well, my chicken," he would say as he fondled her thin face, "my little one is better, yes? Now I tell you everything I have done in every moment of the day. Things they go very well over there. This land is much better than ours. I am making a paradise."

And Agnes, who had been waiting all day for this moment and conserved her strength to be at her best to meet it, would whip herself up to a pathetic simulation of vivacity which might deceive him but by no means deceived her sister. Now that she ate—or attempted to eat—her dinner in bed, these brief moments were the only time of the day in which he saw her, for this gave him the best excuse he had ever had for spending his evenings in the village. If he had watched her all day as she did, Miss Ellen thought, he might have made a better estimate of his wife's condition and marked the change in her. He might have noticed, for instance, her hands, as Ellen had done when she sat dozing in her chair and they lay folded on her lap. Agnes had always prided herself on the beauty of her hands, which were long-fingered and shapely—what some people called 'artistic'. Now their whiteness was bluish and almost transparent, like that of the hands of the dead; one could see the shape of the bones; the knuckles seemed large out of all proportion, and the wedding-ring which had fitted her closely only five months ago looked quite loose on her finger. Agnes must have been aware of this, for more than once Ellen noticed her automatically slipping the ring up and down. She also noticed her rubbing her hands together as if they were frozen and she were trying to bring them to life.

"Why do you do that, Agnes?" she asked.

"I don't know. It's ridiculous. For some reason I don't seem able to keep my hands warm, and sometimes they go numb and tingle. Papa was the same. You remember, he always wore gloves. I suppose it must mean that I have a poor circulation, and that's hardly surprising now that I sit here all day and take no exercise."

"Would you like to try a few steps down the terrace, dear? You could lean on my arm."

"That might be a good idea; but I certainly don't need your support, Ellen. I may be a trifle weak, but I'm not so feeble as that. I only let dear Salvatore carry me upstairs because he insists on it. I feel stronger to-day as a matter of fact. Perhaps I will try a little walk after tea."

It was by the merest chance that Miss Ellen saw this experiment, looking down from the balcony of the room where she was arranging Agnes's bed for the night. It was a pitiful spectacle—not so much because of the painful determination with which Agnes forced herself to perform it, as because of the oddness of her gait, which would have been comical had it not been pathetic. It had a grotesque, high-stepping character. With every move forward she lifted her foot, as though she were afraid of her toes catching on the terrace pavement when she put it down, so that her progress resembled that of a lightly-shod person picking her way through wet grass. Miss Ellen watched it with awed fascination. Even from a distance she could feel the strain of the painful expenditure of will that every step cost her sister. But it would never do for Agnes to know that she had been watched; so it was not until the evening that she dared ask her how she had fared.

"Well, I must confess I found walking rather difficult," Agnes admitted. "I expect you remember my saying that my fingers tingled with pins-and-needles and felt numb? I have the same sort of numbness and tingling in my legs: the oddest sensation—just as if I were walking on springs. Of course that's entirely the result of my laziness in not using them, and the pressure of the chair on the nerves. You know how foolish and helpless one feels when one's leg 'goes to sleep'? It was a little like that, but in both legs at the same time. However, I know the reason; so I shall try again to-morrow."

At the dinner-table Miss Ellen gave the news of these symptoms to Salvatore, who seemed not in the least disquieted.

"Now that you tell me this," he said, "all is clear. Now I understand. This is the same as Don Ludovico. I remember he walk just like that. It is weakness of the nerves and rheumatism."

"Don't you think we ought to insist on her seeing a doctor?" Miss Ellen pleaded.

Salvatore's face darkened.

"Why you say that again, Ellen? You know well that Agnes not like it. Many times she have said she is passionate against doctors, and the doctor in Monfalcone is old and no good. Do you want to frighten her? She is already neurasthenic, and this is the spring, which is always trying to foreigners. When the season, the summer, arrive, she will be better. *Non dubitare.*"

"If you are certain it's only rheumatism," Miss Ellen persisted, "don't you think it would be possible to get her some medicine to help her?"

"Sure. That is a swell idea. Now I go to the pharmacist at the Marina and ask him to prescribe against rheumatism. Then all will be satisfied."

That was hardly true so far as Miss Ellen was concerned, but it was at least a small satisfaction to feel that the bottle of medicine which Salvatore brought back that evening represented some contact, however frail, with the outside world. The thing that depressed her most about Agnes's illness was her sense of being cut off and isolated; her feeling that—largely because of Agnes's prejudices—this malady, trivial or serious, was being allowed to take its course without anyone outside the Castello Inglese even knowing that she was ill. Agnes, too, was delighted with the medicine and took it submissively.

"That was kind of you, Salvatore," she said. "It shows how thoughtful you are. And I must say I quite agree with your diagnosis, particularly after what you tell me about Uncle Ludovic. I know Papa suffered agonies from rheumatism—though of course he never complained—after his retirement from India; so it would seem that I inherit it from both sides of the family."

It was difficult to decide how much Faith had to do with it, but there was no doubt that Agnes seemed to be 'better in herself' during the next few days. Though she was determined to force her recalcitrant legs to do their work, and insisted on taking a walk every day, her fantastic high-stepping gait remained in evidence and, in Miss Ellen's judgement, her muscular power diminished. For all this, she was less depressed, and confident that when the mad March days were ended and the settled summer weather began she would recover completely. She even made plans for the future.

"When I begin to get about again," she said, "I look

forward tremendously to seeing for myself the improvements Salvatore has made in the new property. He has worked so hard and is so proud of it that it will be a great joy to him to show me all he has done. After that I feel both he and I will be entitled to a holiday. I haven't mentioned it to him yet, but I think it would be a good idea if we paid a short visit to England."

"To England?" Miss Ellen gasped. "Oh, that would be lovely!"

"I had not intended that you should accompany us, Ellen. It will be necessary to leave some responsible person to look after Stewart, as I understand that the English customs officials do not admit dogs. But there are a number of reasons," she went on, "why I consider such a visit would be good for Salvatore. For one thing I think he ought to meet Mr. Wilburn, who can explain to him, much better than I can, about the North Bromwich property. I should like him to see London as well. He has never been anywhere outside Italy—except in the United States, which hardly counts, after all—and it would widen his mind to see something of an old, established civilization such as ours and to realize something of the meaning of the British Empire. We should make our headquarters in those nice quiet lodgings in Bloomsbury where you and I stayed when we came back from India. I should show him the Tower and the Albert Hall and the British Museum. And I think I should also take him to the Zoological Gardens. That will be a lesson in Kindness to Animals as we understand it."

Yet the spurt of recovery was short-lived. Three days later—on the tenth after the beginning of her illness—Agnes went down with another gastric attack.

"It is such a disappointment to me and to poor Salvatore," she said feebly. "I was so confident that the medicine was doing me good; but now I can't help feeling it may have been rather too strong. The last dose I took burnt my throat, and my legs are so sore that I can hardly bear the pressure on the calves when Salvatore lifts me, though nothing could exceed his angelic gentleness. I can bear this little new setback for myself, but I can't help seeing how much it distresses him."

"I'ld much rather you stopped taking that horrid stuff," Miss Ellen said. "It isn't as if the man who prescribed it had seen you. Oh, Agnes, how I wish you would see a doctor! Going on like this, day after day, in the dark . . . I feel the responsibility is too much for me. I don't think it's fair."

"Now you are talking quite wildly, Ellen. You must be losing your nerve."

"I think I have every reason for losing it," Miss Ellen said hotly.

"For heaven's sake don't let us have a scene: I'm really not fit to stand it. You know perfectly well there is only one doctor in Monfalcone, and I don't want a man like that meddling with me. He's decrepit, and, according to Salvatore, most unreliable. As for your being responsible: I am in the fortunate position of no longer being a weight on you: I have a husband on whom the responsibility now devolves. Do you doubt for a moment that he feels it?"

"No, of course I don't doubt Salvatore's feelings. It's only that I'm not satisfied."

"One would think that this illness was yours and not mine," Agnes said with a wry attempt at a smile. "Now don't look so hurt, Ellen. Must we even be forced to lose our sense of humour?"

"If there were an English doctor here, you wouldn't mind seeing him?"

"Of course not. Naturally I should be glad to have his opinion."

"There must be one in Naples surely. Couldn't we get him over to see you?"

"From the way you talk one would think I was acutely ill, or that we were millionaires looking for somewhere to throw money about. If my condition were really grave it would be another matter. I felt much better yesterday, and should be quite all right to-day if it weren't for this wretched dyspepsia and the weakness in my arms and legs which, as you know, was precisely what Uncle Ludovic suffered from."

Miss Ellen sighed. "Well . . . I suppose you know best as usual."

But she knew that Agnes didn't in this case. She couldn't understand how it was that neither she nor Salvatore appeared to realize that she was slowly and steadily going down-hill. Were they both of them, she wondered, aware of it and putting on a brave face for her benefit? If they were, if they realized that this was a matter of gravity, surely they wouldn't be quibbling about the cost of calling an English doctor from Naples?—although Agnes, schooled by their hard experiences at North Bromwich, was still inclined to be just a little mean, and Salvatore, since he had begun to handle their money, admittedly resented the spending of every halfpenny that didn't go into the land.

What made his attitude much harder to understand was the fact that she was never in doubt of his complete devotion to her sister. In the earlier stages of Agnes's illness he had occasionally seemed to her inattentive and insensitive, if not exactly callous, taking it rather too much for granted that everything would come right in the end; but of late, since Agnes had grown feebler and looked far more ill than she would confess, nothing could have exceeded his tender solicitude, his genuine unselfishness. It had been touching to see the way in which he had departed from his established habits of life—not merely neglecting the care of the land, which meant so much to him, but going upstairs to sit with her for hours at a time and humouring her morbid irritability with a patience which Agnes had rightly described as angelic. He was always at hand, within call, ready to re-arrange her pillows and lift her if she wanted to be moved. More than that: when Agnes had complained of his mother's cooking, he had insisted on taking possession of the kitchen and preparing, with his own hands, all the invalid food that she ate. If he had been a trained nurse his attentions could not have been more skilful and delicate. He was devoting his life to her. Could any husband living have done more than that?

Up to this point in her sister's illness Miss Ellen had been merely perplexed by its mystery, and distressed by the sense of her own helplessness in dealing with it. It was at the end of the second week that two incidents, which occurred in swift succession, gave her a painful shock. She had been dining alone with Salvatore in the salone—Agnes had persistently refused to let him take his meals in her room: partly because the mere sight and smell of normal food revolted her, and partly because she thought a change from the atmosphere of a sick room would do him good. During dinner that evening Miss Ellen had returned to the attack on the idea of calling the English doctor from Naples. For a while Salvatore had listened morosely, without answering, as though the subject bored him. Then, suddenly, he leapt up from his chair and rated her with a passionate incoherence, all his English going to the winds.

"Why you say all this nonsense?" he shouted. "Why you talk like this to me? What you think I am? I am the God, perhaps, to force Agnes to do what she does not wish? She tell me herself, Agnes tell me, that it is you with your worrying that will drive her right off her head. Now you come between wife and husband. That is a fine thing, I tell you! See here: There is not need of a doctor to say what is this malady. I have seen it before one time, with Don Ludovico. It is in the nerves, as I say. It is in the blood. It is a thing of the family. Now you shut your damn mouth! Understand?"

Miss Ellen said nothing. Her heart was fluttering so fast that she could not speak.

As he spoke he had been striding to and fro and waving his napkin, his face suffused with an angry purple, his tawny eyes blazing, his mouth twisted and cruel. Then, as suddenly as it had risen, his fury subsided and he laughed out loud. With the flourish she knew so well, he tucked the napkin over his arm and came up behind her, just as he used to do when he was waiting at table. He placed his arms about her; his hands closed tightly on her breasts.

"Poor little Elena!" he said in a soft, wheedling voice which she hardly recognized. "What I do? I scare you? There is no need to be scared of me. I am only your brother—eh? And what a nice fat little quail you are! Like a woman should be. See here now: if Agnes she die like Don Ludovico, you not fly away? You like to stay with me? Yes?"

Miss Ellen shuddered. 'Scared' was hardly the word for what she felt now. This was the terror of that panic flight through the olive-grove a hundred times magnified. She gasped feebly:

"Please, Salvatore! Oh, please let me go!"

Salvatore laughed softly, his hands relaxed their grip.

"All right, then. . . . I let you go. But do not forget I have the appetite for the little quails, and I prefer them fat. Now you go and tell the long history to Agnes, I suppose?"

She did not know where she was going nor care, so long as she could get away from him. She scurried out of the salone and into the dark hall, making straight for the stairs. As she ran, she stumbled and nearly fell, her foot catching in some unyielding obstacle that lay in her path. Her mind leapt to it at once that this was probably Stewart, who, ever since Salvatore had banished him from Agnes's bedroom, had persisted in lying asleep in the darkest and most unexpected corners of the house and getting in everybody's way. When he was trodden on he usually growled and occasionally snapped. But this time he did not move. Miss Ellen bent down and patted him, murmuring an apology. He still remained motionless, and her fingers touched something slimy and wet. She hurried back to the door of the salone and called Salvatore's name.

He did not answer; so she opened the door of the salone and looked inside. He was standing there with his arm tightly clasped round Angelina's waist, his face pressed against hers.

"Salvatore!" she called again.

Angelina leapt away from him. Salvatore turned with the face of a frustrated bull.

"What is it?" he said.

"Bring a light, please. It's Stewart. There's something wrong with him."

Salvatore grumbled under his breath and appeared carrying a candle whose flicker illumined the body of Stewart lying with his head outstretched like a camel's, and Miss Ellen's fingers dabbled with slime and blood.

"Oh dear, the poor little thing must be ill," she said.

Salvatore advanced and turned Stewart's prostrate body over with a contemptuous kick.

"The dog's dead," he said brutally. "I will do the necessary, Elena. *Non dubitare.*"

He put down his candle and picked Stewart up by his stubby tail. Then he opened the door that led to the terrace and flung the limp body over the parapet. He wiped his hands on the napkin which was still over his arm.

"If Agnes ask for the dog," he said sternly, "you tell her that he is all right. You understand?"

Miss Ellen did not answer him. She was choking with tears. Having groped her way over the dark staircase she locked the door of her bedroom and stood frozen behind it, listening for she knew not what. She was conscious for the first time of an imminent, incalculable danger—to herself no less than to Agnes. It was as though the earth had opened and a bottomless chasm yawned at her feet.

13

DURING THE hours of nightmare darkness Miss Ellen made up her mind: she determined to take no more risks—even at the cost of offending Agnes or estranging her she was resolved, on her own responsibility, to get in touch at once with the English doctor in Naples and bring him to the house. How she could set about doing this was another matter on which she had only the haziest ideas. No doubt Mrs. Hamilton-Gough knew all about him; but the prospect of inviting another rebuff intimidated her. Perhaps Mr. Potter or Ronnie Sanctuary could help her; but she could not imagine either of them rising very rapidly to an emergency. In the end she decided to unburden her troubles in the capacious bosom of her first friend Virginia Murphy.

The studio at the Marina appeared to be hermetically sealed. As she knocked at the door she realized that Miss Murphy rarely rose before noon and was probably still asleep. After five minutes of anxious hammering she heard sounds of sluggish movement inside, and Miss Murphy, inadequately swathed in her pink wrapper, which she apparently wore day and night, opened the door and blinked at her with a bewildered smile, emitting, at the same time, a concentrated odour of cat.

"Why, honey," she wheezed, "I declare this is a lovely surprise. Come right in, and I'll get you some breakfast. I've no idea what time it is, because I've no watch; but I guess I must just have overslept as usual."

"I'm afraid it's I who am dreadfully early," Miss Ellen apologized; "but I had to come. I'm so worried about my sister, Virginia. I'm afraid she's terribly ill."

"Oh no, she isn't ill, honey," Miss Murphy said cheerfully. "That's where you're mistaken. My Science has taught me that there is no such thing as illness—only wrong thinking."

"I don't quite understand . . ."

"Never mind about understanding. Just remember right now there's nothing whatever to worry about. Eat your breakfast first, and then we will have a nice talk. You'll find it all put quite clearly in the little book I'm going to lend you—that is, if you study it thoroughly. *Science and Health with key to the Scriptures* by our dear leader. And I'll let you have some of the pamphlets as well—that is if I can find any. Now where have I put that tea? I know you English people can't live without it."

Her pink shape disappeared into the dim welter of wreckage at the back of the studio while the ginger tomcat fawned on Miss Ellen's legs.

"I'm afraid it's rather more serious than that," she said. "Agnes is really dangerously ill. I'm thoroughly frightened."

"Fear and pain are both entirely imaginary," Miss Murphy mumbled, still hopelessly ferreting for the lost tin of tea. "They are only the signs of lack of Spiritual Harmony, and, like so-called disease, neither of them can be healed by Material Means. But don't worry, honey; you'll find it all in the book. Ah, there we are! Now wait while I light the oil-stove."

"I was only wondering," Miss Ellen said anxiously, "if you happened to know the name and address of the English doctor in Naples. There is one, isn't there?"

"Well, naturally, *I* wouldn't know if there were," Miss Murphy said reproachfully. "We Scientists don't employ doctors anyway, because we know there's no need for them. Material Healing is powerless to get at the root. Only holding fast to the Truth can do that. 'Stand porter at the door of thought,' Mrs. Eddy says. 'Admitting only such conclusions as you wish realized in bodily results, you will control yourself harmoniously.' And it's perfectly true. You will, honey."

"Yes, I'm sure there must be quite a lot in what you say," Miss Ellen said feebly. "But . . . you see, I want to get something done at once—before it's too late. And if you don't know about the English doctor, I think I had better . . ."

Miss Murphy shook her head sadly.

"Now there you go. Doesn't that just prove that you're still thinking wrongly? It's never too late. If you'll only be patient and cast out fear, I believe I have the address of a perfectly lovely American lady, an experienced Christian Science practitioner who lives either in Rome or Siena, I'm not quite certain which. Why, now that I come to think of it, I do believe it was Florence. If you'll give me time I'm almost sure I can find it, unless it's been lost."

"But even if we could get hold of her," Miss Ellen said, "I'm not at all sure that Agnes would consent to see her."

"Oh, she needn't come here, honey. All we need do is to write her and ask her to do some work for your darling sister. After breakfast I'll set about doing some work for her myself, but if you start fussing and hurrying me this way you can't possibly expect me to have harmonious thoughts. Now *can* you?"

"Well, I'm terribly sorry," Miss Ellen said desperately; "but I feel I simply can't wait any longer without doing anything. You won't think me rude, will you, Virginia? I'm really most grateful. I'll look in again if I can."

She rose and moved to the door. Miss Murphy ponderously pursued her.

"You're forgetting the little book, honey."

"Thanks so much. I'll call for it later if you don't mind."

Miss Murphy had no time to say whether she did mind or didn't. By the time she had recovered from the shock Miss Ellen was already floundering over the sand towards the piazza. As she reached it, the clock in the campanile clanged half-past ten. Though Miss Murphy had failed her, she still had two strings left to her bow. One of them, Mr. Potter, would already be on his way to the Post Office to collect his *Daily Telegraph*. She decided to wait for him there; and before she had crossed the piazza she ran into the second, Ronnie Sanctuary, strolling along with a mincing, gingerly gait, in a Panama hat and a suit of white Capri flannel. When he saw her he threw up his hands in an affectation of delighted surprise.

"Well, upon my soul," he said, "what are you doing down here? This is an unexpected pleasure, dear lady. It's weeks since we've met. How's your charmin' sister?"

"She's ill, Mr. Sanctuary. To tell you the truth, I was hoping to see you. I'm terribly worried about her."

"Indeed? No wonder you look—may I say it without offence?—a trifle dishevelled. Not quite your delightful self. I'm sure I don't know what use I can be; but if there is anything I can do, here I am, at your service as always."

Mr. Sanctuary bowed gallantly and flashed a quick artificial smile, without looking at her. "If the question isn't indelicate," he said, "perhaps you will tell me what's wrong with her?"

"She's been ill for a week—no, nearly a fortnight. At first it was just indigestion, but very severe, you know. Now there's something wrong with the nerves in her limbs. She's losing the use of them."

"Losin' the use of them . . . ah yes," Mr. Sanctuary repeated absently, with a gay wave of the hand and another flash at a handsome young fisherman who at that moment crossed the piazza. "Excuse me . . . a young friend of mine," he mumbled. "What was that you said? Losin' the use? The use of *what?*"

"Her legs and her arms. I'm afraid it must be the nerves. There's a lot of numbness and tingling."

"Ah, tinglin'. . . . That must be the weather. These accursed March thunderstorms. Too much electricity in the air. I must confess I find it exceedingly tryin' myself. Thank your stars you're still in the bloom of youth, dear lady. When you get to my age. . . . But losin' the use of them: that's quite another matter. Look here, now; I've suddenly remembered. Wasn't that precisely what happened to poor old Ludo Vaughan?"

"Salvatore says so. That's what I find so disturbing. You see. . . . Uncle Ludovic died."

"Ah, but that was a different pair of sleeves. Poor Ludo never looked after himself, I regret to say, while your sister's a healthy and virtuous woman. This is odd, you know. Very odd. It might be in the family, mightn't it? The sins of the fathers. . . . I suppose *your* father didn't have the same trouble by any chance?"

"Oh no, Papa had a constitution of iron. What I really wanted to ask you was this, Mr. Sanctuary: do you know the name and address of the English doctor in Naples?"

"Now there you've got me. I'm afraid I don't. I never go to Naples unless I have to. When I want vettin'—and that's very rarely—I get the Italian feller here to look over me. But I tell you what: if I were you I should try to get hold of poor Potter. He's the true-blue Britisher and knows all about that sort of thing; but for heaven's sake don't excite him—the poor old boy's goin' to pieces at an alarmin' rate. You'll have to shout, too: his hearin' gets worse every day. And now, if you'll be so gracious as to excuse me, dear lady, I must get on with my humble shoppin'! I'm after some fish. Poor Potter is bound to be down in another few minutes unless he's popped off in the night."

With a sweep of his Panama hat Mr. Sanctuary minced off rapidly in the direction taken by his young friend. Miss Ellen, thwarted again, hurried across the square to the Post Office. At that moment, the clock in the campanile struck eleven, and simultaneously, as punctual as the midday gun at Greenwich, Mr. Potter swept round the corner carrying a sturdy ash-plant and wearing a bowler hat. At the sight of Miss Ellen he hesitated and turned to take refuge in a smelly side-street on the left, but not sufficiently quickly to avoid her cutting him off.

"Mr. Potter," she yelled. "I want to ask you a question."

"Eh? What's that? I'm sure I don't know."

"My sister is seriously ill, and I think you can help me."

"Ill? I can't say you look it."

"It's my sister, not me."

"Oh, your sister. And why is she ill? To be brief: Italian food. Are their concoctions fit for a civilized stomach? The answer is 'No'. Are they wholesome? On the contrary. But if you'll promise never to tell Mrs. Hamilton-Gough I'll tell you what I will do. I'll let you have the address of the butcher in Naples who posts me my leg of mutton. A roast joint every Sunday with two vegetables. No foreign kickshaws. And plenty of regular exercise. That is the secret of health. Look at poor old Sanctuary. That man started life with a digestion as good as mine, a stomach like an ostrich. But the diet's beginning to tell on him. Will he last out the year? The answer is doubtful. Senility. That is the word. And whose fault is it? In a nutshell, his own."

"What I really want is the address of the English doctor in Naples," Miss Ellen shouted.

"In Naples? Don't trust them. Damned rogues every one of them."

"I believe there's an Englishman."

"If there is, I'm sorry for him among all those scoundrels. Would they allow him to make an honest living? Not on your life! I've never been ill myself because I refuse to truckle to their ideas of feeding; but if I ever wanted a doctor, I should take the first train to England. There's an excellent fellow—I can't just remember his name—in Stony Stratford. M.R.C.S. and L.R.C.P. What do those eight letters stand for? In two words—British Integrity. In one—Honesty. Is the matter arguable? No. You can take it or leave it."

Miss Ellen decided to leave it.

"Thank you so much, Mr. Potter," she bawled. "I'm sure you would have helped me if you could."

"You've forgotten the butcher's address," Mr. Potter reminded her.

"Oh dear. . . . May I have it later?" Miss Ellen shouted as she hurried away without waiting for a reply. At the moment she had no precise notion where she was hurrying; but, as she crossed the piazza once more, inspiration came to her help. Of course. . . . The Pensione. She did not know its proprietor even by name; but it was the house in which most of the English visitors stayed, and he was therefore more likely to know the English doctor's address than any other person in Monfalcone. The palm-shaded garden in front of it appeared to be almost deserted; for its famous wisteria was not yet in bloom, and the flights of elderly spinsters who painted it would not hatch out until the middle of April. Only the thick-set flowers of a leafless Judas tree flaunted their petals of rosy purple against a sea that shimmered like the satiny wings of an Adonis Blue butterfly. At the farther end of the terrace, in full sun, sat an elderly gentleman, his eyes puckered over a newspaper. Something in the cut of his clothes encouraged Miss Ellen to think he was English. No doubt he would be able to help a fellow-countrywoman to find the proprietor and explain her predicament. Though she was still uncomfortably conscious of the cruel reflections Mr. Sanctuary had made on her dishevelled appearance, she decided to accost him. As she approached, he heard her steps and looked up from his newspaper; then rose with a smile.

"Oh, Ben, Ben," she cried. "Why didn't you let me know you were here?"

"I've hardly had time: I only arrived late last night, Ellen. I was planning to come up and call on you this afternoon."

"Thank God, thank God you've come, Ben!"

"Why, what is the matter, Ellen? Are you in trouble?"

"It's not me—it's Agnes. She's terribly, terribly ill."

"What's the matter?" His tone immediately became professional. "What do the doctors say?"

"She won't see a doctor. That is the worst of it. You know how obstinate she can be, and her husband encourages her."

"Her husband? I didn't even know she was married."

"She was married just after you left, Ben. It was all very sudden."

"And who is the fortunate man?"

"It would take too long to explain. His name is Salvatore Ferraro. He was our butler. A Monfalconese."

"Dear, dear. . . . I must say that sounds very surprising, Ellen."

"Nobody was more surprised than myself."

"I can see you don't like him."

"Oh, I wouldn't say that. He's extremely kind to her, and I'm sure she is happy with him. But I'm frightened, Ben . . . desperately frightened."

"I can see that, my dear. You look it." He took her arm gently. "Now come and sit down quietly over here and tell me all about it."

Miss Ellen smiled wanly.

"If you only knew what a comfort it is to see you, Ben. I feel happier already."

He pressed her arm reassuringly and made her sit down beside him.

"Now suppose we begin at the very beginning," he said.

Miss Ellen began to talk. The act of unburdening her mind of all the unspoken doubts and fears that had tormented it gave her an immediate sense of relief. Her first rush of words was confused and disjointed; but as she went on she grew steadily calmer and the process of thought became more coherent. The mere presence of this man, so wise, so serene, so stable, so understanding, gave her confidence. As she spoke, he never took his eyes off her: they were clear, cool, penetrating eyes, and their keenness did not confuse her, for she felt that the brain behind them was not critical of herself but only of what she said. From time to time he interjected a sudden question, the purpose of which she could not understand; but the mere fact that she did not understand it gave her all the more confidence. He was working the problem out by his own methods and to his own satisfaction. It was not for her to worry about what the solution might be. With every word that she spoke she felt the weight of her own responsibility lifting. It was like passing from the black terrors of a nightmare into the light of day.

"That is all? You can tell me no more?" he said at last.

"Yes. . . . I believe that is all. Do you think it is . . . very serious?"

He evaded the question. "I think you were most foolish not to insist on calling in a doctor—even the local doctor. From all that I know of it, Italian medicine is pretty good."

"Ah, but you don't realize what Agnes is! And Salvatore . . ."

"Of course I know nothing about *him;* but even in his own interest he should have been firm. That is a feature in the case which, I must confess, I don't like."

"Can you tell what it is, Ben?"

"From some of the symptoms—the paresis and so on—it sounds like what is called a peripheral neuritis; but there are others which I couldn't possibly diagnose without seeing her."

"You *will* come and see her, won't you?"

"Certainly I will—if she'll let me."

"I shan't give her the chance of refusing; you shall see her whether she likes it or no!"

"I agree that the risk is worth taking. But you must understand that I can only see her as a friend. I'm not licensed to kill or cure in Italy, and I should not be allowed to prescribe for her. On the other hand I should be glad to meet the local doctor—or the man whom you mentioned in Naples—in consultation."

"If you only saw her for a moment I should be happier. Could you come with me now?"

"Of course. I'll ask the padrone to send for a carriage."

"It would be far quicker to get one at the piazza."

He smiled at her urgency: "Very well. No doubt you know best. This is your country, not mine."

On the slow grind up the hill to the Castello Inglese they spoke no word about Agnes. He was tactful, as she guessed, in keeping her mind away from any subject that distressed her: and, though she saw through it, she was grateful. He talked about Egypt: the beauty of Assouan, where he had stayed for six weeks, and the splendours of Karnak and Luxor.

"Still, you know," he said, "I have never seen anything more beautiful, more—how shall I put it?—more reassuring than Monfalcone. Egypt belongs to the past just as much as America belongs to the future. Here I feel that life is only concerned with the present—and that is all that one asks of it when one comes to our age. Which reminds me: have you found me that villa I spoke about?"

"I've heard of one which I believe would suit you perfectly. It's an old *contadino* house, that would have to be reconstructed and modernized of course, on the property next to ours, which Salvatore has just bought."

"So he's a man of means, this husband of Agnes's?"

"Oh no, it was with our money he bought it. I think at one time, it belonged to his family. He's mad about land."

"H'm. . . I see."

The cab pulled up at the gates of the Castello Inglese. They passed in without challenge, since Stewart was no longer on guard, and the long terrace, bleached in the light of the midday sun, lay empty but for a couple of basking lizards that jerked up inquisitive heads and scurried away as they advanced.

"What a charming place you have here," he said.

"Please don't talk," Miss Ellen whispered. "I want to take you to Agnes's room without anyone hearing or seeing us."

She went forward on tiptoe. Sir Benjamin, smiling at her precautions, followed. As they passed through the hall Miss Ellen shuddered as she noticed on the polished encaustic tiles the stain that had been left by poor Stewart's dribbling. With that sight, trifling as it was, the icy shadow of the horror which she had almost forgotten returned, and she quickened her pace. She tapped softly on Agnes's door. There was no answer, and a fear even colder gripped her. They entered in silence.

Agnes was lying on her back, her eyes closed, her mouth half-open. The sun, streaming through the uncurtained window, illumined her face with a merciless light. Once before its colour had reminded Miss Ellen of the keys of the ancient Broadwood piano. Now, she could not say why, it struck her as resembling that of the old mare Rowena's teeth. The lips were bluish and dry, and the tarnished ivory of her brow showed, in this fierce illumination, two patches of bronze. Miss Ellen anxiously turned to look at her companion. His mouth was grave, severe—she had almost said angry.

She spoke softly and timidly: "Agnes. . . . I've brought you a visitor."

Agnes opened her eyes and surveyed them both with an odd, remote calmness.

"Why, Ben," she said. "What are you doing here?" Her mildness was unexpected. Perhaps she was too weak to be anything but mild.

"Ellen met me quite unexpectedly at Montalcone

Marina, and asked me to come up with her and see you. I'm sorry to hear you've been ill."

"Yes. . . . I have been seedy for some time; and it has left me a trifle weak: not a bit like myself. It was kind of you to come and see me. A strange meeting, too, isn't it?—after all these years. I'm sorry I'm not in a better state to receive you."

"Yes, indeed, it is strange, as you say," Ben Dench replied gently. "But I'm glad I came, Agnes—if only because it's possible I may be of some help—not merely as an old friend but as a doctor. Would you mind my asking you a few questions and examining you professionally? I'll try not to tire you, and you'll tell me, won't you, if I do?"

"I should be glad if you would examine me. But don't you think it would perhaps be more fitting if my husband were present? I expect Ellen has told you I am married?"

"She has—and of course I look forward to meeting your husband."

"One has to be careful in matters of this kind: the customs of foreigners are sometimes different from ours, and one has to study their susceptibilities."

"I agree; but, if you have no objection, I'ld much rather he were not here. It's a mistake, on occasions like this, to have too many people in the room."

Agnes sighed. "Well, perhaps, since Ellen is here, it's all right. What do you want me to do?"

"A few questions first, if you don't mind. Ellen has given me a rough outline of your trouble, but I'ld like to confirm it. Perhaps it would be simpler if you told me in your own words. Can you remember when it began?"

"Exactly sixteen days ago."

Agnes's voice was feeble; again and again she was forced to moisten her lips; but her memory was faultless—once again Ellen was amazed by the acuteness of her observation, the clarity and precision of her mind: no detail which she could have supplied escaped it.

"I don't think I've left anything out," Agnes said at last.

"You are an admirable patient. I only wish others were as helpful. There are just one or two more things I want to know. About these gastric attacks—I think 'bilious' was the word you used? Can you associate them with any particular food?"

"I don't think so. There's no accounting for them. Even the lightest foods seem to bring them on sometimes."

"Who prepares your meals?"

"At first it was the cook. My husband's mother has been giving us temporary help in the kitchen. But lately my husband has insisted on preparing them himself, for fear of any possible carelessness. He is extremely particular about little things like that. His anxiety has been most touching."

"I see. . . . And the last of these . . . attacks?"

"It was yesterday. But it wasn't so severe as the others. It passed off quite quickly."

"And it has left you with no discomfort?"

"No. . . . Apart from this wretched loss of appetite. That is what worries me most. You see, if I don't eat, how *can* I regain my strength? The mere smell of food revolts me. You see . . ." She pointed feebly to a cup of some milky invalid food that lay cold and untouched on the bedside table. "Salvatore brought me up this an hour ago, and I simply can't touch it."

"I see. And the bottle of medicine beside it?"

"That was what he got from the pharmacist—as we say, the chemist. The first doses seemed to do good; but the last burnt my throat. I couldn't swallow it."

"Quite, quite. . . . I'll find out what he prescribed later on. Now, if you don't mind . . ."

He began to examine her methodically. First the eyes, which he tested for movement and the reactions of the pupils to accommodation and light. Then the tongue and the lips. "Just smile for a moment." She smiled mirthlessly. He appeared to be satisfied.

"Now clasp both my hands with yours. Can't you grip any harder than that? Well, well. . . . Never mind. Close your eyes." He brushed her arms lightly with a pinpoint. "Tell me quickly when you feel that I touch you." Agnes was silent. "You didn't feel anything then? Nor even now?" She shook her head. "That will do, then. Now you can open them. Next I want to examine your chest—your heart and so on. Don't exert yourself. Ellen will help you to get clear of the night-dress."

Miss Ellen helped her, with trembling hands. It was ridiculous, she knew, but she herself seemed far more nervous than Agnes. How beautifully white and fine-textured, she thought Agnes's skin must have been: but how terribly wasted her figure was now—far more wasted than she had realized!

"That will do nicely, thank you."

She heard the calm level voice of Ben Dench behind her. As she made way for him, Miss Ellen was overwhelmed by a ghastly sense of the situation's irony. To think that the man who now gazed on the nakedness of Agnes's body unmoved by any emotion had once passionately desired her! Did any part of the mind behind those shrewd, cool eyes, whose habit it was to miss nothing, glow suddenly with remembrance of that past emotion? Was it shaken, if ever so little, by the thought of what might have been, reconstructing from those aged and wasted tissues a vision of the young beauty that had been denied him? Was Agnes, too, wondering what he thought?

Miss Ellen saw him take out his watch as he gazed. He was counting the respirations. He bent over Agnes, percussing the outline of the heart, and laid his ear to her chest to listen to the sounds of its pulsations. As she watched this methodical performance of a clinical routine that had become second nature, she realized, of a sudden, the futility of the romantic speculations which had moved her. At this moment Ben Dench was no longer a man but a doctor—and Agnes, to him, no longer a woman whom he had desired but a patient. And perhaps not even a patient: merely a case.

"Now the abdomen, please," he was saying.

As Miss Ellen tucked up the night-dress and pulled up the sheet, she fancied he frowned. She, too, had noticed the coppery discoloration that marred the skin's whiteness. His strong hands were pressed firmly but very gently on the abdominal wall.

"No pain here? Tell me at once if I hurt you," he said. "You've been very patient. I shan't have to worry you much longer. Just the reflexes of the lower limbs, Ellen, if you'll kindly uncover them."

"Oh dear," Ellen thought. "She used to be so proud of her ankles!"

They were nothing, alas, to be proud of now. It was no wonder that Agnes had been unable to walk. Her legs were like shapeless sticks. The muscles of the calves had almost disappeared. When he touched them, gentle as he was, Agnes started with pain.

"I'm so sorry I jumped," she said, "but I couldn't help it. That really hurt me."

"My fault. I won't do it again."

He propped the joint on one hand and with the edge of the other sharply tapped the tendon below the knee-cap. The knee-jerk reflex was absent. He bent back the trailing feet on the ankles. The ankle-clonus reflex also was gone.

"That is all," he said, with a smile. "I think I know where we are now. With your permission, Agnes, I shall talk over the case with your local doctor and get him to prescribe what I want you to have."

"I'm afraid Salvatore—my husband—won't like that," Agnes said.

"That can't be helped. Without an Italian registration I can't prescribe for you myself. I've no doubt that everything can be arranged without his seeing you. The point is that somebody must be made legally responsible, in case of accidents."

"In case of accidents?" Agnes repeated. "You don't mean . . ." She hesitated. "You don't mean that I'm going to die?"

"My dear Agnes!"

The reproachful tone was not convincing. Agnes gazed at him long and doubtfully.

"I would much rather you told me the truth, Ben," she said. "It is not for my own sake. Life has given me as great and perfect a happiness as any woman could ask of it. I am thinking of my poor dear husband. If I . . . didn't get well, it would be so tragic for him. It would break his heart. He is so good, and he needs me so much."

Ben Dench laid his hand on hers: "Put that out of your mind, Agnes. You are suffering from a troublesome and painful complaint which we call—if you must have a name for it—Peripheral Neuritis. You've been much more gravely ill than you realize, and, of course, you are terribly weak. But there's no reason on earth that I know of why you shouldn't get better, always provided—and this is vitally important—provided that your husband and you are prepared to put yourselves completely in my hands. Will you trust me? Will you promise to accept whatever I may decide without question, even if it seems to you hard and unreasonable?"

"Of course I will promise. I trust you implicitly, Ben. But naturally I can't answer for Salvatore."

"Somehow I think your husband is likely to see eye to eye with me when I've had a talk with him. If he doesn't . . . Well, it's no good meeting trouble half-way. Now I'll say good-bye for the time being."

He pressed her bony hand tenderly and Agnes responded with a faint smile.

"You have done me good already," she said. "Though I wouldn't confess it even to myself, I was beginning to feel rather hopeless. Now I'm full of new hope and confidence, and so anxious to be better. If you'll help me, Ellen, I think I could drink that gruel."

"No, I wouldn't do that if I were you," Dench interposed quickly. "Ellen will warm it up for you or make you some more. We'll take it down with us. I may as well take this bottle of medicine too." He slipped it into his pocket. "Now I'm going to have a talk with this dear husband of yours."

Downstairs, in the salone, he waited, while Miss Ellen went to look for Salvatore. She found him, as she had expected, in the kitchen, lazily gossiping with his mother and the new dark girl whom she had noticed at work in the olive-groves.

"An old friend of ours has turned up unexpectedly to see Agnes," she told him.

Salvatore scowled. "Agnes cannot see nobody. Tell him that. I will not permit her to be disturbed."

"I'm afraid he has seen her already," Miss Ellen said calmly. "Now he wants to see you. He is waiting in the salone."

Salvatore's face darkened.

"How dare you let him see her without asking me? Who is he, this friend?"

"His name is Sir Benjamin Dench."

"Ah, now I can understand. That is the name I heard before. This is the man you said would rent the villa I make in the new property. That is good. He has much money? Yes?"

"I really can't say. He wants to talk about Agnes. He's a doctor, you know."

"A doctor?" Was it possible that Salvatore went pale? If he did, it was only for a moment. "Very well. Now I come."

Ben Dench was sitting in Agnes's chair. Beside him on the table, stood the half-empty bottle of medicine and the cup of cold gruel which Miss Ellen had brought downstairs. As his eyes fell on them, Salvatore blinked and his face went red.

"Excuse, Signore," he said. "Let me remove the cup and saucer. The persons of service in this house are impossible: so untidy and careless. They leave everything about. Permit me . . ."

He put out his hand to take them but Ben Dench forestalled him with a protective gesture.

"That can wait," he said. "You are Mr. Ferraro?"

Salvatore bowed. In a moment he had become once more the perfect manservant. It was extraordinary, Miss Ellen thought, how quickly and without effort Ben Dench had established a subtle superiority.

"Won't you sit down, Mr. Ferraro?" he said pleasantly. "I want to have a few words with you about your wife. As Miss Isit has probably told you, we are old friends."

For a moment Salvatore hesitated. As she saw the two men gazing at one another, Miss Ellen was frightened of what might come next. Almost as if he were aware of this anxiety Ben Dench spoke to her.

"I think, perhaps, it would be better if you left us alone, Ellen." As she went, he turned to Salvatore again. "Mr. Ferraro, I asked you to sit down."

Salvatore sat down.

"Now I want to talk to you seriously," he went on. "You understand English, don't you? Mr. Ferraro?"

"Well enough, Signore. I have been a long time in America."

"Excellent. In that case I shall not have to choose my words. I should tell you, by the way, that I am a doctor . . ."

"That is understood."

"Very well. I have examined your wife, with her permission, of course, and I find she is gravely ill—more gravely ill, it would seem, than you realize. I am surprised that you haven't thought fit to call in a doctor before."

"Eh, you do not understand, Signore. I have already seen this illness. It is a thing of the family. Her uncle, my master, the Captain Vaughan, he was the same; but the doctors, they say it is the nerves, and they can do nothing . . . nothing at all."

"And Captain Vaughan died?"

"He was an old man. What will you, Signore? We must all die."

"You were serving him at the time, I believe?"

"For twelve—fifteen years I serve him faithfully. And he do me very bad." Salvatore became excited. "He promise to leave me this villa; and when he die, there is no testament. It is a scandal. Everyone laugh at me."

"A great disappointment. Yes. . . . I can well believe it. But if your wife should die of the same illness, the identical illness, you would not be so disappointed? The property—I should say rather her share of it—would become yours?"

Salvatore waved his hands. "That is a thing of the law. How should I know? I am an ordinary person, not a lawyer, Signore."

"But surely . . . ? However, we'll leave that aside for the moment. You were devoted to Captain Vaughan, Mr. Ferraro?"

"What must I say? He was my master and friend. I am faithful by nature. I am attached—how you say?—to the house."

"That is fairly evident." Ben Dench paused. "I suppose. . . . I suppose you attended to him, during that last illness of his, with the same devotion which I gather you have shown to your wife?"

"She is my wife. That is different. I am a good husband. I love my wife."

"We take that for granted, naturally. But to be more explicit—to go more into detail . . ."

"Continue. I understand."

" . . . I suppose you prepared all his food with the same touching care and devotion as you have shown in the case of your wife?"

Salvatore rose angrily:

"Why you ask all these questions?" he cried. "I am not here to question! These things are not your affair. I tolerate it no more. I am not the man to be tormented in my own house!"

"In your wife's house, to be more exact."

"It is the same thing, Signore. I come here to talk of my wife who is ill, and you waste the time talking about the Captain Vaughan who is dead. What is that to do with it?"

Ben Dench gazed at his angry face fixedly, a faint smile on his lips.

"Very well. We will leave Captain Vaughan for the moment and talk of your wife. You had really better sit down again, Mr. Ferraro."

"I do not wish to sit down," Salvatore said sullenly.

"Let us go on, then. I have examined Mrs. Ferraro with a good deal of care, and I find she is suffering from what we call peripheral neuritis in a serious degree."

"That is nothing new. Have I not told you it is the nerves? That doesn't help any."

"I entirely agree. It doesn't. This neuritis is only a symptom, if you understand me. What we want to find is the cause."

"That is not difficult. I speak now of private things. My wife—it is not worth the pains to deny—is an old woman for being married. There is the strain on the nerves—is it not true?—and the time of life. There is also one thing you do not understand. The air of Monfalcone is too strong for foreigners. This is a thing well known. They are habituated to suffer from the nerves if they stay here too long. Sometimes it is worse. There are many I can remember who go out mad. *Escono pazzi.* What you call crazy."

Ben Dench shook his head.

"I don't think we need stress the Monfalcone air as a probable cause of this illness, Mr. Ferraro."

He took up the medicine-bottle, then read the label and put it down again. With the same idly meditative air he moved the cup of cold gruel a little nearer to him. Then he leant back in his chair and put the tips of his fingers together.

"This disease, peripheral or multiple neuritis, is always associated with the action of certain specific poisons in the blood." Salvatore started. "The toxins, for example," he went on, "of Diphtheria and Influenza, and to a certain extent Enteric Fever, which you, I believe, call Typhus."

"Then that can explain . . ." Salvatore began.

"No. Unfortunately it can't. There is no history of anything of that kind. Apart from these toxins of infective disease there is another group of poisons. Alcohol is the commonest. But I should be surprised if you told me that your wife habitually drank to excess."

"She always drink wine," Salvatore said hopefully,

"and the wine of the Castello Inglese is well known to be strong."

"But she is a temperate woman. I don't think we need have any doubt about that. There remain the metallic poisons. Lead and arsenic. You will be happy to know that your wife has none of the usual symptoms of lead-poisoning. As for arsenic. . . . Its presence cannot be ascertained by a cursory physical examination; but if we proceed to laboratory tests—you understand me?—it can easily be isolated from the natural secretions. If we take samples and send them to Naples. . . . Why, what is the matter with you, Mr. Ferraro? I must really beg you to sit down . . ."

He took Salvatore's arm and supported him while he sank down into the chair. He was deathly pale and breathing heavily.

"It is nothing . . . nothing," he said.

Ben Dench laughed: "Upon my word, I thought you were going to faint!"

"It is nothing," Salvatore muttered. "This is a thing that sometimes happen to me. It is, perhaps, the heart."

"Don't try to speak till you feel better. Let me do the talking. Since you first came into the room I have been examining you closely with a doctor's eyes. I don't want to frighten you, Mr. Ferraro; but I think it is only fair to tell you that you are not so strong as you look. That brings me to what I have been intending to say to you. You are listening?"

Salvatore nodded. His face was still livid, his breathing rapid and shallow; the fire had died out of his eyes.

"You are an ill man, Mr. Ferraro—much more ill than you realize. That is quite understandable. In the short space of two years you have had to deal with two cases of serious illness in people to whom you were attached by an exceptional devotion. The strain has told on you, Mr. Ferraro: It has told particularly on your nerves. A man in normal health, you'll agree, would not have turned faint, as you did just now, in the middle of a quiet discussion about the causes of peripheral neuritis. The real reason, of course, was your natural concern for Mrs. Ferraro's health."

"You are right, Signore." Salvatore broke in, "I would give the two eyes to see her recover. If it is a matter of money . . ."

"In my own case that doesn't arise. I have seen her as a friend, an old friend of the family. But if you do what I tell you—as Mrs. Ferraro has promised me she will—I think I can guarantee her complete recovery. My prescription may seem difficult and possibly painful to yourself."

"Truly, Signore, I do not understand. If there is anything I must do, there is only need to ask me. *Non dubitare.*"

"Well then, let me explain. After seeing you both, it has become perfectly plain to me that you have been too much together. Without realizing what was happening, you have been getting on each other's nerves."

"We have never quarrelled, Signore. Not so much as a word . . ."

"No, I don't suggest that. What I mean is this: that your obvious anxiety for her health and her equal anxiety for the distress it caused you have had a bad effect on both of you. She is in need of complete isolation; and you, I feel sure, are in need of a change. I think you should go on—what shall we call it—a holiday."

"I do not believe that Agnes would ever consent to it."

"I have told you she has promised to do whatever I may decide."

"This is a busy season on the land. It is necessary to tie the vines. This is difficult. See here—it will be all right if I stay here and do not see her?"

"No, no. I'm afraid that won't do. I don't want you to be in the house or even in the village. I want you to go right away from Monfalcone."

"To leave Monfalcone? I think the Signore is joking!"

"You must realize, Mr. Ferraro, that this is no joke. I am deadly serious."

"But I am a man of Monfalcone. This is my home. Where can I go?"

"I suggest America."

"America?"

"If there is any difficulty about money—though I imagine you are not badly provided for—no doubt something can be arranged. I'll undertake that myself."

"But. . . . . America? You do not know what you're saying. This is a thing not heard of, unpardonable. To separate husband and wife!"

"Precisely. I am proposing that you should go at once. No doubt you will have certain arrangements to make. Let us say to-morrow morning."

"This is a menace. . . . What you say threat?"

"No, no. I am merely advising you."

"And if I refuse?"

"You will have to reflect on the consequences. I consider that if you stayed here they would be serious to your wife. You are an extremely intelligent man, I think, Mr. Ferraro—sufficiently intelligent to realize that they might be even more serious to yourself. I am going to protect my patient's life in any case. I also want, if I can, to avoid a scandal that would give her and her sister enormous pain. As for yourself, you can go to the devil for all I care. As a first step, I'm proposing America."

For a moment Salvatore was silent.

"The return ticket to New York is two thousand lire," he said, with a disarming smile. "And living there is expensive."

"You are even more avaricious than I thought, Mr. Ferraro. When I hear you have reached New York, I undertake to refund you the third-class passage. Not before then, and not a cent more."

"I must see my wife first."

"Oh, no, that won't do. I am taking no risks. From this moment nobody will go near her but myself and her sister. I will make that quite clear to her, as tactfully as I can."

"And if I refuse to go?"

Ben Dench rose and slid the medicine-bottle into his pocket.

"That is a question to which I think you have guessed the answer. You will certainly know it to-morrow morning if I come up and find you still here. I shall be obliged," he went on without any change of voice, "if you will be so kind as to find Miss Isit and say that I'ld like to see her."

Salvatore stiffened himself and bowed with the studied politeness of a well-trained butler receiving a guest's command.

"Si, Signore. I find and send her at once. *Non dubitare.*"

He went to the door and opened it. Strange to say, Miss Ellen was standing immediately outside.

. . . . .

Soon after dawn on the following morning, between half-past five and six, Salvatore Ferraro shot himself in a straw hut, a *pagliaro* as it is called, in the grounds of the Castello Inglese. Nobody who heard the shot paid any attention to it. The report of a charge that blows a man's head off is no louder than that which wings a nightingale.

14

THE EFFECT of the news which shook Monfalcone that day was brief. In that countryside, where every contadino carries a gun with him to work, shooting-accidents are by no means uncommon, as numerous mutilated hands and fingers testify. Fatalities, of course, are rarer—but what can be expected of a man who is so careless as to clean a loaded gun with the safety-catch off and the barrel pointing at his throat? Moreover the victim, in this case, was not popular. He came of a 'bad family', a *mala razza*, and among the more sober inhabitants of the village, which is to say the majority, had always been regarded as a scapegrace. Young men who go to America for any reason other than earning their living by the sale of potatoes are no more respected than those who support themselves by marrying for money outside their own race and class, and, on the strength of this, consider themselves better than their neighbours. It was unfortunate, of course, that any man—even Salvatore Ferraro—should die so young and so suddenly. Yet the people of Monfalcone, who are more than half Greek, have an ingrained respect for what their ancestors called 'Phthonos'—the jealousy of the gods for too-easy prosperity—and a wholesome belief that, sooner or later, pride comes to a fall. In their eyes a bad lot had, appropriately, come to a bad end.

Nor were the police unduly excited or worried over Salvatore's death. It relieved them of the supervision of a *pregiudicato*, who had 'done time' in Naples for a criminal offence. In their books he was known as a *ruffiano*—which, in Italian, does not mean 'ruffian', but a man who lives on the immoral earnings of women. It was true that the case showed peculiar features: it was unusual, for instance, for a man to go out shooting at dawn in a pearl-grey lounge-suit, by Hawkes of Savile Row, and patent-leather shoes. But the question of suicide could not arise. Men who committed suicide were either embarrassed for money or crossed in love; while Salvatore, at the time of his death, was carrying a wallet well-stuffed with yellow-backed dollar bills of a value equivalent to five thousand Italian *lire*, and had certainly not been unlucky in his love affairs. On the contrary. . . This was, in short, a plain case of accidental death, and the victim was entitled to be buried without any fuss and in the odour of sanctity—as he duly was, two days later, at Miss Ellen's expense. In accordance with her social station, the funeral was costly.

At the Castello Inglese life went on much as usual. No echo of that fatal gunshot had been allowed to reach that sunny bedroom where Agnes, attended by her sister and visited, every day, by Ben Dench, continued to make a slow but sustained recovery. It was most fortunate, Miss Ellen reflected, that the impact of the blow on Agnes had been postponed by his having explained to her, the evening before the tragedy, that he had insisted on ordering Salvatore to go away on a month's holiday for the sake of his nerves. Agnes had been indignant, at first, that Sir Benjamin had not allowed Salvatore to see her before he left, and was anxious to be assured that he had been well provided with money. It was even more odd, she thought, that he had neglected to write to her after his departure. She only accepted this omission because she knew that, for all his talent for compound arithmetic, he was a laborious writer. And indeed, in the mental twilight of exhaustion, tactfully increased by the sedatives which Ben Dench prescribed for her, her brain was too feeble and confused to sustain the effort of consecutive thought.

For a week after her husband was buried she lay in a state of half-consciousness in the dim borderland between life and death. In the second week her spirits began to revive. Though she was still too tired to talk or even to think, her appetite improved, and Miss Ellen was delighted to find that the food she prepared no longer disagreed with her. In the third week, her colour became more normal, and the strength so far returned to her hands that she could feed herself. Her mind, too, became clearer. It was still worried and hurt, as Miss Ellen guessed, by Salvatore's silence; but she often spoke of him and looked forward eagerly to the time when he would return, counting the days as they passed, like a schoolgirl impatient for the holidays.

"Though I felt it hard at the time," she said, "I am ready now to admit Ben's wisdom in insisting on Salvatore's going away. I don't think either he or I realized how ill I was, and I am truly thankful that he wasn't allowed to see me at my worst. He would have been heart-broken. He had nursed me so long and so faithfully, and I, in my selfishness, thought nothing of what he was suffering. I doubt if I can ever repay him."

Whenever she spoke about Salvatore or Stewart, Miss Ellen took fright and evaded her questions, in terror, lest some unguarded word should arouse her suspicion. As a rule she managed to shift the burden of answering them to the broad shoulders of Ben Dench, whose calling had made him more skilled in the arts of evasion than herself. Indeed, during that long and fretful convalescence, she came to rely on his tact and wisdom more and more. He was a wonderful man, she thought. In the old days of Moogly Meringapatam they had laughed, she was ashamed to remember, at his stolidness and lack of imagination. Now time and experience and the dignity of his honours had not merely mellowed his mind but given him a self-confidence and an ease of manner that filled her with an admiration which, apart from all considerations of gratitude, she couldn't believe Agnes did not share. In his relations with her sister there was no trace of the awkwardness one might have expected. He even teased her! She had never known anybody who had dared to tease Agnes before. And, wonder of wonders, Agnes appeared to enjoy it!

In these circumstances it was only natural that Miss Ellen's mind should return to its habitual vein of romantic speculation. After all, though poor Agnes wasn't aware of it, both she and Ben Dench were now free to marry. Of course custom and decency would demand that such a marriage should be preceded by a period of mourning; but, once that convention were satisfied, what in the world could be more fitting, more truly right, than that Agnes should give her hand to the man who had not only saved her life but had loved her faithfully for nearly thirty years? That indeed would be a Romance in Real Life! And how lovely it would be for herself to have Ben, whom she admired more than any man on earth, for a brother-in-law!

As the time of her sister's complete recovery and the day on which she expected Salvatore to return drew near, Miss Ellen was compelled to contemplate this rosy vision with less confidence. Agnes herself became increasingly excited.

"Do you think," she said, "Ben would allow me to go downstairs to receive him? I have made such a delightful plan. Of course it will be difficult to calculate the exact hour of his arrival; but I am sure he will be eager to come home as early as he can. I should like to be sitting in the loggia all alone—except for dear Stewart, of course—so that he won't know I'm downstairs until he comes to the door. And then. . . . Oh, Ellen, I can hardly bear to think of it: that meeting will be such a great happiness for us both!"

"You will have to ask Ben about that," Miss Ellen said.

"Of course. I will ask him when he comes up this evening."

When Ben Dench arrived, Miss Ellen was waiting for him at the gate and told him what Agnes had planned.

"We can't put it off any longer," she said. "I'm afraid you will have to break it to her to-night. It's awful, isn't it? Do you think she is strong enough to bear it?"

Sir Benjamin sighed.

"I hope so. It's impossible to say how she will take it; but your sister is a remarkably courageous woman, Ellen."

"It will be terribly difficult, Ben. I feel so sorry for you."

He smiled. "That is kind of you, Ellen. Situations of this kind are only too common, unfortunately, in my gruesome trade. I'm used to them."

"You won't want me to be there?"

"I'ld much rather you weren't."

She accompanied him to the hall and watched him going upstairs. Then she heard his unhurried, confident steps as he passed down the corridor and the sound of his knocking on Agnes's door.

Miss Ellen stood still for a moment, listening to the silence. Then she went out into the garden.

Ben Dench entered the room. Agnes welcomed him with a smile. She was sitting up in bed with a shawl round her shoulders.

"You are almost beginning to look like yourself," he said. "Nothing new to report?"

"Nothing at all. I feel splendid. Of course I am naturally excited, thinking about to-morrow. You'll allow me to go downstairs, won't you?"

"We'll talk about that later on. Do you mind lying down, while I take your pulse?"

She obeyed him. He sat down beside her and took out his watch as he laid his fingers on her wrist.

"Of course it's likely to be a little more rapid with my excitement this evening, isn't it?" she said.

"Not too bad, not too bad," he murmured.

He slipped his watch back in his pocket, but still held her wrist. More firmly.

"I want to talk to you, Agnes," he said. "Rather seriously."

"About myself?"

"About your husband."

"You've heard from him? He's not coming back to-morrow? Ben. . . There's nothing wrong? Tell me quickly!"

"I'm afraid you must be prepared for bad news."

"You mean he is ill?" She gazed at him anxiously.

Ben Dench shook his head.

"You don't mean . . . ? You're keeping something back from me, Ben!"

"I want you to be your brave self, Agnes, as I know you will."

It was strange how, in moments such as this, one was always forced to fall back on trite, conventional phrases! He went on slowly:

"There was an accident with a gun . . ."

"When? When?"

"It was nearly a month ago."

"Why didn't you tell me, Ben?"

"I couldn't. It might have killed you."

"That would have been better."

"No, no. . . . You mustn't say that, Agnes. I thank God you're alive."

"You don't know, you don't know. He was all the world to me, Ben. Did he suffer much pain?"

"No, Agnes, I'm quite sure he didn't. None at all."

"It was cruel, cruel of you, not to let me see him."

"If you had seen him, my dear, you couldn't have done anything. There was nothing to be done. If there had been, it would have been done. You can be quite certain of that."

She was silent.

"Now I am going to leave you," he said. "Unless you want me to stay?"

She shook her head and pressed his hand feebly. He bent over and kissed her forehead.

"Would you like me to send Ellen to you?" he said.

"No," she whispered. "I don't want to see anybody. I would much rather be alone." Her voice broke. "I shall always be alone now," she said.

As he moved to the door, she called him.

"Ben!"

"Yes, Agnes?"

"You saw him once, didn't you?"

"Yes, just once, when I talked to him that evening."

"I'm glad you saw him," she said slowly, "if it was only that once. There was nobody in the world like him, Ben. So gentle, so loving, so strong. . . . And I was so proud of him. He was a wonderful man and a perfect husband, Ben."

15

AGNES DID not go down to the garden next day. Another week passed before she sat up in bed again. It was a terrible week for Miss Ellen. Day after day her heart was harrowed by the spectacle of her sister's mute grief. At night the atmosphere of Agnes's room with its tall wax candles was that of a *chapelle ardente*. In its silence she felt as if she were watching over the dead. The strain of that silent vigil told on her. Indeed, but for Ben Dench's sympathy she would have broken down under it. He was always the same. No matter how depressed or hopeless she felt, she seemed able to draw courage and cheerfulness from the unselfconscious strength, the quiet serenity that his mere presence radiated. If he had saved Agnes's life, she felt he had saved her own reason.

At the end of that dreadful week, as the result of a surprising exercise of will-power, Agnes came suddenly to life. Having once decided to live, she began to talk with interest about the domestic affairs of the Castello Inglese and the care of the estate.

"There is no need for you to sit with me any longer, Ellen," she said. "You have been shut up in the house far too much. Though I cannot see for myself, I want to know everything that is happening outside, and I rely on you to tell me."

Miss Ellen was thankful to be released from imprisonment. Every day she walked out to inspect the work on the land and brought back reports of all that was being done. It was strange, she thought, how the routine processes of husbandry, which poor Salvatore had controlled with such jealous importance, had continued in his absence. His cousin, Francesco, appeared to be a capable and industrious young man. All the vines had been pruned and tied as carefully as if he had been there. Some of them were already beginning to sprout, and the smell of their bronzy leaves tipped with rose had a faintly vinous savour. Spring was over. How swiftly it had passed! It pained her to think that she had missed seeing the billows of cherry-blossom tossed on lascivious winds of April against the blues of sky and sea. It was as though six weeks had dropped out of her life: six exquisite weeks that could never now be recovered. . . .

Often, when she stepped out of the house, she found Ben Dench waiting for her on the terrace, and he went with her on her wandering tours of inspection. In his company she never thought of the lost days of spring. He kept her mind busy with his eager interest in everything, demanding exact information which she sometimes found difficult to give him. For a man of his age, she thought, he was extraordinarily young and alive and stimulating: such a gay and charming companion. She had never had much human contact with a man before. All her relations with men had been formal, and she had been rather afraid of letting herself go with them, because she never quite regarded herself as their equal. But Ben Dench was different from any other man she had known. He encouraged her to express herself, and when, sometimes, he smiled at her simplicity, his smiles were kindly. Had Salvatore ever talked to Agnes like this? Had Agnes known this delightful companionship, this innocent sharing of a delight in simple, homely joys and humble beauties? Had Papa and Mama ever known the like of it? Was this what married life meant? Miss Ellen wondered.

By the end of another week this Eden was snatched away from her by the arrival of Agnes downstairs. She was still weak in the limbs and dared not venture further away from the house than the belvedere at the end of the terrace; but the grotesque high-stepping gait which had horrified Miss Ellen was gone; a faint colour of health had returned to her cheeks and her face was no longer strained and haggard. On that first evening Miss Ellen watched her walking the terrace on Ben Dench's arm, and was conscious of an emotion which she had never experienced before. She wanted to walk beside them and hear what Agnes was saying—and even more what he replied. They walked close together and spoke in undertones. Was it possible, she wondered, that the dream of a romantic reunion which she had cherished for so long was beginning to come true? Miss Ellen was shocked to discover that she no longer desired it, and knew that this was wicked.

"I may as well face the truth," she told herself: "I have changed. I am jealous. I mustn't be jealous. I won't be jealous. Oh, dear God, let them be happy!" she prayed. "Please let them be happy!"

She forbade herself to watch them any longer for fear that her presence might embarrass them. It was only right that Ben should marry Agnes. They were made for each other. He had always been hers and she his, if they had only known it; but she couldn't help crying a little, all the same, as she lay there with Waifie in her arms.

A maid tapped at her door. It was Assunta's successor, the dark Angelina.

"Dinner is served, Signorina," she said. "It is past seven, and the Signori are waiting for you."

"The doctor is staying to dinner?"

"Si, Signorina."

So the worst—the best—had come! There was no avoiding it: she would have to go down and face them. "But I must make myself look happy," she thought. "It would be dreadful if they should see that I have been crying."

She bathed her eyes in cold water and went downstairs to the salone. Ben and Agnes were already seated. He was sitting at the head of the table, where she had last seen him at the end of his mysterious interview with Salvatore. This seemed to her significant. It was just as if he were already the master of the house.

"You were so late that we decided not to wait for you," Agnes said with a hint of her old severity.

"I'm so sorry, Agnes. I was tired. I must have fallen asleep."

During the meal, which she found hard to eat, they talked of ordinary things. It seemed to her that Ben gave her far more attention than was necessary, and she felt herself compelled to discourage him—so chillingly that at length he gave it up as a bad job. He seemed to her as gay and natural and serene as usual—not in the least excited—but Agnes's face wore a sombre look that she knew well of old and feared. It was clear that she had something weighing on her mind, and was not disposed to fall in with his cheerful mood.

At the end of dinner he helped her to rise, with a charming courtliness, and offered her his arm.

"Thank you, Ben," she said. "I don't need any help. I must learn not to be dependent on anyone now. Will you come with us into the studio, Ellen? I have something I want to discuss with both of you."

Agnes went first, with some effort, Miss Ellen thought. It had been naughty and ungracious of her to refuse his arm. Ben and she followed slowly. "If Agnes won't take my arm," he said mischievously, "perhaps you will?" Miss Ellen blushed and drew away from him. She felt this was no time for joking.

Angelina, who was waiting for them, made a bob and opened the studio door; and Agnes, without acknowledging the obeisance, went on towards the divan. As she sank down on it, Miss Ellen was aware of Uncle Ludovic's picture of Salvatore, which had been restored to its easel, but was still veiled. Ben Dench innocently took the chair which had always been occupied by Salvatore. At the side of it stood Salvatore's brass spittoon, which he stared at with what seemed to Miss Ellen a tactless curiosity, though Agnes, fortunately, appeared not to notice his interest in this odd piece of furniture.

"I have been talking matters over with Ben," she said at last, "and I think it is right that you, Ellen, should know what I have decided, since it affects you. As soon as he considers I am fit to travel, I am returning to England."

"To England?" Miss Ellen gasped.

"To 'The Cedars'. All the time I have been lying upstairs I have been wondering if I could bring myself to stay here. When I came down on to the terrace this evening I knew at once that I couldn't. This place is so steeped in memories of past happiness that I cannot bear it. Everything I see, wherever I look, brings a pang to my heart, reminding me of my dear one. There is no need, as Ben wisely agrees, for me to force myself to suffer unnecessary pain. He assures me that Time is the greatest of healers, and perhaps he is right. I don't know. I only know that I cannot be happy as long as I stay here."

"In that case, of course, I must go with you, Agnes," Miss Ellen said.

"Will you think it strange and unsisterly of me, Ellen, if I say 'no'? It isn't really that. It's not easy to explain; but for the present there is only one desire in my poor heart. I want to be alone with my memories and my great grief. I do hope you will understand."

"I can't bear to think of your going alone, Agnes dear. Won't you let me go with you? I feel it's my duty to be by your side in this great unhappiness. Nobody else understands you as I do. And, as Ben says, you may feel differently after a time."

Agnes frowned. "That only shows how little you do understand me. I shall never feel differently, however long God chooses that I shall live. Please don't argue, Ellen. You know it will only exhaust me, and I've made up my mind. I shall never come to Monfalcone again."

"But Agnes . . . The house? The property?"

"I have considered all that. I have no idea what they may be worth; but that doesn't really matter: there is quite enough money for both of us to live on without any privation. What I suggest is this: we will divide Uncle Ludovic's money between us, as was his intention. As for the property, I shall be quite content to take 'The Cedars' if you are content to take the Castello Inglese. If you prefer it, of course we can ask Mr. Wilburn to decide whether the division is fair to both of us, and he can prepare the necessary adjustment. Even if he considers the Italian property is more valuable, I shall not complain. I have always felt rather guilty in deserting 'The Cedars' for so long. Somehow I can't help feeling that Papa would have approved of what I suggest. And now, if you'll kindly give me your arm, after all, Ben, I think I will go to bed. This talking has tired me, and I am anxious to muster all my strength for the journey."

Agnes left the Castello Inglese for England five days later. Miss Ellen had implored to be allowed to go with her as far as Naples, but she would not consent.

"It is no use prolonging good-byes, Ellen," she said. "I would much rather make a clean break of it. When the carriage leaves the house I am determined not to look back. I shall close my eyes until it has crossed the mountain. It will be like starting a new life—though it will not be a very happy one, I fear, and I hope not a very long one."

"Oh Agnes," Miss Ellen pleaded, with tears in her eyes, "you must not talk like that!"

"I have always preferred to tell the plain truth, Ellen. Papa taught me that. Not that I blame you—but there is nothing here that does not speak to me of death, so it's natural that my thoughts should dwell on it. Even poor little Stewart! I was devoted to him—and yet how small that seems now!"

The carriage was to leave the Castello Inglese early in the afternoon, in order that Agnes should reach the station at Naples in time to catch the night train for Paris without having to go to an hotel. Ben Dench, who had charged himself with all the arrangements, came up for luncheon. Agnes, strange to say, was looking remarkably well in the black satin which had always suited her. Since the moment when she had made up her mind to break with Monfalcone she had seemed to be immune from all minor troubles of life. Though Miss Ellen had relieved her of the physical labour of packing, Agnes had insisted on superintending the whole proceeding and had showed no signs of fatigue. When the luncheon-gong boomed in the hall she appeared, ready dressed for the journey, at the foot of the stairs. It was unfortunate—and characteristic—that Miss Ellen was two minutes late.

"We have exactly twenty-eight minutes," Agnes said, as they entered the salone. "The carriage should be at the gate at two precisely. I have told the servants that I don't wish them to see me off. They are much too emotional. We will have the coffee served in here at the table. I don't want to enter the studio. Angelina will let me know, Ellen, when all the luggage is on, and then I shall leave you and Ben, if you don't mind, sitting here. Do have some more wine, Ben. It is extremely wholesome, you know: we make it ourselves. This is last year's, isn't it, Angelina?"

"*Si, Signora . . . dell' anno scorso.*"

It was delicious, Ben Dench agreed. Miss Ellen hoped

he didn't see that she drank three glasses right off. It couldn't be helped if he did. She felt she needed them. She really needed more.

At ten minutes past two Angelina appeared with tears running down her cheeks to announce that the luggage had been loaded. Agnes rose from her chair, extraordinarily handsome and slender in her black satin. She bent over Miss Ellen and kissed her without any word. Ellen returned the kiss passionately, conscious of the heat of her wine-flushed face and of the tears which had begun to flow. Then Agnes, still without speaking, took Ben's hand and pressed it. She sighed and smiled faintly. The tall, queenly figure passed slowly out of the room. Miss Ellen tried to steady her twitching features, but it was no good. She buried her face in her hands and cried quietly, her hot tears dripping into the finger-bowl in which floated a single flower of orange-blossom.

"I can't help it," she sobbed. "I'm sorry, Ben, but I can't."

He stood behind her and put his arms round her—just as Salvatore had done, she thought, but oh, how differently!

"Of course you can't, my poor, sweet child," he said. "Don't worry. I'll look after you."

THE END

Talland.
February 6*th*, 1942.